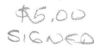

D1082600

DEATH OF
INNOCENCE

P.S. Hunter

To the OIF/ OEF Veterans and their loved ones, we stand in awe of your courage and sacrifice.

To my wife Emily, thank you for putting up with me spending way too much time on this

To TIM

KEEP YOUR HEAD

DOWN. MUCH LOVE

BROTHER

B Hunter

Death of Innocence
by P.S. Hunter

Prologue

No one survives war. People experience it and some make it to the other side. It has been called a crucible. There is not a more accurate depiction. When forging steel, raw iron is heated. Impurities are burned out. Then the impurity, carbon, is added. Pressure is added in a violent rhythm. Under fire and pressure a new alloy is made--steel.

War makes people in the same way. What comes out the other side will never be iron again. People born of war can be a steel girder holding up the world, only stronger for the experience. Others become like the weapons they used. Now, it is possible to hammer a nail with a .45. But it feels as awkward as it sounds. And thus, some people are just never going to be good at anything else anymore. And no matter what the steel is used for, it will never be iron again.

Sergeant Samuel Parker considered the ramifications of his forging. He was steel and he knew it. But sitting in this car he could not help but question where it all went wrong. Somewhere in the forging process something had gone terribly wrong or, perhaps, far too right. Samuel knew he was exceptional at violence. Men in at least two countries had learned to fear him firsthand. Samuel was a weapon. He was technically and tactically proficient. The fresh and old scars on his body throbbed as he sat. That meant the hydros had started to wear off. He reached into his jacket and pulled out the bottle and poured a couple in his mouth. He washed it down with the beer in the cup holder. He didn't bother counting them anymore and, besides, tonight was a special occasion.

November 10, 1775, he was born in a tavern. This was his birthday. Not his actual birthday. It was every Marine's birthday and tonight he was celebrating the memory of his honored dead. Those that had come before him had lost more men. He didn't doubt that. But the truth was that was little comfort. Nothing was comfortable anymore. He tried to think back to when had been the last time he was comfortable. He chuckled to himself as he thought, *Must have been in the Iron Age.* The age before the wars. Samuel had trouble remembering anything anymore, but he especially had trouble remembering the times before. He figured that's how the drugs worked though. You can't be haunted by memories that escape you. And if the good times escape with the bad, fuck it, maybe they weren't as good as you thought they were.

Samuel knew that was wrong though. Samuel had grown up in the height of the Pax-Americana before any of the bubbles crashed, planes crashed into buildings, or the fates of a generation of warfighters crashed into the deserts of the Middle East. Perhaps that was the problem ultimately. Samuel grew up too comfortable. Upper middle class by any standard, he had the world on a platter. But he decided to shake his fist in a romantic fury and run off to *Fight his Country's battles.* He could not help but smirk when he realized where he was. He was in the parking lot where so many important moments in his life had happened. This strip mall could honestly define everything about him that was not related to combat.

Samuel took a long pull out of his beer bottle and finished it. He opened another as he watched some blue lights race by in his rearview mirror. For a moment he considered what it would be like to get one last gunfight in. Not a bad idea other than the fact that some dude just trying to make a living would be on the other end of it. That would be a bitch move, to go out fighting some beat cop. Besides, if Samuel was certain of any portion of the equation, it was not that he had not seen enough combat. He thought for sure that every generation looked back to their elder's wars and thought, *That was real combat.* But Samuel was certain he could snatch any dude from Hue City in Vietnam and put them in Iraq and they would have felt right at home.

Samuel heard his cellphone vibrate in the passenger seat. He looked over and saw it was a text message from Samantha. He knew she was worried about him. That's all she did anymore, worry about him. Honestly, it was exhausting. As if he needed any other reminder that he had tied her to a corpse. Samuel Parker, the consummate nerd from high school, had bagged the homecoming queen. If he had stayed in his lane, he could just be dead and gone by now and she wouldn't have a broken heart. He reached past the Glock 21 in his passenger seat and grabbed his phone.

I hope you are having fun!
I wanted to talk to you about
going to a thing with
my mom and dad tomorrow.

Samuel read the message and rolled his eyes. He could not think of anything to reply so he did not intend to at all. He put the phone down and took another pull from the beer bottle. Samuel thought to himself how much of a selfish piece of shit he was. He stayed alive so *he* could come back to be with *her.* The noble thing to do would have been to bleed out and slip slowly into a deep state of nothingness. Now, he had to rely on pills to keep himself from killing her in his sleep. And even worse, now that she expected him to be out of danger there was no way for him to gracefully exit the stage. No matter what, she would be devastated.

A fleeting thought entered his mind with the semblance of an emotion attached to it. Samantha would be no less beautiful in a widow's cowl. There was no doubt in his mind that Samantha was the most important person in his life. Loving her was his life's greatest accomplishment. The problem was that the man that loved her was iron, he was steel. Steel is cold and unmoving. He could love her, he did not know how to make her feel it anymore. How does one express emotion when they do not know how to feel?

If he could do it over again what would he change? In a strange way, he was certain he would have still joined the

Corps. Samuel believed there was a demon inside him. It had always been there; he just did not know the demon until war brought it out. Samuel had made peace with the demon. So much so that the demon drove the bus now--all the time. Only the pills kept him on a leash. But there were Marines alive today thanks to the demon. Erasing that part of his life could erase the lives of several good men. That's not up for negotiation.

No, this war has much more humble beginnings. This war Samuel was fighting now started in this strip mall. *Remember that time you ruined the life of the best person to have ever walked the Earth?* Samuel thought to himself. That must undo any good he had done in his life. Samuel looked over to the empty bay where the ice cream parlor used to be. *My war started there,* he thought to himself. Samuel heard his phone vibrate in the passenger seat. He reached over and grabbed the pistol and moved it over to his lap. Then he reached for the phone.

Mac said you never showed up.
Where are you?

Busted, Samuel thought. He knew what the inevitability of his life was. He could not have lived without the demon, but he could not let the demon live with Samantha. And the pills made it so he was hardly alive. This was the end of the alliance with the demon. It had to end here, and, if nothing else, the demon had proven nothing could destroy him. That really only left one inevitability. Samuel had to go. Samuel reached down and picked up the pistol. He checked it to make sure there was one in the chamber. Old habits really do die hard. He put the business end in his mouth. He wasn't slow about it. No need for dramatic pauses.

He heard the phone vibrating again. This time it was a phone call. Samuel tried to put the distraction out of his mind. The steel from the slide was cold on his tongue. His eyes cut back to the empty bay where the ice cream parlor had been. *This is for you, Samantha,* he thought as he shifted his mind back to the task at hand. The only sound in the car was the vibrating of the phone. *Time for us to go old friend,* he thought as if speaking to the demon.

Suddenly his mind raced. He felt. For only a second. He felt regret that the last thing he had said to Samantha was, "See you later." He pulled the pistol out of his mouth. She at least deserved an "I love you." He picked up the phone and said, "Hey Sam."

"Hey Sam," he heard her reply. Her voice was soft and sweet as always. She let out a soft sigh of relief as she said, "I understand you might want to be alone right now, but tomorrow's Veteran's Day and my father wants you to come to this luncheon at his country club. I just need to know if we can be there."

CHAPTER 1
CONFIDENCE

Samantha saw Samuel walking towards the door holding the pizza box. Their late afternoon ritual was a comfort that she had grown so accustomed to that she did not realize how much she enjoyed it until it had been interrupted the day before. Samuel had gone to school with her since... forever. And since they both got jobs the summer before junior year, they had worked in the same strip mall. Samantha worked at a frozen yogurt shop and Samuel worked at the pizza parlor a few doors down. Samuel brought a small pizza that the two of them split every day that they both worked. It was an unforeseen friendship that developed between the two of them. They were not in the same circle of friends. Samantha had been homecoming queen and Samuel was in the crowd of people that everyone knew everyone else was going to be working for someday.

Samuel opened the door taking a deep breath. Samuel had a crush on Samantha and they both knew it. It took the already awkward task of making conversation and increased the tension to near intoxicating levels. Samuel was feeling quite good today though. He had big news. He was nervous, but excited. He finally felt like the worst thing that could happen in his life was not embarrassing himself in front of Samantha. Samantha was wiping down the counter smiling at him as he walked in. She was easily the most beautiful girl he knew, and what made it worse was that she seemed blissfully ignorant to the fact.

"Hey Sam," he said with an unusual gusto for himself.

Samantha replied, "Hey Sam."

She noticed his changed demeanor. He seemed like he had just found out there was a mix up and now he was graduating top of the class instead of third.

"Where were you yesterday?" she said jokingly, "I almost starved to death."

Samuel slid the pizza on the counter and opened the box. He turned around and hopped up onto the counter. Samantha was taken aback. This was not like him at all. He was normally a quiet and reserved type that followed all of the unwritten social norms such as not sitting on counters.

"Well I actually have some big news," he started.

Samantha was intrigued. She had learned through their two year friendship that his clique had just as much drama as hers did. There were break-ups, flirting, love triangles and everything else. Samantha grabbed a slice out of the box and said, "Do tell."

Samuel felt more nervous than when he had told his parents. It was peculiar. The pair of them had an entirely platonic relationship, but he somehow loved and valued her opinion more than most in his life. Life has a cruel joke that it plays on young men. At the most formative period of their life, hormones begin flooding their body and clouding their mind.

"I wasn't at work yesterday." Samuel finally uttered.

Samantha replied with a joking snide remark, "I'd hope not. You'd better not cheat on me and take pizza to some other girl."

"Well," Samuel started. He paused to increase the tension, "I was enlisting in the Marines."

There was a long palpable silence in the room. Samuel looked back at Samantha to see the face of pure incredulity.

"You're messing with me," Samantha said.

"Not even a little bit." Samuel said as he took a slice of pizza out of the box.

"Sam, you know there's a war going on right?" Samantha

exclaimed.

"There wouldn't be much of a reason to join if there wasn't, would there?" he snapped.

"Sam. You have never even been in a fight," Samantha said in an uncharacteristic swipe at his masculinity.

Samantha had always been careful to make sure she treated Samuel like he was any other guy. She never liked thinking that she was the archetype other girls were torturously compared to, so she never felt like it was fair to make him feel the contrast of him to the guys she usually dated. For some reason she felt an immense amount of dread at the thought of him being in harm's way. Samantha had grown very comfortable having Samuel in her life. Sure, that would end when they went off to college anyway. But this seemed far more final and that seemed frighteningly real.

Samuel was trying to hide that he was wounded by that comment. He slid off of the counter and turned to face her.

"Sam, I don't think getting drunk and fighting at high school parties qualifies someone to fight a war."

He studied her face. He did not expect what he saw. She looked visibly shaken by the news he had given her. Samantha was a sweet person, he knew that. But he did not expect her to have such regard for his future.

"Why?" She uttered finally.

"Why what?" Samuel asked.

"Why you Sam?" she said.

"Why not me?" he asked.

He had calculated that response to that exact question since he first spoke to the recruiters. Samuel knew it was a veiled statement of moral superiority. There was not a response anyone could give without backing themselves into a trap.

"You can do anything you want, Sam. You had your pick of colleges" Samantha stated in frustration.

Samuel knew that this wasn't fair. Samantha was brilliant, unfairly brilliant for someone who was as beautiful as she was. She would have known by saying that that he was now able to lay into her in such a way that she would either have to insult him or servicemembers to back out of it. Samuel decided to go easy on her.

"Maybe that means I could make a big difference."

Samantha knew Samuel had not given her the full effect of what he could do with his words. If Samuel had a most attractive quality it was his ability to verbally destroy someone in a polite and tactful way. His brain just seemed to function several steps ahead of everyone else's. It made him frustrating to disagree with, but his wit was incredibly entertaining to watch.

"Maybe, are you going to do something with computers or something?" she asked.

"No, I'm going to the infantry," Samuel replied, somewhat sullenly.

"So, like the front line," Samantha replied with clear disdain. Before he could even reply she interjected with a bitter tone, "Why am I just hearing about this?"

Samuel was caught off guard. It was an entirely valid question. He had been thinking about how much their relationship had blossomed into a friendship that, at face value, was something unique.

"I'm sorry," Samuel said softly, feeling guilty.

He had not told her any lies, but that was the most honest thing he had said to her since he walked in. Samuel had been in the process of enlisting for nearly a month. He had plenty of chances to tell her of his intentions, but instead, he sprung it on her after the deed was done. In truth, this was part of the reason he had joined in the first place. Their friendship was the first thing about his life no one could have predicted if they would have looked at his qualities on paper. He was not the kind of guy that talked to the homecoming queen daily. It had become one of his favorite parts of his existence. Now he was the guy that talked to the homecoming queen daily and the guy that was volunteering to fight in the deserts of a far-off place.

There was a deafening silence in the room.

Samantha finally broke the silence by saying, "Well, when are you leaving?"

She studied him while she waited for a reply. She felt like she was waiting to hear how long she had to know him. Samantha noticed features she had not before. Subliminally, she felt as though she had taken him for granted.

"Middle of June," he replied softly.

Any tranquility Samantha had started to feel abandoned her again. "Sam! I'm leaving for my trip the second weekend in June!" she exclaimed.

She did not know why that made her so angry, but she could read all over his face that her tone was soliciting a reaction from him.

"So?" he said coyly.

Samantha did not know why, but she felt as though she needed to save face.

"Who is going to bring me pizza then?" she said in a forced laugh.

"Sam, you are gorgeous. Any guy in this city will bring you pizza anytime you want," Samuel said with a certain air of disbelief.

Samantha felt the blood rush to her face. It was fairly obvious Samuel had a crush on her. But he had never been so forward before, ever.

"But I'd have to train someone else on how I like my pizza and who has time for that?" she said, again trying to force a laugh that embarrassingly came out as a giggle.

Without a moment's hesitation, Samuel said, "Pepperoni pizza. It is the most popular pizza choice in the world. There's a solid ninety-five percent chance he would guess right."

That was it. That was the quickness Samuel operated at. Not a moment to catch your balance in a conversation. If someone said a single thing that was slightly counterfactual he was going to catch it and throw it back.

Samuel could not understand why Samantha seemed so perturbed. Their friendship was going to come to an end soon anyway. He was supposed to be going to Georgetown or Holy Cross. She was going to Ole Miss. They were graduating next week anyway. He also knew she was not the type that would ever use someone for food. The whole ritual had started as a joke anyway. He was a thoroughly neutral, platonic, male pair of ears that could listen to her complain about the flavor of the week. The first time he brought pizza he was listening to some drama when he interrupted and made the announcement in a feminine tone, "Girl, let's discuss this over pizza." But no matter how much she was trying to hide it, he could see her blushing. Had he missed some veiled cue through the years? Had she fallen for him in some subliminal level of consciousness and now, at the end, he was finding out?

"I guess we'll just have to cram our fill of pizza dates into the next few weeks," Samuel said.

He felt like he was walking in a minefield even calling their ritual a "pizza date". Samuel knew he was not good at hiding his obvious attraction to Samantha.

"That or I'm going to have to find a way to get myself and a pizza to Iraq every time I have boy drama," Samantha replied.

She could not hide her expression from Samuel though. He knew that she was intentionally throwing the comment of other guys in there now. Suddenly, years of anxiety, nervous sweating, and hormonal insecurities vanished. He thought to himself that it did not matter anymore. The two of them had their expiration date either way.

"Maybe we could actually hang out outside of a yogurt shop between now and then," Samuel said.

Samantha was reeling. For reasons she did not fully understand, she was an emotional wreck. This boy, who she knew she could have had anytime she wanted, was soon to be out of her life. In the last few minutes he had carried himself with more confidence than he ever had. She had never felt like he was a bad looking guy, but she had never thought she was attracted to him. But here and now, after finding out he was going to be gone, and seemingly for good, she was a wreck. He was smiling at her waiting for a response. She watched as the smile slowly slid from his face. It was at that moment while studying his features as if for the last time, she realized she never answered him.

"Of course." she spouted abruptly. "Come to Sarah's with me this weekend."

She went back to the box for another slice of pizza as her face got hot again. She knew she was an open book. But she had to do something to distract him, or maybe herself, from her obvious emotional state.

Samuel was dumbfounded. He was not one to be at a loss for words but in this moment he was. Contrary to popular belief, he was not a loser. He had been to high school parties. He had even been invited to some by girls that gave the impression of interest in him. Samuel had simply been someone more focused on his future than the fruits of high school romances. There were past girlfriends. But in his mind if those relationships interfered with school, work, or extracurriculars, they were nothing more than a distraction. But he was not a robot. Anyone with a pulse would have a reaction to being invited to a party *with* Samantha. She was the type of beautiful that you genuinely feared corrupting. She was not a dolled-up debutante. She was a natural beauty with a glowing personality that perfectly complemented her flawless features. And as if in God's own twisted sense of humor, she had developed incredibly young. Here and now, at 18 years old, Samuel was looking at a woman, with a woman's body.

"Yeah sure." is all he could muster in response.

The time for their accustomed meal and gossip was coming to an end. Samantha strangely wanted it to end sooner rather than later. A few minutes before she saw him coming in and was waiting to harass him about missing yesterday. Now they had a somewhat official date and very official end date. She was actually worried if he did not go back to work and give her a chance to catch her breath they would end up in the walk-in freezer exploring other feelings she never knew she had for him. And that was *if* she really had those feelings. A part of her was not certain that she did. Perhaps it was shock and some weird form of grief that had escalated this to the point it was at now.

"Well, soldier boy, I expect you to be on time." she said firmly. "I will be there at nine."

"Marines," he replied laughing, "I joined the Marines and I'll meet you there."

"Same difference." Samantha said going back to wiping the counters. "Just so you know, there's probably going to be quite a few guys there who are going to hear you are going to the service and take that as some kind of challenge. Maybe you'll get in a fight before you graduate after all."

She had some inner hope that the comment would make him come to his senses and rethink this whole fool's errand of deciding to join.

"You always did date guerrillas." Samuel said as he walked out the door in a last twist of the knife.

She paused and took a long blink. She should have known better than to leave him low hanging fruit like that. He was not wrong--the guys she was thinking about behaving in such a barbaric manner could all claim the title of ex-something to her.

Friday night arrived with the surety of passing time. Unexpectedly, Samuel was only really nervous *for* Samantha. He was not oblivious to the realpolitik of high school cliques. Samantha was at the status where she was only to be courted by the golden boys. Star athlete, nice guys with perfect hair could go to parties with Samantha, not first runners-up for salutatorian with an affinity for punk music and a propensity for snarky comments. By now, word was out that Samuel had enlisted into the military. So, Samuel thought, at least Samantha could claim patriotic duty for being seen at a party with him. As Samuel arrived at Sarah's house, he thought to himself that there was perhaps never a better cross section representing the progress of human civilization than the attendees of an upper middle class high school party circa 2006. Samuel always marveled that there was at least one representative from every race and ethnic group. Just about every particular subculture was represented, except perhaps the goth group. Social gatherings were kind of contrary to their particular ethos. He could see the representatives of each tribal sect of the school coming and going when he parked his car and started up the driveway.

Samantha found herself increasingly distracted. Nervous would have been a harsh description of how she felt waiting for Samuel to arrive. But she was certainly out of her comfort zone. She had not felt so much like a fish out of water in a long time. She had not told everyone that Samuel was coming, but she had also made a careful point not to make it seem like she was ashamed by telling a few. Samantha was truly a kind person. She was inclusive to all people and did not ever wish to hurt anyone's feelings either way. So this precarious situation was exhausting. If she had been too boisterous about Samuel coming, she was worried, it would have seemed as though she was somehow using his recent enlistment as the reason she was interested in him now. But she was just as worried that if she did not tell anyone and he just showed up, it would seem like she was not enthusiastic about his being there. The truth was somewhere in the middle.

She definitely felt as though she had taken for granted how important he had become to her, but she was not head over heels for him either. It was as though a cruel quickening of the passage of time had rushed events to a fever pitch. All the girls in school knew Samuel was the kind of boy that was going to grow into a man that you marry. He was kind, gentle, not bad looking, and wildly successful, as much as a teenage boy could be considered successful. Anything he decided to do he seemed to excel at. She had known him, or at least known of him, through the boy scout years, science fairs, etc. Samantha even remembered back to middle school when he was a pretty good soccer player. Once they got to high school though, he just got hyper focused on school. And to high school girls exploring and craving what attention from boys was like, there was very little reason to chase the boy who would skip time with you to work on some honors project.

Samuel opened the front door and walked in. Immediately there were more than a few out of place salutations from people that were either shocked that he had actually come to a high school party or people that just wanted to confirm the rumor that was already circulating that he had enlisted. Sarah, the girl whose house it was, was a latch-key child. Her parents were about as inattentive as they come. The parties here were frequent enough that even Samuel had been to one before. But he expected that tonight, like then, he would blend into the woodwork and neither she nor most of the other attendees would know he was there. Besides, he was here to see one person. He looked around the house to find Samantha.

The house, like most of them that all of these kids grew up in, was larger than a family of four needed, but not extravagant to the point of ridiculous. Like everyone else, they all grew up with more than most in a time of plenty. But seeing as how graduation was so close, the house was packed more than usual. Samuel thought that perhaps after 18 years of making sure their children didn't get into too much trouble, most of the parents must have just stopped caring and let them roam. Samuel took stock and tried to find Samantha in this horde of delinquent juveniles. He was strangely calm. He had completely adopted a "no worries" attitude about the whole situation. He looked up the staircase and saw Samantha standing in the foyer area. She was surrounded by her usual crowd of sycophants and suitors. Describing them as sycophants was not a cruel mischaracterization. Samuel had often tried to explain to Samantha that she was the glowing source of energy to her crowd. Most of her friends basked in it. At least she used her powers for good. There was an uncharacteristic friendliness from the "cool sect" of their high school which was undoubtedly due to Samantha and a couple others' genuine kindness rubbing off on the rest of them out of osmosis.

Samantha had watched Samuel walk in. He may have been unusually forward the other day, but he was still very predictable. Samuel would not come into someone else's house through any other door but the front door. It was a part of his strange adherence to every social convention that was in place. Her stomach was strangely in knots. She had zoned everyone else out.

She must have been staring when she heard Michelle say, "I guess he showed up after all."

Quickly, Samantha looked away from her stare to look back at Michelle.

"Yeah, I guess he did."

Michelle was one of Samantha's closest friends. The thought kind of made Samantha laugh inside. Samuel had burst the bubble on most of her friends like Michelle when he explained that she was really just a sycophant after sharing some drama that had happened between all of them with him. He was right. Michelle was not someone that Samantha trusted emphatically. Samantha had come to realize that female politics could be absolutely toxic. Samantha prided herself on being independent in mind and spirit. Michelle seemed to respond by being independently tied to whatever opinion or decision Samantha held. Samantha knew Michelle was on the edge of her seat trying to decide if she was supposed to like Samuel now after Samantha had told her he was coming to the party. A torrent of questions had spewed from Michelle ever since Samantha told her.

"Really? So are y'all like a thing now? I thought he just brought you pizza. Did you know he was joining the Marines? Do you think he did that to impress you?"

It had gotten exhausting.

Samuel saw that Samantha was talking to Michelle.

Samuel was not usually a very judgmental person, but he despised Michelle. In general, Samuel was of the opinion that however someone saw fit to navigate the minefield of a path from adolescence to adulthood was probably acceptable. The amount of hormones coursing through the body during that phase was probably enough physical evidence to merit an insanity plea in court for any misstep one might make. But Michelle was the epitome of a parasitic human being. Samuel thought she must not have been hugged enough as a child because she was the type that would do quite literally *anything* for attention. And to his own demise the person she sought attention from the most was Samantha. Samantha looked beautiful as always though. He got the impression that Samantha had gotten somewhat dressed up for the occasion. He began to feel more than a little flattered at the thought that perhaps she had gotten dressed up for him. To be fair, he only ever saw her at school or at work. So, she might always dress like that on the weekends. But she was in a sundress with her hair down. There is not enough that can be said for the beauty of a woman that is neither shy nor flaunting in her wardrobe. And that is precisely how Samuel would describe how Samantha looked. She never overdid the make-up and she never wore something that advertised a level of sexuality that seemed inappropriate, but she also was not going to wear longer shorts just because someone's grandmother thought hers were too short. Her choice in fashion reflected her personality--genuine.

When Samantha looked back she saw Samuel looking up at her. There were butterflies in her stomach. He was staring up at her and smiling. She smiled back and waved for him to come up the stairs to her. For the first time, Samantha began to think about more than just what tonight meant. He was here and she intended to treat the night as the first night of a courtship that had evolved naturally. What she did not know was what that meant in any length of time. He looked as invariably professional as he always did. A polo, jeans, neatly combed hair, that was exactly what you could expect from Samuel.

Samantha knew one thing: Samuel had become incredibly important to her. How ferociously selfish must the human race be, that the only time someone realizes how important someone else is to them is upon learning the news that they will be gone soon. For no less than two years she had ample opportunity to explore this person. But now there is an impotence of time. But to confuse matters worse, the lack of time proposed an even more futile endeavor. What was the point when in a few short weeks the cast and crew of this potential love story would be changing?

Samuel made his way up the stairs. In his head he was rehearsing his introduction. *Hey, babe.* Samuel was fairly certain sounding like a total tool was not a good choice. Whoa to the fates that now, when it is too late to turn around and go home, that nerves take over. Samuel felt sick to his stomach as every step took him closer to the decision of exactly how to make this most difficult greeting.

Now, standing outside the tightly packed circle of people around Samantha, he uttered the only thing he could force his mouth to say, "Hey, Sam."

The circle of human mass quickly jerked their heads to see what unworthy serf would deign to speak to their queen.

"Hey, Sam." Samantha replied in her customary sweet tone with a glowing smile on her face.

The people who not a moment ago had not noticed his ascent were all now staring at him. One by one they looked back to Samantha as if to see if Samuel was accepted into this social group. Upon seeing her smile, they all slowly slid their scowls into smirks and shuffled to the left and right to allow him a small space to waddle into.

Samuel mentally noted how few people had probably ever been allowed to stand in this circle freely.

Before he could take a moment of pride in his current situation he heard a shrieking, "Hey, Sam!" from Michelle.

She was like a parrot that just attempted to repeat whatever her keeper said.

"Hey, Michelle," Samuel said forcing a smile and cordial tone.

In some weird ritualistic offering, one of the guys in the circle held out a beer as if to say *Here new one, share in the spoils of our last hunt.* Samuel looked up to see that it was Paul Carver.

Samuel took the beer and gave a cordial nod, saying, "Thank you."

Yes, great hunter, Samuel thought to himself, *I am grateful for your offering of friendship.*

Samantha was not surprised by Samuel taking the beer. They had talked before about how funny they thought it was that alcohol was a necessary, but ridiculous, social lubricant. Samuel had drunk before, but she knew he was the type who had probably never been the worse for wear due to drinking. She looked on smiling though. She wished she knew what was going on in that witty mind of his. Samuel was always cordial and polite in his conversations. But Samantha felt like their many pizza date conversations had given her a unique insight into his mind. Samuel was an observer. He had a keen understanding of everyone, their roles in particular settings, and most importantly their inner motivations. And on top of that he was actually quite funny in his comparisons and commentaries on people. Samantha was trying to imagine what funny thoughts must have been playing in his head as he was almost like some alien talking to a group of humans for the first time.

"So I heard you joined the Marines," Paul said as Samuel took the beer.

That was fast, Samantha thought to herself.

"Yeah," Samuel replied abruptly.

"What made you decide to do that?" Paul asked getting right to the point.

"Well," Samuel started. "You know there's just a—" Samuel said before being interrupted.

Samantha was listening intently as she had not yet heard the answer to this question herself.

"Don't you know that it's dangerous?" Michelle voiced

loudly.

Samantha was not sure who was more annoyed by the interruption, Samuel or herself. Samuel's face twisted as if he had just been asked the dumbest question in the history of spoken language.

"Yes, Michelle, the danger had occurred to me," Samuel said in response even though he did not see a reason to respond to such an insolent question asked at such a rude time.

But these were Samantha's friends and there was no reason to offend her by being rude to any of them, even Michelle. Paul seemed eager to probe Samuel more after having his last question go unanswered. Paul was a track star and a wrestler. He was a good enough guy, but he was clearly established as one of the more alpha types out of all of the guys in their school.

"I just never picked you for the type," Paul said.

Samuel had been waiting for a softball like that for a while.

"What type is that Paul?" he asked looking back towards Samantha.

Samuel wanted to make sure that she heard his crushing response to this question since he had mentally rehearsed a full dialogue encompassing any response Paul might give.

Before Paul could even answer, Michelle interrupted yet again, "Well, like, what if you have to kill someone?"

Samuel felt his heart sink. He looked around and everyone in the group was staring at him intently waiting for an answer. Samuel was disconcerted. He had not really considered the possibility. He was a southern boy. He was pretty sure he had killed a duck before. But to kill another human being was certainly something more visceral. Killing a person, to snuff out any possible continuance, carried no romantic overtones.

Samantha could tell that the question made Samuel uncomfortable. His face twisted and his head sank. This seemed to confirm a suspicion that she had about the whole choice he had made. He must have been uncharacteristically immature and impetuous in his decision to join. He was never a violent or confrontational person. He must not have thought this through. But Samuel broke the silence in typically brilliant fashion.

"I would hope it would accomplish something," he said softly but with a certain level of determination.

Samantha noted how simple yet wise the answer was. What more could anyone ask of any task? Does a surgeon not attempt high risk surgeries that could very well result in the death of the patient simply hoping it accomplishes something? Samantha had never considered that the taking of life might accomplish something until that moment. But she definitely understood how, in something as unsavory as war, killing someone might accomplish something. But here in the upper middle-class suburbs, the idea seemed very alien.

The silence was palpable. Samuel could judge by the silence that his dignified answer to that most ignominious question must have struck a chord. And he felt that he had avoided the obvious follow-on question "what if he died?" Samuel could already feel the strains of war and he had not even begun his training. He was already some alien species being interrogated.

Ah, yes, little green man, we understand your species still engages in armed conflict. What's that like? he thought to himself. He had grown up with these people. He was raised with them and had all the same influences. But now, after espousing his values that they all should seemingly share, he was foreign to them.

Samantha started to feel even more uncomfortable at the situation. It was as though Samuel was a novelty. She did not understand why he was offering himself up to a dangerous and violent endeavor, but she could fathom it. The feeling amongst most of middle-class suburban America was that *they* started it. Everyone watched in horror, not even five years before, as the peaceful world they had all grown up in was shattered. She could understand Samuel being angry and wanting to do something about it. Being a girl, she never felt compelled to *do something.* But she could understand that he might. She could feel her face getting flush with anger.

"Let's go get some air," she said, determined to escape the gawking onlookers.

Samantha grabbed Samuel's hand and pulled him towards the stairs. She looked back at Michelle to express her disdain and to signal that it was not okay for her to follow.

Samuel was not sure what to think. He had never had physical contact with Samantha for this long before. She had hugged him before and, flush with hormones, that made him uncomfortable enough. She had simply reached out and taken his hand and led him away. In this moment she seemed like a titan of strength and decisiveness. Overawing him and everyone else, she had ended an awkward conversation as if by decree. And now the sea of people simply parted as she approached while she pulled her willing captive to, well, wherever she wanted. Samuel knew she could feel the perspiration on his hand. But she not only did not seem to care, the further they got away from her friends, the more obvious it was they were going somewhere private. Samuel was stupefied with disbelief. The pace of the evening seemed to be relentless.

Samantha had a rush come over her. With every person they passed, she only saw more gawking faces staring at Samuel intent on subjecting him to more undignified conversations. She was not worried where they all might have thought she was taking Samuel, or the reason. She only felt a primal desire to protect him from her immature peers. She was reminded how all of these people had never been like Samuel. This uncouth rabble re-enforced her new, or at least newly recognized, attraction to Samuel even more. They reached the door leading out to the garage of the house and she stormed through it. The smell of marijuana smoke hit her in the face indicating that they were still not clear of all of them. By now Samantha was thoroughly flustered. She continued dragging Samuel out of the garage into the driveway. By now she really had no reason to continue holding his hand, but she also liked doing it.

Samuel was beginning to grow concerned about where exactly Samantha was taking him. As they reached the point where the driveway met the sidewalk, he planted his feet to keep her from dragging him any further. As he pulled her back to him, she turned around. She looked like she had tears forming in her eyes.

"I'm sorry," she gasped. "I shouldn't have made you come."

Samuel instinctively pulled her close and hugged her, trying desperately to comfort her in some way.

"It's ok," he said softly, "I can go."

Samantha pulled her head back away from his chest to look him in his eyes and said, "Sam, I should have not been so selfish and made you do what I do on the weekends."

Her smile indicated that she could read his mind. Samuel was worried he had embarrassed her. But with a simple disarming smile, Samuel was reassured that it was her friends that had embarrassed her.

"You are important to me, Sam," she continued. "You are the one running off to start a new life for a good cause. I should have gone to do...." she paused, "whatever you do on the weekends."

Samantha had perhaps not ever felt so vulnerable to a boy before in her life. She was not a maneater, but she did not let herself feel encapsulated by any guy. She was desperately trying to make sure that Samuel felt appreciated by her. Samuel let out a chuckle.

"Well, Sam," he said laughing, "I had a riveting evening planned initially, practicing a few songs on guitar and to wind down from that ruckus I was going to read some of 'Caesar's Commentaries on the Gallic War' to see if I could divine any tips to get ready to fight an insurgency."

Samantha felt a smile come back to her face. He still had his arms around her which she liked and she remembered that Samuel was fairly impervious to the opinions of others as he was completely aware and comfortable of his stereotypical nerd status.

"But then," he continued, "I remembered that I wasn't even going to college beforehand, so I would not have the unfortunate task of having to develop a strategy anyway."

Samantha was staring into his eyes wishing she could have gotten an answer to Paul's question. But now, she did not want to bring it up again.

"All the tests are done, Sam," Samuel continued sullenly.

He dropped his arms from around her in a rapidly shifting mood.

"All of the projects are turned in. Everything I would normally be doing with my weekends is over."

Samantha felt like in that moment she got the answer to the question. Samuel's whole life had been one long stream of tasks to get him ready for college so that he could pick a major, to get a career, to complete some long stream of tasks until he died. He had never taken time to enjoy any of it; not his hard work or the admiration of his peers, he had never stopped to smell the roses. Maybe this whole impetuous decision was not a fool's errand but an escape.

Samuel began to reflect that his entire academic career had been a waste of time. Holding Samantha just then was probably the highlight of his time in high school. What had any of it meant? Here he was standing at the end of a driveway with the most gorgeous girl he had ever known. They were probably best friends in a weird twist of fate. They laughed together, shared secrets with each other, and if she wasn't attracted to him at all she at least tolerated him enough to let him put his arms around her. He could have spent the last four years happily passing the days with Samantha, but instead he had spent his time packing his resume to be the ideal candidate for some university to accept into an honors program.

"Maybe you've earned the right to find something new to do," Samantha said in a characteristically positive tone.

She had a way of overcoming someone's negativity with pure positivity. She dropped her arms finally from around his waist. But she did not step back to create any more space.

Samantha had made up her mind that she was going to spend the next few weeks trying to rehabilitate the workaholic standing in front of her and find some joy in his life before he left.

"So," she said in a chipper voice, "what does Samuel Parker like to do?"

"First off," he said rolling his eyes and smiling, "Samantha Wallace, I think you misunderstand. I enjoyed tests and papers and projects."

"Well, if you want," she replied, "we can run and go get the MCAT prep books or something."

"No." he scoffed back.

"Yeah," she said while considering the reality, "you would probably do really well on those practice tests and it would really piss me off."

Samantha wanted to go into the medical field. Samuel had always been on the track to be a lawyer and everyone knew he would make a good one. Junior year, a law school had brought a practice L-SAT for his AP Government class to take in some vain attempt to scare them about law school, and Samuel scored higher than the majority of their law school students.

"Well, come on, Sam," Samantha said feigning desperation in her voice, "you have got to work with me here."

There was a long pause.

"Well," he said, "for the last two years, the highlight of my day has been eating pizza with you and hearing you talk about your day."

Samuel had no idea why he said that other than it was true. He was not smooth, especially not with Samantha. But he could read the expression on her face and it told him it was exactly the right thing to say. She was looking at him like he imagined he usually looked at her. The reality was it made him feel sick. He was afraid. Somehow in the course of a few days he had gotten this woman's undivided attention and in a matter of weeks he was going to leave her for an undetermined amount of time. Samuel thought to himself that this is why women grow to be cynical consumers of B-list romantic comedies. It must be some fantasy world they get to live vicariously through, where everyone lives happily ever after. Samuel was going to be the dagger pointed right at her heart all while pulling her in for a fatal first kiss. Not that he was her first kiss, but since he knew all of her innermost secrets, and judging by the way she was looking at him now, he was fairly certain it might be the first one that broke her heart. The old adage that "nice guys finish last" was merely a half truth. Samuel considered himself a nice guy, but he was not finishing last. He was setting up the utter destruction of a genuinely nice girl. And if every "nice guy" that ever crossed her path in the future never got a chance again, it would probably be due to her entirely reasonable defense mechanism. At least with assholes a woman knows what to expect.

"Then let's go get pizza" she said finally, as if to confirm his suspicion that his line had worked.

If Samantha had any doubts about how she felt about Samuel prior to that comment, she had none anymore. There is an inevitable downside to the sexual liberation. While the stigma of sexuality might have subsided, it is automatically assumed in modern times that physical attraction supersedes the magnetism that develops between two people. And that was probably the best metaphor to describe the way Samantha felt for Samuel at that point. Slowly over the past two years, the magnetic pull of his personality had pulled her towards him. Once Samuel openly declared his affection for her, it was like two magnets that had gotten close enough to stick together. It was not an instantaneous, love at first sight, storybook romance. It had developed organically. But Samantha was not stupid or naive, she was fully aware that this was not a good time for either of them to chase the dream of a relationship. But Samantha was also not the type to fly in the face of adversity. She was not afraid of space or time and refused to be a slave to either. She knew that Samuel had feelings for her and she would not lie to herself and deny that she had feelings for him regardless of the potential struggles of a long distance relationship or with long intervals of loneliness.

Samuel looked at her with a smirk for a long while until he finally said, "Ok. Let's go."

The pair rode in relative silence while they looked for an open pizza parlor. Samuel felt an immense amount of pride at the fact that Samantha had all but abandoned her friends without any regard for what that might mean to her relationship with them. She was sending and receiving text messages throughout the trip, and Samuel gathered that they were to the girls Samantha had just left at the party. But Samantha also seemed both annoyed by and entirely uninterested in the contents of the text messages.

Samuel did not know how to make small talk with Samantha. In a very strange way, she knew everything there was to know about him, and he was confident that he knew all that there was to know about Samantha. In the classic romances, the star-crossed lovers always want to know *everything* about each other. And that was the premise of their relationship, but for Samuel and Samantha, they already knew *everything* about each other. The contemplation of that reality coupled with the nausea that he still felt kept Samuel unusually quiet.

Samantha felt the burden of the silence in the car. She desperately wanted to know the answer to Paul's question. Why had Samuel joined the Marines? She secretly wondered, if it was for a bad enough reason, if she might be able to convince him to back out and the two of them could start their happily ever after. Several times the question was on the tip of her tongue. But she was still mortified by the circumstances of the party earlier. She felt completely responsible for Samuel getting spoken to and treated like a specimen. She was not sure if she had over-reacted or if Samuel had under-reacted, but she could not bring herself to probe him any further for answers.

She was comfortable with the idea that his reasons were his own and could accept them, even in anonymity. What Samantha was more interested in was how deep Samuel's feelings for her ran and what that meant moving forward.

"Well this is awkward." Samuel said breaking the silence.

Samantha looked over at him. He was looking at her while changing gears. She must have been staring at the road with what she imagined was a petrified look for a long time. She could not help herself. She burst out in hysterical and uncontrollable laughter.

"You look like I just gave you a prison sentence," Samuel continued joining in her laughter.

The two of them were laughing to the point of tears until about the time that they pulled into the pizza cafe.

In between breaths Samantha managed to force out the words, "Two days ago—." She paused, both to catch her breath and to consider her next words carefully. "We...were best friends... and now you are going to war..." She took another long pause to laugh and fight off tears and because the thought was funny. "And we are..."

Samuel was laughing uncontrollably too. It was possibly the most ridiculous course of events he had ever witnessed.

"We are what?" he asked laughing.

The two of them looked at each other in the eyes. The laughter died down until they both had a serious look on their faces. Samuel could nearly read every involuntary twitch of Samantha's face by this point in their relationship. He knew she was fighting back laughter. There was a long pause of silence and the tension rose in the car. Samuel could not hold it back any longer. He smiled and shrugged his shoulders. Samantha mimicked his motion exactly and the two of them went back to laughing uncontrollably. Samuel knew there was no way to, nor any reason to attempt to, define whatever was blossoming between the two of them. At the moment, he was comfortable with her knowing that he had fallen for her and he understood the fact that she had feelings for him.

After a few long minutes of laughter, Samantha finally said, "Well, let's go discuss what we *are doing* over pizza."

Samuel nodded in agreement as Samantha was already sliding out of his car. Samuel observed all of the social customs like opening women's doors. But Samantha, on the other hand, seemed to intentionally break any that involved her behaving a certain way because she was a woman. Samuel thought to himself how it was just another level of strange considering the fact that they were here together now. Samantha was walking about a pace and a half in front of him.

If he did not know her as well as he did, he might have been offended. It might have seemed like she was eager to get the whole thing over with. But Samuel was marveling at the fact that she was out with him at all. Technology had turned every teenager into paparazzi. Anyone that saw them together could send a text message bulletin to twenty-five people who could tell twenty-five people until everyone knew. And the on scene reporter could even snap a picture on their phone as proof of the affair. The implications were not lost on Samuel.

But just then, about halfway across the drive in the front of the parking lot, Samantha looked back at Samuel with a huge smile on her face and said, "Come on."

His gaze drifted downward until he saw she had her hand out for him to take. He slid his hand into hers and she jerked him quickly towards the front door of the store. But she didn't drop his hand.

Samuel was looking into her eyes again. Samantha could feel her heart about to beat out of her chest and she was positive that Samuel could feel her pulse through her hand he was holding. She enjoyed him touching her. Unlike any boy she had been with before, she did not feel like she had to be on guard to make sure he did not try to create more physical contact. She was actively trying to solicit more physical contact and she really was not sure where she wanted it to stop. She definitely wanted Samuel to hold her again. She was fairly certain she wanted Samuel to kiss her though, not by the end of the night, right then.

Samantha did not feel like the two of them had any time to waste and ultimately, she felt like it was her fault. Had she had these feelings for Samuel the whole time and just refused to recognize them? She had known for years Samuel was attracted to her, but she never once stopped to think if she was to him. Her mind was racing back to memories of throwing M&Ms and other toppings from behind the counter and Samuel trying to catch them in his mouth while she laughed. She remembered the time she told Samuel she had gotten back together with her ex-boyfriend, who was nothing but trouble. Samuel pretended to storm out mad and said she was in time out. The very next week she was telling Samuel how the boyfriend had again tried to have sex with her and she was done with him. Samuel did not rub it in or say "I told you so." He just listened intently. She could have had that as a foundation to a romantic relationship all along but now there was no time.

Samuel and Samantha had been staring into each other's eyes for quite a long time, holding hands in silence. Samantha finally pulled away towards the door still holding his hand.

"Sam," Samuel said pulling her back towards him.

He shocked even himself as he pulled her towards his planted body. Like an unstoppable force she spun all the way back around facing him and melted right into his arms. Their lips met and for the first time there was no denying that what was actually transpiring between them. Whatever it was that they were doing together, it was not a continuation of the friendship they had shared for the years previously.

Intro to Chapter 2: Teufelshund

War is a place that brings man to find religion. Recent generations questioned the dogma of religion. The idea was that there were no miracles to be found. Men like Samuel knew the truth. If you were looking for God in a world of men, you would come up short. God hid himself amongst the mundane. But the devil, the devil made his presence fucking known.

The first time someone feels the earth shake from an explosion, all doubt is released as to the existence of the devil. Only at times like that can someone know that God had been with them all along. If the devil is real, then God must be real, because nothing else could keep that fury at bay. Samuel knew God was real because he had gotten to spend time with an angel before he shipped out. Samantha was his proof, and now, watching Doc go to work on a fellow Marine in a seemingly futile attempt to keep him alive, Iraq was his proof. The devil was real, and God was real.

Mac was not in his chipper mood, making jokes and keeping everyone happy.

"You asked about Fallujah?" Mac said to Samuel, "It was a fucking lot like this."

Samuel did not know how many guys were hit, but he knew they were up shit creek. The platoon had been en route to hit a bomb maker, "the intel was sound," they were told. En route to the target, second squad found one of the target's bombs. His squad, first squad, got ambushed when they stopped so the platoon commander could get a situation report. His squad leader was over in a corner screaming at the platoon commander. Poor guy, the platoon commander was wide eyed, he had ordered the squad into this building so he could take stock of the situation, now they were dead center of an L shaped ambush with second squad and their casualties trying to fight through two streets to make it to this building.

The devil is real, Samuel thought, *but I left God with Samantha.* All the same, truth be told, he was relieved at the thought in a strange way. Better that all the forces of heaven be protecting her with all the forces of hell busy here. He could die on this cross. An explosion rocked the building. It was an RPG. Samuel snapped out of his inner dialogue. God wasn't here, Samantha wasn't here, and he needed to get his head in the game.

"Corporal!" Samuel shouted to Mac, "We need to get the fuck out of this building."

Mac looked towards the Platoon Commander who was shouting at the squad's radio operator to relay information to headquarters.

Mac looked back at Samuel and said, "No go Pony Boy. Second Squad is en route to us. This is a Casualty Collection Point now."

We're all about to be casualties soon, Samuel thought as the building shook again.

The Platoon commander shouted to the Marines in the room, "We got a lot of ass oscar mike, just hold them off!"

Samuel was putting out some suppressing fire out one of the windows when the third RPG hit the street and kicked up a whirlwind of debris. The dust and dirt and sand kicked into his eyes.

Samuel closed his eyes for a moment. A voice in his head said, "Sometimes you send the devil to do God's work." He had heard that before, although he was not sure where. He took a deep breath and exhaled slowly. A song started playing in his head. Samuel opened his eyes and was calm. It was his 20th birthday, and suddenly he knew exactly what he wanted. Well, what something inside of him wanted, he wasn't sure what it was. He did not want to survive. He did not want to get out of this building. He wanted the agents of the devil outside to fucking fear him.

As Samuel popped his head around the door that led to the street, he opened his eyes. He saw several gunmen. Instinctively, without a single thought, he poured rounds in their direction. Their bodies fell to the ground like rag dolls, indicating that, now, three were no longer a problem. Samuel

took a few steps out the door. His weapon was one with himself. He scanned the top of the two-story buildings across the
street. He saw and dispatched a man loading an RPG on top of
one of the buildings, precision shooting. He continued on his
way until he reached the other side where the corpses left over
from his initial burst lay dead. He looked back across the street
briefly and saw that a few of the Marines in his squad had
made their way out of the building and were joining in his new
offensive.

Suddenly, Samuel had a strange feeling. Jealousy. He was
going to jealously guard his kills. Not for glory, simply because
he wanted the kills more. He burst through one of the doors
on the side of the street where he was now. Samuel's squad
was to his west, second squad was two streets further west
fighting their way east towards them. Third squad was far to
the north coming at the target from the north side. One cross
street north there was an unknown number of enemy fighters.
Samuel understood the entire layout, but he was not sure how
he knew it. But he knew he was going to push out to the street
to his east and ambush the ambushers, as they would be trying
to push further south and completely envelop the two squads.

Samuel's instincts served him well, as he was pushing
through the building he was in, he saw two men emerge from
the entryway leading from the rear of the building that led to
the street he was trying to get to. He let out a burst and made
quick work of them. The second man ripped the curtain down
from the entryway. Samuel could see daylight from the doorway leading to the street to his east. Samuel felt himself smirk
as he made his way outside.

Samuel looked to the north and saw a small group of
men unloading boxes of ammunition out of a car with rifles
slung on their backs. He let out a burst to ensure that they did
not complete their task. By this time Mac had caught up to him
and joined in the shooting.

"Get some, Parker." Mac said, "We can hit them from
this side while the rest of the squad hits them from the other

street." Samuel simply nodded as he saw the rest of the fire team emerge from the building. He was disappointed. They had ambushed the ambushers. But something felt off. Samuel had released something inside of himself. And whatever it was had a bloodlust.

CHAPTER 2 BEGIN PLANNING, ARRANGE RECONNAISSANCE, MAKE EXCUSES...

The last two weeks had been like a whirlwind. In a strange way, Samantha felt like she and Samuel had spoken much less than they ever had before. But, they spent every available moment together, the difference was every moment they spent together their lips were locked and no matter what they did they could not find the willpower to create any distance between them. Graduation Day had come and after they had spent their time with their families, they met each other and spent hours together. Samantha had all but abandoned her school friends, no parties, no pool visits, and no late night phone conversations with "the girls." She would go to his house and spend hours with him in his room until they had to smuggle her out of the house as it was an unreasonable hour for a teenage boy to have a girl over. Other times he would come over to her house and it was effectively the same smuggling but with him as the contraband. She had taken to bribing her little brother to not say anything to her parents and help them smuggle him in and out of the house. They had not talked about what they were as far as titles were concerned and quite frankly, she did not care. Samantha did not want to waste any time having to go through the ins and outs of meeting parents or showing off the new boyfriend. Typically, introducing a boy to her father was the sign that it was a serious relationship, but it seemed so trivial for her to do that with Samuel.

Samuel felt very much the same way as Samantha did. He was drinking up every drop of her he could. Anything else was a distraction. Samuel felt like his family had been treating him as a pariah since he told them he was joining the Marines anyway. He found nothing but irony in the duality of the mood in his house. His mother and father and sister all carried themselves like he had contracted some fatal illness and wore a visible depression on their persons. Meanwhile, Samuel was floating everywhere he went. He would come to dinner, eat as quickly as possible with very little conversation, bolt to put his dishes up, and then escape to meet Samantha.

Samuel had already quit his job at the pizza parlor. It was another unneeded distraction from Samantha. Their clandestine time together was all that mattered to him. But then, one day, the young couple's luck ran out. Samuel was walking Samantha down the stairs of his house, stopping every other step to kiss again. They must have gotten careless in their stealth because Samuel heard footsteps coming from the direction of his parents' room. Before they could scramble the rest of the way down the stairs and get her out of the door they were greeted by "Hello." and the lights turning on. It was Samuel's mother. Samuel hung his head in disappointment.

Samantha watched Samuel's head sink into her chest. She could not help but feel that this was probably the first time he had ever been caught with a girl at his house and she could not help but find the whole situation cute. She leaned over and kissed his forehead and said in a sweet bubbly tone, "Hello Mrs. Parker."

Mrs. Parker leaned forward squinting to see who had just greeted her instead of her son.

"Samantha?" Mrs. Parker said in a loud surprised tone. All at once it sounded like the house came alive. There were now sounds coming from Samuel's sister's room, from his parents' bedroom again, and even the dog could be heard clicking his nails on the hardwood floor to come investigate who this stranger was in his house.

Samantha heard a muffled "Fuck my life." come softly from Samuel who still had his head on Samantha's chest. Samantha fought to keep back laughter as she put her hands on his face and lifted his head to look at him in the eyes. She gave him a look as if to say, *We have to deal with this now.* Samuel gave her a look like a toddler that just found out he had to go brush his teeth. As if they were having a completely non-verbal conversation he was replying *Do we have to?*

Samuel turned slowly to see his mother standing there with her mouth wide open in shock.

"Mom, this is Samantha Wallace." He uttered in despair.

"I know who she is." His mother snapped back. That was all the reminder Samuel needed that he had spent the past two weeks carrying on a sorted affair with the Homecoming Queen.

"I'm sorry dear," She said changing her tone to her normal sweet motherly voice, "If my rude son would have told me there was going to be company in the house I would have cleaned up and I would not be standing here in a nightgown right now."

Samuel could see the embarrassment on his mother's face. Maybe a heads up would not have been such a bad idea, after all he was 18 years old now and would be leaving to go fight a war soon. What was the worst they would have said if he had told them a girl was going to be visiting him regularly until he left?

"What's going on out here?" Samuel heard coming from behind his mother. It was his father. Before he could even respond to that inquest he heard

"Mom, who is that?" coming from his sister's room. Samantha seemed to find the whole situation frustratingly comical.

"Hey Carrie," Samantha said back to her, "It's Samantha Wallace."

"SAMANTHA WALLACE?" Samuel's sister shrieked in disbelief.

"Carrie go back to bed!" Samuel yelled to his sister in anger. There was a long quiet pause as every living thing in the house sat motionless in disbelief.

The silence was broken first by the dog standing at the bottom of the stairs sniffing loudly trying to figure out what was going on.

"Well why don't y'all come into the kitchen for a moment?" Samuel's mother said finally, "we can at least get a proper introduction."

Samantha looked at Samuel's face to see if that was what they were going to do or if they needed to make a break for the door. Samuel took her hand in his and began to lead her the rest of the way down the stairs. She wanted to console him and make sure he understood that she did not find this to be the end of the world. By the time they got into the kitchen she could see Samuel's father standing by the coffee pot making a new pot. He had his back to them. Samantha was not sure that she had ever met Samuel's father. She had not seen Samuel's mother since probably 5th grade at some school event, but she at least could have picked her out of a crowd.

About the time they shuffled into the kitchen, Mr. Parker turned around. His face was pure shock when he saw Samantha. Samantha felt her face get flushed and red hot. Samuel's mother had retreated to their bedroom evidently to freshen up. Mr. Parker at long last broke his incredulous stare and stuck his hand out towards Samantha and said, "Hello, I'm Mr. Parker. I'm Samuel's father."

Samantha took his hand and shook it gently saying, "I'm Samantha Wallace."

Mr. Parker smiled warmly at her and said, "Pleasure to meet you."

Samantha cordially replied, "Pleasure to meet you too, sir."

Samuel could read his father's face. He was not angry, he was impressed. Samuel had always thought anything with a pulse could recognize that Samantha was gorgeous, and Samuel did not take any offense to anyone recognizing that she was way out of his league.

But his father's face cut towards him in a scowl as he asked both of them, "Coming or going?" Before Samuel could analyze what would be the best response to that question Samantha interjected, "Samuel was walking me to my car."

Samuel gathered Samantha had a greater insight into this situation from experience than he would ever have.

"Been here long?" His father continued with his inquisition.

"Not terribly long," She said sweetly, "I just wanted to see Samuel after a long day, I don't get to see him as much as I'm used to with school being out and him not working next door anymore."

Samuel thought she was really good at this. There were a lot of truths and deceptions in that answer. The truth was they saw each other far more than they ever did before. She had not been there a terribly long time, and they were leaving. When she called Samuel to say she was coming over she had said she had a long day and needed to see him.

"Yes well, when he told me he was quitting his job," Samuel's father started as he turned around to get coffee cups, "I didn't really see much reason why he should continue. The Marines will give him food, shelter, and a paycheck soon enough."

That had been the only real conversation of choice around the house for the past month and every conversation somehow seemed to lead back that way.

Samantha hated being reminded that Samuel was leaving soon. She had come to pretend like it was not reality. The truth was it was a couple of short weeks away. Samantha noticed that Mr. Parker had gotten four coffee mugs down. She presumed that this meant that they were going to be expected to stay and talk at least as long as it took to finish a cup of coffee. Samantha spotted two stools on the other side of the counter next to the sink. She led Samuel around to where they could sit down. She knew this would send the signal to his parents that they were not trying to escape. She looked at Samuel in an attempt to communicate that this was all ok and that it was just a small hurdle that they would have to clear. Mr. Parker looked across the counter to where the young couple was now sitting.

"If I would have known about you," Mr. Parker said, "I wouldn't have even tried to talk Samuel out of going to the Marines."

Samantha felt wounded. Had he already made up his mind that she was some poisonous influence sinking her talons into his son?

"If you couldn't convince him to stay." Mr. Parker continued, "his mother and I never stood a chance."

Samantha believed she had figured out where Samuel had gotten his gift for flattery. She had been blushing since the moment Mr. Parker had first spoken to her and it did not appear that was going to change anytime soon.

Samuel saw his mother coming back into the kitchen, she had clearly combed her hair and had changed from a nightgown to one of his father's sweatshirts and sweatpants. He knew it was not fair to have sprung this on her. His mother had been through a lot these past few weeks. Her baby boy had graduated, signed up to fight a war, and had just brought a girl home. She was a wreck when his older brother told them he wanted to go to the Airforce after college and fly planes. He had not even committed to anything yet as he was about to start his junior year. Most people considered that to just be a prudent move for someone that wanted to be a commercial pilot anyway. But his mother had still taken that news very hard, and a couple months later Samuel dropped the Marine Corps on her like a ton of bricks.

She must have heard his father's comment because she said as she was entering the kitchen, "There's never been talking Sammy out of anything."

Samuel looked over at Samantha sitting next to her. She had an uncomfortable smile on her face. Samuel was not sure if she was uncomfortable with the conversation or the situation or both.

"You don't have to convince me of that." Samantha said smiling and looking back at Samuel.

"Samantha, we are a house of coffee drinkers here," Samuel's father said, "so please pardon my assumption that you would want a cup."

"Oh, thank you," Samantha replied in her sweet voice. Samuel recognized that she was talking to his parents the same way she talked to customers in the yogurt shop.

"Cream and sugar?" His father asked.

"Yes, please." she said.

Samantha was studying the interaction of Samuel's parents. They were like a well-trained assembly line. Without making eye contact or speaking a word, Mr. Parker would pour the freshly made coffee in mug after mug and Mrs. Parker would come behind him dumping a spoonful of sugar. Then Mr. Parker came back with cream and Mrs. Parker stirred each one after he had poured in the cream. Samantha saw in the way these two interacted with each other the genesis of Samuel's work ethic. They were hyper-focused on the task at hand and, even though it was such a menial task. The efficiency with which they finished the task made Samantha feel as though her coffee making skills were amateurish. Mrs. Parker slid a coffee mug in front of Samantha. Conspicuously, she was served first as the guest in the house.

"So, what are you kids up to tonight?" Mrs. Parker asked as she put Samuel's mug in front of him.

"Apparently not sleeping." Samuel said taking the coffee in his hand and holding it up as the punchline to his joke. Samantha saw Mrs. Parker roll her eyes in disapproval, but her smile was disarming to Samantha.

"Well, I was going to ask if you have any embarrassing photos of Samuel as a child, since we are all here now." Samantha said. She was hoping that she could steer this conversation away from talking about Samuel leaving.

Samuel was okay with sitting here looking at pictures, anything to stop questions about the two of them or discussion about him leaving soon.

"Oh, I have plenty of pictures of little Sammy." His mom said looking at him.

"Mary, we are not embarrassing our son any more than he already is." He heard his father say. Samuel looked at him, surprised by the sudden display of loyalty to him. His father was standing behind his mother and as he took a sip from his coffee he winked at Samuel. Samuel was abashed by this display. Telling his father that he had decided to defend his nation on the frontlines only brought harangues accusing him of being immature and not thinking anything through, but getting caught sneaking the homecoming queen into the house after hours and suddenly he was Samuel's staunch defender.

"So, Samantha," Samuel's mother started, "how long have you two been..."

Samuel felt his stomach turn. They had not discussed what they even were to each other and now they were having to discuss those facts with his parents.

Samantha was half expecting some questions like this. She knew that they had not openly discussed if they were *official*. Official was the colloquial way of saying that they were together as boyfriend and girlfriend and that they each would be afforded the rights and privileges of those titles. At that age, in that time of suburban America, there was much ado about whether two people were official. It was almost like a court legal status. Was one person in the wrong for talking to another person in what could be construed as a non-platonic way? Well were they *official.* Friends of one party or the other could be expected to be friends with the counterpart if they were *official.* But if they were not, a friend being accused of being rude to the counterpart almost had a legal defense by stating, "It's not like you two are official." Strangely, they had been spending so much time with each other exclusively there had not been any situations arise necessitated them defining anything.

But Samantha was certain her years of boy drama had prepared her to navigate these rough seas. "Well we've been friends for years now."

Samuel nodded his head in agreement. He felt like this was a good start to answering the question and he was completely comfortable with letting Samantha do all the talking.

"And a few weeks ago, I guess, we started spending more time together." Samantha continued. Samuel nodded again in agreement. So far so good. Nothing she had said up to that point would raise questions or indicate that they had been sneaking in and out of each other's houses for weeks now.

"I guess our friendship just blossomed," Samantha said in conclusion, "so it's kind of hard to say how long exactly."

Samuel was satisfied. Samuel looked at his mother and she appeared satisfied. Samuel looked at his father, he had trouble written on his face.

"So, did he tell you he was going to join the Marines?" Mr. Parker asked. Samantha's heart sank.

"No, not until he already had." Samantha said sullenly. Mr. Parker shook his head in disbelief. Samantha was not sure if he thought that she knew before-hand and approved or had somehow been a catalyst to his decision to go, but she felt a need to clarify.

"We actually didn't start really hanging out until after I found out." Samantha said.

Immediately she regretted it. It certainly sounded like now his joining the Marines influenced her decision to be with him. That was not entirely false, but not for the perceived reason. Sure, the knowledge of him leaving gave her the kick necessary to start a relationship with him in earnest, but it was not like she was only now attracted to him because he was rushing headlong into a dangerous future.

"Well, I was proud of him before," Mr. Parker started his reply, "I thought it was more than a little impetuous to throw away his future in college, but I am proud he wants to make a stand."

Samantha was starting to feel better about what she had said, she looked over at Samuel. His face was glowing. She gathered this was the first time his father had expressed that to him.

"But when I was his age," Mr. Parker continued, "if they'd have told me it would have gotten me a date with you, I would have volunteered to be on the first boat to Vietnam."

Samuel could feel that he was blushing perhaps more than he ever had in his life. He glanced over at Samantha and she was blushing just as much.

"WILLIAM," His mother shouted slapping his father on the shoulder. "Samantha, forgive him, he's a pig." She said.

The only word that was coursing through Samuel's mind was "escape." Escape, by any means necessary. He could not be subjected to this torture anymore. There were a few long beats of silence other than Samuel's father laughing and murmuring something to his mother that Samuel both could not understand and was fairly certain he did not want to understand. Finally, his father walked up to the counter with his mug raised as if to solicit a cheers.

"Samantha dear," He started "as long as your parents know where you are and are ok with it, you can come whenever you want and stay for as long as you want."

Samuel was in shock. His father had basically just given his blessing to the sneaking around. The young couple slowly raised their coffee mugs to touch Samuel's father's.

"I for one," He continued, "all jokes aside, feel better

knowing he will have someone worth fighting to come back home to."

His father's voice almost sounded like it was cracking. Samuel believed he meant what he said. His father believed some romantic notion that a man fighting to get home to a beautiful woman would fight that much harder to make it through.

Samantha was both mortified and flattered. This Parker flattery took some getting used to. Mr. and Mrs. Parker shuffled out of the kitchen with a passing "Goodnight" and the young lovers were once again alone. They sat in silence and in awe and disbelief for a few moments. Samantha was deep in con-templation.

Was she really Samuel's best hope for survival? How much stock could she put into that notion coming from a tired father of a teenage boy who was leaving to a war that filled the newspapers everyday? Perhaps he was clinging to any idea that could comfort him. But on the other hand, Samantha felt as though she would gladly be his lighthouse guiding him back home when it was all said and done. Samuel was a sweet boy who would never hurt a fly. If she needed to be his motivation to do what he needed to do to make it home, she could do that. She slid her hand along the counter and took Samuel's hand in hers.

"I am so sorry," he said. "I think there is a gland hidden in the body that just spits out embarrassment. That gland stays dormant until you have high school aged children."

Samantha smiled as she replied, "They were sweet." Samantha pulled his hand up to her lips and kissed his hand gently.

"I see where you get your ability to make me blush though." She said quietly.

Samuel laughed and leaned over in his stool and kissed her.

They both finished up their coffee and made good their escape. There was a more relaxed atmosphere over the next few days, at least at Samuel's house. They were still sneaking around at Samantha's as they kept the clandestine arrangement there. Samantha had explained to Samuel that when it came to her father, he was going to demand an incredibly formal meeting, probably a background check, and a blood test before he gave his blessing to date his little girl. Samuel did not protest, and still avoided too much interaction with the two of them and his parents. Carrie, his sister, had become incredibly obnoxious. She was a freshman in high school and basically saw proximity to Samantha a credible boon to her own social status. On more than one occasion Samuel had to put his foot down and get Carrie to leave them alone. Samantha was a good sport as always though. She had swapped numbers with Carrie and at least put on a good show of being friends with her.

Samantha was getting to the point where she could not think of anything but the impending doom of Samuel leaving. She had tried to cancel her senior trip to give them three more days together. Samuel would not stand for it though. He had begun acting weird in general, but Samantha chalked it up to the same depressing overtones she was dealing with. They were down to 4 days together. Samantha had come over to his house and they were thoroughly exploring their feelings for each other in his bedroom. Samantha was a virgin. And she knew Samuel was too. Samantha had always felt like the first time should be with someone really important, not that she necessarily needed to wait for marriage. Samantha had thought a lot about it and had made up her mind that she wanted Samuel to be her first. There was never another person as important to her as Samuel was. So, hot and heavy and flush with hormones, Samantha decided to make a pass at taking it further. Samantha knew Samuel would never initiate it himself. She was working his pants off when he grabbed her hand without his characteristic gentle touch. Samantha stopped kissing him and looked while he shook his head no.

"Sam," He said softly, "I don't want you to waste your first time on me."

Samuel sat quietly staring at her for a moment. He really did feel like it would be a waste. He knew he had let this whole thing go too long as it was. He was fairly certain he could not keep from breaking her heart already, but he knew if he took her virginity he would ultimately crush her. The thought of that was too much to bear.

"It wouldn't be a waste," Samantha whispered, "I think I love you Sam."

That pierced like a dagger and tore open his insides. Samuel's head sank in utter defeat. How could he have been so selfish to have not called this off before it got to this point?

Samantha spoke again as if pleading with him, "I know I love you."

Samuel softly whispered, "I know I love you too. I always have."

Samantha took her hands and lifted his head up to look into his eyes.

"Then it's not a waste." She said.

Samuel could not look at her. He dropped his head again. Every fiber of his being wanted nothing more than to give in. But the conscious part of his mind reminded him what that would mean. In four days he would be leaving for at least four years. He had chosen to put the normal cursus honorum of suburban middle America on hold to go on an idealistic crusade. He would not drag her along with him. She was brilliant and hard-working and she belonged in college chasing her dreams, with boys chasing her, without a locket picture boyfriend keeping her from experiencing it all.

Samantha just assumed Samuel was afraid. The truth was she was scared too. But, she thought maybe she could help get them both through it. She reached for his pants again, and Samuel snapped at her, "No."

She reeled back again. She was wounded. She did not know if it was her or not.

"Sam," he whispered. "I cannot be the one who breaks your heart."

She felt a tear form in her eye.

"Well you're doing a pretty good job of it right now." She said fighting back the tears. For the first time since their first kiss his presence felt completely cold.

"Sam," Samuel continued, "... I know, and I am sorry." Samuel's voice sounded like he was fighting back tears himself. "I should not have been selfish enough to let it get this far. I am leaving, I may never make it back."

"Samuel," Samantha said loud enough to get his attention. "I will wait for you. For as long as it takes."

There was a long silence in the room, and somehow, Samantha felt him get even colder.

Samuel could feel his sorrow turn to frustration.

"I don't want you too." He said in a snide tone. "I couldn't really claim to love you if I wanted to rob you of the whole college experience."

The tears started pouring out of Samantha's face.

"Well don't I get a say in the future that I want?" She said.

"Of course you do, but don't you understand that no matter which one you want I am not there." Samuel said back. His brain had started turning the wheels. He was in full debate mode. This must be his most convincing argument of his life. Everything had led him to this moment. He had to argue the side that was against his own self-interest, the sign of a true debater. He had to convince the woman of his dreams that she was not in love with him, and that she was better off without him as baggage. It was a novel position but he felt up to the task.

"Samuel," she said, "you make it sound like you are already dead."

Samuel knew he could not relax the pace.

"What if I am Samantha?"

Her face sank into her hands as she began sobbing.

"What if this time next year I am just another casualty of some fighting in some shithole desert?" He continued, "What if I get my legs blown off?"

Her sobs were getting louder.

"Even worse," He continued, "What if I get my dick blown off and the last time you get to have sex was also your first time?" Samuel knew he had to give a knockout closing argument

"Because I know you better than you know yourself. You are a sweet person and loyal-- to a fault. You would wait for me Samantha. Until the end of time if you had to. You would take up the widow's mantel if something happened to me. And when the time came to give another man a chance, he would never get a full chance because he would live in the shadow of your perceived memory of me. I would be your impossible and untrue standard that you would compare the rest of the world to. And I cannot, with a loving heart, leave you standing by a mailbox waiting to hear if that's your fate or not. I believe that you would wait Samantha and that is why I am begging you not to."

Samuel was satisfied. That had been his delivery of a lifetime and still he felt like he lost. Samantha's crying subsided slowly until she was not crying at all anymore. She finally lifted her face out of her hands and looked at him.

"It's just not fair." she said.

"No, it's not," Samuel said.

"Stupid fucking war." She said. Samantha did not cuss often so when she did it carried that much more influence. Samuel put his arm around and sat next to her upright on his bed. They sat there in silence. Samuel was sure that he had made his point and convinced her, but he did not feel better for it. Finally, she broke the silence.

"Promise me one thing." Samantha said.

Samuel waited to hear the promise.

"When you make it home, come and find me." She said.

Samuel was about to say how he could not do that. He was going to explain how her waiting for him to come find her was the same thing as her waiting for him.

But she cut him off and simply said, "You owe me that much." Samuel hung his head. "No matter what condition you are in, I deserve to see you again when you come home." She put her hand on his face and pulled it towards hers to make him look her in the eyes.

"Besides," She said smiling, "I deserve to get a second chance before some slut looking for a soldier boy gets a first chance." Samuel was not happy about it but considered it a fair compromise. So, he nodded his head and said, "I promise."

Samantha knew that Samuel was the type that he would never allow himself to break his promise. As they both sank down into the bed, Samantha considered the terms she had just agreed to calmly. Effectively, he would leave, and when he came back home they would get a chance to rekindle their love. She rolled over and put her head on his chest and closed her eyes. She thought about how in the meantime, Samuel was demanding that she simply go to college and continue with her life as though the last few weeks had never happened. That seemed surprisingly reasonable. But still she felt heart broken. She wandered off to sleep as she began to fantasize about the day Samuel returned to her and swept her off of her feet.

The next morning the young couple shared a long sweet kiss as they said goodbye for what carried the potential to be the last time. Neither of them felt good about walking away, but Samantha was reassured by Samuel's promise to come and find her again. Samuel felt reassured that within a couple sorority formals and college boyfriends she would forget about that boy she almost had sex with that went to the Marines.

Intro to Ch. 3: Pride

Pride is something inherent in the warrior culture. The Marine Corps has embraced the mantle of "the Few and the Proud." The entire award system of the military is inherently designed to recognize acts of gallantry amongst the ranks. To recognize people for something to be proud of. Then they give you some piece of cloth to wear on your uniform as something to be proud of. Often lost behind the colored ribbon is the story. The combat action ribbon does not tell the story of the combat. The unit citations do not tell of the men who died. And the medals of valor only imply the price paid in blood.

Samuel questioned the sanity of taking pride in murder. He was proud that he was a Marine. He was proud that he had not cracked under the pressure of combat. Samuel was proud that he had saved lives in his conquest of those two streets. But something felt wrong about the idea that he would be getting decorated for killing those men, because he enjoyed it. The thought made him sick to his stomach. He had gone through that door with the intention of being recognized, of being feared, but only by his enemies. But this felt contrary to honest living. The platoon commander had told him he should be proud, and that he was writing a citation for a medal of valor. Samuel knew what pride felt like. The day he got his Eagle, Globe, and Anchor, he was proud. The night Samantha took his hand in public and they shared their first kiss, he was proud. That was something to be proud of, kissing the homecoming queen in front of a pizza shop.

Mac walked into the hooch.

"Corporal Mac." The Platoon Commander greeted him, "I was just commending Pony Boy here. You raised a hell of a Marine."

"Damn straight sir," Mac said, slapping Samuel on the back, "he decided it was time to give as good as we were getting and took it upon himself to make that happen."

The platoon commander chuckled and said, "His explanation was he saw an opening and he took it. I'll be doing a write up on him for that. That's precisely the type of decisiveness we like to see from our Marines."

The platoon commander took his leave so it was just in the two of them in the room. Mac was staring at Samuel and smiling.

"Next time you say something like 'We need to get the fuck out of this building' I'll know," Mac started, "you're plotting some shit."

"That shit wasn't planned," Samuel replied, taking a seat on his rack.

"Hell of a birthday present," Mac chuckled.

"What's that?" Samuel scoffed, "Dead men?"

"No, they're all going to make it," Mac replied, "Doc said they're all outa' the weeds now."

"That's not who I was talking about," Samuel said.

"Fuck 'em." Mac said, "These fuckers ain't worth a second thought. Believe you and me they would've loved nothing more than to send you home to little miss homecoming in a box with a flag on it."

Samuel thought for a moment what that meant. Maybe surviving was worth being proud of. If all war is hell, no one should be ashamed if the demon inside pops out to get you home.

"Don't dwell on that shit Pony Boy." Mac added, "It'll eat you alive. You speak your peace about what you see here to me, or little miss golden pussy, or your momma or somebody. And you let that shit go. In the meantime, you don't give a fuck about who needs to die so you can get home. You ain't dying in this shithole you hear me. You gotta' go be a senator or some shit so you can keep folks like me from ruining this world."

Samuel pondered if it was Mac's experience that was making what he was saying make sense, or some inner desire he had. Was he projecting that it made sense so that he wouldn't feel as guilty? Samuel only knew one thing: he enjoyed killing those men in the moment. Maybe nothing was wrong with him because he sure did not enjoy it now. But maybe something was. Maybe Mac was right about his future though, it was not a stretch of the imagination to believe that Senators enjoyed dooming men. If they weren't sadists why did this war keep going?

CH. 3 SEMPER FIDELIS

Samantha was sitting in her dorm room staring at her computer screen and studying when her phone lit up. She checked to see that she had a new text message. It was from Sarah. Samantha had not talked to Sarah in months. Sarah, ever the under-achiever, spent high school more worried about offering up her house for parties and establishing her social status than doing school work. As a result, she was back home going to the community college trying to build her way into following everyone to the universities. Samantha had gone to Ole Miss like planned. Samantha's life was back on the predictable path. She read the text message:

You remember that time you dated
Samuel Parker for like two weeks

Yes

Well you are going to be
upset you ever called that off

We called that off mutually.

He was a sweet guy.

Why do you say that anyway?

I just ran into him.

OMG girl he got HOT.

    Samantha felt her heart drop out of her chest. Was he back? The reality was she still found herself thinking back to their last night together. It was the second month of her second semester of her sophomore year of college so that meant, it was getting close to two years ago.

    Samuel had been right about some things. He was her gold standard when she thought of how she wanted a guy to treat her, and the truth was no one ever quite measured up. Samantha really had not been that focused on guys since she got to college. She was pretty absorbed in making sure she had a good shot at medical school. There had been a few guys here and there, and even one that was pretty serious, Cameron.

    Cameron seemed so sweet. He had acted like Samuel so much for months, at first. Surprise visiting her and listening to her worries, flatteries and compliments, everything felt like a guy that was like Samuel. But after about two months of them dating in earnest, it was like Cameron got bored and he cheated on her. Samantha had convinced herself that if a "real" Samuel was still out there she was not going to find him if she was looking, they would just happen. The thought that *a* real Samuel, would be *the* real Samuel felt too much like a romantic comedy to be real life though. So, Samantha had given up on that idea. She must have been zoned out for a while because she got another text message from Sarah.

If you are trying to find him on Facebook he
doesn't have one I already checked.

                      Lol. Thanks. Where did you see him?

He was up at Luigi's with Will Han.

    Samantha thought to herself that Sarah, bless her heart,

was not the sharpest tool in the shed. That and Sarah was completely in the clique of high school popularity that did not bother themselves with the interpersonal relationships of kids like Samuel. So, she would not have ever known that Will Han was one of Samuel's best friends from high school. And Luigi's was the pizza parlor Samuel worked at. Samuel was back making his rounds. Samuel's other best friend was Michael Morton. Michael was thoroughly in the growing cult of chronic social media posters. Michael would post pictures of Samuel and give a full itinerary of their moves if they were together. Samantha found Michael's page and, sure enough, there was a picture of Samuel.

The post:

"Just hung out with this American Hero.

Samuel's back in town."

Samantha stared at the picture for a good few minutes. She was sweating. It is unfair that women should develop so much faster than men she thought. She kissed a boy goodbye outside of his house two years ago. This was a grown man. To begin with he looked like whomever this was, ate Samuel. Samuel was always a kind of scrawny kid. This guy's arms were easily bigger than Samuel's waist ever was. His shoulders were broad, his chest was brawny. Samuel's neatly combed hair was replaced by a military cut. His face was showing a couple of days of growth. He had a devilish smile on his face and his face was full and square. The only give away that it was Samuel was that he had the same piercing light green eyes that even through a computer screen looked like they were peering through your soul.

Samantha could not believe he had grown up so.... well, Sarah was right, hot. Samantha found herself absorbed like a detective trying to uncover all the evidence she could about who this new Samuel was, where he had been, and how long he would be here for. She looked at every page she could think going through as many posts as she could find. His sister had changed her picture to a picture of her hugging him in uniform three days ago. Was that when he got back? She picked up her phone and scrolled down to Carrie's number. She then slammed her phone closed. She could not believe she was about to call his sister out of the blue after she stalked everyone he ever knew online. She guessed that he had forsaken his promise, or forgotten it entirely. Young love is often deep and sincere. But that tends to have young lovers swear oaths and vows they would never be able to keep.

Samantha finally sent Sarah a message to end the conversation and put the whole notion to rest:

> Go to Michael Morton's page you can
> drool over his picture there

Good work. OMG. He wasn't interested in me
anyway. He kept asking about you though.

> WHAT?!?

Samantha felt her heart jump into her throat. She waited for what she felt like was twenty minutes for a response from Sarah. She needed to know what he asked about and more importantly what Sarah had told him. The suspense got to be too much for her to handle so she called Sarah. Of course, she did not answer, so, she just called her again. Finally, Sarah answered.

"What is it, Psycho?" Sarah answered.

"What was he asking you about me?"

"Geez, Sam" Sarah said in a snide tone, "I didn't know you had it that bad. I mean he's hot now and all, but you are blowing up my phone at work."

Samantha realized that perhaps she did look a little too desperate for news about Samuel. But the truth was she was that desperate. It was like she had been consumed by a torrent of unresolved, two year old emotions.

"Sarah, I don't have time to explain what's going on. What did he say?" Samantha said forcefully.

"Well I was giving him everything I had," Sarah started in a relieved tone, as if she had missed this type of drama from her life,

"And he was just smiling and being his normal polite self, just like smoother. And then he was like, 'What's Sam up to?' So, of course, that was a buzzkill. Giving it your best and he asks about some other girl. But anyway, I told him you were at Ole Miss being great at everything like always. He just laughed and said something like 'I'm supposed to catch up with her later.' I asked him what was up with that. And by the way, kind of mad you never told me you kept in contact with him. But, he just said the same thing you said that he didn't have time to explain. So, you tell me what's going on."

Samantha was overcome with anxiety. Somehow knowing that he was going to be coming soon was worse than her thinking he'd forgotten about her. He had changed so much, at least physically, and if anything, she had gained a couple of pounds. She did not know if he was going to like what he saw when he was there in front of her.

"Sarah," Samantha started still in shock, "I haven't spoken to Sam since a few weeks after we graduated. I don't have a clue what's going on."

Samantha could hear Sarah say "What the..." As she ended the call.

Samantha sat there staring at the ceiling of her dorm room contemplating. She half expected to hear a knock on the door and for this nightmare to hasten it's pace. Samuel never wrote her, called her, or told her how she could contact him. He decisively cut her out of his life as though they had a bad break-up. She had never resented him for it, and she did not consider it a bad break-up, she never forgot about him. Apparently, he had not forgotten her either. She knew she would not be getting any sleep until she knew how this was going to play out, but she was merely a slave to time. She could not speed up the process and she could not make it slow down or go in reverse.

Samuel had been on U.S. soil for a grand total of seventy-two hours. He had been back home for approximately twenty-four of those and home felt no closer to home than the streets of Iraq. He had spent the last two months talking about plans with the guys about what all he was going to do when he got home.

The most important thing should have been to readjust but that, of course, was never considered. The great wide world had started talking about things like PTSD. Samuel believed in it plenty, but he did not consider himself to be experiencing that. No human being is going to go from the violence of Iraq to not in Iraq and not have some literal and metaphorical ringing in the ears. He wanted a comfortable bed, he wanted real food, he wanted to catch up on nine months of pop-culture, but he really wanted to have a conversation that was not between two people in a warzone. Not that Samuel particularly disliked warzone conversations, they were usually deep, meaningful, funny, ghastly, relevant, or if nothing else distracting. But he wanted to be a normal guy for a little while. He had done his duty now he wanted to be himself for a moment.

Samuel had met up with Michael earlier to go fishing. Michael was glued to his phone and was too much on that "Home of the free because of the brave" bullshit. Samuel understood he had a little bit of local celebrity to his name now as he was the first one to have, well, to quote another Marine "gone to an interesting place full of interesting people and killed them." But Michael just reminded him every second of how "Badass" it was. Then he had met up with William and gone to Luigi's. He owed William quite a lot. Apparently, Carrie had let him know he was going to be back. William got a flight from Michigan to be here for the cookout. Carrie had changed a lot too. Her relationship with Samuel had done a one hundred and eighty degree turn. Samuel was her hero now. She did not want to let him out of her sight and had done everything she could to make his homecoming a big deal. The manager at Luigi's would not let Samuel pay for anything. The whole day just served as a reminder that there was never going to be a sniff of normality in his life ever again.

But then out of nowhere Sarah Littleton walked in. Samuel thought it was funny, but he could tell she did not know how she recognized him. She would not have talked to Samuel much two years ago anyway, but she knew who he was. They had interacted plenty in high school. She was staring at him in a way that would have made the Samuel of two years ago blush. She was undressing him with her eyes and trying to stand in a sultry pose. Samuel was sitting at a booth with William with the manager hovering over the table going on and on about how Samuel was always such a good boy.

Finally, Samuel just said, "Excuse me." He heard William laugh from behind him as he walked towards Sarah. Then he heard the manager say to William, "I get it, after a year in Iraq, I'd be more interested in that too." Sarah was standing at the counter looking down at the menu pretending not to see Samuel walking up to her. Samuel knew Luigi's had not changed their menu in fifteen years, no one from this area did not know the menu by heart so he was fighting back laughter.

Sarah did look good but that was not what he was after at all. Make no mistake the man just spent nine months in the company of men as filthy as he was, trying not to get blown up, and therefore he would take whatever came his way in that regard, but he was looking for an escape from the droning conversations more than anything.

"Chef salad no eggs no onions add chicken fat-free Italian on the side." He said standing next to Sarah.

Sarah let out a giggle and began to say, "You're good."

As she turned to look at Samuel and her mouth opened gaping wide. Samuel let out a loud laugh genuinely amused by visibly watching the amorous expression on her face change to one of pure shock.

"Samuel Parker." She shrieked.

"In the flesh." He replied. Samuel was well aware of the fact that he was a scrawny kid and now he had the body of a professional athlete, so the shock value of his transformation was not lost on him.

"What have you been up to?" He asked hoping that he could dictate the course of this conversation and keep it from the war, or the Corps, or the lot.

"You know," She said nervously moving her hair behind her ear and looking down again, "Work and school. What-- what about you? what are you up to?"

Bingo, Samuel thought to himself. Sarah was so un-interested in him in high school she seemed to have forgotten, never found out, or never cared that he went to the Marines. He would at least keep this conversation going for a while.

"Not much, just in town for a little while." Samuel replied.

The two carried on a back and forth for a few minutes with "remember so-and-so" and "What are they up to now?" Sarah was taking advantage of the continuing conversation to move closer and closer until at one point she had put her hand on his arm while laughing at some comment Samuel had made. He knew she was dramatizing how funny the comment was, which annoyed him a little. Not that she touched him, more at the dishonesty.

Until finally she said, "I haven't spoken to you since that party right before graduation."

His mind snapped back to that night. That was the first night that he ever kissed Samantha. He remembered every single detail of that night and he never talked to Sarah that night. In his mind that was strike two for this conversation.

"No, we didn't talk at all that night." Samuel said bluntly. Sarah's face contorted. "To be fair," Samuel continued, "I wasn't there very long. We left really soon after I got there."

Sarah was trying to recover from her obvious misstep,

"Yeah, that's right. Samantha just like freaked out and made you take her somewhere else, right?"

That was strike three. This was over as far as Samuel was concerned. Fortunately, for him the fastest way to end this conversation was to get straight to the point he wanted to get to anyway.

"No, everyone was treating me like some kind of science experiment because I joined the Marines and she didn't want me to sit there and take it."

Sarah's face looked like her brain had just short circuited or like the little hamster in her head had a heart attack. She had just realized or remembered or cared where he had been.

"How is Samantha anyway?" Samuel added, twisting the knife. In general women do not want someone to ask about other women when they are flirting with them. But Samuel knew to ask her about Samantha was one million times worse. Samantha was frustratingly formidable to anyone, but Sarah had been in competition with Samantha for adoration since elementary school.

The truth was Samuel wanted to know about Samantha. He was certain she was happily settled down with some serious boyfriend, and he had no intention of screwing that up. But, he did intend upon keeping his promise to drop by and see her.

"Well," Sarah started, "You must have rubbed off on her. She, like, only cares about school. She had a boyfriend, but he cheated on her and now she just, like, doesn't do anything but study for her pre-med classes."

Samuel felt his nerves jump. He felt like tears were going to come into his eyes and he was fighting them back. It was not the news that Samantha was single that was forcing the tears. It was visceral. For nine months, he had only known a few emotions. Rage, fear, and occasionally regret.

Before that moment, that solitarily unimportant moment, of finding out his ex was single, when he felt nervous it was usually because he had *something* to be nervous about.

He felt nervous now, but he was not half expecting to have to watch his buddies get blown up. This was what Samuel was looking for. Samuel wanted to feel nervous about a woman or happy about her approval, or really anything that he did not have time for when he was in combat.

"Interesting." is all he could say. "I'm supposed to see her soon anyway."

Sarah looked at him dumbfounded as if he had just wasted her time by not telling her he was supposed to see Samantha soon anyway.

"It's a very long story Sarah." Samuel said hugging her, "but I really have to go, there are a lot of people I am still supposed to go see."

At that, Samuel walked back to the table and collected William and they left the parlor. While Samuel was walking to the car, it was like a very old wheel in his head started turning again. It was like the rust that was holding it in place had broken off and it was slowly gaining momentum to move at the speed it was supposed to. That wheel was the one that turned for women, and romance. That wheel was the sinew of thinking in poem and desire, staring into a woman's eyes and doing nothing else for the day. War had jammed that wheel.

In combat you need all of your brainpower for the task of surviving. Everyone daydreams on post and their minds wander to places filled with women that love you. But that is almost a defense mechanism to boredom. When someone is living in the rubble of a war-torn city the true belief in those daydreams is impossible. Samuel just realized he had made it out of the crucible, he was allowed to believe in daydreams again. That wheel was free to spin again. And his wheel had only ever spun for one woman.

Samuel's family, mostly his sister Carrie, had been planning this cookout for a long time. His dad had been working all day since the very early morning to get the smoker ready. They were having slow cooked pork. Samuel reveled in the glory. One of the worst things, he thought as a southern boy, about being in the Middle East was the lack of pork. For his entire life pork had its own spot in the food pyramid. So, he was excited to get to eat it tonight. His father had taken barbecuing seriously for as long as Samuel could remember. It was going to be a welcome consolation to the house packed full of people. In attendance were: four grandparents, five aunts, four uncles, nine cousins, his mother, his father, his sister, her boyfriend, his brother, his brother's fiancé, and six high school friends. Samuel felt like the main attraction at a Vegas show, and he had never much been one for being the center of attention. But he was ready to dutifully go on with the show, because his family had worked so hard putting the whole thing on.

Samuel was sitting on the back porch drinking a beer with William and a couple other friends that made the trip, and watching his dad perform the rites and rituals to get the pork to taste just right. Carrie came bouncing up to in front of him. She sat in his lap and hugged him.

She had hugged him every time she had seen him since he got home. Samuel was not sure if she felt guilty for years of mistreating him, or if she broke something of his while he was deployed, or if she was just genuinely glad he did not die. But, he accepted that he now had a loving affectionate sister, for whatever that was worth.

Samuel looked up and saw a young teenage boy standing in front of him. His shirt was wrinkled and his stringy black hair was almost completely covering his eyes. *The boyfriend,* he thought, *emphasis on boy.*

"Sammy," Carrie said jumping up to stand next to her show-and-tell, "this is Logan."

Samuel stood up for full effect. Samuel was neither tall nor short but he was a good head taller than this kid.

He stuck his hand out and barked, "Pleased to meet you."

The kid was visibly shaking. He stuck his hand out in an awkward manner as if he had never shaken a man's hand before.

Partially out of comedic value, and partially to re-enforce the kid's fear of his girlfriend's older brother, Samuel squeezed the kid's hand until he was satisfied that it hurt a little.

"P-pleased to meet you too sir." the scared little deer said.

"Calm down dude." Samuel said, "I work for a living. The oldest is the one becoming an officer." Samuel continued, pointing to their father out by the smoker, "And he's the boss around here. Just call me Samuel."

Samuel looked at Carrie and smiled. She smiled back in appreciation that all of the niceties were satisfied. She hugged Samuel again and they scurried off. Samuel sat back down.

"You were saying." Samuel heard. Samuel looked around the group confused. Everyone was looking at him wide-eyed. Samuel was quickly gathering that he must have been talking about something before and he zoned out. He felt his face get hot. He was beginning to feel embarrassed that he could not remember anything that was being said before.

He must have had his embarrassment all over his face because William stepped up and saved him. "You were telling Landon a story about going to post one night."

Samuel remembered, he was telling a story and then he saw his dad slap the pig over and had lost his train of thought thinking about some dead body or another. Or perhaps it was the smell of the roasting pig. But either way that was several minutes before his sister walked up. They must have been staring at him for a while.

"Well yeah," He said, "We have this Staff Sergeant in the COC that always said the same dumb shit when he was giving you your post briefing. He'd always be like, 'You just need your rifle, your PPE, and a water source. Don't bring any other shit, no i-players, no titty magazines.'"

Everyone was captivated again so he guessed that's right where he left off.

"So my buddy Torres," he continued, "was like fuck that guy. So, we get back to our hooch and we're getting our shit together and Torres strips down butt ass naked. Puts his flak and Kevlar on grabs his camelback and his rifle and walks straight to the COC to report for post." Everyone started laughing. Samuel continued, "By the time I caught up to him, Torres is getting his ass chewed and he's like, 'Staff Sergeant I brought exactly what you told me to.'"

Samuel was a little freaked out that he had completely zoned out when he was telling the story. But he was confident in the fact that he had a million funny stories like that one to keep everyone entertained without having to get into any bloody or gory details about the war. He knew he had a few stories that if his sister heard she would never stop with the hugging thing. And he certainly did not want his mother to hear most of the stories funny or not.

Just then he heard a voice say, "So how does this work do you salute me yet or not?" Samuel looked over and saw his brother Ryan standing in the doorway.

Samuel shot up and yelled, "Asshole, I'm never saluting you."

Ryan smiled and leapt towards him. They came together in a loud thud and hugged.

"Don't think just because you are a Marine now, I can't still kick your ass." Ryan said. The two started play-wrestling around on the porch.

"Boys stop," They heard their mother yell from inside, "if y'all break one of my planters I'm going to tear you both a new one."

The two brothers stopped and hugged again. Ryan had finally accepted a commission from the Airforce and was going to flight school when he graduated in May. Samuel was proud of his brother and was particularly glad he was going to be a couple thousand feet off the ground when it was his turn in the sandbox. Samuel saw a stunning blonde standing smiling behind his brother.

"I don't know why you are marrying the rude brother." Samuel said reaching his hand out to her in a greeting.

"Ha-ha. Jerk." Ryan said in a sarcastic tone.

"You must be Katie." Samuel said pulling her hand up and kissing it.

"Ok Casanova." Ryan interjected, stepping between them, "dude gets a little shrapnel and suddenly he's a lady's man. You used to not have the courage to talk to the lunch lady." Samuel laughed knowing he was telling the truth. Ryan continued his insult, "Hell, I always figured if I didn't carry on the Parker name it was going to die with us."

"Yeah, yeah, yeah." Samuel said putting his arm around Ryan. He looked past him and said, "Sweetheart, it's a pleasure."

Samuel led Ryan away from the door towards the other side of the porch.

"Cool it with the shrapnel talk dude," He said in a low tone, "you're the only one that knows about that."

"Shit dude," Ryan replied, "My bad, I just figured since you were out of there now it was all good."

"I just don't really want to talk about it, you know." Samuel replied.

"They are going to see the scars or the purple heart eventually you know, like at my wedding." Ryan said.

"Yeah," Samuel scoffed, "but I can tell Mom that it's like a boy scout merit badge for being kind-hearted, She'd never know the difference."

Ryan hugged Samuel again and said, "I'm just glad you're home dude. I didn't want to try to find another best man."

Carrie had made her way back out to the porch. Samuel whispered to Ryan, "Wait until you meet this kid Carrie is dating."

Ryan's head shot up and he yelled, "Who the fuck is trying to date my little sister?"

About that same time Carrie joined into the hug and made it a group hug. All of Samuel's high school buddies died with laughter as Logan stood nervously next to Katie. Samuel could not help but smile as he saw the sheer terror on the kid's face.

"Be nice." Carrie said.

"Oh I'll be nice." Ryan said as he stormed off towards where the poor kid was standing. Carrie was scurrying after him when Samuel grabbed her arm and pulled her back.

"Ryan is not going to hurt the kid.... Too bad." Samuel said.

Carrie looked back and rolled her eyes.

"Hey," Samuel said, "Mom told me you pretty much put this whole thing together. Thank you."

"Of course." She said as tears welled up in her eyes, "we are all super proud of you."

She hugged Samuel tightly. She cried loudly in his arms.

"Carrie what's wrong?" Samuel asked squeezing her tighter.

"I just used to sit and watch the news and hear all those stories and see all of those guys' pictures and it scared me so much."

Samuel picked Carrie up and just whispered, "I'm home now." Everyone must have found their sad moment too much to handle. The whole backyard was empty except for them and their father who was completely absorbed in his barbecue ritual. They stood there in silence for a while. Samuel desperately wanted to change the subject and break the silence.

"You, uh," He cleared his throat, "You ever talk to Samantha?"

Carrie smiled and replied, "Yes, I talked to her quite a bit for the first year after you left."

Samuel's head twitched and he gave her an inquisitorial look.

"I would try to give her updates on you," Carrie continued, "but, I don't know if she was just trying to be sweet or if it was too hard for her to hear, she made it a point to change the subject."

Samuel grew a sullen look on his face. He did not really know what he expected to hear. But that's not what he wanted to hear.

"She used to give me advice on boys and high school," Carrie said, "and once you deployed I never really talked to her again."

Samuel stood silently for a moment contemplating. On one hand it was stereotypical of Samantha, the sweetest person to have ever lived, to make sure that the 14-year-old that idolized her was reassured that she was not using her for information about him. On the other hand, it was well in the realm of possibility that she really did not care and had moved on completely. Either way, he had a promise to keep and fully intended to before he had to go back to the fleet.

Carrie must have used some sibling extra-sensory perception to read Samuel's mind. "If you want, I'll drive to Oxford and pick her up and bring her back--if you want." She said.

"There's a novel idea." Samuel replied. "I'll just use my sister as my pimp to arrange my soirees."

They both laughed loud enough for their father to actually notice and look up from his sanctuary.

"What's my take?" Carrie said.

"Fifteen percent." Samuel said.

"Twenty" Carrie replied.

"Deal." Samuel said sticking his hand out. They shook hands and he said, "What's the going rate for a washed-up Marine anyway?"

"Not much," Carrie laughed.

"Well good she's a college student anyway, she probably can't afford much." Samuel said with a ponderous look on his face. Carrie started walking towards the door. Samuel began to panic thinking she might take the joke too far.

"Carrie, wait." He shouted, "Don't be ridiculous." Carrie looked back at him with a confused look on her face. "She doesn't want to see me." he said.

Carrie tilted head in disbelief and said, "Really, who's being ridiculous?" Samuel paused for a moment. Truthfully, he was enjoying the feeling of being nervous to see her again. Maybe her being the one that got away was enough to make him feel like he belonged among the living. Maybe, this was his last connection to who he was before he was dropped in the forge of combat and molded into an entirely new substance. He was worried that if, when he saw her, there was no spark, it would mean he was a new person entirely that could never go back.

"Either way," He uttered, "I don't know that now is a good time. I'll be leaving again in a couple of months." Carrie shrugged her shoulders and went back inside. Samuel grabbed a new beer and sat back down on the rocking chair to gaze out over the yard.

Samantha's phone lit up at a little after eight. She was so anxious the pressure was consuming her. She reached on the nightstand next to the bed and grabbed the phone. She saw it was a text message and looked to see who it was from. It was from Carrie. Samantha shot up in the bed. She looked at it two more times to make sure she was not dreaming or that somehow her mind was projecting the message to be from Carrie. She flipped the phone open to read what it said. It was a long message:

Hey Sam, I'm really sorry I
didn't text you earlier. I feel
really bad. Sam's home from
Iraq. We are having a BBQ
tonight. I would have invited
you but no one knew how
many people Sam was going to
want around. But he's been
asking about you and I
think he really wants to see
you. He's just too scared to
call you.

Samantha threw her head back and stared at the ceiling. She pulled a pillow over her head and yelled into it. It was now established that he wanted to see her. Samantha knew she wanted to see him too. That should have been the end of it. But it was not that simple. She had not felt so much like a little girl since well before she qualified as a woman.

What was she going to do if he was not impressed? *The man just got back from war*, she thought, *is he really going to be picky?* Samantha thought to herself that he still sounded like the sweet shy boy she had known years ago. Too scared to call her. That sounded like Sam. Samantha tried talking her way through it. "Ok," She said out loud but by herself in the room, "If you don't call him he will never come and see you. And you will never get a chance to get back together." She nodded her head realizing the logic. "But!" She said, "If you do and he sees you and he is not impressed, that's it. You blew your chance." She took a deep breath not liking that option. "Or we could pick up right where we left off."

Samantha typed out several different responses, but finally decided to send:

Thanks, I would love to see
him too. What's his number?

A few short seconds later. She got a reply from Carrie:

He doesn't have a phone
yet. You can just call me
or the house phone.

Samantha thought to herself that this girl was going to be the death of her. She had just made the torturous decision to call him and now, she was telling her she was going to have to choose between calling his little sister to talk to him, or calling the home phone and most likely talking to his parents first. *Hey,* she thought to herself, *I'm looking for Sam this is his now twenty year old high school girlfriend. RIDICULOUS.*

Samantha sat in bed torturing herself. She finally just made the decision she was going to call the house phone. Why not? It was ridiculous that a grown man did not have his own phone. So, if anything he should be embarrassed by it, not her. She dialed the number took a deep breath and pressed send. She could barely hear the ringtone over her heart beating so loudly. Suddenly, she heard a ruckus on the other line. It sounded like the phone had been placed in the middle of a music festival. She heard Mrs. Parker on the other line.

"Hello!" she said loudly. "Everyone shut up for a second I can't hear the phone" She yelled.

"Uh Hello," Samantha said. She thought about hanging up for a moment, but she was worried about explaining that when they called back. She heard a deep masculine voice say "Mom who is it." She was not sure if that was Samuel or not.

Samantha could hear Mrs. Parker say, "I don't know. I can't hear over all of you"

Then she heard the voice again on the line, this time clearly talking into the phone, "Hello." He said. Her throat stuck as she said, "Sam."

"Hold on," He said in a stern voice. Samantha laughed as she heard him yell, "Everyone shut the hell up." Then she heard him, say "Hello," again.

"Sam?" she said as the butterflies almost took her away.

"No." the voice said abruptly. Samantha felt like could die right then. *Who* had she been talking to? "This is Ryan, his brother" he said, "let me get him."

"Hey Jarhead!" he yelled. "Someone is on the phone for you--Yeah. I don't know." She heard Ryan continuing. Ridiculous is the only word she could think of to describe the situation. "No, go take it upstairs, it's too loud down here." Several long seconds passed, each one feeling like an hour to Samantha.

Suddenly she heard a voice over the phone, "Hello." It was Samuel.

"Hey Sam," She said softly.

"Samantha?" Samuel said surprised. "Oh my god, how are you?" Samuel asked her as his tone softened.

"I'm good." Samantha said, "Carrie told me you were back in town. I wasn't sure if this was a good time or place to call you."

Samuel huffed into the phone. "Yeah I'm sorry about that, the ever-prudent Parker clan decided me coming home was worth celebrating so a bunch of two beer queers are like six deep." Samuel said. "I cut my phone off before I went down range, I'm getting another one tomorrow."

Samantha felt like he sounded very frustrated. And she was beginning to regret calling him.

Samuel was happy that she had called, but he was embarrassed by the entire situation. "Carrie talked to you huh," Samuel said in a flustered tone.

"Yeah," Samantha said in a very soft sweet voice. Samuel was worried his tone had conveyed the wrong message.

"I was really looking forward to talking to you," Samuel started, "and I told her as much. Ryan and I let her have a couple beers and I guess she decided to take matters into her own hands."

Samantha was smiling ear to ear. Hearing his sweet voice put all of her worries to rest. He was the same sweet boy she remembered.

"Carrie Sam's going to kill you." She heard Ryan's voice say. He had not hung up the phone when Samuel took the call upstairs and had been listening to them the whole time.

Samuel said, "One second, Sam." She could tell he had tried to cover the receiver but she could still hear him yelling through the phone, "Katie get your boy or I'll make you a widow before y'all even get married." Samantha thought to herself, maybe he was a little more forceful than he was before but still seemed like the same sweet guy at heart.

Samuel did not think this could have gone worse. But he was so happy to hear Samantha's voice again. "I am really sorry." He said.

"It sounds like you have your hands full over there." Samantha said.

"Yeah," He snickered "I'm wildly out numbered."

Samantha laughed loudly.

"Sam, I really want to catch up with you," Samuel said, "but can I call you tomorrow? And then you'll have my new number too, so you won't have to deal with these savages the next time you want to talk to me."

"Of course," Samantha said sweetly. And as if to suck all of the doubt and humiliation from the whole course of the phone call out of his mind she ended by saying, "Maybe we can talk about evening out those odds."

Samuel felt his heart flutter as he said, "I can clearly use the help. I'll call you tomorrow."

Intro to Ch4. ...Do You Want to Live Forever?

Courage is not the lack of fear. Courage is the ability to act in the face of fear. Sometimes courage is the resolve to try something new. Sometimes courage is finding the intestinal fortitude to ask the homecoming queen to go on a date. Other times courage is running under fire to a commanding position and laying waste to a city block. In any regards Samuel had proven he was no coward. But does the manner in which someone finds the courage to act belittle the display? If you have to get hammered drunk to ask that girl out, are you as brave as the sober man? Is it courage if you channel a berserker fury fueled by blood lust to run under fire? Or is that some form of psychosis?

The Mujahideen were no push-overs, they were not undisciplined farmers, but they were not professional soldiers either. If they had been this ambush would have been a much bigger problem than it was. Samuel knew that. But it did not quell his anxiety. The distinctive cracks of bullets passing over head were a reminder that danger was all around. Samuel knew what had to happen next. He needed to find a spot to spew hate and discontent in the direction of his adversaries with his Squad Automatic Weapon.

Vasquez, his assistant gunner, came running up to Samuel. "Let's go dude!" Vasquez commanded, "I think we can get on top of that house and un-alive these fuckers."

Samuel knew what Vasquez expected. Last week Samuel had done some real war hero shit. He just about massacred a squad by himself. He popped out behind the guys ambushing his squad, allowing them to get, well un-alived them was not a bad way of putting it. He had a reputation ever since. He did not know how to tell the guys that it wasn't him. That had been his twentieth birthday and something just snapped inside of him. A dark force took over him and guided him to violence.

Samuel looked at Vasquez for a moment. He wanted to tell him he did not know how to bring that back out. Suddenly a bullet cracked the wall behind Vasquez. Vasquez hit the ground. Samuel felt his heart skip. He reached down and grabbed Vasquez with one hand and started to pull him towards him.

"What the fuck?" Vasquez screamed, "Am I good dude?"

Samuel looked him over quickly. He saw no sign of gore, no blood. "I don't know bro, are you fucking good?" Samuel pleaded.

Vasquez smiled and said, "Yeah--yeah I'm fucking good." Vasquez slid his leg under himself and took a knee next to Samuel.

Samuel felt a calm rush over his body as he watched Vasquez knock the dust off of himself. Samuel looked over to the house Vasquez had identified. The roof was not but about 8 feet off the ground, with a low wall running off the side. As he looked at it, it seemed to be getting further away. Samuel tried to remember how close it had been before the ambush started, because now it looked like it was 200 yards away, and he knew that wasn't right. Suddenly Samuel knew what he had to do.

Alright Motherfucker, He thought, *Time to eat. I know you're hungry.* Samuel closed his eyes and took a deep breath. He let it out slowly as he began to hear a melody in his head. His mind cleared, he felt his heart rate plummet. He opened his eyes and saw the wall was about 10 yards away, the house was another 5 yards after that. The song played on. Samuel looked at Vasquez. Vasquez had a slightly disconcerted look on his face.

Samuel popped out of cover and faced the direction the enemy fire was coming from. Time had slowed to a standstill. He saw the Marines from his squad scattered about, some shooting from behind cover, some behind cover that was getting pelted with automatic gunfire. Samuel raised his weapon stock up to his cheek. Staring down the barrel he saw one of his enemies silhouetted on the top of a building. He let out a burst. Samuel watched the man's rifle falling to the street as he turned to make his break for the low wall.

Samuel sprinted. As he approached the low wall, he

didn't take cover. He was enjoying the sound of the cracks be-hind him. *Can't catch me.* Samuel thought. The gunfire was like a roaring drum matching the tempo of his song, taking cover behind the wall might disrupt the cadence. As he approached the point where the wall met the house Samuel spun his weapon towards his back on its sling. Samuel leapt. He planted his foot on the low wall and pushed off. Samuel reached up and grabbed the roof of the house and began to pull himself up. As soon as he was high enough over the ledge, he started to roll over the edge. Samuel felt a bullet strike his "Day Pack" on his back.

Step one complete. Now for the fun part. Samuel rolled to his back and pulled his weapon up. He gave it a quick inspection to ensure it was still ready. Samuel rolled back over to the prone position and began scanning for victims. He saw that the majority of the shooting was coming from one building, a store of some sort at the top of the T- intersection.

Ok, Samuel thought to himself, *Fuck that entire building then.* Samuel opened up with a cyclic burst. Slowly the cracks of bullets coming towards his squad subsided and the only sound was the outgoing shots from the Marines. First amongst those sounds was the rattle of Samuel's S.A.W. sending a mani-festo of violence. This was not a letter to the enemy. It was more of a "To Whom it May Concern: Play time is fucking over."

Step two complete. The Marines had fire superiority. But Samuel, or whatever force was now in control of Samuel was not satisfied with that. Step Three was what got him on this house. The song in his head was reaching its crescendo. It was raining bullets on their enemy. But the dark force wanted blood. Whatever was driving Samuel's bus wanted to quench the parched deserts with torrents of blood.

"Parker!" He heard from the side of the house. He looked over and Vasquez was crouched behind the wall. Vasquez had his hand raised towards Samuel for help up. Samuel reached down and Vasquez jumped up to grab his arm. Samuel pulled Vasquez up who took his position next to him.

"Good call," Samuel said, "This was a good spot."

Samuel then heard the platoon commander call up to him, "Parker, you two keep that position as an overwatch, the rest of the squad is going to push forward to clear this area out."

"Roger that." Samuel shouted back in disappointment. Samuel wasn't sure why, but he found himself a little let down that he was not going to personally take part in the potential slaughter to come. Being relegated to overwatch was normal, but the dark force was hungry and he wanted to let it out.

"Oh and Parker..." The platoon commander called back to him.

"Sir?" Samuel inquired.

"What the actual fuck was that?" the platoon commander asked.

"Pony Boy decided he'd had enough sir." Samuel heard Mac shout in a joking tone. Samuel scanned for more enemies to vanquish unamused by the comment. Then he heard another Marine, shout, "He ain't Pony Boy anymore, he's the fucking god of death." Samuel smirked as he considered that analysis.

CHAPTER 4. HOMECOMING QUEEN

Samantha spent the whole day in a strange dichotomy between floating on air with euphoria and running to the nearest bathroom, so nauseous she felt like she was going to vomit. Samuel had called her, and they talked for six hours...straight. It was as if their old pizza dates had just been paused and the two of them had to binge to get their story caught up to present time. They talked about his friends he'd made, and the suitors who never quite measured up to him. Mostly, she caught him up on pop-culture and the exploding world of technology.

She had tried to convince him that social media was a worthwhile investment of his time. Samuel was far from a luddite, but as he put it to Samantha, he was not sure how he felt about a whole page of original content specifically designed to advertise a particular digital version of himself for the consumption of relative strangers. Samantha tried to explain that the fun was that it was like people watching, but you could do it from your couch. By the end of their marathon conversation Samuel had resolved that he was going to drive to Oxford to see her, and in an unusually decisive nature for him, he was coming the next day, which was today.

Samuel had found the interaction he was starved for and it was in the form of his first love. Samantha Wallace had always had a spell on him. Samuel had not felt right since the plane touched down on U.S. soil, and he had spent the last few days feeling like his condition was degenerating. There was talk before they left the sandbox that some battalions had started putting their Marines on a limited restriction for the first couple weeks when they got back. They slowly weaned the guys into being home. Now, having experienced coming home, he was not convinced that was such a bad idea. He could not help but feel like there was no real way to reconcile one's humanity when you are stuck in reality where savagery is rewarded with survival, and the only people you interact with are playing the game by the exact same rules. Then when the savage returns to civilization he is no longer human enough to interact with in normal day-to-day life.

But since he talked to Samantha, he felt like he was back on track to some degree of normality. She was a lifeline cast out to the sea that could lead him back to shore. He was not going to make the mistake he had before, he was not going to waste a single moment he could be spending with her.

Samantha was at least comforted by the fact that she had a solid time that he was supposed to be there. Samuel was going to arrive "no later than two thirty." She felt like that was a weird way to tell someone when he was going to arrive, but it was strangely definitive. At two thirty-one she would know something was wrong. She had not been very active with her sorority at all this year, but she had to admit she was glad to have them around when she called some of them in complete panic that Samuel was coming. A whole crew had showed up like she was a movie star.

They must have brought an entire store worth of make-up and forty different wardrobes to make sure she was perfectly ready. They had experimented on her with different looks and different styles until there was a consensus that Samuel would not be able to keep his hands to himself. To her surprise they had even established different wardrobe changes for different scenarios. She had an outfit for if he decided to go to the movies, one for staying in, one for "staying in," and one for doing something outdoors. They had even established one to go dancing, but Samantha was fairly certain nothing would have changed Samuel enough to make dancing a reality.

Samuel had made the trip to Oxford a few times before. He was reminiscing about the last time he went, which was in high school. He had a mock trial. Samuel felt like this was the place for Samantha. Ole Miss seemed to have a never-ending supply of beautiful southern belles, but his thoughts turned more... sour as he remembered that it also had a never-ending supply of preppy country club guys to go with them. Samuel was vehemently opposed to the idea of being jealous. But he had to admit he had a wash of inferiority coming over his thoughts. These guys she was surrounded by now had considerably much less of a chance of getting blown up than he did, they had already started a path towards some type of fruitful career, and worst of all they were close and not going anywhere.

But Samuel consoled himself by remembering even if he was only a welcome distraction from "Jody" for a day or a week or more, it was still more time than he ever thought he would have gotten with Samantha. Looking at the book of his life the highlight was the few weeks he had spent with her before shipping out, and the idea that he could add a couple pages to the highlights was well worth the risk.

"Sam" the phone said blinking in Samantha's hand. She was almost paralyzed. Samantha had missed feeling this way. Her first college boyfriend had been the closest she had felt. The butterflies, anxiousness, and the lack of certainty were the best and worst part of a fledgling relationship. Of late, the only thing she had gotten excited and nervous about was an anatomy final. She took a deep breath and answered, "Hello." Samantha wanted to throw up for sounding like a giddy little girl when she answered.

"Hey," Samuel said, "So, uhh, I'm lost"

Samantha felt like she had gotten a temporary reprieve, so she was not upset.

"I thought you'd been here before," She said breathing a

sigh of relief.

"No," Samuel replied laughing, "I've been to the campus before, I have no idea how to find the entrance. There's fifteen doors that require a keycard, and I keep waiting for someone to come out so I can get in, but they just storm out and the door shuts before I can get in."

Samantha felt all of the dread come back over her as she said, "The one with the two spirally trees isn't actually locked you can just come in there." Samantha mouthed to herself "spirally" dumbfounded she used that word while talking to, objectively, the smartest person she knew.

"Ah," Samuel replied, "I remember those they are-- that way." he said.

"Ok," Samantha said abruptly, "When you walk in take the staircase to the right to the second floor. Go right, I'm the second door on the right."

"Got it," He said, "walking past the spirally tree's right now."

Samantha estimated she had about forty-five seconds. "See you in a second, bye." She said hanging up. She leapt up and ran to the mirror for one last look over.

Samuel did not ever remember Samantha being nervous about anything for as long as he knew her. He smiled as he hung up because he could tell that she was now. He was flattered but not surprised. He was nervous, and he prided himself on having ice water in his veins not a month ago. He was happy that his imperturbability had subsided. As much as this was a quest to reunite with his first love, he felt like this was a quest to reunite with himself.

He climbed the stairs smiling. Samuel knew some things would never change back to the old ways. As he went up the first flight, he looked to the first landing and then straight up to the next landing to the point he was almost walking backward going up the first flight. Anyone who had ever heard a shot from the top of a staircase they were climbing would never climb a staircase the same way again. But Samuel was happy that he was more worried about seeing Samantha again than getting ambushed in the staircase. And that, he thought, was definitely progress towards normality.

Samantha heard a knock at the door. A rush of excitement took over her. She was not nervous anymore and was not going to let herself be psyched out. She rushed out of her room and to the doorway. Samantha did not even pay any attention to her roommate sitting on the couch watching TV. She flung the door open with a huge smile. The first thing she noticed is that Samuel was not standing there. She stuck her head out into the hallway and looked left. He was not there.

Then from the other way she heard "Hey sorry." She whipped her head around and her mouth went from a smile to wide open. She saw a pair of brown boots standing next to the wall. Samantha slowly lifted her gaze taking in every inch. Samantha saw blue jeans, and more blue jeans. They were stretched tight. When she got to the thighs she noticed that each one was like a decent size tree. That quickly shifted to a small waist. As her gaze went higher she saw a forearm that was bigger around than her neck, and a bouquet of flowers blocking the other arm. Samantha was in complete awe at the specimen standing in front of her as she ever slowly lifted her head. She saw the bicep not covered by the flowers that was about as big as her waist. His chest was so big it looked like the green polo shirt was struggling to keep the one button that could be buttoned in place. Then she expected to see a neck, but it was just a mountain of flesh that went from his two-person wide shoulders to behind a square jaw. Then Samantha saw the most unbelievable sight. The same boy she had known in high school's face atop this machine that was in front of her. Only his piercing green eyes were unchanged and staring at her behind what appeared to be a nervous grin.

Samuel thought to himself that she was exactly like he remembered. He was flattered as he could tell she had put on make-up. The entire time he knew her he only remembered her wearing make-up to a dance. Her brown hair was pulled back and cascaded down her shoulders in waterfall curls. Her perfectly formed face was on display. Samuel felt his nerves jump and twist the longer she studied him. Samuel had gone to bootcamp at one hundred and thirty-five pounds soaking wet, at the physical before they left Al Asad, he was one hundred and ninety-seven pounds. So, it was not lost on him that he looked quite a bit different. But he was beginning to worry that Samantha might have preferred a scrawny, nerdy looking kid. She finally took a step out into the hallway. She was wearing a white sundress that, Samuel noticed, was a little shorter than what she would have been two years ago. Her golden tan legs seemed to go on forever. Samuel started to feel a heat rush over him. He was prepared to see his first love, whom he had considered a woman. But, the Samantha in front of him now irradiated sexuality.

"I-- Uhh," He started to say, "brought you some--" Samantha cut him off by jumping into his arms.

Samantha could not help herself. Certainly, he looked a lot different than the boy she knew once, but the sweet features and shy charm was still there. She felt overcome by the emotions she had not felt since the last time she left his house nearly two years previously. Samantha could not believe that she had almost forgotten how she felt for him.

"Flowers." Samuel said. His face must have been covered by her hair because Samantha felt her hair flicker when he said it. He brushed her hair aside with his free hand and then put both arms around her. Samantha felt completely absorbed in the mass that was the new Samuel. Samantha could not speak, or at least she did not know what to say. He held her off of the ground for what seemed like forever. Finally, he leaned over and her feet touched the ground. Samantha found herself wishing he would just pick her back up. She leaned back to look at his face again. Samuel was blushing, and she thought it was an adorable display of boyishness from what otherwise was an object lesson in masculinity. As she was gazing and smiling Samuel put the flowers in her face. Samantha let out a laugh.

Samantha thought to herself that the Samuel she remembered had probably read a book somewhere that explained: "When rekindling an old relationship make sure to bring her flowers," and he was not going to be able to proceed until she acknowledged the flowers.

"They are beautiful," Samantha giggled pulling them down so she could see his face again. He dropped his arms and Samantha took a step back. She took another long look at Samuel. Samantha had seen her share of guys that wore clothes that were too small. She felt like they were all trying, poorly, to imitate this. His chest and arms were too big for the shirt to the point that it looked like drapes over the rest of his torso. But the shirt was comically too small for his neck.

Samuel was beginning to get a complex from Samantha's staring, but it gave him an opportunity to stare at her more, which seemed like a decent consolation.

"Let's go put these on water," Samantha finally blurted out. She reached down and grabbed his hand and yanked him through the doorway. Samuel felt as though it was a blast from the past. Samuel had fallen in love with the girl who was strong and decisive. The Samantha from his memory and dreams knew what she wanted and was not going to wait for someone to offer it. Samuel had fought a war and been through the charnel house of modern combat, he knew he was tough as nails. But he was butter in the hands of this five-foot six inch, twenty-year-old coed. Samantha could pull him anyway she wanted, and he was powerless to resist, and all it took from her was one look and one smile. But Samuel felt at ease for the first time in as long as he could remember. Samantha pulled him through the doorway and into the kitchen area of her student apartment. Samuel had felt drunk with euphoria, but stone-cold sobriety hit him when he saw one of the two girls sitting on the couch in front of him was Michelle Raleigh. He did not know why he was surprised she would have followed Samantha to college, but having her here now was rapidly turning his dream into a nightmare.

Samantha was obliviously looking for a vase to put the flowers into when she heard from behind her, "Je... sus." She turned around. From the kitchen there was an opening to the living room where she could see into the room. Michelle had apparently come out and was sitting in the oversized armchair. One of her other roommates, Lucy, was sitting on the loveseat with a bowl of cereal. Lucy had been the one who made the remark because the spoon was up about half the distance to her mouth and her mouth was wide open. Lucy was staring at Samuel. Michelle looked like she had seen a ghost and her mouth was sealed shut. Samantha was fairly certain if Michelle opened her mouth the only thing that would come out was a shriek. Samuel was staring at Michelle. Samantha had not thought to tell Samuel that Michelle was one of her roommates. Samuel had always hated her with the fire of a thousand suns, but Samantha thought that was a long time ago. In a very uncharacteristic flair of jealousy Samantha had decided that Lucy had stared at Samuel a little too long.

"Lucy this is Sam." Samuel heard Samantha say from his left side. Samuel shook his head to snap to his senses and took a step towards the girl he did not recognize.

He put his hand out and said, "Samuel. Nice to meet you."

The girl just stared up at him without moving and finally said, "I'm eating cereal." She had not blinked since he walked into the door. Samuel thought that was a rude reason not to shake someone's hand. He was not sure if this was some type of high school drama way of saying that she did not approve of the fact that some boy from the other side of the tracks had come to date her friend.

Samuel paid it no mind. He had been in a renegade affair with Samantha before and did not expect this to be any different. Then he cut his eyes over to Michelle. She was staring at him like he was some incarnated horror here to steal her soul. She had pure terror written all over her face. He could not pass up an opportunity to torture her. He walked the two or so steps to the armchair. She was sitting with her legs up on the chair. Her hair was thrown up in a bun and she was in a sweatshirt in some shorts. He mentally noted that she would never have been caught by any boy from their high school seeing her not done up.

He leaned over and hugged her and said, "Michelle so good to see you again." He fought back a snicker. Mentally he pictured himself twirling a handlebar mustache and yelling, "dastardly." *Yes, I have come back to steal your friend.* He thought, *You may have to come up with an original thought soon.*

"Hey--Samuel." Michelle finally squeaked out.

Samantha thought to herself that everyone had grown up. Samuel did just hug Michelle. She went back to the task of finding a vase for the flowers and floating away in her bliss.

"I hate to do this but," She heard Samuel start. Samantha turned quickly in despair wondering if he was leaving already. "But I have been on the road and I really need to make a head call." He continued.

Samantha stared at him completely confused. The room was dead silent. Samuel closed his eyes and put his hand on his head and said, "Freaking boot." as he sighed. "I have to use the restroom." He said as if he was ashamed.

Samantha was not sure what just happened, but she was actually happy he asked as she had cleaned the bathroom five times in preparation for the occasion.

"Just in that hall, it's the door straight ahead." She said, nodding towards her bathroom and smiling. He took his leave and Samantha went back to filling the vase with water. She was having to keep herself from actually humming. Lucy shot out of the chair and rushed into the kitchen to the point that she was standing uncomfortably close to her.

Samantha was thinking of a sly way to comment on her disapproval at Lucy's staring when suddenly Lucy spouted, "Samantha!" Samantha looked at her. "You said," Lucy continued, "we were all helping you get ready to see a boy from high school."

"He is." Samantha replied going back to arranging her flowers.

"Girl, that is a MAN!" Lucy barked. A smile came to Samantha's face as she thought, *He certainly is.* "My little brother is a boy," Lucy continued, "That is a hulking... beautiful man." Samantha rolled her eyes and looked at Lucy.

"He grew up." Samantha said, "That's what boys do."

Lucy slammed her hand on the counter and said forcefully, "My brother is not going to grow into that." Lucy threw her hand towards the hall Samuel had retreated to. "Shit, my dad never had a chance to grow into that." She continued, "and I'm sitting here in pajama pants," Lucy continued with her tirade pulling on her pajama pants, "and eating fucking cereal." She pointed to the bowl that was now in the sink. "You need to warn a girl before you bring-- Superman to the apartment." Samantha smiled and smelled the flowers that she had finally gotten arranged.

Samuel came walking out of the hallway and saw Lucy scurrying from the kitchen with a scowl on her face. She looked up at him and smiled nervously as she nearly planted her whole body against the wall to get past him without touching him. Samuel smiled back at her and watched her go into the room on the right. She barely opened the door and squeezed through the crack and shut the door right behind her. Samuel was fairly certain she was just talking to Samantha about him, but Samantha did not seem phased by it, so he was not worried about what was said.

Samuel thought she looked like some ethereal being or wisp floating around the kitchen, glowing and smiling. She was calling to him with her beauty and all he wanted to do was touch her again. But he then remembered the intruder in the room. He looked back and saw Michelle. She had not moved a muscle. Her eyes were as wide as when she first laid eyes on him. Samuel figured this situation was not going to resolve itself. He moseyed into the living room and sat down on the loveseat where Lucy had been sitting. He glanced over at Michelle and verified that she was still staring at him. He puffed up his mouth with his lips sealed in an awkward face and nodded his head while glancing at her trying to match his face to the palpable feeling in the room.

"You know I am not here to kidnap her." Samuel said unable to take the silence any longer.

Michelle smiled and said, "I-I know."

They were making direct eye contact. Samuel smiled and shrugged his shoulders. Michelle let out a giggle and finally blinked.

"You just," Michelle started. Samuel looked over and saw Samantha walking towards him. "Look so-- different." Michelle finished.

Samantha sat down next to him on the couch. The fact that she sat so close they were touching was not lost on Samuel. He hoped that meant that she felt the need to touch him as much as he felt the need to touch her.

He was studying Samantha sitting next to him, and as his eyes moved up his saw Michelle still sitting there and realized he had not replied. "Same old Sam," He said shrugging his shoulders.

Samantha was convinced it was the same old Sam. He was no more used to his body than any of them were. If he had wanted to, he could have had Michelle apologizing for years of talking down to him. Michelle used to interrupt their pizza dates. She would usually make some rude comment to him, and once even looked him dead in the face and said, "You know she's not into you right." Samantha always stuck up for Samuel when she did that, which solicited the appropriate apology. But right now, he could get a genuine apology.

Samantha knew Michelle was not bad at heart. Michelle had always been a slave to the culture that told girls what they should look like and how they should act. Samantha was one of the few people that knew she had struggled with an eating disorder early in high school. Samantha always hoped Michelle would grow out of it, and in a lot of ways she had. Michelle no longer associated rudeness with beauty. That idea was always packaged and sold. Samantha assumed the logic went something like: celebrities are beautiful and they do not have time for regular people, so if someone does not have time for "regular" people they must be a celebrity and thus beautiful. Unfortunately for Samuel, most of the world would have thought he was a regular person when he was eighteen. Unfortunately for Michelle, at twenty years old he was anything but a regular person. But in typical sweet Samuel fashion he seemed entirely ignorant to that fact. Samantha hoped this would be a morality lesson to Michelle.

Samuel was starting to get frustrated. Samuel was sure that it was a shock to Michelle's central nervous system that the guy that was sitting in front of her could pick up the boy she remembered and use him as a weapon to destroy every guy she had ever dated, at the same time. But she was cutting into his time with Samantha. He did not know how to get her to leave without being rude. And he knew nothing was a bigger turn off to Samantha than someone being rude.

"So, what's there to do around this town?" Samuel asked hoping Samantha would suggest somewhere they could go to be alone.

"There's a party tonight." Michelle exclaimed. Samuel felt disgusted that a moment ago the girl was silent as the grave and now she was going to throw out ideas like she was a part of this relationship. Samuel looked over at Samantha. Samantha's face showed the faintest indication of displeasure. He was thinking of a way to get out of that idea when Michelle interrupted his train of thought by saying, "I forgot Samuel doesn't like parties."

Samuel felt a rage come over him. He wanted to stand up and yell in Michelle's face for having the audacity to say what he did and did not like. Before his brain could roll through the possibilities and come up with the best possible response his mouth blurted out, "I love parties."

Samantha snapped her head towards Samuel in disbelief. Samuel did not like parties, at least the Samuel she knew had never liked parties.

Samuel continued though, "Every night in the barracks was basically a party." Samantha would have preferred to spend the night alone with him, but she figured he had not really gotten to experience college parties while he was gone. Samantha would give up a night alone with him to get to see what it would have been like had he gone to college instead. And Samantha was fairly convinced that he would be so uncomfortable with the insanity of an Ole Miss party that she would not have to worry about him wanting to go to another one while he was with her.

"Sure," Samantha said. She had decided if she was going to give up the night alone with him, she had earned something in return. She took his hand and interlaced her fingers in his. She saw Samuel blush. Samantha marveled at how much things had not changed between them. He responded to her the way he always had. Well truthfully, things had changed for her. She was back to being the girl laying in his bed offering herself up, which had been a recent development at the time. Samantha was certain she had loved him then. Samuel was her best friend, her confidant, and her adoring beloved when they last saw each other. A war had torn them apart, but here he was now, and he did not seem any worse for it. If anything, he was more developed.

Samuel could not believe he had let his temper get the better of him. He was not like that. Samuel processed every word and considered every option before he ever uttered anything. Here he was having put his foot in his mouth. Samuel hated parties. He accepted them as a necessary social liturgy, but he thought that it was a display of debauchery and pageantry married into one ridiculous human mating ritual. But when Samantha took his hand, he felt his mood shift. He had a calm come over his whole person. He had not felt this calm in his life. Their time before carried the anxiety of knowing he was leaving and, quite possibly, never coming back. But now he felt like the worst was behind him. And the one that had gotten away was serendipitously back in his life. Samuel would face a thousand nights of parties if it meant she never let go of his hand go again.

"It's a plan then." he said.

"Ok we'll go at nine." Michelle said in an overly excited tone.

Samuel was relieved that Michelle jumped up and scurried to her room after that.

Samantha was ecstatic that they were finally alone. "So, what do you want to do until nine?" Samantha said with a smile. Samantha wanted him to take her up on her two-year-old offer, but she figured that was still out of the realm of possibility. Samuel looked at her with a devilish smile. Samantha was beginning to think that it was not out of the question.

"You know," He said.

Samantha leaned in closer hoping she did know.

"I have not watched TV in almost a year." He said with a grin.

To say that Samantha was disappointed was an understatement.

"You want to watch TV." She said with incredulity.

Samuel nodded. Samantha picked up the remote and turned on the TV still in shock.

"What do you want to watch?" She said leaning back in defeat.

Samuel was beginning to wonder if he had not been direct enough. They used to sit in his room and turn on the TV so his sister could not hear them while they made out. He thought she would catch on since the other two girls were in their rooms.

"No preference." he said thinking that would get the point across.

He was not even paying attention to what she stopped on. She had a perturbed look on her face. He was certain if she would look over at him, she would understand. She was just staring at the screen.

"Uh, do you want to turn it up a little bit?" He said softly.

He was certain that she would understand then.

She slowly turned her head towards him and said, "Ok." She looked like he had just shot her dog in front of her.

Samantha was trying to be understanding. The man wanted to watch TV. That sounded like a perfectly reasonable thing to want to do when he had not watched TV in over a year. But she was starting to lose her patience. When he said he did not care she picked some ridiculous dating reality TV show, exactly the kind of thing that he always hated. That would be her way to pry some other activity out of him. But then he asked her to turn it up.

"That good?" She said rather snidely.

"Should be." He said. Samantha was seething. She pulled her hand away from him and put it back into her lap. This is not the way she saw this going. Then she felt his hand back on hers. Before she could pull her hand away, she felt two fingers from his other hand on her chin. He gently pulled her face towards him. When she was finally looking at him, he leaned in for a kiss. Samantha's eyes got wide as she finally understood. Samuel kissed her.

Samantha pulled back and exclaimed, "WATCH TV."

Samuel laughed and said, "Exactly."

Then he leaned back in.

The two had fallen straight back into their typical exercise, as if they were high school lovers again. They were passionately intertwined. Neither one knew or cared how long they had been there.

Suddenly they heard a voice from the hallway. "Are y'all clothed?" It was Lucy.

Samuel was at least thankful for the warning.

"Yes," Samantha giggled.

Samuel was not sure why Lucy did not like him, but he was certain she did not. Samantha reached for her phone while Samuel lifted himself off of her and got back to his side of the couch.

"Holy shit." She said laughing.

"What?" Samuel said concerned.

"It's almost six." She said.

They had apparently been catching up on that lost time for hours. Lucy finally came walking out. Samuel could tell she was intentionally not looking in their direction as she walked into the kitchen.

"Michelle said we are going to a party." Lucy said from the kitchen.

"Yes," Samantha let out with a giggle while looking at Samuel.

"Will they have food there?" Samuel asked.

Samantha looked at him with a blank expression. Samuel was not sure why that solicited that response, it seemed like a valid question.

"You're adorable." Samantha said smiling at him. Lucy walked briskly into the room.

"What planet are you from?" She said looking at Samuel.

Samuel was fairly certain she was the rudest person he had ever met.

"Iraq, I guess," He said in a sarcastic response.

"Sweetheart," Lucy said, "no college fraternity is going to have a pizza party."

Samuel laughed realizing in retrospect that it was a pretty dumb question.

Samantha found the whole notion that he had thought that there would be food there cute. She looked up and saw Lucy mouth, "Oh my god" to her while fluttering her hands at her face. Samuel, who had not seen it, was oblivious to the fact that Lucy found it equally adorable. Samantha reflected that the first time they kissed was after a party where everyone was treating him like an alien creature. But whereas before she felt like it was undignified, it was happening again, but everyone was flat out enamored by him.

"We can go get something before if you want." Samantha

said.

"Please," he said laughing "I have a little more to feed than before."

Samantha smiled at him feeling that she already knew the answer to the question, "What are you in the mood for?"

Samuel rolled his eyes at her and said, "Really?"

Samantha laughed and leaned over and kissed him.

"I hate you." Lucy said as she walked away to her room.

Samuel slipped his boots back on and the two were on their way. Samantha was not sure what she was more excited for, getting to relive their pizza date ritual, or getting back to the room in time to pick up where they left off before the party. Their romantic rendezvous left nothing to be desired. Samantha laughed like she had not in years. Samuel, in typical fashion listened to every word she had to say like it was gospel. She noticed he was not as forthcoming with details about his life since they had last seen each other but, it felt really good to have her best friend back. They had been so lost in conversation they lost track of time. When Samantha realized it was time for them to go back and gather their companions she was distressed, but they made their way. When they arrived, Lucy and Michelle were waiting for them in the living room.

Lucy immediately barked at Samuel, "You may be able to go out in whatever you want, but us mortals have to get ready."

Samantha laughed realizing they had not left very much time to get ready. She had explained to Samuel earlier that Lucy was in love with him, and did not hate him, so he had only bashfully smiled when she said that. So, Samantha kissed Samuel a temporary farewell and dutifully joined the girls in one of the bathrooms. Samuel made his way to the loveseat and sat down.

Samuel jolted awake looking for his rifle. He must have startled the girls as much as he had been startled because they were all looking at him wide-eyed.

"Sorry," He exclaimed, "I must have dozed off."

Samantha leaned forward and kissed him on the forehead. He felt his heart rate plummet. He did not remember having a dream. He had not slept for more than a couple hours at a time since he had gotten home. Samuel had not slept long enough to know if he was having nightmares but, having them was one of the things he feared most.

"It's ok," Samantha said sweetly, "Let's go," She whispered.

Samuel stood up and took her hand.

Samantha had heard of veterans having nightmares and getting jostled when someone woke them up. Hearing about it and experiencing it though were two different things. Samantha had heard of guys waking up and getting violent or pointing guns at people. But what affected her was the look of sheer terror on his face when he woke up. It broke her heart to see him look around the room not recognizing where he was, he had even looked right past her. Samantha was not sure what nightmare he had woken up from, but she wanted to know. She wanted to know all of his nightmares so she could kiss them away.

As they all started out of the door and down the corridor, Samantha held Samuel's hand tight. She was beginning to wonder if this was a foolishly bad idea. They were going to an over-crowded house with flashing lights and train horns going off and loud music. Samantha thought to herself that it might end up being a reason for them to leave early, but then felt disgusted with herself. She could not believe she would want his war weary debilitation to be her excuse to get him alone again. Samantha resolved to walk in silence as a penance for her most implacable thought.

They all walked through the campus to an old Victorian house. There was loud music coming from inside, but he was a little disappointed there was no other cliché imagery establishing this as a college fraternity party. They went walking up the stairs and he saw a police officer standing there and some kid with a money box.

"ID's" the cop barked. Samuel looked over at Samantha

and she gave him a smirk. Samuel pulled out his wallet and grabbed his driver license from behind his military ID. The cop reached out and touched his hand before he could get it out. Samuel's heart rate jumped, and he pulled Samantha behind him while he squared up.

"It's all good, devil dog," The cop said.

Samuel could feel his heart beating out of his chest. He looked at the man in the face and saw an old grizzled face. The cop rolled up his sleeve to reveal an eagle globe and anchor.

"Sorry man." Samuel said.

The cop looked over at the kid with the box and said, "They're good."

"Do they need a wristband?" the kid replied.

"I said they're good!" the cop barked back at him. Samuel's heart rate started to slow.

"How much?" Samuel asked the kid.

"Your money's no good here." the cop said.

Samuel looked over at him and saw him glaring at the kid.

"Thanks." He said to the grizzled officer. The girls all shuffled inside. As Samuel was walking by the officer, he clapped Samuel on the shoulder and said quietly to him, "Just get back." Samuel nodded. "It gets better." He said.

Intro to Ch 5. Men Die, Machines Break, But Marines...

Every culture has a coming of age ritual. A time when a boy becomes a man. After completing the ritual the boy is recognized as an adult member of the community. Other men will treat him as an equal, and the boys suddenly pay him the respect of a grown man. The Spartans used to send their boys into the wild without food. Many Native American Tribes had a rite involving a display of pain tolerance, such as standing in an icy river for some length of time. The Jewish community makes their pubescent boys sing in front of the whole community at time in their life when they are most likely to have a cracking voice. Western civilization as a whole seems to consider a boy a man when he has sex for the first time. Samuel only considered three rites he had been a part of as a moment when he could become a man: when he graduated Parris Island, when he graduated high school, or, ironically enough, when he refused to have sex with Samantha.

To Samuel, his forethought to abstain from sex with Samantha was a sign that he was adult enough to put his logic and reason before his lust and emotional desires. But to the Marines in the company one thing secured his status as a "full grown man," -combat. Specifically, his proficiency at ending lives. His legend was quickly growing around the battalion. Random Marines were calling him the god of death when he would walk by them. He had now committed exceptional acts of violence and made multiple displays of physicality on the battlefield when his unit was in a precarious position. His celebrity was approaching if not equal to the Fallujah vets in the unit. Samuel considered it a gross mischaracterization.

Samuel and Mac were in the gym working out when some other Marines came to give Samuel some "attaboys." Samuel was uncomfortable with the flattery.

"Take it easy god of death," one of the Marines said as they walked away.

"His name is Pony Boy," Mac said sternly. Mac looked over at Samuel and smirked. "You may be a death-dealer, but you're always going to be Pony Boy to me." Mac said.

"Just as well." Samuel replied as he bent over to pick up the bar to continue his deadlifts.

"Just as well." Mac said in a mocking tone, "see what the fuck I mean, you talk more proper than god damn British Marines. I swear you ain't from Dixie boy, I don't care what you say."

Samuel smiled as he continued his set.

"You figure this is what it's always been like?" Samuel inquired.

Mac looked around and smiled and said, "Hell, I think we built some gyms two days into the invasion. There might have even been a little juice before and after Fallujah but not during."

"No," Samuel stated as he put the weights down, completing his set, "I mean with warriors moving up in so significantly in status after combat. Or is that just a Corps thing?"

Mac smirked as he said, "Hell, I figure Pompeii's men were a little starry-eyed facing down Caesar's, knowing what they had done in France."

"Gaul?" Samuel asked.

"Fucking exactly," Mac said, "Shit ain't called Gaul for a fucking reason. Pompeii's men knew why."

"It just seems a little contrived to me," Samuel replied, "everyone is fighting the same war."

"Look devil dog," Mac said as he picked up the bar to take his turn lifting, "when you get back to the real world, people ain't gonna' know what you did here." Mac grunted out through his reps, "Some people are gonna' think it was worse. Others will think you were fucking camping. There's a sacred bond between those who've seen it, that those that ain't, won't never understand."

Samuel guzzled some water as he considered the prospect of what Mac was saying.

Mac finished his set, put the weights down, and looked at Samuel. "I know you don't get it," Mac said, "That's why you're the Pony Boy. These cats are paying respects. Not everyone jumps on top of some shack and starts laying waste to a fucking squad of enemy foot mobiles in a building while under fire."

Samuel smiled and let out a scoff as he went back to the bar to start his next set.

"I ain't got to tell you not to let it go to your head," Mac said, "but I do have to tell you to stay golden."

Samuel cut his eyes at him while he started his next set.

"You can get addicted to this shit," Mac added.

Samuel quietly contemplated whether Samantha would have ever understood what he did. He was thankful that she would not have to. Not dragging her into this was the most adult thing he'd ever done. It was a dangerous game, but Samuel considered that he was still playing at it, nonetheless.

CHAPTER 5. NO BETTER FRIEND, NO WORSE ENEMY

Samuel was surprised how well he was taking it. The horn was annoying, but it did not sound anything like the mortar alarm. It was loud, but he would have felt uneasy about that long before going to Iraq. Samuel had always felt like the ability to verbally communicate was the greatest gift of mankind, so he found any situation where people could not talk to each other as uncomfortable, at best.

The lights were flashing, but as long as he was not on the dance floor there was enough other light to keep him from getting discombobulated. Not but a few seconds after walking in, the horrible rap song playing on the music system had a gunshots with rapid secession, and -nothing. Samuel could tell it was not real. He smiled to himself and thought how he was fine. He may have picked up a few quarks and jitters but he was fine. It helped that all the guys took one look at him and parted like the Red Sea for him. In truth he was marveling at the whole situation so much that he was that he was relatively unaffected by the sensory overload. He was holding hands with the most gorgeous woman in a house full of gorgeous women. And for the first time since he had been back, getting reminded of his veteran status had not been obnoxious, but instead had gotten them in for free and without the under twenty-one wristbands. Samuel was feeling pretty good.

Samuel was looking around taking it all in. He was impressed by how "professional" everything was. They had a cop working security. The dance floor looked like something out of a music video with lasers and lights. Samuel scoffed thinking back to the time they made a "dance floor" by the smoke pit back in Twenty-Nine Palms. That was a couple of broken down MRE boxes with a two CD changer boombox. But it was still a cherished memory of his whole squad, drunk off their asses, making fools of themselves dancing.

Samantha looked back to Samuel as she drug him towards "the bar." The bar was really just a counter where the kegs were set up. Everything with college fraternity parties was about liability. An off-duty police officer was hired to check ID's and kick people out. They gave underage people wristbands. Everyone knew that they were just going to take them off and drink, but that was not the fraternity's "fault." And the alcohol was kept in one location so they claim it was not drunk people serving drunk people. Each trick had probably been learned by some lawsuit or another. Samantha thought Samuel looked cute as he was looking around in wonderment. Samantha was glad to see he appeared to be taking it well, and since he was getting to satisfy some curiosity, she was happy they were here.

They finally made it up to the counter. Samantha recognized several of the boys at the counter. Samantha pulled Samuel closer to her, she was not usually a fan of showing off, but this was too good of a chance to let pass.

Jake handed her two cups and said, "Who's the monster?" just loud enough for her to hear.

Jake was Cameron's "little brother" in the fraternity. Cameron was her ex-boyfriend, who had cheated on her. So, she was happy to explain who the "monster" was.

"This is Samuel," Samantha said holding up Samuel's hand.

"Sam and Sam," Jake said putting the rest of the cups down, "cute."

Samantha saw Jake was staring Samuel up and down.

She looked back and saw Samuel was obliviously, looking around. Lucy was standing next to him staring at him too. Samantha wondered if this is how Samuel had felt about her all of those years, the center of most people's attention, and she just wanted him to herself.

"Cameron is upstairs," Jake said,

Samantha turned back around sharply and said, "I don't care, Jake."

Samantha felt like it was rude even as she said it, but she really did not care. She was not here to rub Cameron's face in it, that was just an added bonus.

Samuel felt Samantha tugging on his sleeve. He turned around and saw she had a cup full of beer in her hand. Samuel had not realized they made it to the bar as she never once let go of his hand. There was some level of dedication to holding his hand if she had gotten two cups, filled them up and was now handing him one.

"Thanks," He said smiling. When he looked up from the cup, he noticed why she did not let go of his hand. On the other side of the counter and on both sides of it there was a pack of polo wearing hyenas, salivating staring at them. Samuel had to fight back a chuckle at their faces racked with inferiority as they studied him.

Yes, scavengers, he thought, *you will go hungry tonight, the lion is not sharing.* As if karma for his internal arrogance, Samuels heart jumped into his throat. The songs changed and the bass made a thud, thud, thud sound that was loud enough to shake his organs. Samuel fought to keep his cool, not wanting to show that it had disturbed him. He quickly took a long pull from the beer as if to play off whatever he expression he might have made. Samantha was trying to say something to him. He could not hear here so he leaned in as close as he could.

"Let's get out of the way." She giggled in his ear. Her breath danced along his ear and down his neck. Samuel felt calm again. Samuel pulled back and kissed her in appreciation. Samuel thought how she may not ever know how therapeutic she was for him.

Samantha was not sure if Samuel kissed her to "stake his claim" in front of the boys or not. Normally, she would have abhorred that type of showmanship. But in this case, she was comfortable with the idea. Samantha led him off to a less crowded area kind of near the dance floor. She put her arm around his waist and they waited quietly for Lucy and Michelle to catch up. Samantha was staring up at Samuel when he finally looked down at her. Samantha stuck her bottom lip out imitating a sad baby's face.

Samuel leaned in and whispered in her ear, "What's wrong?"

His voice in her ear was almost too much for her to handle.

She shuddered and pulled him close while she whispered in his ear, "I want to be able to talk to you."

Samuel leaned back and looked down at her and smiled and nodded.

Samantha looked over at Lucy who was making her way with Michelle to where they were standing and gave her a look to communicate:

Keep Michelle and do not follow us.

Samantha could tell she understood because she huffed and rolled her eyes at her. Samantha took his hand and led him through the house to a back patio. Normally this area would have been reserved for members and their dates, but Samantha was confident she could charm her way past any would be nuisance that might try to turn them away. She opened the door and began to lead Samuel out. There was a solitary light on the porch lighting up the otherwise pitch-black night. There were a few guys out here smoking cigarettes. They looked over at them with disconcerting expressions on their faces.

Samantha recognized a few of them so she quickly blurted out, "Sorry guys." Samantha took a dramatic gasp, "I had to catch some air."

One of them said, "Oh it's just you Sam." One of them chimed in by saying, "Thought we were going to have to kick someone's ass." Several of them laughed and some of them turned around. But Samantha noticed some of them had not, and they had locked eyes with Samuel. Samantha started to feel a panic come over her realizing this might not have been the best idea.

"Who's this?" one of them said.

Samantha felt a lump in her throat as she tried to answer. But Samuel shot the rest of the way through the doorway revealing the rest of his mass, which was too big to make it through the old narrow doorway abroad.

"I'm Sam," He said cordially. Samantha could see the panic she had felt had been completely absorbed by all the boys on the patio. They had all turned to look at the specimen fully visible to them now.

Samuel understood that he was invading the world of these guys. He was not here for confrontation, he just wanted to spend time with Samantha.

"This is my fault guys," He said, "I just got back from Iraq and thought I could handle a party, but I needed some space." That seemed to do the trick as the guys' body language instantly changed from cornered dog to content.

"When did you get back?" one of them said.

"Just about five days ago," Samuel laughed.

Another one just said, "What branch?"

"Marines." He said. He started to feel like he was at a press conference as he heard a slight murmur coming from them and then another one said, "Do you know my cousin Richard Wilson?"

Samuel shook his head and said, "Sorry dude, it's a great big Marine Corps." Before anyone could ask him another question he said, "I don't mean to impose we can find somewhere else if-" A ruckus of protests came from the guys. Samuel smiled and said, "Thanks."

He turned back around and saw Samantha staring up at

him with adoration. Samuel smiled at her to convey his surprise that had worked.

"Everyone seems to know you around this place." Samuel said putting his hands on the railing of the porch.

Samantha hugged his arm closest to her and said, "Long story." Samuel knew that meant it involved one or more of the boys here, which did not bother him at all. He had fallen in love with her listening to her complain about boys she had dated.

"I've got time." Samuel said taking another drink from his beer.

Samantha sighed and said, "My ex-boyfriend is in this fraternity. He's an asshole and he cheated on me, and I haven't really been here since."

Samuel looked down at her with her head on his arm and said, "Wow, you are right. How could you have wasted my time with that long drawn-out tale?"

Samantha looked up at him and rolled her eyes. Samuel had never been judgmental, least of all to her. Samantha had made plenty of mistakes when it came to her choice in boys. Samuel was quick with advice and honest assessments, but he never belittled her about them. He would listen and make jokes when appropriate. But if she had been telling him about some guy that seemed nice, he would council patience, or another chance. She did not know how he had operated with such an apparent lack of envy for as long as had. Samantha had just gotten him back and the thought of who might have had him in the intervening time was more information than she cared to know.

She sighed and said in reflection, "No one ever quite measured up to you." Samuel blushed and looked at her. He leaned over and their lips locked. She did not care about the spectators she was not going to stop if he did not.

Their moment was ruined by a voice next to Samuel. "Hey man." For a moment she thought their public display of affection had spoiled the peace Samuel had just won for them. Samuel slowly pulled away from her, visibly annoyed by the disturbance.

"What's up?" he said not even deigning to look in the direction of the interloper.

"I just wanted to thank you for your service." It was Paul. Samantha did not know him well. He and Cameron were the same age, so a year older than Samuel and her, and apparently, they had been closer friends before she dated Cameron.

"Thanks," Samuel said in an uncharacteristically discourteous tone sticking his hand out to shake Paul's hand. Samantha knew that only she knew him well enough to know that Samuel not showing social niceties was cause for concern. As if to make matters worse, Paul leaned on the rail next to Samuel not taking a hint to leave.

"I mean it man, we really appreciate you." Paul said in a magnanimous tone. Samuel looked over at Samantha and rolled his eyes. He picked up his beer and finished it. Samantha laughed silently to display her amusement. Paul started some long monologue about how they could only do what they did because of guys like him. Then Paul noticed that Samuel's beer was empty.

"Hey Sam." Paul said. "Will you go get us a couple more beers?"

Paul was holding his empty cup up as well. Samantha saw Samuel's knuckles go white. He would have been willing to fight over as much in high school, the problem now was he would be able to murder Paul and every single one of the guys on the patio with no problem.

Samantha, eager to diffuse the situation, put her hand on Samuel's arm and said, "I'd love to." in her best sweet voice. Samantha grabbed the cups and retreated inside hoping that if she was quick enough Samuel would not take the slight as anything more than a minor inconvenience.

"Just walk up to the back and tell them one is for me." the prick standing next to Samuel yelled to Samantha as she walked through the door, "They'll serve you first."

Samuel could feel his anger welling. He wanted to smash

the guy's face into the support column next to him... repeatedly. Samuel stared out into the darkness and tried to control his breathing. Destroying this guy would only make him feel good until he saw Samantha's disgust at the sight.

The prick started up again, "Like I was saying..." he continued on, but Samuel was not listening. Samuel saw that the guy was pulling a pack of cigarettes out of his front pocket while he was droning on. Samuel thought for a second some nicotine might help save this guy's life. Besides if he was going to be subject to this guy stealing perfectly good oxygen that Samuel could have used, he was going to take perfectly a perfectly good cigarette from him.

"Hey man," Samuel said, "You mind if I bum a smoke off of you."

"Sure," the guy said eagerly, "I get it don't want to smoke in front of the lady."

He opened the pack and Samuel took a cigarette out and nodded at him in appreciation. The offering and referring to Samantha as a lady had bought him a few more minutes. The guy held the lighter up as if he was going to light it for Samuel. Samuel kept thinking of the Caesar quote, "I could kill you faster than I could threaten to kill you." Samuel must have given him a look like he was insane, because the guy let out a nervous chuckle and turned the lighter around handing it to Samuel. Samuel lit the cigarette and took a deep long pull. The noxious, life giving fumes hit Samuel's lungs and he believed he now had the willpower for this guy. Whatever-his-name-was, lit his own cigarette and continued his "Look how patriotic I am" spiel. Samuel reflected that he was proud that he had the self-control not to rip the guy in half.

"You know I was going to join..." Samuel heard whatever-his-name-was say. Samuel thought to himself, *But,* as he flicked the cigarette out into the yard. Samuel finally looked over at the guy. Samuel stuck his left hand out and clapped the guy on the shoulder with his right hand.

"What was your name man?" Samuel said. The guy

switched the cigarette to his other hand and grabbed Samuel's hand with the now free hand.

"Paul." He said smiling.

"Paul..." Samuel said as he squeezed his hand. Samuel stopped just shy of where he thought the guy would scream out in pain and with his right hand, he squeezed Paul's deltoid until he could feel the muscle twitch. "I really don't fucking care." Samuel said calmly. Samuel loosened his grip and slapped Paul on the back hard enough that he almost went over the rail they had been leaning on. Samuel turned his back on him as if to say, *I dare you.* Samuel walked back into the house with complete disdain.

Samantha had just gotten the beers and was walking back towards the porch. She was eager to get back to make sure nothing had escalated. She saw Samuel walking up from the direction of the porch. His face was calm, and he did not appear to be in a hurry. Maybe he had used his brilliant mind to escape. He looked at her and smiled. But then Samantha saw him look down at the beers she was carrying, and his face went blank. For a moment Samantha was worried that the beers were a reminder of his recent homicide.

As he walked closer Samantha tried to look past him with a worried expression to see if she could see a crime scene behind him. Samuel calmly took both of the beers out of her hand and threw them both in a trashcan next to them.

"Fuck that guy." Samuel said with a smile. Samantha was really worried now. Samuel tried to lean in for a kiss.

Samantha reeled back and demanded to know, "What did you do?"

"Thought about you," Samuel said, "and then came to find you." In between his arm and his body Samantha saw Paul lurking in the doorway of the porch. She was glad to know he was alive. Samantha saw he was shaking his hand and had a distinct look of worry and despair on his face. Samantha smiled figuring only Paul's ego had been hurt. She looked up at Samuel and leaned in for that kiss she had denied him a moment ago. Then she heard Samuel whisper in her ear, "Let's go watch TV."

The next morning Samantha woke to the room filled with daylight. She tried to calmly crawl over Samuel. She had four missed calls, twelve text messages, and it was eleven twenty. Samuel was fast asleep, and she did not want to wake him, or leave him. She decided it was best to let him sleep, remembering the night before when he fell asleep sitting upright on the loveseat. Samantha slipped on some sweats and quietly opened the door and snuck out into the apartment. Samantha walked towards the kitchen to get some water and saw Lucy sitting in the living room. Samantha was waiting for the stinging barrage of quips at her leaving them at the party. Lucy's crass personality was too funny to be offensive and too playful to not be endearing. Samantha glanced up from the sink to see Lucy squinting at her. Then she saw Lucy leap up and race into the kitchen. Lucy got right next to her. Samantha looked up and rolled her eyes knowing some ridiculous pass at her loyalty was coming.

"You had sex!" Lucy said loudly.

Samantha gasped and hushed her.

Lucy changed her volume to a whisper and said, "He's still here because you had sex!"

Samantha felt her face go completely red.

"That is none of your business." Samantha said forcefully in a whisper.

"You can't deny it because you did," Lucy exclaimed and then asked, "How many times?"

Samantha looked at her side eyed with a blank expression.

"I don't know how many that is-five." Lucy inquired.

Samantha just rolled her eyes.

"Six!" Lucy exclaimed.

Samantha went back to filling up her glass of water.

"If it gets to be too much to handle you know you can tap me in girl."

Samantha put her glass on the counter and gave Lucy a stern look to make sure that she understood the joke had gone too far.

Samuel woke up to the sound of a woman yelling something. He had not slept so hard or for as long, probably, in years. And to make the whole thing even better he did not wake up startled. His eyes just kind of opened. He knew exactly where he was. He also heard Samantha's voice whispering on the other side of the door, so he knew where she was. Samuel slowly raised to a sitting position and thought how it was a nice change of pace that the only thing he did not know is where his clothes were. Samuel ran his fingers through his hair and laughed to himself as he realized he had not gotten his bag out of the car.

Yesterday's clothes it is he thought. Samuel got up and got dressed. Samuel smiled in remembrance as he found each article around the room next to some article of Samantha's. Finally, clothed to an appropriate level Samuel slipped his cowboy boots on. That was the biggest change to his wardrobe in his life. Samuel had grown accustomed to boots but, refused to wear combat style boots when he didn't have to. Samuel refused to do a lot of things now. He refused to wear dirty socks or underwear, as he remembered diapers and five-day-old socks on deployment. So, he knew he needed to go get his bag so he could put some clean ones on.

Samantha heard the door to her room open softly. Samuel came out with a big smile on his face.

Lucy, standing next to her, was staring at him walking out and muttered, "I hate you," to Samantha.

Samuel said, "Ladies," in salutations.

Samantha's heart was pumping out of her chest. She raced over to Samuel and jumped into his arms locking lips with him.

"I was trying not to wake you." Samantha said softly.

He put his forehead on her forehead and said, "Thank you." He swung her around for a moment and then put her down.

Then he said pretending to smell himself, "But I really need to find a place to take a shower and put on some clean clothes."

He had a smile on his face, but Samantha was wounded. She wondered if she had been too presumptuous to assume that he was staying. She did not want him to leave, ever. As far as she was concerned, they had five people living here now.

Lucy's crassness came in for the save when she said from behind Samantha, "I would be honored--honored... if you would stand naked in my shower."

Samuel's face turned fire engine red as he chuckled and said, "Thanks Lucy, but I could not impose on your private space."

Samantha knew that was a low hanging fruit for Lucy's disgusting mind, so she blurted out, "We insist," before she had a chance to say whatever she was thinking. "It's our bathroom. And, if we have to, we can use Michelle's. Our other roommate has been at her boyfriend's since the beginning of February."

Samuel looked into Samantha's eyes and smiled, "Let me go get my bag."

Samuel thought it was a good time to check his messages while he went to the car seeing as how it was going to be a hike. He read a couple of text messages from a few Marines saying they had gotten his new number through the grapevine with a typical Marine harangue and insult. He was scrolling through laughing to himself and replying to them, when he saw he had a voicemail. He listened to the message.

"Hey Pony Boy, it's Mac. I called your house and some fox named Mary gave me your new number. They let me out, dude. I am Oscar Mike to Ol' Arkansas. I am going to stop by and see you on the way. Or I am going to stop by and see Mary. Either way call me dude, you should have my number now. Stay gold."

Samuel laughed through the message. Mac was probably his best friend. They thought Mac was going to be able to come see them when they landed, but they had sent him off to some specialist for some kind of final medical check at Walter Reed that week, so the last time Samuel saw him was in the Medevac that picked him up and took him away in Iraq. Samuel had made it to the car and retrieved his bag, so he called Mac for the trip back. Samuel listened in laughter as Mac had set a ring-back tone. In typical Mac fashion the song was the ever classy, "Titties and Beer." Samuel knew Mac probably paid $1.99 a month to have that feature and was proud to do so. He blew his money on stupid things like that.

"Pony-boy," Mac said as he answered the phone, "What is your pos, over?"

"Damn," Samuel said laughing, "Let me call you back the song was just getting to the good part."

"You like that?" Mac said laughing back at him in his deep southern drawl, "I got a little bored laid up in the hospital all that time. If I'd 've known you were calling, I'd 've changed it to 'Raining Men' for ya'."

Samuel had missed talking to Mac. Mac was the type of guy that could find humor in anything. If there was any person in the world that could get him to leave Samantha's side for even one minute, it was Mac.

"Where the hell are you dude?" Samuel inquired.

"Oh, you know somewhere around Knoxville." Mac said.

"Damn son," Samuel said, "You're hauling ass aren't you."

Mac laughed. Mac always liked it when Samuel imitated his southern accent and word choice.

"Damn straight," He said, "Figured, I better get gone before the big green weenie figured out a way to keep me around longer."

"Well look as entertaining as the thought of you being my stepdad is you aren't going to get to see Mary this trip." Samuel snickered to Mac.

"Damn."

"You are coming down to God's country brother." Samuel said.

Samuel thought to himself that if there was one person from his life that he wanted Samantha to meet it was Mac. The thought of his two favorite people together with him made him smile.

"Damn son," Mac sneered, "You run off and desert?"

Samuel laughed and said "What?"

"Hell, everyone knows Mexico is God's country." Mac said confidently.

Samuel burst out with laughter.

"Cocaine and senoritas," Mac continued, "I guess Iraq made a man of you after all. I'm just proud to think I might 've had something to do with this."

Samuel caught his breath for a second and said, "Yeah, you always were a bad influence."

"Shit," Mac said continuing in between Samuel's laughter, "you're gonna have to scope out an ADA accessible bar. I can't limp my ass up in any Ol' cabana."

Samuel felt the beginnings of a tear forming in his eye. The thought of how bad Mac might have gotten mangled was a frightening prospect to him.

"Well they have plenty of them," Samuel said recomposing himself, "in Oxford."

"Hell son," Mac said laughing again, "I sure as hell can't swim."

"Mississippi, idiot." Samuel said. "Oxford, Mississippi."

"What the hell are you doing in Oxford, Mississippi?" Mac said abruptly. There was a brief pause then Mac blurted out, "Oh shit you went and saw that dude Sam."

Samuel scoffed into the phone. It had been a long running joke for Mac that Samantha was a guy and Samuel was too stupid to come up with a name other than Sam, which he just changed to Samantha.

"Samantha, yeah." Samuel laughed.

"Look brother," Mac continued with his harassment,

"I'm out now you can just admit it."

Samuel shook his head thinking that he was going to be floored when he actually saw her.

"I mean," Mac said, "I hope y'all can get married someday. Really I do, everyone deserves to be happy."

"Macintosh," Samuel barked, "Shut the fuck up."

Mac quietly said, "Man used my Christian name, must 've struck a nerve."

Samuel rolled his eyes. He wanted to cut to the chase as he was back at Samantha's building and wanted to get up there to tell her the news if she would be meeting this slightly domesticated animal or not. "You coming or not asshole?" Samuel said.

Without hesitation Mac said, "Of course, I got to pull over and figure out where the hell Oxford, Mississippi is and how to get there, but I'll give you a shout when I'm about an hour out."

"Alright dude," Samuel said in relief, "I'll find a place for us to throw down."

"Out," Mac said hanging up the phone.

Samantha was sitting on the loveseat when she saw Samuel come through the door. Samantha could not help but feel that she missed him in the short time he had been gone. Samuel's face expressed that he was deep in thought, but he was smiling, so Samantha thought it must have been good thoughts.

"What's up?" She inquired, getting up to greet him at the door.

"I've got some big news." Samuel said, turning his head slightly. Samantha got a confused look on her face.

Lucy blurted out from the armchair, "If she says no, I will say yes."

Samantha and Samuel both looked at her with an incredulous look on their faces.

"I just figured," Lucy continued looking at the TV, "If it was that you decided to settle down and get married... you know." Lucy widened her eyes and said, "I'm game."

Samantha had made the mistake of telling Lucy about last night, and the even bigger mistake of telling her that he was shy and incredibly uncomfortable with flattery, while he was gone getting his bag.

Samantha just looked back at Samuel and rolled her eyes. "What is it?" Samantha said, throwing her arms around his neck.

"My best friend from the Corps finally got released," Samuel paused briefly "and he's going to stop by here tonight."

Samantha could tell that this was good news for Samuel. She was happy to see that he was happy about something.

"That's great!" She said, "Do you want to know some places y'all can go?"

Samuel's face morphed instantly to disconcerted.

"I was hoping you would want to meet him." Samuel said.

Samantha felt herself drifting away in euphoria with the realization that Samuel wanted her to meet the people that were important to him.

"Of course," Samantha said smiling. She reached up and kissed him. "I just did not want to impose." She said.

"I have a question." Lucy said from the living room raising her hand.

Samuel looked at her and rolled his eyes. He had caught on that she was always going to say something inappropriate to him.

"Do they like manufacture you guys?" Lucy asked, "Is he just like you?"

Samuel looked at Samantha who was rolling her eyes again.

"There's no one like Mac." Samuel said thinking to himself about the potential between the two of them. Lucy sat there in silence. Samuel thought for a minute. He did not know how bad Mac had gotten torn up. He was able to drive and walk, and if he could do those two things, he was always willing to chase skirt. But Samuel did not want to embarrass him by having him get turned down by some college girl who could not get past his injuries.

Samuel considered the best way to approach this and then added, "I tell you what, let me get a few drinks into him, and convince him not to drive the rest of the way to Arkansas tonight, and we'll give you the cue to make a dramatic entrance." Samantha had a big smile on her face when he looked back at her. "I don't really know where to go though." Samuel added.

Samantha looked up to the ceiling deep in thought for a moment, then she said, "One of our sorority sisters works at a bar off the square. It's pretty low key and if she's working tonight, she would serve us."

"Tell her we have plenty of deployment money and tip lavishly." Samuel said thinking that it sounded like the perfect place to take Mac.

Intro to Chapter 6: Situation, Mission, <u>Execution</u>, Support, Command and Control.

If war has an upside, it's the friendships. "We merry band of brothers" is a resounding line for a reason. Something about the shared experience of toil and turmoil brings people together in ways that cannot be copied. Samuel knew instinctively that He and Mac were lifelong friends. He was fairly certain that Mac was the only person on the planet that knew him better than Samantha did. The truth was Samantha may not know him at all anymore. Samuel had only just recently discovered the demon that he kept chained up inside himself. Samantha would neither care to meet that side of Samuel, nor would she understand it. Mac, however, knew that side as well as he knew the nerdy over achiever.

The battalion had gone mobile. They were living out of vehicles cruising the deserts looking for a fight. Samuel and Mac were sitting in their truck. Samuel was on radio watch and, well Mac was just bored, so he was up talking with Samuel while the rest of the fire team slept. Nighttime in Iraq was a unique experience. It was cold, especially compared to the scorching days. Light discipline was strictly enforced, seeing as how there was miles of visibility in all directions.

"So, what's her name again?" Mac asked.

"Samantha." Samuel replied as he spit tobacco into a bottle.

"And you never fucked her?" Mac asked.

"No bro," Samuel laughed, "No matter how many times you ask."

"You got a picture?" Mac inquired.

"If I did, I wouldn't let you see it." Samuel said sternly.

"Damn dude," Mac replied, "Usually you get the pussy before you get whipped by it."

Samuel laughed. They had, had this conversation a thousand times.

"You're going to, right?" Mac said.

"I'm supposed to go see her when I get home." Samuel

explained.

"I expect a phone call immediately afterwards!" Mac exclaimed.

"No man," Samuel said sullenly, "I don't think I will."

Mac lifted his head up and looked at him, "After all this time I, got to know if it's good or not." Mac explained, "I got to know if it was worth the wait."

"No," Samuel said, "I do not think I will engage in a relationship with her... Physical or otherwise."

Mac contorted his face in disbelief.

"What the fuck am I going to do Mac?" Samuel asked, "You don't understand this girl man. It's like she's on another plane of existence. She's not something you fuck, or fuck up. There's a special place in hell for the men that break her heart." Samuel resigned, remembering he had already broken her heart once before.

Mac laughed out loud for a moment and finally said, "Well that sounds simple. Just fucking don't break her heart, moron."

Samuel chuckled as he thought to himself., *An impossible task, to live up to be the man she deserves.*

"You know I joined the Corps because of her." Samuel said.

"Bull--shit." Mac said. Samuel nodded silently looking off into the distance.

"Shut the fuck up." Mac said.

"I did." Samuel replied, "Eighth grade, we were sitting in math class and the announcement came on." Samuel looked over at Mac. He continued, "Telling us planes had crashed into the World Trade center."

Mac nodded in understanding. In some regard everyone that joined after that, joined in part because of that.

"I remember looking at Samantha," Samuel said looking out into the distance, "she sat right beside me. She was covering her face and crying. She looked so hurt. Genuinely hurt, by the news that people had gotten hurt." Samuel looked back at Mac, "Can you imagine? 13-years-old, already the most beautiful person I had ever seen, and she had that much compassion." Samuel spit into the bottle again as he contemplated. "I think the demon was born that day," Samuel said.

"Oh, don't start with that shit again," Mac said, "just because you are exceptional at killing doesn't mean you're fucking possessed by some demon."

"No," Samuel said, "but I like it." Mac looked at him for a long moment. "Somebody hurt her Mac," Samuel added, "When I looked at her, she leaned over and threw her arms around me. Looking for comfort, I guess. It wasn't a conscious thing, but a part of me resolved that day to do everything I could to make sure I was standing between her and people that might want to do that shit again. Anything to keep her in the place she was before that announcement over the intercom." Samuel and Mac sat in silence for a moment. Even Mac could not make a joke out of that.

"Sounds to me like you're the only man in the world that belongs with her if she got you out here slaying bodies... where you belong." Mac said. Samuel thought for a moment. That was a novel idea indeed.

"Mac she's gone off to college," Samuel found himself slipping into a southern twang, a sign he was tired and not thinking before he spoke, "We both know 'he who lives by the sword.....'"

"Dies by the motherfucker," Mac finished.

"I'm gonna' die out here," Samuel said, "If not this desert some other one. I'm just going to take a lot of motherfuckers with me."

There was a long silence until Mac finally said, "Or..." Mac looked over at Samuel and said, "You can stop being a whiny little bitch and realize someone upstairs wants you to get through this shit, and that's why you are good at what you do. You can get through this shit and get home, fuck miss golden girl like a rabbit...." Mac smiled and said, "Excuse me, make sweet, sweet love to her, and live happily ever after."

Samuel smiled, he knew Mac couldn't understand, Samuel might live, but he could not make plans of being in heaven with Samantha while he was rotting in the depths of hell.

CHAPTER 6:
BLOOD STRIPES

Samantha thought it was adorable that Samuel was visibly giddy with excitement as they walked up to the bar.

"Ooo," He said looking up at the marquee, "live music tonight."

Samantha could tell that Samuel had been understating what this friend, Mac, meant to him. He looked like a kid on Christmas morning. Samantha was reflecting that she might not have ever seen him act so childlike in his movements.

"Yeah," Samantha said attempting to match his excitement, "they usually have someone pretty good too."

They walked in and Samantha began looking for Kristen, her friend that worked there. She had sent a text message earlier, letting her know they were coming. She saw her across the room setting a drink down. There was always a little anxiety when drinking underage. Something could always go wrong. Samantha had a fake I.D. but Samuel did not. He did not have a baby face anymore, but there was always a possibility that the manager or someone else might catch on and throw them out. Samantha waved to Kristen when she finally looked their way. She waved back with a big smile and came quickly to where they were by the door, The two girls shared a "Hey" and hugged.

"You look so good," Kristen said sweetly.

"Thanks," Samantha said.

Kristen's eyes shifted over to Samuel. She looked at him

for a long second with a smile and her eyes got a little bigger. Samuel was scanning the room, and then saw her look at him and smiled. Samantha laughed to herself at how oblivious he was to his effect on women.

"I'm sorry this is Sam," Samantha said. Samuel leaned in and hugged her and said, "You must be Kristen. So nice to meet you."

Kristen's face slowly turned back to Samantha with the same big smile while he was hugging her. Samantha could read Kristen's thoughts on her face. She was uncomfortable with how much she enjoyed that hug, even being the southern church hug that it was.

Samuel was certain that was amongst the most awkward hugs he'd ever received. But Samuel wanted to make as good of an impression on Samantha's friends as he could. He knew eventually he was going to have to head back to the fleet and he was already planning for that future. He did not intend on cutting ties again. He knew he was comfortable with long distance and he felt pretty good about Samantha's future loyalty. So, he figured he needed to have allies in Oxford.

"Right this way." Kristen said.

The bar was kind of a dive bar. There was a guy on the stage to his right sitting on the stool with a ginger beard and a bald head that appeared to be strumming a sound check. The three of them walked through the center of the bar towards a back corner.

Samuel noticed the bar was sparsely populated, perhaps about a fourth of the tables had anyone at them. The girls were walking in front of him chit-chatting. Kristen leaned over to Samantha and whispered and they both laughed. Samuel caught himself returning to his wartime habits. He felt like he should have been focused on getting involved in their conversation, but he was too distracted. He noticed the exits and found himself scanning every person in the whole place in a threat assessment. By the time they reached the corner table he was satisfied that it was a safe enough place.

Samantha was listening to Kristen while they walked to the table.

"So really don't worry, nobody is going to come ask him for his I.D." Kristen said.

"I really didn't think so." Samantha said in reply, "But you never know."

"He is definitely an upgrade," Kristen leaned over and whispered to Samantha. They both shared a laugh.

Samantha said, "That's an understatement."

"Cam will definitely be jealous." Kristen said.

Samantha thought how she truthfully did not care if he was or not.

"Well," Samantha said as they arrived at the table, "truth be told Cam was just a distraction until he got back to me." She put her arm around Samuel's waist and looked up at him. He was looking around the room with a stern look on his face.

When he felt Samantha's arm around him, Samuel looked down and smiled. He leaned over and they shared a kiss.

"I'm so happy for y'all." Kristen said with a smile. Samuel stuck his arm out for Samantha to scoot into the booth.

Samuel sat down next to her and Kristen said, "Let's make this official," as she was putting down napkins.

Samantha got her fake I.D. out of her clutch. Samuel had a shocked look on his face. Kristen looked at him blankly. Samantha put her hand on his arm and smiled. He had probably never been in this situation before she thought. There was so much of the college experience that was foreign to him. Samuel looked like he caught on had he went for his wallet and pulled out his I.D.

Kristen picked them up and pretended to study them for a moment and then said, "Alright, what are we drinking?"

Drinking, even underage, in the Corps was a way of life. The golden rule was do not get a DUI, that was a career-ender. The runner up was do not get busted drinking underage. It was known by everyone at every level of command that it happened-- every night. But you were not to get caught. So, drinking out at a bar, with a fake I.D. or a wink and a nod was only for the bravest, or dumbest. So, Samuel had been nervous when Kristen had asked him for his I.D. Now he was unsure what he was going to order. He pondered for a moment and then it came to him.

"Crown and sprite." He said smiling.

The first time he had ever gotten really sideways was with Mac. Samuel had only been checked into the company for a couple of weeks. Mac had effectively taken him under his wing and decided to get him drunk, on Crown and Sprite. It was a good night.

Samantha ordered a whiskey sour and Kristen left to go get the orders. Samuel looked over to Samantha.

"I am really glad you are here." He said.

Samuel felt a little flutter in his stomach. He had meant to think it, but it came out as he was thinking. Samantha had her arm wrapped around his and was holding his hand on the table.

She leaned over and kissed his arm and said, "You have no idea how glad I am you are here."

Samuel gave her a long kiss on the forehead thinking to himself how thankful he was to have survived if only to be here now.

"Sam?" Samantha heard the voice of dread while Samuel was kissing her forehead.

She knew it was Cameron. She looked up and saw him. Samuel looked nothing more than annoyed at the interruption.

"Cameron." Samantha said blankly.

Samuel's head shot around to look at him. Samantha had told Samuel he was the one who had cheated on her. She was frustrated that Kristen had not given her a warning that he was here, she would have preferred to avoid this situation. Cameron sat down in the booth across from Samuel. It was typical fashion for him to act as though he could sit anywhere he liked.

Samuel immediately snapped, "Sure dude, have a seat."

Cameron got a smug smile on his face.

"I heard you met Paul last night." Cameron tilted his head and looked satisfied, "You did the world a favor. I always knew his mouth was going to get him in trouble, so I am sure he deserved that. He swore you broke his hand."

Samuel sat there staring at him unblinking.

Cameron said, "He's fine if you are worried. But don't be offended if I don't offer to shake your hand."

About that time Kristen walked up she was looked right at Samantha and mouthed "I am so sorry." to her. Cameron saw Samantha looking at her, so he interjected, "Kristen put these on my tab."

Samuel seized the opportunity to disarm Cameron. "Well, hell if I'd have known that was happening, I'd have ordered a double," Samuel laughed.

Samuel had grown up around kids like this. They think they are smooth and suave. They are used to throwing daddy's money around and getting what they want. Which was fair enough, generational douchbaggery deserves generational money. They were really easy marks. They were never one quarter as intelligent as they believed they were. Their motivations were always the most base imaginable. It was fun to tear them down.

"What brings you down big guy?" Cameron said.

"Oh, just came to see this one." Samuel said.

"Oh, are y'all a thing?" Cameron inquired.

Samuel had to keep himself from laughing in his face as he thought to himself *Gotcha.*

"We are." Samuel said in an endearing tone.

Cameron smugly smiled again, "We have something in common. I don't know if Sam mentioned it, but we used to be a thing." Cameron was standing on the trap door now.

"No, she hadn't mentioned it." Samuel lied.

Cameron looked down at his drink and said, "I doubt

that."

That's what Samuel was waiting for.

"Why?" He immediately snapped back.

Cameron's face twisted in shock. Samuel had put him on the spot to comment on what made his relationship with Samantha remarkable.

Samantha was not much one for macho displays. She knew what was going on though. She had witnessed Samuel destroy the guys at their high school for the smallest discourtesy towards girls. He was a disciple of chivalry and gentlemanly behavior. She was worried now though, before it had always been verbal. However, she was worried that it was verbal then because that's what he was capable of. Now he was definitely capable of more.

"We just dated for a while." Cameron said, taking a drink nervously.

"How long?" Samuel asked immediately.

They had dated for two months, so not that long. Samantha knew he was putting relentless pressure on Cameron. That's what he was best at. Samuel's brain worked too fast to go toe to toe with him. He would press someone until they slipped up and then unleash a barrage of words that left the person feeling small and insignificant.

"Let's just change the subject." Cameron said.

"Sure, you brought it up." Samuel said taking a drink.

He looked over at Samantha and gave her a wink. She did not feel very reassured.

"So, where you down from?" Cameron asked.

"Iraq." Samuel said blankly.

Cameron smiled smugly again. Samantha started to feel hot. She wanted to escape this situation. She knew Cameron was about to mess up big time.

"Got to go back soon?" Cameron asked, licking his lips.

"Eventually." Samuel said blankly.

Cameron just looked down at his drink and said. "Samantha did always have a soft spot for those less fortunate."

Samantha was seething with anger. She officially did not care about what happened to him now. It was belittling enough that he was talking about her in the third person, but he had no right to say what she had a soft spot for.

Samuel abruptly turned to her and in the most calm voice imaginable said, "Can I destroy this guy now?"

Samantha let go of Samuel's hand and crossed her arms in preparation for the first punch and said, "Certainly."

Samuel watched Cameron flinch back in the booth as soon as she said "Certainly." Samuel laughed loudly. "You think I would waste the calories on you."

The boy kind of lowered his hands to see what Samuel meant by that. Samuel was going to enjoy this. He began his destructive harangue in the calmest voice he could muster:

"But that's the big secret isn't it. Daddy and mommy gave you anything you wanted, so now you assume the whole world is going to give you what you think you deserve, because you know you certainly deserve to get your ass kicked. The reality is you will never be anything other than insignificant. The privilege of being a spoiled rich kid will get you a job, hell it will probably get you a wife. But like mommy and daddy's attention the privilege is just another drug you get addicted to. You believe your life can only get better, because it only ever has. Until one day it doesn't get any better. You'll find that you've reached the limit of what your privilege can get you and you'll never get anymore because you never learned to earn anything. So, you feel empty and try anything. Next thing you know you are banging your twenty-something-year-old secretary, thinking you still got it. But your wife leaves your cheating ass and half your money goes with her. The twenty-year-old secretary leaves you because you're old and no longer wealthy enough to spoil her with material things, and she does not need your old broke ass. And when you go to pick up your kids on the weekend you have to hear them say they want to grow up to

be like me, one of the less fortunates, who went and fought a war while you pissed the best years of your life away. Because nobody grows up wanting to be a forty-year-old divorced account executive at some white-collar job."

Samantha saw the horror on Cameron's face. That was Samuel's style and it had not changed one bit. Samuel had nailed every bit of what he said. Cameron had never done an honest day's work in his life. And Samuel had basically described the exact reason that Cameron cheated on her to begin with. He would get bored and decide he wanted more. Cameron was never sorry he did it, he was sorry he got caught, and actually expected Samantha to forgive him. Cameron considered her wrong for not taking him back. Cameron was speechless. Whenever Samuel unleashed on someone, he said so much so fast there was no way to respond to any one thing. And it always came out mere seconds after something they said.

It felt so good to Samantha to see Cameron get put in his place.

Cameron started to get up out of the booth, Samuel snatched his wrist and said, "Don't forget to pay for those drinks on the way out. I'd hate for someone to think you can't afford them."

Cameron snatched his arm away and started towards the bar.

"Thanks for the drinks Cam." Samuel shouted.

Samantha was thoroughly turned on by the whole display. She found his restraint to be the sexy part. Samuel could have used his bran to cause Cameron more pain than he had ever felt before, but he did not need to. Samuel looked at her and put his hand back out on the table for her to take back.

"I'm sorry," he said.

"No need to apologize to me," Samantha said putting her hand in his, "He was insulting you as much as me."

"No," Samuel chuckled, "I'm sorry I ever left you alone to

be preyed on by pricks like that."

Samantha smiled and kissed him on the cheek.

"I forgive you." She said, then imitating a stern voice she continued, "Just don't ever do it again."

Samuel felt like this was as good of a time as any to talk about the future.

"I'm yours for as long as you'll have me," he started.

Just then his phone started ringing. It was Mac. He looked at it for a second. He wanted to finish his thought. He wanted to talk about what was going to happen when he had to go back.

"Well, get it." Samantha said smiling. Samuel smiled back at her and answered the phone.

"Hey boy." Mac said.

Samuel looked towards the door waiting for Mac to be walking in. He saw Cam walking out, so he laughed when he said, "What up dude?"

"I'm limping my ass your way." Mac said, "Had to park in Alabama though."

"So, we'll see you Tuesday." Samuel said.

"Hell, boy, I can still make forty miles a day." Mac said.

Samuel laughed and said, "See you in a minute." Samuel hung up and kept an eye on the door.

Samantha said, "Oh, no. He sounds like a character."

"You have no idea." Samuel laughed.

Just then he saw the door fling open wide. In stepped Mac. He did not look as bad as he expected. The left side of his face had some scarring. Samuel knew his injuries, but he had not seen them for himself. Burns to the left side of his face, fractured pelvis, fractured both femurs, compressed spine, and a collapsed lung. Mac's heart stopped twice on the bird. Samuel knew Mac's injures better than his own. Mac's limp was pretty bad, it looked like a waddle more than a limp. But he appeared to be in pretty good shape other than that.

Samantha felt Samuel shoot up out of the booth and drag her by the hand he was still holding towards the door. He was moving so fast it scared her. She hoped he saw Mac because otherwise it seemed like there was some type of danger.

They made it about half the distance to the door when she heard a voice yell, "PONY BOY." It was so loud the singer paused and everyone looked over at them. Samuel let go of Samantha's hand and threw his arms out wide for a hug. Samantha could not see past Samuel's huge frame to get a look at Mac.

Then she suddenly saw this man appear to slide over to Samuel's right side. He had both of his hands up on Samuel's shoulder. Mac, she assumed, had dark hair in the same kind of cut as Samuel. He was about an inch or two taller than Samuel. He was enormous too. Samuel might have been slightly bigger, and this guy's stomach was not as flat, other than that he was about the same size. Samantha saw he had some scars on his face and most immediately identifiable, was a baseball size lump in his jaw, that was obviously chewing tobacco. Then suddenly the guy kneed Samuel in the thigh with all the force he could muster. Had she avoided seeing a fight between Samuel and her ex-boyfriend only to have to watch him brawl with his supposed best friend?

"Mother--fucker!" Samuel yelled. The whole bar was on edge as these two massive men appeared to be starting a fight, and no one there was big enough to break them up.

"Turn around bitch." Mac said smiling, "I heard. That's why I drove all this way. To haze you one last time."

Samuel shuffled around so that he was facing Samantha. He had a nervous smile on his face, which made Samantha feel better, but no less confused. Mac was now gripping Samuel's other shoulder. Then he kneed him in the other thigh. Samuel's face twisted ever so slightly in pain.

"Congratulations!" Mac said and the two hugged each other.

Samantha felt like it was safe to approach now.

Samuel looked over at Samantha. She had a very nervous smile on her face.

Samuel started, "Mac this is-"

"Shut the fuck up!" Mac shouted.

Mac said, looking at Samuel.

Then Mac looked back at Samantha and said, "Did he kidnap you? I'll kill him if he kidnapped you."

Samantha blushed and started smiling.

"Are you being held against your will?" She started laughing as Mac started waddling closer to her. "Blink twice if you are being held against your will."

Samantha started laughing harder. Mac threw his arms around her in a bear hug and picked her up off the ground.

"Are you Sam?" He asked as he put her down.

She covered her mouth with her hands. She was laughing too hard to answer so she just nodded. Mac put his arm around Samantha and looked at Samuel. He waited until Samantha stopped laughing enough to hear his comedy routine.

When he was satisfied his audience was back he said to Samuel, "I fucking hate you." Samantha started laughing again, "The only reason you were tolerable," Mac continued, "Is because you were horrible at picking up women."

Samantha was back to laughing hysterically and Samuel was on the verge of hysterics himself.

"And then you go and introduce me to this." Mac said. Mac gave his audience time to recover and then he said, "Where we sittin'?"

Mac still had one arm around Samantha as she led him towards the table. Samuel figured that was half, part of his comedy routine, and half, hiding his limp.

When they got back to the table Mac took his arm off Samantha. She loved him. He was one great-big giant ball of energy. The entire bar reacted the moment he walked through the door. She was curious what happened to him. The whole walk to the table she could feel him put quite a bit of weight on her, and now, watching him crawl into the booth, he appeared to move like a very old man. Samantha and Samuel had already sat down by the time Mac completed the task of getting upright in the booth. Mac looked at them both with a blank look on his face.

"Abandoned already, huh," Mac said. Samantha got a confused look on her face then Mac looked at her and shook his head while he said, "I thought we shared something special."

Samantha started laughing as she said, "We did but I'm already his."

Samuel started laughing too.

Mac started laughing and said, "Not you honey, him." Then Mac looked at Samuel and said, "That explains how this happened, walk this girl to a table and she thinks it's something special."

Samantha had to wipe the tears away she was laughing so hard.

"What did you do hold the door open for her?" Mac added.

Then she heard Samuel say, "Don't worry you'll always be first in my heart."

Samantha looked down to see Samuel holding Mac's hand on the table. She got a blank look on her face. It was not a common sight to see two massive men that dripped with masculinity holding hands across a table from one another while staring into each other's eyes. Mac pulled his hand away and turned his head like imitating a scorned lover as he made some protest. Samantha started laughing again. When she stopped enough to be able to see Mac again, he was looking right at her.

"If I could figure out how to leave myself for you I would." He said.

Samantha saw that Kristen was back at the table. They all ordered a round. Mac always had something funny to say about everything. Samantha felt like her face hurt from laughing so much. Samuel was even funnier with him here. It was like Mac's energy brought out some energy from Samuel that she did not even know existed.

Samuel had missed Mac's banter. Mac was enjoying himself telling Samantha stories and picking her brain about the young version of Samuel.

Mac started in on Samuel pretty hard at one point by saying, "You know I gave him the name Pony Boy." Samantha looked at him with interest. "You know from the Outsiders," he said.

Samantha shrugged her shoulders to indicate she did not get the reference.

"So, there's the preps, or the soc's as they call them." he started, "and there's the greasers. They are the kids from the wrong side of the tracks."

Samantha leaned in and took another sip of her drink intrigued.

Mac continued, "So there's one kid, called Pony Boy, that hangs out with the greasers, but he's smarter than they are. He's got a chance to get out and get him a nice girl and go to college."

Samantha nodded in understanding.

Mac pointed at Samuel and said, "Pony Boy!"

Samantha nodded and said, "I get it."

Samuel said, "Yeah, I didn't fit in until y'all needed someone to talk to the cops."

Mac laughed, "Yeah, that's why you were Pony Boy. All us greasers were staying in trouble and you were like," Mac changed his voice to a mocking nerdy voice, "Come on guys maybe we shouldn't do this. This seems like a bad idea."

"Yeah," Samuel laughed and said, "Because it was usually a bad idea."

Mac raised an eyebrow and said, "When did I ever have a bad idea?"

Samuel got an incredulous look on his face and said, "Vegas!"

Mac replied, "Vegas was a great idea!"

Samuel laughed loudly at that claim, "Then why did I have to talk that deputy out of taking y'all to jail."

Mac paused for a minute in disbelief. Samuel felt like he had him cornered. He looked over at Samantha to silently celebrate his triumph.

"We weren't going to jail!" Mac said, "That FEMALE deputy," Mac looked over at Samantha, "was just trying to get you alone so she could give you a blow job in her cruiser."

Samuel felt like there was a lump in his throat. Nothing had happened with her but he still felt like he was stupid to have brought it up.

"Don't worry." Mac added to clear the air, "Pony Boy was too stupid to even realize it."

Samantha had no problem believing that some woman was hitting on him and, had even less of a problem believing that Samuel was oblivious to it.

Mac continued though, "Let me tell you something this boy is in *love* with-- you."

Samantha felt her face get hot and her heart started to flutter.

"That's the real reason I named him Pony Boy." Mac said pulling out a tin of tobacco and packing it. "The first time he came in, I was drilling him about girls."

Mac pulled opened the tin and put a big wad in his mouth and continued, "He told us all about this prom queen that was perfect. And how his dumbass had left her to go fight with the rest of us slops. And anytime we'd ask him after that, same shit. Sam's back home, I told her I'd come see her."

Samantha took Samuel's hand. She was on the verge of tears thinking of Samuel talking about her for nearly two years while she was dating douchebags like Cameron.

Samuel knew what Mac said was true, but he also knew he was being a good wingman. "You know," Mac added, "Sam's special."

He was staring at Samantha. Samuel could see the booze was hitting him.

"I know." Samantha said sweetly hugging Samuel's arm tighter.

Mac held up the tin of tobacco for Samuel to see.

"Welfare bear?" He asked.

Samuel shook his head and Mac shrugged his shoulders.

"Sweetheart," Samantha said, "You're a grown man. If you want to dip, dip."

Samuel looked at her with a nervous look. He was feeling the alcohol and desperately wanted some nicotine. She motioned her head towards Mac's hand. Samuel smiled and went to the task of putting a wad in his mouth.

"No," Mac continued looking at Samantha, "My granmomma' used to say some people are touched by God."

Samantha looked at Mac curiously.

"Sam's one of *them*."

Samuel looked up at Mac with an angry glare. He knew where this was going. He shook his head no at Mac.

Mac scoffed. "You haven't told her have ya?'"

Samantha looked over at Samuel in confusion. She felt like she had been betrayed, what had he not told her?

"She's going to see those scars in the light of day sometime." Mac said.

"I don't want to talk about this." Samuel said. Mac threw his left arm on the table to expose the burn marks on his outside arm.

"I don't want to talk about this in present company." Samuel said.

Mac laughed, "Boy you really are stupid you know that."

Samantha started to feel really concerned as the tension at the table rose.

"I've seen the way that girl," Mac said motioning his head towards Samantha, "looks at you. Pony she can handle the truth, the whole truth. She still gonna' look at you with those doe eyes like you hung the moon."

Samantha felt tears start to form in her eyes, she wanted to know what the secret was.

Mac leaned over to Samuel, "Parker you don't want to talk about it. And I told you not to hold the shit we seen in. It would only eat away at you. Happened to me after Fallujah."

Mac looked back over to Samantha, "See God's got a plan

for Samuel. God wants the Pony Boy for something big, that's why he ain't as fucked up as I am."

Mac pointed to the burn mark across his face. "We were in the same truck that day."

Samantha's heart sank. Mac told the story with his eyes glazed over:

"We were running out to catch up to the rest of the squad. We had got separated pushing through some bullshit village. It was our fire team and our usual driver. I was up front Vasquez was in the back behind me, Wilson was up on the turret, and Moore was driving. But I always put Sam in the back behind the driver. That door was fucked up, so you had to hold the door closed. His big ass could do it and hold a S.A.W., and not bitch about it too much. Anyway, we were cruising and the next thing I knew I was on the side of the road. Me and Sam got blown out of the truck. Sam got a little bit of shrapnel under the armpit and a mild concussion and, well I got all this."

Mac made a motion towards his body. Samuel did not want to hear any more about it. Samuel started looking around for Kristen to order another round.

"The truck looked like it got hit by a semi-truck," Mac continued.

"Mac!" Samuel yelled at him to get him to stop.

Mac grabbed his Samuel's arm and started crying. "Man, we watched our buddy burn alive."

Samuel grabbed his arm back and said softly, "I know man. I couldn't get up either," tears started coming out of his eyes, "I tried. I thought-- all of you were in the truck still."

"If we don't talk about Willy," Mac said, "screaming for help in that turret. That's all you're ever gonna' hear man."

Samantha was on the verge of sobbing. These two pinnacles of masculinity were crying reminiscing about the worst day of their lives. Her entire life had seemed so trivial by comparison. Samantha had no idea how to console Samuel. In some vain attempt she rested her head on his shoulder and rubbed his back. There was nothing but silence for a few long moments.

Mac finally broke the silence by putting his hand on her arm, "Pony Boy being Pony Boy," Mac said clearing his nose, "He was back in the fight in like a day and a half." He pointed at Samuel and said, "Don't let this shy calm exterior fool you, this man is a death-dealer."

Samantha smiled and chuckled assuming Mac was saving face for Samuel.

"No," Mac said shaking his head at Samantha, "Parker here is a freaking poet of violence. When it's 'go' time, this guy gets scary calm and just starts murdering like he's ordering a fuckin' pizza. Just like 'You guys want extra cheese? Yes, extra cheese please'."

Samantha looked over at Samuel. He had a slight smile on his face as he took a drink. She gazed back at Mac, he was not laughing.

Samuel finally broke the silence by looking at Mac and chuckling, "I fucking hate you."

They both started laughing hard and Mac said, "I love you too."

Samuel felt like a wall had come down. Samantha had heard the worst there was to hear. But Samuel also believed that Mac was right, he was the one who really did not want to hear it. But they were able to speak more freely, he did not have any secrets left from her. Mac was a nutjob but he was not a psycho. They did not go into any details about killing or corpses. But they could talk about the close calls, jokes told, and strange happenings freely. Samuel felt like he was not having to pick which version of himself to accept. Mac could see the sweet boy in him that was basically defined by being in love with Samantha. Samantha could see the stone-cold warrior that was feared and respected by Mac. About another hour passed of swapping stories when Samuel looked at his watch.

Mac was telling Samantha this story about Samuel getting in a brawl with some Marines that threw a rock in the "chimney" of a porta-potty, while Samuel was using it, so that all the waste and blue liquid would splash up on him.

Samuel realized they were supposed to call Lucy. He was thinking that he wanted to talk to Samantha before they called her though. He wanted to make sure that Lucy was not going to freak out about a little bit of scarring and embarrass Mac.

"So, Sam's standing there," Mac was laughing, "pants around his ankles looking like a Smurf from the waist down."

Samuel looked at Samantha who was in tears, again, laughing at Mac's story as he continued.

"Sam snatched one of them up and was chasing the other ones that had run away. But his pants were around his ankles so he just, WHAM, ate shit. Like five feet from the porta-shitter. Sam's got the one in a headlock though, so he yells to the other ones that were running away, Come back here and take your ass beating or I'm going to kill him."

Samuel started laughing remembering the story, but not having heard it from another perspective.

Mac had to catch his breath but then continued, "That's when I come running over thinking we 'was getting mortared or some shit. Sam's sitting there red-faced, bare blue-assed, with some Marine in a headlock. I see the other guys who had stopped and looked back at Sam. And I wanted to go catch one of them, you--you know that's my boy, gotta' give 'em a hand. But I can't because I'm laughing too damn hard. Then I hear one of the other guys say, 'Sorry bro,' and another one said, 'I'll tell your mom you died in combat' and they took off running."

Samuel burst out with laughter considering how it must have looked for a group of guys that fancied themselves to be elite warfighters to behave like that. He decided it was time to talk to Samantha though, before another story started. He gently gave Mac a little kick under the table. Mac looked at him. Samuel cut his eyes towards Samantha and then motioned his head away from the table. Mac nodded in understanding.

Samantha had finally caught her breath.

Mac suddenly said, "Folks, I gotta' go see a man about a horse."

Mac started working his way out of the booth. Samantha anxiously watched him get up. As soon as she saw Mac had walked away, she turned to Samuel and locked lips with him. She could not believe all the stories she had heard were about the sweet boy who used to bring her pizza every day. Suddenly, she felt Samuel pull away, he was studying her with a smile.

"Well, one second," he said as he went back in for more. Then he pulled away again and said, "So what do you think?"

"I love him," Samantha said.

"No," Samuel replied, "I meant with Lucy."

Samantha had entirely forgotten about the deal Samuel had made with him. Samantha thought for a second. The two of them would be a dangerous combination. They both had a great sense of humor. Samantha quietly nodded with a smile.

"She's not going to freak out about his burns or his limp?" Samuel asked.

Samantha rolled her eyes, realizing that even these guys were not immune to insecurity.

"No," Samantha snapped, "She'll probably make jokes about them."

"That's probably how Mac would prefer it." Samuel said with an expression that he was deep in thought.

"She will definitely try to jump his bones though," Samantha said laughing, "If he'll let her."

"I heard he was hitting on the flight nurse that took from first field hospital to the transfer point after we got blown up. And she had just brought him back to life." Samuel said snickering.

Samantha giggled imagining that scene.

"I'll text her." Samantha said.

Intro to Chapter 7. Locate Close With and Destroy

Throughout the history of armed conflict, participants have had to deal with the "Fog of War." That is the parts of the battlefield that are not visible to the participants. The uncertainty has decided the fate of countless battles throughout history. If the commanders guessed what was in the fog correctly, they could win a war. Underestimate what hides beyond the veil and entire armies could get swallowed up. Theoretically however, to the American military, the entire battlefield is visible. So, one might believe the uncertainty is gone. Nothing could be further from the truth.

The Marine Corps has a motto that gets thrown around a lot: "Semper Gumby," always flexible. Samuel's battalion were "straight leg infantry," dismounted infantrymen. They had trained during the work up in vehicle operations, but they were focused on dismounted urban fighting, that was their mission. Well, that mission went relatively well, and they got a new mission. Tour the desert looking for people that needed killing. That seemed pretty straight forward. But a battalion of Marines that had just spent six months without vehicles were now operating in them exclusively. "Improvise, Adapt, and Overcome," a familiar adage in the business world that found its roots in the Marine Corps.

"Dude where the fuck did they go?" Mac asked.

Moore shook his head letting him know he did not know. Samuel was sitting in the back seat laughing at them.

"Willy," Mac yelled to Wilson in the turret, "You see the rest of the squad."

"Not a fucking clue where they are," Willy called back.

Samuel looked over to Vasquez and smiled.

"Mierda!" Vasquez called out to Samuel.

They hit a bump in the road and Samuel's door flung open. Samuel scrambled to pull it closed again.

"Yo," Mac said, "You fucking fall out we're leaving you."

Samuel laughed and said, "I might find the rest of the squad first."

Everyone in the truck started laughing. Samuel looked at the door, the zip-tie holding the door closed broke, and he didn't have another one on him.

"You know if this fucking squad could follow a route that would be outstanding," Mac shouted.

Samuel looked back out to his sector as they were passing through, what passed for, a village, again. Samuel saw an older man standing off the road smiling at them as they passed by his hovel.

Mac shouted back to Samuel, "Ask that motherfucker if he's seen any Americans pass through here."

Vasquez started laughing. Samuel felt his stomach sink low. Something was very out of place about this situation.

Willy shouted, "I see their dust clouds, they are on our heading but at about 3 o'clock."

Mac looked at the map for a moment and then crumbled it up and threw it on the floorboard,

"Fuck it if they don't want to follow the route neither will we." Mac shouted.

Samuel could not hear anything. The expression is "ringing in the ears." Screeching is a better description. Samuel did not think that he lost consciousness, but he had no idea where he was, or what happened. Samuel scanned his surroundings. He saw the smoke first. The truck was burning. Samuel was laying on top of his door. He felt something sticking out of his side just below his arm pit. As he checked it, he felt a small piece of metal sticking out. Samuel looked back to the truck as tears formed in his eyes. He tried to get to his feet, but he could not seem to get his legs to find their place underneath him. Then he saw Willy. He could not hear him, but he saw him. His arms were flailing, through the thick black smoke that was pouring out of the turret hole.

Samuel tried to scream out to him. But with the screeching in his ears, he was not sure if any words were coming out. Samuel tried to crawl towards the truck.

"Mac!" he screamed.

Samuel thought for a moment. If he could channel his dark compatriot, he might be able to muster the strength to get up and get to the truck. Samuel closed his eyes; he took a deep breath. But no music started playing. Samuel thought back to the man standing by the hovel. He closed his eyes again. He took a deep breath. *I'm going to kill that motherfucker.* Samuel thought to himself. Suddenly the music started in his head.

Samuel stumbled to his feet and found his S.A.W. The buttstock was sheared off and the spring was out. Samuel stood there and thought for a second. He threw the weapon on the ground and drew his knife off of his flak. *I'll fucking gut that piece of shit.* Samuel resolved to himself. As Samuel stumbled towards the truck, he could not see Willy's arms flailing anymore.

The heat from the truck was intense. Samuel made his way slowly, but as fast as he was able to, around the truck. He saw Mac on the ground smoldering. Samuel looked back down the road to where the old man had been, then he looked back to Mac. The choice was obvious, he could not leave Mac on the ground to die alone while he went to murder the man who had at least known it was going to happen. The demon might have been hungry, but Samuel was still in control. He was not going to leave his best friend here alone. Samuel dropped his knife, and with it the rage that was keeping him on his feet left his body. Samuel collapsed to the ground. He crawled to Mac's side, about the time that the rest of the squad pulled up to find what had happened.

The squad leader had gotten a bad feeling when approaching the village and taken a different route. The truck died momentarily, which is why they had gotten separated from the rest of the squad. The radio in their now blown out truck had dropped its encryption when the truck died so they did not receive the radio traffic to take a different route. The small convoy was not used to maintaining convoy integrity. But they had improvised convoy operations, adapted their route, and now Samuel had to overcome the loss of his whole team.

CHAPTER 7. IF YOU GIVE A MARINE A BOWLING BALL...

"Lucy." Samuel proclaimed. Samantha looked towards the door and saw her standing looking around the room for them. Samantha could tell that she had put some serious effort into getting ready to come out. She was dressed to kill. Samantha smiled as she thought that no matter what, having Mac and Lucy at same table would be fun. Lucy finally saw Samuel. She waved to them and began to strut over to them. Mac was trying to turn around to look at her, but his size and his injuries made it hard to turn around towards the door.

Lucy finally made it to them and announced her presence with, "Jesus could y'all have sat farther away from the door."

She studied the table and saw Mac. Samantha noticed she had an unusually shy look about her. Samantha figured a part of her audacity with Samuel was that she knew she did not really have a chance with him. With Mac there was not only a chance but an expressed intention. Mac was staring at her grinning from ear to ear. There was no such subtle shyness with him.

"Holy shit," Samuel heard Mac say, "I guess I'm going to be putting that GI bill to use after all."

Samuel started laughing and took a drink.

"Yeah?" Samuel asked. Mac was staring at Lucy and smiling.

"Hell," He said as he scooted over to let Lucy sit down, "I'll figure out something to study."

Lucy sat down, but she would not look over at Mac. Samuel gathered that she was not avoiding making eye contact with him because he was abhorrent. Quite the opposite, she was acting like a girl sitting next to her crush.

"I guess I've always been a Rebel at heart." Mac continued.

Samantha chimed in to make the introduction, "Mac. This is Lucy. Lucy this is Mac."

Lucy finally looked over at him. Mac was sprawled out against the wall with his arm along the back of the booth behind her.

"Your parents named you Mac?" Lucy asked in an icy tone.

Mac just smiled and said, "My parents named me Aaron and I never forgave them for it. So, I decided to just go by Mac."

Samantha could tell Lucy was caught off guard by finally conversing with someone who made just as ridiculous statements as she did.

"Is that short for something?" Lucy asked.

"Macintosh." Mac said.

She stared at him for a second.

"Sweetheart," Mac said finally, "I ain't attached to any of those names. You can call me whatever you want."

Samuel started laughing really hard at that comment. Around that time Kristen came to the table. Her and Lucy shared a greeting and Kristen took Lucy's drink order. Mac announced he would be paying for Lucy's drinks.

Lucy blushed and said, "You don't need to do that."

"The hell I don't" Mac said, "Me and Pony Boy here got Iraq money to burn. What the hell else we gonna' spend it on if not beautiful women?"

Lucy was back to not being able to look at Mac. Samantha thought the whole display was very cute. She looked at Samuel and he was smiling at the two of them too. Samantha leaned over and kissed him on the cheek.

The mood changed rapidly, though, when Mac said, "Sweetheart if it's the scars that you can't look at, I can't do much about them."

Samuel and Samantha gave each other a nervous look. That was an abrupt way to bring it up.

Lucy turned around immediately and snapped back, "I hardly noticed the scars, I'm having trouble looking at that baseball you are smuggling in your mouth."

Mac looked at Samuel and Samantha with his mouth wide open.

Then he looked back at Lucy and said, "Forgive me please."

Mac made a scene about taking the tobacco out of his mouth and stuffing it in a beer bottle.

"Poor ol' white trash like me ain't used to being around gen-u-ine southern belles." Mac said.

Lucy's face went back to cherry red as Mac took her hand and asked, "Can you find it in your heart to forgive me?"

Lucy stared at him for a moment. Samantha knew she was trying to think of something witty to say.

Finally, a smile came to Lucy's face as she said, "That's a good first step. If you can be house broken, I'll let you pay for my drinks."

Mac without missing a beat said, "I could give up the streets if I can sit on the couch and sleep in the bed."

Samuel burst out laughing at the conversation that was transpiring between these two. For as long as he'd known Mac, with as many women as he'd seen him interact with, he had never seen one that could go tit-for-tat with him and he gathered that the experience was new for Lucy as well.

Lucy said, "Well you'll need a bath first... you know fleas."

Mac looked at Samuel wide eyed with a shocked look on his face.

"Are you gonna' hose me off?" Mac asked, "Or don't you

high class women wash their dogs off in their bathtub?"

Samantha leaned over to Samuel and whispered into his ear, "Oh, God. What have we done?"

Lucy looked at Mac for a minute studying him and pondering a decent come back.

Samuel interjected, "Just going to warn you."

Lucy looked at Samuel as if she was expecting some actual dire warning.

"You feed him once he's never leaving."

Lucy started laughing.

"That's what happened to me," Samuel added, "a couple table scraps, and he was just hanging out on my porch waiting for me every morning."

Lucy laughed as she asked Samuel, "Did you ever teach him any tricks?"

"Not really," Samuel said, "but he's a hell of a guard dog."

He held up his glass for Mac in a cheers.

"And he's a damn good friend."

Mac raised his glass and tapped his to Samuel's. The two men touched their glasses to the table and took a drink. Lucy giggled as she leaned back to where her shoulders were now touching Mac's arm. Samuel caught the shift in body language and the skin-to-skin contact. Samuel had always been hyperaware of people's body language. Lucy's subtle shift might as well have been an "Open for Business" sign to him.

But subtlety was obviously not Lucy's style because she immediately turned to Mac and said, "Well in that case. You hungry boy?"

Mac choked on his drink and Samantha muttered under her breath, "Holy crap!"

Mac sat his drink down and said, "Always!"

Samantha's mouth was wide open. Samantha had never experienced such blatant and sudden sexuality between two people. She always knew Lucy was far more comfortable with her own sexuality than she was but these two had met each other for approximately three minutes had, through thinly veiled innuendo, effectively planned out a rendezvous.

"Well," Lucy said, "I'm going to let you buy me those drinks first."

Samantha was considering the prospect that her apartment was being invaded by Marines, as it seemed like in a very short time there was going to be two of them there, at least for the night. Samantha looked at Samuel who was taking another drink with a smirk, looking very proud of himself. Samantha noticed Mac was staring at Lucy with a new level of intensity. He was spellbound to her looks and her wit.

Samuel must have been able to read Samantha's mind, or he had been thinking the same thing, because he suddenly blurted out, "There's a lot of stairs you know."

Mac broke his gaze and snapped his head back at Samuel as if he was completely annoyed by the interruption.

"What are you talking about?" Mac demanded.

"At their apartment." Samuel said leaning back and putting his arm around Samantha.

Mac got a sour look on his face and leaned back turning to Lucy.

"It's ok," He said going back to his infatuation, "I checked into a hotel before I met y'all here."

"Really?" Samuel said surprised.

"I knew I wasn't goin' to be able to drive all the way back to Arkansas tonight if I was drinking with you. I'm not that dumb." Mac said.

Samantha saw Lucy's face twist with concern as if she thought the whole course had been a joke upset her.

Samuel was not surprised that Mac had gotten a hotel, he was surprised that he had not told him. Samuel was surprised that Mac had not already tried to talk him into coming and staying in the hotel with him. Mac had not known there was going to be another woman in the picture until moments before she arrived. And Mac was like a giant 13-year-old boy. If there was not a girl in the picture, he wanted the guys to get together and do stupid stuff together. His entire Marine Corps career had been a camping trip with his best friends. Mac was the kind of Marine that would keep the whole hooch awake making finger puppets all night trying to get a laugh out of one of the guys. Mac always assumed everyone was having as much fun as he was and just wanted to hang out like he did.

Samuel assumed Mac must have really believed Samantha was special if Mac automatically knew the teenage slumber party was out of the question. Lucy was looking at him with a worried look on her face.

Mac in almost complete ignorance said, "I got blown up. Stairs are not my friend anymore."

Kristen arrived and delivered the next round which now included Lucy's drink. Lucy remained silent as she took a sip. Mac finally looked like he caught on to her dismay.

He added, "Besides, you can check me for fleas and not have to worry about your furniture."

Samuel looked at Samantha and smiled. She laughed and hid her face from them behind Samuel.

Samantha was glad to know that they had somewhere else to be, even though the entire idea of how they arrived at these plans was *ridiculous*. But Samantha also reflected that it was incredibly sad that their apartment was out of the question due to his wartime injuries. They were in a very old building that did not have an elevator. Samantha considered how much of Mac's life had been changed forever due to the war. How many situations would he face for the rest of his life that were going to be more challenging simply because he had volunteered to go in harm's way, and harm found him? He was twenty-two or twenty-three-years-old. There was a lifetime of not being friends with stairs ahead of him. But Samantha thought to herself that if anyone was equipped to face it, it was Mac. His personality was the type that he would never let it dampen his spirits. She was so grateful though that it was not Samuel in his shoes. She hugged Samuel tight.

The, now seemingly, double date continued on for a while longer. Mac and Lucy treaded into the realm of normal conversation. Lucy had sent Samantha text messages through-out the night explaining that she thought Mac was "Hot" and funny. Lucy considered his scars rugged and sexy and in typical Lucy fashion was "only worried that his injuries might cause him to underperform."

Samantha knew that neither Samuel nor Mac under-stood their attractiveness to young impressionable college girls. College girls were used to college boys, and college boys were not like them. College boys tended to be obsessive about establishing themselves, and it put their insecurities front and center. The most obvious example was college boys' near homophobic need to display that they were not gay. Mean-while, these two made near homosexual comments to each other every other sentence. They were secure with themselves and who they were. It was ironic that the two most "alpha" dogs in the whole bar seemed to have no need to assert that status. But the really attractive quality was that they did not seem to take women for granted.

Samantha was not sure if it was a lack of women in their normal day to day life or if it was that they had just recently experienced a year-long near death-experience but, they both seemed to listen to every word either Lucy or her had to say. They gave compliments, and they gazed longingly at their re-spective interest. College boys seemed to have all taken advice from the same jerk that said, "Seem like you aren't inter-ested." Whoever gave men that advice was a complete idiot. No human being wants to feel like they are not appreciated. Maybe somewhere there is some woman with some type of complex that works on, but in general Samantha felt like that was just a horrible display ignorance.

Samuel could not help but feel like this is how life was meant to be spent. There was no war to worry about, there was just friends sharing drinks, stories, jokes, and love. As the night wound to a close Samuel could not help but feel foolish for passing up a life full of this to go on some idealistic ad-venture. Each moment was sweet to him. He was overjoyed to know that for Mac's adventure was over. It was nothing but sweet moments left. Samuel would have to go back soon, but Mac had earned his peaceful life and he already seemed to be enjoying himself to the max. Samantha and Samuel had come back to the table at one point and found Lucy straddling Mac in the booth making out with him.

But at least this night, was quickly becoming history. Kristen had come and closed out the tabs. Samuel and Mac both tipped her $200. She freaked out. But Mac gave a very... eloquent explanation to what "Iraq rich" meant. And added that he was now on full disability, so she need not worry about it. Samuel was not worried about money either. Unlike many Marines, he had never bought a new car at twenty-nine percent interest. He had a modest sum of money saved up. And to Samuel there was not a price too steep for the night they had all shared together. Finally, the time came for everyone to stumble out.

"You two." Mac proclaimed at Samantha and Samuel in front of the bar, "go populate the world with beautiful babies."

Samantha laughed at the comment as she hugged Mac goodbye. Next was Samuel's time. It was an emotional goodbye, as they bear hugged and shared "I love yous." As Mac wandered off arm and arm with Lucy towards his hotel he called back to Samuel, "Stay gold Pony Boy!"

The next morning, well early afternoon really, Samantha woke to find Samuel not in bed with her. She checked her phone to find several messages from Lucy and one from Michelle. Lucy was bragging and sharing too many details from her night; Michelle was complaining about the noise coming from Samantha's room. No message from Samuel though. Samantha checked her missed calls. To her dismay he had not called her either, but more concerning she had three missed calls from her parents. Samantha's parents were the type to show up suddenly at her door if she did not answer the phone. Samantha resolved to call her mother, as she was the more understanding of her parents. Samantha was a daddy's girl, which meant he was not comfortable with the idea of her growing up.

The idea that Samantha had drank enough the night before to wake up late was entirely reasonable for a college student on the weekend. But, in her father's mind, she might as well still be a little girl that was more concerned with tea parties. She called her mother quickly, half expecting to have to talk them into turning the car around.

"Hello." Her mother answered in a stern voice.

"Hey," Samantha said in her best sweet voice. Samantha heard her mother speak in the background to her father, "Yes it's Samantha... John she's a college student maybe she wanted to sleep in."

Samantha knew her mother would be the voice of reason.

"What are you doing?" Her mother asked. Samantha panicked for a moment realizing that the whole truth was too much information for her mother to hear. She tried to think of something between "Nothing" and "Waiting naked in bed for my boyfriend you haven't met to come back to bed" that would satisfy her mother's curiosity.

"Uhh," Samantha stumbled, "Just woke up and waiting for my friend to call."

Her mother always seemed to know everything. There was a pause and she could hear her mother walking, Samantha assumed she was walking away from her father.

"I presume this *friend* is a boy." Her mother said.

Samantha felt her face get flush. She did not like Samuel getting referred to as a boy, and she was uncomfortable that her mother had figured out that there was a boy so quickly.

"Yes." Samantha giggled reflexively. Samantha was not a good liar, so she rarely did she even bother trying.

"Samantha," Her mother gasped, "That's great," she added with her voice rattling with excitement. Samantha pulled the blanket over her head realizing that it was now inevitable that she would have to take Samuel to meet her parents.

Samantha was not opposed to the idea in the slightest. But it seemed like a tax on Samuel. Her father could be a little much. The fear of his daughter growing up included a proclivity to being opposed to guys dating his daughter.

"You haven't dated anyone since Cameron." Her mother added.

Samantha knew that was true, but hearing it said made her feel sick to her stomach. The night before she had seen the sharp contrast between them. They were both male, that was where the similarities ended.

"Yeah," Samantha squeaked out.

Samuel was walking up the stairs to return to the apartment. He had gone for a run and managed to talk some kid into letting him in the student athletic center to get a workout in. He had not intended to be gone for as long as he had, but he got carried away and had spent two hours in the gym, not to mention the time he spent on his run. He got back in the apartment and turned his iPod off. He heard Samantha in her room talking to someone. He walked over and quietly opened the door and saw her sitting up in the bed with the sheets pulled up to her neck. She squinted her face at him and mouthed the words, "I'm sorry," to Samuel. Samuel shrugged his shoulders to make sure she knew he had no idea what she was apologizing for.

Samuel snuck over to the bed. Her eyes got huge like she was worried. Samuel knew he was pouring sweat. Samuel knew it was probably gross, but over the past two nights she had more than enough of his sweat drip on her.

Samantha covered the phone and mouthed, barely making a sound, "I'm on the phone with my mother."

Samuel threw his head back and silently laughed. Samantha's parents were incredibly protective of their little girl. He had never met them as a love interest before. Samuel in a dramatic sneaking motion tiptoed closer to the bed and gently and silently pressed his lips to Samantha's forehead. Samuel considered his being locked in silent purgatory for the duration of the phone call and figured it was a good time to take a shower. He grabbed a towel out of his bag and snuck back out of the room silently.

When Samuel returned from his shower Samantha was sitting in the same spot dumbfounded at her inability to avoid anything she had just agreed to. She looked at him with her face squinted.

"Hey Sam," She said sweetly.

"Hey Sam," Samuel said back to her in the same tone he had always said it in. That had been their greeting since the earliest days of their relationship, long before it was anything other than platonic. Their greeting had become a romantic re-minder to how long their relationship had been going on.

"I'm really sorry." Samantha said to him. Samuel looked at her confused as he walked over to the bed and sat down.

He got a decisive look on his face as he said, "I forgive you."

Samantha needed to give him the news but before she could say anything, he was kissing her, and she knew he was not wearing anything but that towel. It took all of her will-power to fight the distraction of her desire.

She pushed him off of her and said, "Seriously though."

Samuel looked at her with an even more worried look on his face than before.

Samantha exclaimed, "We have dinner plans." Samantha pulled a pillow over her face to hide her shame.

Samuel laughed as he said, "Awesome, one less plan for the day."

Samantha without removing the pillow from her face said, "With my parents!" She was so ashamed to have sprung that news on him so suddenly. Samantha was not sure how it had happened. Her mother had brought up Cameron, Saman-tha had explained Sam was so much better, her mother said she wanted to meet him, Samantha said she would soon, her mother asked what they were doing for dinner, and suddenly they had dinner plans. Samuel pulled the pillow off of Saman-tha's face slowly. Samantha looked into his eyes. Samuel was smiling and did not seem the least bit phased by the news.

He softly said, "What do I need to wear?" Samantha smiled back at him.

Samantha could not contain herself any longer, "We'll worry about that later." she said as she pulled him on top of her locking her lips to his.

As the two of them drove home, Samuel considered the prospect of meeting Samantha's parents. It seemed like a natural progression for young lovers. Samantha had met his parents long before. Samuel considered this an act of more significance. If Samuel made a good impression on Samantha's family, they would ask about him regularly. They would become a constant reminder to his absence from her life. Or if he made a bad impression, they would remind her of his unwelcome presence in her life. His parents did not hold such sway over his perception of Samantha. He was in love with her and that was that. But Samuel was nervous about meeting her family. He figured it was make or break. Samuel thought to himself that there was no way that the people that raised such an amazing person as Samantha were anything but amazing themselves. Samuel was just not certain of his own charm. He was worried that war had left him as brutish company to be in.

"Any subjects I should steer clear of?" Samuel asked Samantha.

Samantha was terrified her family was going to embarrass her. Samantha adored her father, but he was a far cry from the kind of man Samuel was. Samantha had known for a long time that there were different kinds of men. Some men were rugged and tough. Some men were gentle and sweet. Some men were entertainers, and some men were stoic. But for the first time in her life, Samantha felt as though she knew a man that was not the type of man that her father was, that may very well be a better man than her father.

Samantha's father was funny, and sweet. He was an entertainer. Samantha's father could light up a room. He was thoroughly devoted to his family. But the man had come from an upper middle-class family to raise an upper middle-class family. He was white collar. He was an amazing man who, through no fault of his own, had never faced any adversity. As a result, Samantha had come to realize, his perspective on a lot of things was very one dimensional. Samantha's mother was less of a worry. She was sure if anyone was going to get along with Samuel it was her. Samantha's mother thought of her father like Samantha thought of hers, their fathers were their idolized concept of a man in their youth. But Samantha's maternal grandfather was a veteran. In fact, Samantha thought, Samuel had a lot in common with her grandfather. He was sweet beyond compare. He was kind-hearted and quick witted. And her grandfather adored his grandmother. Samantha was certain that when they saw the way Samuel looked at her, they would both fall in love with him. It had never been a secret that Samuel was in love with Samantha. But now she was certain she was more in love with him than he was with her.

"Just be yourself," Samantha smiled as she tried to assure him.

Samuel was certain that Samantha had no idea what that meant. Samuel was not so sure he knew what that meant. Samantha now knew the worst thing that had happened to him, but Samantha had no idea what the worst thing he had done was. Samuel snickered to himself as he imagined grabbing a belt fed weapon and hosing down some Jihadists in the courtyard between dinner courses and yelling, "Mr. Wallace shift your fire to the right." That was who he was now. He was, amongst whatever else he might be, a warrior. Samuel had earned his reputation as a Marine who commanded fear and respect from friend and foe alike. Samuel was cut from the cloth of "shooters." They were men who lived and breathed modern combat.

But Samuel was fairly certain that Samantha wanted him to be the boy she had known before, whatever was left of him anyway.

Samuel smiled and said, "Are you sure about that? I've

always been a bit of a nerd." Samantha pulled his hand to her mouth and kissed it.

"You're my nerd now though." She said sweetly.

Samuel was confident he could maintain the demeanor of normalcy throughout the evening, he would just have to carefully consider every word before he uttered them.

Before the two could go on to dinner they had to stop by Samuel's house so that he could get a change of clothes. Samantha had not been to his house since before Samuel left for boot-camp. Samantha was far less nervous about this reunion than she was about Samuel meeting her family for the first time. When they arrived, Samuel started explaining that Carrie had become very affectionate towards him, but other than that the family was all the exact same.

He opened the door and they walked in. The memories rushed over her. She remembered discovering the feeling of love and being loved for the first time in her life inside these walls. The first one to greet the young lovers was the dog, Avery. He walked up and sniffed the Samuel and wagged his tail. Then he walked over to Samantha and sniffed her for a few moments. He must have remembered her because he opened his mouth and looked up at her while he wagged his tail. He let out a solitary bark as if to communicate that he wanted her to pet him. She knelt down to pet his head.

"Hey, Avery." Samantha said, "You remember me don't you."

Then Samantha heard a commotion coming from upstairs. Carrie made her way from her room to the top of the landing. Samantha looked up to see her standing there.

The girls shared a smile as Carrie cried out, "Sam!"

Samuel sat at the bottom of the stairs waiting for the coming embrace. Carrie bolted down the stairs. Samuel stood there with his arms slightly open. Carrie ran straight past him and threw her arms around Samantha.

"Glad to see things are back to normal around here." Samuel laughed while looking at Samantha. Samantha giggled in response.

"Hey Carrie," Samantha said finally.

"Hey Sam." Carrie said as she walked over to give Samuel a much less enthusiastic hug. Samuel gave her a tight squeeze. The girls rushed off to the kitchen while Carrie interrogated her about the happenings of the last year. Samuel followed a step behind them smiling and thinking about how the situation had played out.

Samuel waited until he could get a word in to ask, "Where's mom and dad?"

Carrie explained that they had gone to the hardware store to grab some things to work on the house. Samuel kissed Samantha and headed upstairs to find clothes to wear. It had not occurred to him that his "nice" clothes no longer fit. Samuel went back downstairs and broke the news to Samantha that he was going to have to go to the store to pick up something to wear. Samantha offered to go with him, but Samuel figured he would leave the girls to catch up.

Samuel finally returned after about an hour. Samantha was marveling at how comfortable he was with her just being around his family. She would have freaked out if he had been left alone to her parents and her brother. But Samantha knew the difference was clear. To Samuel's family, her being in the house today was the return of the prodigal girlfriend. They showered her with compliments and questions. Her parents had never met Samuel--by design. Samuel walked into the kitchen and smiled when he saw his mother talking to Samantha with an old photo album out.

"I see Dad didn't have my back this time." Samuel said announcing his presence.

Samantha held up the album so he could see a picture of himself from Halloween dressed up like a soldier, Samantha guessed he was six years old. Samuel smiled at her and rolled his eyes.

"Samuel Parker," Samantha heard Ms. Parker yell, "How dare you leave this poor girl alone!"

Samantha looked back at Samuel about the time he had closed the distance between the two of them. He leaned over and kissed her. Samantha was not expecting such a display of affection in front of his mother, but when it happened it made her heart sing, it was further confirmation that he was hers and she was his.

"Samantha is a strong independent woman mother." Samuel said when he pulled away from her. He started walking towards the refrigerator and added, "She does not need me to protect her from the Parker clan."

Samantha watched Samuel pull out some orange juice and start pouring himself a glass. She was starry eyed thinking of his confidence in her, and in their relationship, and his family's feelings towards her. The contrast to her nervousness about him meeting her family was stark. Samantha felt a little guilty.

"Samuel Parker!" Ms. Wallace said, "Don't you twist my words."

Samuel just smiled at his mother and said, "Love you Mom."

Samantha looked back at Ms. Parker who was now smiling at her son from ear to ear. Samantha thought she could see a slight mist forming in his mother's eye. Samantha got the impression that she had only recently joined a club of women, or people perhaps as she considered Mac's relationship with Samuel, that adored Samuel for the man he was now. She resolved to herself to have confidence that her parents would be in the same club. Samuel announced that he had to go get ready and Samantha turned back to the photo album and asked, "Do you have any of these pictures you could part ways with?"

Into to Chapter 8 DFAC: Chow Hall, Mess Tent, Cafeteria

Everyone knows the military uses a lot of acronyms. CO: Commanding Officer, AO: Area of Operation, ETA: Estimated Time of Arrival. It is, rightfully so, the punchline to many jokes. The confusing part is that many acronyms have multiple meanings. BG: Brigadier General, or Battery Gunnery Sergeant. Another double meaning acronym is CLP. CLP: Cleaner, Lubricant, & Protectant, the oil used to clean weapons. CLP also means Chow, Liberty, and Pay in the Marine Corps. Those are the tools the Marine Corps uses to raise and lower morale. For a Marine deployed to an active combat zone, liberty does not exist, and no one knows if they are getting paid. So, the only way to raise spirits is to offer up a special meal.

Samuel had just gotten released from medical. The battalion was "refitting" at one of the larger bases in Iraq. The truth was morale had taken a hit, so they were letting the guys get a shower, a couple decent meals, and letting them sleep under a roof for a couple nights. That's where Samuel caught up with his company. Samuel had gotten a plate of food and was sitting by himself eating. He had intentionally sat away from the rest of the company, not because he did not want to see them, he did not want them to see him. He was not fully healed and if anyone saw him eating with his left hand, they might send him back to medical. The Company Commander came walking over to him and sat down across from him.

"How are you doing Parker?" the CO asked.

"Amongst the living sir." Samuel replied without looking at him.

"I know, dumb question," The CO replied, "but to be honest, I really did not know what else to say."

Samuel allowed his face to crack a smile in sympathy for the man's predicament.

"Well, I came to tell you," the CO continued, "the Battalion Commander has seen fit to meritoriously promote you to Corporal."

Samuel glanced up from his food to the CO and said,

"Whole new meaning to the word blood stipe isn't it, sir."

The CO scoffed and said, "Parker you earned the promotion a long time ago. That paperwork has been with battalion for months."

Samuel closed his eyes and thought for a moment. He knew what he had to say, but it was not what he wanted to say.

"Thank you, sir," Samuel finally forced the words out, "I'm glad you think I am ready to be an NCO."

The CO smiled at him and reached across the table and slapped him on the shoulder and said, "Are you kidding? You could run this company if you wanted to. Probably better than me."

Samuel stared with a blank face to hide the fact that he was in pain from getting slapped on the shoulder on the same side as the injury he was claiming was no longer an issue.

"I won't let you down sir," Samuel said.

"Well, the promotion ceremony is tomorrow morning." the CO said, "you got anyone you want to pin you."

Samuel knew the CO did not mean to be insensitive, but there was only one person he wanted to pin him, and no one was sure he'd be alive in the morning.

The CO must have realized he put his foot in his mouth because he quickly changed the subject, "I also wanted to tell you Parker, I am looking for a job for you with higher headquarters. Something that will keep you close to us, but you won't have to slog through the rest of this deployment."

Samuel did not care what he should have said this time, "What kind of message will that send sir?"

The CO scoffed and said, "Hell Parker, every Marine in this battalion knows you are a tough son of a bitch. Two days and you are already back. Everyone knows you deserve a break."

"With all due respect sir," Samuel started, "I don't give a fuck what the Marines think."

The CO was obviously taken aback by the statement.

"What message does that send to the chicken shits that

are planting I.E.D.s?"

The CO appeared to be in contemplation for a moment, then he said, "Well I doubt that they know who you are Parker."

Parker took his fork up with his right hand with resolve. He did not care how bad it hurt he was going to show the CO and himself he was ready to get back in the fight.

"Well the way I see it sir," Samuel said, "I've got about 3 months left to make sure they know my fucking name."

The commanding officer leaned back and shook his head. "Alright Parker," He said, "I'll find a squad to fall in on."

Samuel said, "Thank you sir," as he took a bite.

CHAPTER 8. "NEXT MAN IN"

Samuel had picked up flowers for Ms. Wallace when he left to get a new shirt and slacks. He considered the reality that he had not been as nervous as he was now when he cleared, probably, a hundred houses, and he went into those houses full well expecting to find someone that wanted to murder him inside. He was not nervous about the prospect of meeting the family, he was nervous about his ability to maintain the façade of normalcy. Samuel looked up at Samantha's house. He remembered parking his car several doors down and coming in through the back door. Samuel thought it was ironic that this might be the first time he ever came in through any other door. The young couple walked towards the door that led from the garage to the house. Samantha looked back at him and gave him one last smile before she opened the door. Samuel took a deep breath and broke the threshold.

A different class of fatal funnel he thought to himself, chuckling.

Samuel noticed Ms. Wallace had spent a good bit of effort getting the house "ready" for his arrival. Or so he assumed. There were candles burning, everything was in ordered placement and there was not a speck of dust to be seen. They were greeted in the living room by Mr. and Mrs. Wallace. They were standing in front of the fireplace in what appeared to be a staged meeting arrangement. Mr. Wallace was standing slightly behind Mrs. Wallace and they were both smiling.

It looked like they were posing for a Christmas postcard.

He could almost see the words "Merry Christmas from the Wallace Family" framing them now. Samuel considered that the meeting place was not poorly chosen. The room was warm and inviting and it was set up in such a way so that whenever someone turned this corner they would be in center view of where the Wallaces were standing now. Samuel thought that if he was going to ambush someone coming into this house he would stand where they were standing now and point his rifle the direction they were facing. *Merry Christmas from Cpl. Parker,* Samuel thought to himself, *Smile and wait for the flash.*

Samantha knew her parents had a couple of glasses of wine today. Whenever her mother would get deep into a cooking ritual, especially if her father had a couple glasses of wine, her father would bring her into the living room and slow dance with her to no music and sing Frank Sinatra to her. It was endearing and sweet, but she needed them to be on their best behavior. Samantha noticed her father's smile slowly melted and morphed to an open-mouthed stare. Samantha's mother's smile only got bigger as she saw Samuel holding the bouquet of flowers.

"Mom and Dad," Samantha said proudly, "This-" Samantha reached behind her until she found the small of Samuel's back and pushed him forward, "is Samuel."

Samuel trotted forward slowly. Samantha noticed that the man she had become accustomed to had changed instantly. She was used to his impeccable stature exuding confidence. His head was usually high, shoulders square, and chest stuck out. But Samuel had reverted back to a shy boy. His back was slightly hunched, and his head hung slightly low. Samantha thought it was cute that he had decided to be shy now.

He just slowly raised the flowers and said in a soft voice, "Mrs. Wallace."

Samantha watched her mother's smile get as big as it possibly could, her whole face was smiling. It really was a throw-back gesture to a time of gentlemen and old south sensibilities to bring a woman's mother flowers. Samantha had never brought a boy home who had done it, to say the least. Samantha's mother grabbed the flowers and hugged Samuel.

"Thank you, Samuel," she said glowing, "It's so nice to meet you."

Samantha's eyes shifted to her father. His face was sheer horror.

Samuel softly said, "Nice to meet you too."

He would not say that his feelings were hurt, but it stung a little bit that Mrs. Wallace did not remember that she had met Samuel many years ago. Samuel shifted so that he was facing Mr. Wallace.

Samuel stuck his hand out and said, "Mr. Wallace."

Mr. Wallace's face had terror written all over it. Samuel's mind raced with the reasons why. Samuel presumed Mr. Wallace could think back to when he was Samuel's age and figure out that he had been sleeping with his daughter. No amount of flowers and gentlemanly behavior softened the blow to a man's psyche of realizing his little girl had sex. Even long after the realization that it was a reality, men mentally blocked those kinds of thoughts. Samuel was beginning to feel like he had had his hand out for longer than an appropriate time to wait. Finally, it was like Mr. Wallace snapped out of his horrible nightmare and the smile came back to his face. He grabbed Samuel's hand and began to shake it. Samuel was careful to give the proper grip that communicated the right message. *Your daughter is safe with me, but I am not challenging you.* Mr. Wallace's smile got bigger and he put his other hand on the Samuel's and continued shaking his hand.

"Johnathan," Mr. Wallace said, "Or John. Please, anything but Mr. Wallace. That makes me look around for my father like I'm in trouble."

Samuel gave him a nod. Samuel felt like it had been more than a little awkward but that it had been a good first impression.

Mrs. Wallace said, "I guess we can just start the tour in here. This is the living room."

Mrs. Wallace chuckled in a surprisingly girlish manner. She had not stopped smiling and Samuel thought to himself that her face must be tired by now. Samuel felt like he was going to be sick to his stomach as he instinctively said, "I remember."

Samantha was too distracted by her father's behavior to even respond to Samuel basically confessing to their high school human smuggling operation of getting Samuel in and out of her house. Samantha's father had never once in her 20 years told one of her friends, let alone boyfriends, to call him John or Johnathan or anything other than sir or Mr. Wallace. And he had made a joke that it made him look for his father. Samantha was flabbergasted. Her father was enamored with Samuel. Samantha was beginning to get worried that she had been replaced as the apple in the eye of her father. Her father would normally have blown right past any boy and greeted her first, but he was actually walking away from her now to follow her mother on the tour of the house.

"Daddy!" Samantha said in frustration.

Her father turned suddenly as if her proclamation was a reminder that she was even there.

"Angel!" he said as he walked over and gave her a big hug. "I missed you so much." her father said.

"Did you?" Samantha said in an annoyed tone.

"Of course, I did." he said.

The two of them squeezed each other tightly. Then they both stared at Samuel and her mother going from picture to picture. Samantha thought that it looked like Samuel was being guided through a tour of a museum and her mother was the art expert telling him about each piece.

Samantha's father lowered his tone to ensure Samuel could not hear him, "He's quite a bit different than the children you usually shuffle out in front of me."

Samantha felt herself blush considering the fact.

"Yes. He is." Samantha said smiling.

"Where'd you meet him exactly? He looks like a middle

linebacker." Her father inclined.

Samantha's father was a diehard Ole Miss Rebels football fan. She would not be honest if she did not admit that he was a big influence on her going to Ole Miss in the first place. She considered it was probably going to disappoint him that she had to break it to him that Samuel did not play for them.

"We went to high school together, Dad." Samantha said.

"Your mother said he just got back from Iraq?" He asked.

"Yes," She said softly, "he's a Marine."

Her father leaned over and whispered, "Don't tell your grandfather that. He was in the Army. The only time I think I ever heard him cuss in front of your mother was when he was talking about Marines."

Samantha smiled thinking about the idea of hearing her mother's father cuss at all, let alone in front of her mother.

Samuel was enjoying being shuffled around looking at pictures. It was sweet revenge on Samantha for her going through the old photo albums. Samantha's whole family was beautiful. Samuel could not help but think that they looked like a senator and his family. Not a hair out of place on anyone's head.

His thoughts, like they naturally seemed to do since the war, went dark as he considered any one of these pictures could be on some true crime show. *Suburban family savagely murdered* the tag line would read. These pictures would flash across the screen to generate shock value as the audience considered the horror that something bad happened to such a beautiful wholesome looking family. Samuel's own family pictures usually had Samuel rolling his eyes, or his sister looking like she'd rather be anywhere else, or Ryan intentionally ruining the picture with some stupid gesture.

"This one was from seventh grade I think." Mrs. Wallace said.

They walked up to a picture of a young Samantha with her hand on her hip and her arm around Michelle posing for a picture at the school field day.

"Sixth." Samuel said. Her mother looked at him funny for a second.

"I remember." Samuel scoffed.

He pointed at the picture. Just off Samantha's left shoulder a few feet behind her in the picture was Samuel. He was looking right at Samantha. Even then, so many years ago, his adoration for her was all over his face.

Mrs. Wallace looked at the picture and then looked at Samuel and said, "Oh my gosh. It is you."

Samuel gave her a forced smile to hide is discontent with the fact that she had not remembered him. The pair finished the rest of the tour and Samuel tried to fake surprise at things he had seen before.

Dinner was served a short time later. Samantha sat next to Samuel. He appeared like a fish out of water. But he was being his cordial and polite self. Samantha's father had been keeping him busy with small talk and she had not had an opportunity to talk to him about how he was taking the night. Her family might have been oblivious to the fact that two weeks ago he was in a warzone but she had not. She found herself much more concerned about his mental well-being since she had heard about the explosion.

"Wine?" Her father offered.

Samantha had only had alcohol with her mother and father one time, last New Year's. They were not a family that shunned the consumption of alcohol, but it was not an everyday occurrence in the house, and it was rarer still for alcohol to be offered openly in defiance to the law.

"No thank you, sir." Samuel said as he looked over to Samantha nervously.

Samantha tilted her head to try and communicate to him that it was not a taboo he needed to worry about.

"Samuel, call me John," her father said, "and we are not prudes around here. Any man that decides to serve his country deserves to enjoy a glass a wine with dinner."

"Can we compromise on Johnathan?" Samuel asked.

"Only if we seal it with a toast." Her father said.

"Sounds like a deal to me." Samuel said looking at Samantha in a form of shame.

Samantha knew Samuel well enough to know that the idea of calling any older man, let alone her father, by his first name was hell on his sensibilities.

Samantha's father came to the table with two glasses. Samantha considered the reality that Samuel might be considered old enough to drink by her father for serving, but she was not. Her father sat a glass in front of each of them and then went back for glasses for himself and Samantha's mother.

Samantha's mother led them in a prayer over the meal and they officially began the dinner. Samantha's father discovered that he, indirectly, worked with Samuel's father. Samuel explained that his father was in logistics; and Johnathan figured out that the company Samuel's father worked for was the company that he used to handle their logistics.

Samantha had been having female telepathic conversations with her mother the whole time. Her mother would make a face indicating that Samuel was nice, and Samantha would make a face indicating *yes, yes he is*. Those sorts of conversations. It was a skill that women learned instinctively when men run off on tangents talking to each other about business or sports. Samuel, being ever the gentleman, would direct the conversation towards including them, but the truth was her mother and her were enjoying their silent conversation with each other about him. Finally, the moment Samantha was worried about came, and sooner than expected.

"So, you just got back from Iraq?" her father asked.

"I did." Samuel answered.

Please don't ask what that was like. Please don't ask what that was like. Samantha thought to herself.

"What was it like?" Mr. Wallace asked.

Samuel considered how to answer the question. It was not a strange question to him. Curiosity is perhaps the greatest of human qualities. Humans can know that the answer is something horrible and they would still prefer to know the answer than live in ignorance. Samuel considered it reasonable to want to know what the war that flooded the news was like from someone who lived it.

"Hot," Samuel laughed, "Sandy," Samuel looked over at Samantha to make sure she knew how he had really felt most of the time, "Lonely," Samantha smiled at him sweetly as if to tell him home was lonely too. "Boring most of the time," and then Samuel looked back at Johnathan to make sure that he was satisfied with the answer, "And absolutely terrifying the rest of the time." Samuel felt like that was the most honest answer he could give in sensible brevity.

"Well, we are glad that you are home," Mrs. Wallace said smiling.

"Here, here," Johnathan added raising his glass.

Samantha put her hand on Samuel's leg as she said, "I will drink to that."

They all tapped their glasses. Samuel, in ritual, touched his glass to the table before taking a sip from his glass.

When he realized everyone noticed he chuckled and said, "Sorry, old sailor tradition."

He figured he was outed to Samantha's parents to having drank before, but he did not see how it would surprise them to know a Marine had drank enough to develop such a habit. If civilians had three stereotypes for Marines it would have to be crazy, drinkers, and fitness nuts. Samuel could probably be called all of those things by an honest person.

Johnathan did not seem to dwell on Samuel's slip of judgement because he asked, "So what's the best thing about being home?"

Samuel pondered for a second.

Johnathan interjected, "I'll save you the obvious answer. Other than my beautiful daughter, what is the best thing about being home."

Samantha felt like her father was behaving curiously. He was never one to seem comfortable with guys being affectionate towards her. Here he was giving Samuel decent lines of flattery in relation to her.

"Thanks Daddy." Samantha said, taking a sip of her wine.

"Well, sweetheart I want to know the less obvious answer. Something you'd have to go to know you took for granted." Her father answered.

Samantha thought for a moment. Perhaps there was nothing to read in to. In general, they were not in the community that had a lot of people that had gone. A few guys every graduating class had joined up. But not in the kind of numbers that made it common to come across someone who had been to Iraq. And Samantha's father certainly did not work with anyone who had been. Samuel appeared to be very deep in thought. Everyone at the table was waiting intently for the answer. Samantha assumed her parents, like her, were guessing the answer in their head. She believed she knew Samuel better than anyone, and she thought the answer would be pizza.

Finally, Samuel said, "Green."

He nodded his head with certainty at his answer.

Samantha was not sure if he'd just had a stroke. She had just studied stroke symptoms and was certain that this was a sign.

As she began to look him over for other signs he continued, "In Iraq the whole color pallet is yellow, brown, gray, and shades of gold."

Everyone at the table leaned back in their chairs taking in the unexpected answer.

"There's grass in some places, but it's just overwhelmed by the yellows and browns and golds. When we got back to Lejeune it was like a sensory overload. I swear the parade field where we got off the bus had more green than the whole country did."

Samantha was surprised but not disappointed that his answer was not pizza. Samuel had always been the type of deep thinker that would pick something like a color pallet to be the biggest difference.

Samantha's mother stated with a ponderous tone, "That is definitely something I take for granted."

Samuel looked at her and smiled a big smile. Samantha may not have gotten the answer right, but she believed she knew what he was thinking now. He was thinking about what he had seen. That was the secret answer. The color pallet was a euphemism for the horrible images he had seen.

Samuel was willing to continue talking about whatever Samantha's family wanted to talk about. He was there to make a good impression. He needed their support for the future. Her parents were gracious enough. They seemed to carry her same sweet demeanor and they felt warm and inviting. He did not feel like a foreign invader in their home, but certainly a passing guest. His only goal was to transition to some place of permanence.

"So, Samuel," Mrs. Wallace began, "you and Samantha went to school together, basically the whole time?"

"Yes ma'am." Samuel replied.

"Why didn't you two date when you were in high school?" She continued.

Samantha choked on her wine. Samuel chuckled to himself trying to hide it from her parents.

He put his hand on Samantha's leg to assure her he was not upset that she had never mentioned him being with her before.

"Well," Samantha started, "Uh-"

Samuel decided he had tortured her enough and said, "Mrs. Wallace I was about a hundred and thirty-five pounds in high school. My life was centered around mock trial and knowledge bowl. I did not really make time for girlfriends. And Samantha should not be faulted for not pursuing me."

Samuel turned his head to Samantha and gave her a wink. Samantha grinned back at him. It was not a whole lie. But they could keep the other part of the story their little secret. There was a cliché about talking walls that was a cliché for a reason.

Johnathan said, "I cannot imagine you at a hundred and thirty-five pounds."

Samuel looked at him and chuckled, "Well there are a few pictures around for proof."

"What are you now?" He asked.

"Johnathan," Mrs. Wallace said slapping him on the arm.

"What? He's not a woman," Johnathan replied, "A man in his shape should be proud."

Samuel looked at Mrs. Wallace to give her the face of approval at the question, "Last weigh-in I was one-ninety-seven."

Johnathan's mouth opened wide.

"I tell you what," he uttered, "if you need a job after you get out, I'm just about certain any SEC team would pick you up as a conditioning coach."

"Not a chance," Samantha snapped.

Samuel looked back at her with an slightly shocked look. Samuel felt like she was reverting back to her old high school protectiveness. She was always quick to defend Samuel.

"Samuel is going back to school and then going to law school." She added.

Samuel had not ever told her that. But he was perfectly ok with her speaking for him.

"Law school?" Johnathan asked with a certain degree of incredulity.

"Samuel out-scored most college seniors on the practice L-SAT as a junior in high school." Samantha said with pride.

Johnathan looked at Samuel and asked, "You were a hundred and thirty pounds and some kind of kid genius. Why did you join the Marines?"

Samuel looked at him for a second. He knew what he meant, and he did not mean it to be rude.

Samantha could not even be bothered by the rude manner her father asked the question. Samantha had never heard Samuel's answer to this question. She had made assumptions, she had good guesses, and she had heard other people's guesses, but she had never heard it from him. She desperately wanted to know why she had lost him for so long. She wanted to know why he had to endure so much loss and misery. It seemed like *the* question she needed an answer to. Her father was right, it seemed like a ridiculous prospect.

But before she could get an answer her father had a flash of courtesy.

"I'm sorry Samuel." her father said, "That was rude of me to ask, and certainly like that. I would not like it if someone had asked me why I became an executive at a sales firm. The question carries a very judgmental connotation."

Samuel looked like a weight had come off of his shoulders. Samantha had so selfishly wanted to know the answer she forgot to think of how it felt for Samuel to be asked like that. Samantha thought back to their first real "date" when he faced the same question. It seemed like an uncomfortable subject to him. There were probably a million reasons and no one deserved to pass judgment on even one of them, not even her.

Her father in an attempt to save face and grace said, "Samuel, just know I for one am glad to know that there are men like you willing to answer the call. I guess the war is just so far away we forget that it's our neighbors going to fight it, just the same as people we have never met."

Samantha looked at her father and smiled. He had made a profound statement. It was easy to forget about something on the news. She had not thought much about the war when she did not know anyone in it. Once Samuel had left, she found herself pausing when the channel was on the news talking about the war. There might be a million college-bound suburban kids serving in Iraq, but until it's someone familiar to you that's there, you just kind of assume that wars are fought by people not-like you.

They all continued their dinner. The conversation shifted from Samuel and his military service to more mundane conversation. Samuel was glad too. He wanted his relationship with Samantha to be grounded in a reality that made sense to everyone. If Samuel was to be defined as a Marine, that would leave room for his relationship to be a novelty, a passing story about that time she dated that Marine. He was nice and she was happy, but it was not meant to be, instead of, Samuel is a good partner for Samantha who happens to be gone serving right now.

Samuel began to get worried though, Samantha's father was continuously refilling their wine glasses. He considered that it might be some type of test. Perhaps he was getting him too drunk to drive to see if he would. How would he adapt anyway? It seemed ridiculous that he was going to be staying there, but was it rude to refuse his host's offer of a full cup? Was it not gentlemanly to point out that he needed to be able to leave? But before he had the opportunity to formulate a plan of action to deal with the arising issue; Samantha's brother, Brian, returned home. Brian was a new complication.

Once upon a time they had taken to bribing Brian to not tell Samantha's parents about his after-hours visits. Samantha started to worry that his new amicable relationship with her parents might get destroyed. Brian walked into the dining room and looked at all of them strangely.

"Hey honey," Samantha's mother said in excitement.

The poor woman was three sheets to the wind and it showed. Samantha looked around the table and realized all of them were showing signs of inebriation. Brian just stared at all of them in disgust.

"What's wrong?" her mother asked him.

"Nothing." Brian said blankly, "It's just not every day you see your parents getting drunk with your sister and the hulk."

Samantha thought for a minute he might not recognize or even remember him, that was certainly the best-case scenario.

"Hey bud." her dad said. He snatched Brian up and put him in a headlock "Don't be rude. The hulk here has a name."

Brian pushed back and tried to get out. They played like that regularly. But she was on pins in needles because she was worried that if Brian got too frustrated, he might just blow the lid on them just because he was frustrated.

Her dad walked Brian, still in a headlock over to where Samuel was sitting and said, "Meet Samuel, also known as the Hulk. Be glad he's nice he might not be as gentle as I am."

"Samuel?" Brian said in a questioning tone. Samantha was certain they were busted.

Samuel assumed all of his work warming the Wallaces up to him was undone in that instant. There was no way he was going to win them back over when they learned he had lied to them about Samantha and his relationship in high school, that he used to sneak into their house, and bribed there then 15-year-old son to keep it a secret from their parents. Mr. Wallace let him out of the headlock.

"You two know each other." Mrs. Wallace asked confused. Brian looked at Samuel studying him.

Come on kid be cool Samuel thought. Brian looked at Samantha for a second and smirked, then looked back at Samuel.

"Of course, mom," Brian said. Samuel braced himself for the betrayal. "We did go to school together."

Alright kid you decided to be cool. Samuel thought.

Brian looked back at his mother, "Sam here is a legend anyway."

Brian looked back at Samuel. "He made Tucker Harris cry after he called some girl fat in the cafeteria. He embarrassed him in front of the whole school." Brian said with a smile.

Alright kid you decided to be really cool. Samuel thought to himself. If the kid was planning on blackmail Samuel figured he deserved every penny.

"What did you say to him again?" Brian asked.

Samantha chimed in with a laugh, "A lot of things."

Samuel looked over to see she was in disbelief at her brother's loyalty.

"I told him he peaked in high school and was only heading downhill from here." Samuel said smirking.

Samantha was pleasantly surprised. The story was true. Samuel had made Tucker Harris cry in the cafeteria. But the three of them knew how Brian knew Samuel.

"On behalf of the uncool kids of the school, thank you." Brian said, "the popular kids are still worried one of us will do to them what you did to him."

Samuel laughed and shook Brian's hand.

"My pleasure." Samuel said.

"Didn't you go to the Marines?" Brian asked.

"I did." Samuel said.

Samantha got the feeling that perhaps Brian's adoration was genuine and that she had unnecessarily bribed him with chores and a couple of video games before.

"Cool." Brian said.

He took his leave from the dinner party and went upstairs to his room. Samantha and Samuel shared a look of relief.

"It's amazing," her father said, "you have two kids. From the same two parents and they are so different."

Samantha laughed to herself thinking of the truth of that statement.

Samuel nodded and said, "My brother, my sister, and me are all completely different."

Her father shook his head and said, "How does that happen?"

Samuel shrugged his shoulders.

"Samantha was the homecoming queen, popular girl." Her father said. Samuel smiled and looked at her,

"Everyone wanted to be her or date her." Samuel added.

Samantha felt her cheeks get red as she put her hand on Samuel's leg to let him know the compliment was not missed.

"Exactly." Her father said, "But that one," He pointed up towards the stairs, "He thinks of high school as some prison. It would suit him just fine to never see any of them again."

Samuel scoffed and said, "I could try to tell him not to try to grow up so fast, but he won't listen."

179

Samantha's father pointed at him and then put his hand on his shoulder as a sign of agreeance. Samantha was not certain she had ever seen her father this drunk before.

Samuel felt for Samantha's father. Samuel felt for all fathers to be honest. There was no instruction manual for kids. Mothers had to deal with moody teenage girls. But boys loved their mothers, at least in Samuel's experience. Boys would not do things to hurt their mothers, intentionally. Girls adored their dads, but fathers could not understand girls. Not in a million years with a million daughters would a father ever understand the way their daughters thought. But their boys, who they think they should understand, end up so different from them they are almost as alien as their daughters. So they just have to roll the dice and hope that keeps everyone this side of pregnant and jail.

Samuel's father was a reserved amiable man. He was soft spoken and kind-hearted, just an all-around average, hardworking family man. But Ryan had been a class clown popular kid who stayed in trouble. Samuel was, well Samuel. His father had no idea how to control either one of them.

Samuel noticed Mr. Wallace was getting misty eyed.

He looked over at Samantha and said, "That's my little girl."

Samuel felt uncomfortable. He was not sure where this conversation was heading.

"She's been my little angel since she first opened her eyes." He continued.

Samuel looked over at Samantha to discover she was just as uncomfortable as he was. Johnathan looked back at Samuel.

"But that's what this is all about." He said, "as much as you want them to just stay the same age, they grow up eventually."

Samuel was completely incapable of saying a word.

"One day you're shopping for prom dresses, and then the next they bring a man home."

Mr. Wallace was truly on the verge of tears now. Samuel

was not certain that was how it worked, but he gathered Mr. Wallace was drunk and emotional and assumed it had to do with Samuel being there. Mr. Wallace patted Samuel on the shoulder again and said, "A good man."

Samantha did not know if she should be embarrassed, happy, or flattered. Her father was drunk, that was apparent, but he had complimented Samuel. But whether it was a dream or a nightmare it did not matter because it was not over yet.

Her father continued, "I know I've had too much wine. Which means you have had too much wine."

Samantha saw Samuel's mouth open as he searched for a protest of some sort.

"Ah, ah, ah." Her father said.

Samantha looked at her mother who was smiling looking at her father. Samantha did not understand how she could be smiling at this. Her mother finally looked at her. Samantha was trying to give her the *stop this now* face. Her mother just winked at her and smiled. Samantha worried that she had missed that day of the female non-verbal communication class. If she was not supposed to be worried about where this conversation between her father and Samuel was going, she was anyway.

"Mi casa es su casa." Her father finally said.

Samantha's mouth opened wide.

Samuel was not sure if Mr. Wallace understood Spanish. He thought he might need to tell him that he had just told him that his house was Samuel's house. As he contemplated the ramifications of explaining that to him. The man continued as if to add more questions to this enigma of a conversation.

"And I know you'll take care of my daughter," Mr. Wallace said.

Samuel felt the need for clarification, "I appreciate that Mr. Wallace-."

"Ahp, ahp." he replied.

"Johnathan," Samuel corrected himself. Samantha's father nodded his head. "I have learned to sleep just about anywhere. I can grab a spot on the cou-"

"No, no," Mr. Wallace said, "Have you not been listening?"

Samuel looked at Samantha who was equally confused as he was.

"It's not my business where you sleep," Mr. Wallace said definitively.

Mrs. Wallace was sitting there staring at her husband smiling. Samuel gathered that this was one: a huge step for him, and two: some previously discussed topic between the two of them because Mr. Wallace looked back at her and gave her a *There I did it look.*

"Come on honey." Mrs. Wallace said, "Let's go to bed." Mrs. Wallace looked at Samuel and Samantha with a big smile and led her husband from the table.

Intro to Chapter 9 ACE Report

Statistically, the latter portion of a deployment is the most dangerous. In the home stretch, servicemembers start to get worn out, complacent, and distracted. "Complacency kills." That is not incorrect. To the higher headquarters that's exactly what it looks like. Non-combat related injuries go up, everything looks a little sloppier, and the atmosphere gets a little too relaxed. From the ground level though, something else begins to take hold--worry. It is often said by many servicemembers that they tended to enjoy many aspects of a deployment. One commonality is the lack of "bullshit." In general, the daily stress of paying bills, managing a household, and maintaining relationships takes a backseat when your concern is more centered on staying alive.

Towards the end of a deployment, guys begin to worry about returning to the "real world." Samuel was no exception. The idea of returning home was something of an enigma. The only thing anyone seemed to talk about was what they planned on doing when they got home, and thinly veiled under the plans was a general anxiety. Samuel's worry was that he had no plans. He had not really written anyone. Samuel knew he would see his family, he knew he wanted to see Samantha, but he had no plans past that. What happens after you see someone, if nothing happens after you see someone? Is that the end? A memory.

Samuel was with a working party inventorying gear to hand over to the incoming battalion replacing his. Sgt. Raffaleno was his counterpart from the incoming battalion. Samuel was picking his brain about what was going on state side while, he was picking Samuel's brain about everything that was going on in Iraq.

"I'm telling you dude," Raffaleno said, "everyone's getting smartphones, not just rich folks."

"That seems dumb," Samuel laughed, "why waste all that money?"

Raffaleno replied, "Man it ain't just Myspace anymore.

Everyone's got a Facebook. The world is online my friend, all the fucking time. Go up to a cell company tell them you want a two-year contract and you'll leave there with the internet in your pocket."

Samuel may not have known what he was going to do when he got back but he was certain making an online version of himself was not going to happen. That would be way too many people to fucking juggle. The demon, Samuel, online Samuel, not a chance in hell.

Raffaleno pointed to the center radio in one of the trucks, "What the hell is that?"

"Yeah that's the new PRC," Samuel explained, "The radios aren't bad, but the batteries on them are hot garbage. Trust me change those fucking things out every chance you get because the trucks are complete shit. Solid chance the truck won't be powering it, even if the truck is running. And if the radio goes down, you'll lose your fill and won't be talking to anybody. Your best bet is to try to get your hands on some SKLs and have some Comm Marines teach your guys how to fill a radio. That way if you go down you can reload your own crypto and be able to talk again."

"Solid fucking idea," Raffaleno replied, "I'll tell main body to get their hands on as many as they can."

"You can also wire an iPod through the speaker if you want." Samuel added, "It's pretty easy to do believe it or not, basically the same thing as running old Comm wire. You just need some headphones you don't give a shit about."

Raffaleno laughed in response.

"I heard Derek Jeter died?" Samuel inquired as they continued walking through the motor pool.

Raffaleno laughed again.

"Nah dude, he's alive," Raffaleno answered, "Sounds like wishful thinking, you a Red Socks fan?"

"Not a sports fan honestly," Samuel responded.

"Well the socks won the series if you didn't hear.," Raffaleno laughed.

Samuel stopped dead in his tracks.

"I know, crazy right." Raffaleno said.

"Are y'all getting those flight suits?" Samuel asked.

"I don't know." Raffaleno said.

"You make sure your guys get those flight suits," Samuel said sternly, "these fuckers have started putting incendiaries in their I.E.D.s."

Samuel looked around the motor pool for a moment. He realized in a few short weeks he was not going to be worried about flight suits and bombs. This *was* his real world. But sooner rather than later it was not going to be. Samuel felt a knot form in the pit of his stomach. He wondered if somewhere along the way he had gotten into his last firefight and not realized it. He wondered if he could put the demon to rest for good in a few weeks. Half of his Marine Corps career was over, and, perhaps, his war story was coming to an end. He had let go of any fleeting hope that a love story came next a long time ago, but now he had no idea what story came next.

CHAPTER 9
WARNING ORDER

The morning after the most interesting dinner party came early for Samuel. Samuel made his escape from Samantha's bed and he snuck downstairs. He considered that if he was up early enough and already about, Samantha's parents would be reassured he had not dishonored their daughter, at least not last night, in their house. Samuel made his way to the kitchen and decided to make coffee. A smile came to his face when he heard a stirring coming from her parents' room. Mrs. Wallace came sleepily into the kitchen.

"Good morning Samuel," she said with a smile.

"Good morning Ma'am." Samuel replied, "Coffee?"

"Oh yes," she replied.

Samuel made her a cup and handed it to her.

"Thank you, dear." she said. "Sorry about John last night."

Samuel smiled at her deciding it was better to pretend like it was nothing unusual to him,

"It was a very emotional night for him." She continued.

Samuel kept his silence and simply nodded in understanding.

"When I told him, you were coming he started asking if I thought you had been staying with Samantha down in Oxford."

Samuel nearly spit out the coffee that was in his mouth. Samuel looked back at Mrs. Wallace to see her smiling.

She got a reassuring look on her face as she said, "I told

him that was none of his business." Mrs. Wallace took a sip of her coffee. She got a surprised look on her face like she had forgotten she did not like black coffee. She walked over to the counter and began to prepare it to her taste.

"John, of course, started with his 'it's my little girl it is always my business routine' but," Mrs. Wallace continued, "I reminded John of how he met my father."

Samuel was captivated as he listened to her.

"My parents came to visit me at college," she continued, "This was a time when people did not have phones at all times, we did not even have one in our dorm room. We just had one in the common area."

Samuel thought of life in that simpler time, a time when human interaction was thrust upon people.

Samuel saw Mrs. Wallace smile, "So when there was a knock at the door, we both just assumed it was his friend coming to wake him up and tell him it was time for them to go back to their campus. John nearly had a heart attack when he opened the door in nothing but his boxers and my father was at the door."

Samuel laughed silently to himself.

"We were twenty then too, you know." Mrs. Wallace said. Samuel thought to himself that Mrs. Wallace looked back on the situation fondly. Samuel started to have a new perspective on the course of events from the night before.

"Samantha is very much in love with you, Samuel," Mrs. Wallace said snapping Samuel out of his deep reflection of the previous night, "As her mother I am not supposed to say that. But I know you are too. So, I'm going to invoke my privilege to say what I want."

Samuel looked at Mrs. Wallace and smiled.

He meant to think it, but he ended up saying it out loud, "I always have been."

Samuel and Mrs. Wallace shared a moment of silence together. Samuel gathered that she shared a lot of traits with him. They were the type that enjoyed conversation greatly but treated it as a finite resource. There was no need to spoil silence with unnecessary words. This was one of those times that required no words. The two of them stood in the kitchen sipping coffee thinking.

Mrs. Wallace finally shook her head and let out a sigh, "I better go give the rest of this to the cry baby. He's going to be whining about his hangover... and the fact that his little girl is a woman, all day."

She started back towards their room with an aura of dignity.

"Mrs. Wallace." Samuel said in reverence.

"Call me Martha, dear." She replied, "I have a feeling we will be seeing a lot of each other in the future."

Samantha awoke and the young couple gave their farewells to her parents. They drove back to Oxford. Samuel filled Samantha in on his early morning revelations with Samantha's mother. Samantha found the whole thing hilarious but, did not like hearing details about her parents' apparent hookup. As much as parents do not want to think about their children growing up, children do not want to think about their parents being young.

While in the vehicle just outside of Oxford, Samuel pulled the car over, in the middle of their conversation. Samuel looked at Samantha with a very serious look on his face. Samantha got worried that he was about to break some horrible news to her. She was bracing herself for Samuel's words informing her that he had no intention to keep this going indefinitely. Her mind went back to the time she was laying in his bed with him and he had given her similar news.

"Samantha," He said, "I still love you. I always have and I always will."

"But." Samantha said softly.

"No buts," Samuel said, "I just felt the need to make sure you understood that." Samuel started to put the car in drive again.

Samantha shouted, "I love you too" as she threw herself

across the car to kiss Samuel. She threw caution to the wind and accepted that she really had the man of her dreams and he wasn't going anywhere.

Samuel and Samantha spent the next couple weeks in a casually romantic routine. Samuel had basically moved in and become another part of the apartment. Samantha would go to class and Samuel would go work-out or jog. Samantha thought she had learned the secret to his size, all he seemed to do is eat, exercise, and spend time with her. She would come home, and Samuel would help her with studying and exercise. Samantha was still frustrated by how intelligent he was. He had not been in school for almost two years, and he still seemed light years ahead of her. On the weekends they dated like young couples did and often went home to spend time with her family or his. It was an intoxicatingly pleasant existence that the lovers found with each other.

Samuel knew that they were slaves to time again. Samuel was going to be returning to Lejeune soon. There was no stopping it. Samuel had resolved before that this time was not going to be like last time. He had been laying the groundwork for what he thought would be a happy and healthy long-distance relationship. They had talked about it in passing during their time together, that he would be leaving again. It was simple, and simply true, for them to cast off the discussions with a "don't want to think about that now" comment from one or the other. But the time had come where they could not avoid it.

One night they were sitting on the loveseat. Samantha had her head on Samuel's lap reading some notes for class.

Samantha suddenly said, "You know I could go pre-med just about anywhere."

Samuel looked down at her knowing where this conversation was heading.

"Yeah," he said. She was looking up at him with an innocent smile, "but you can't pack your family and your friends up and bring them with you."

"They'll live." Samantha replied plainly.

Samuel appreciated her sentiment. But he did not agree with her. Samantha had a life here. Samuel had met his share of Marine's wives. They came in all forms, but they all shared one thing in common, they were Marine's wives. That was their identity. Apart from the occasional idiot that married some stripper in town, Marines plucked women from all over the country straight out of the ground and drug them to shithole military towns, and then said bye. Samuel thought it might be different for some jobs in the Corps, but as a grunt, in wartime, if they were not deployed, they were training.

They would send the battalion to 29 Palms for six weeks at a time regularly, or they would send small groups of Marines to some school or another for months at a time, or, as he knew was in his immediate future, they would send individual Marines to professional military education for months at a time. All the while the dutiful wife or girlfriend was stuck in the shithole town alone with no one to keep her company but other wives. Samuel did not want that for Samantha. He wanted more for her.

This time felt different to Samantha. She was not going to accept the excuse that he was protecting her from heartbreak. They were too invested in their relationship together for Samuel to leave again, and there was no way she was just going to just move on if he did anyway. There was no way she would not be wrecked. Samantha would move across the galaxy and never set foot back on planet earth if it gave her another hour with him. This was not her first high school love anymore. This was her soulmate, her spirit burned with a fire of love for him. Samantha put the book she was supposed to be studying down on the floor and sat up so that she could look him in the eyes.

"I won't though." She said. Samuel looked at her with a confused look. "I won't live if you leave me again." Samantha said, "I may live and breathe, but I won't be alive. Last time you left a standard that could not be reached again. This time you will leave a hole that can't be filled."

Samuel hung his head slightly and said, "I'm not leaving you again Samantha. It won't be goodbye. It'll be 'see you later.'"

Samantha put her hand on his face and said, "But it doesn't have to be as much later."

Samuel could not explain why he did not want her to come. Samuel argued with logic and reason. Samantha believed something. She believed that their love was strong enough for her to deal with the challenges. And Samuel could not logically convince her that she did not because he did not want it to be true. What he wanted to explain was that he was no happier than she was about the prospect of turning their relationship into one of distance and time separating them more than it had to. But Samuel was willing to sacrifice seeing her to leave her in a familiar place with friends and family.

"I think we love each other enough for distance to not be an issue." Samuel said smiling at her.

Samantha frowned and got a disconcerted look on her face. He knew he had struck the right chord.

"Sam, give it a little time." He added, "If it gets to the point that it makes sense then transfer to a school out that way."

Samuel had always heard wise men that he trusted say that the key to a healthy relationship was compromise. He felt as though he had struck a decent compromise. If his career slowed down enough, maybe it would make sense, who knows maybe the wars would end. But if they did not and she started hearing first-hand how often he was not around she would make the decision not to throw her life away and follow him.

Finally the day came for him to leave. It was the most bitter departure Samantha ever experienced. But she clung to the deal that they had made. If it made sense for her to come to school in North Carolina that's what she would do. Samantha had started doing intense research into schools out there. She was looking for which school she could go to that would be close and take the maximum amount of her credit hours and that was not too expensive for out of state students. Samantha kept herself busy with that, her schoolwork, and with their nightly hours long phone calls. Apart from that Samantha's life consisted of missing Samuel. He let her raid his clothes for some things to keep. She kept one of his Marine sweatshirts, a few t-shirts, and some sweatpants. She hid them away to keep them from accidentally getting washed. She wanted them to keep his smell. When she missed him a lot, she would put one on and lay in bed with her eyes closed. Sometimes it was almost like he was in the room.

When Samuel got back to the fleet his battalion was in a buzz. There were new joins, old hats had gotten out, and there was a new word taking over the whole grunt community, Afghanistan. One of the battalions in the division had just gotten back, and the word was it was a different war altogether. Apparently, the Afghani's liked to get down. There were still IEDs and it was guerrilla fighting, but they wanted to fight, and they wanted to fight in large numbers, against large numbers of U.S. servicemen. The truth was that war had really been an army dominated theater for the past few years. This meant one thing to the combat vets: if the Corps was stepping up its presence in Afghanistan and Iraq showed no signs of stopping, the deployments were going to double. It was simple math really.

Samuel seemed much less excited than he normally did when he called Samantha. Samantha knew he had been very busy with Corporal's Course. When Samantha asked what that was, he had simply said it was "a hazefest" but he seemed more upset than simply dealing with that.

"What's wrong babe?" she finally demanded.

"Just a lot of rumors floating around."

When Samantha heard rumors, she imagined women talking about each other behind their backs. It seemed an odd thing for a male dominated warfighting organization to be spreading those kinds of rumors. And Samuel was never one to put stock into those kinds of rumors, so her curiosity peaked.

"What kind of rumors?" She asked.

"The more deployments kind." Samuel replied. Samantha's heart sank. Samuel and her had talked before he left about the possibility of him doing a second tour. Samuel had told her honestly that there was a pretty good possibility of another deployment, but on the current schedule he expected it to be a year or so off.

"Oh." She replied somberly.

If Samuel had been forced to give an honest answer three months ago, he would have probably said he enjoyed Iraq. He did not enjoy some of the things that happened for sure. But he preferred it to garrison life. He did not want to lose any more of his buddies. But to be honest it was still lonely, boring, and he had zero control over anything. At least in Iraq a Marine had a purpose. Infantrymen had two jobs: kill people and train to kill people. Doing is always better than training to do.

But He had restored his life with Samantha and now he dreaded the idea of going back. He did his job. He had killed people. Samuel had been injured and decorated. He had nothing left to prove to himself or anyone else. He had something to live for now. A part of Samuel felt like that made a man weak. Samuel had lived like he was already dead on his last deployment and it worked out pretty well for him. Hell, there were a few men in his battalion that owed their lives to the fact that he had zero regard for his own.

"So, I'm just getting kind of worried about what that's going to mean for us." Samuel said.

Samantha was filled with terror. She needed to see Samuel right then. She needed him to put his arms around her, but he couldn't. Samantha felt tears come to her eyes.

"Yeah." She said.

"Baby," Samuel said, "It's not a death sentence, it just sucks. And it sucks even more because the Corps is not going to tell anyone anything."

Samantha did not even like hearing the word death. It did not make her feel better to have him say that.

"Well, have you heard any rumors about when?" Samantha said.

"No," Samuel said, "not even sure where."

Samantha considered to herself the possibility of some-where else. She would take anywhere but Iraq. They talked for a while longer and concluded their conversation with their normal goodnights.

Samuel hung up the phone and put his head in his hands.

"This is what happens when boots get meritoriously promoted." Samuel heard. He turned around to see his room-mate for the course on his phone laying on the top bunk. His name was Meres. He was from another battalion. He was a good guy, but salty. "You never know half of what you need to know."

"Yeah, eat shit Meres." Samuel replied.

"Look dude." Meres said, "We all know we're going back. You just want to be able to plan some shit in your life."

"What do you know about it?" Samuel sneered.

"A fucking lot," Meres laughed, "You talk loudly to that girl every night."

Samuel laughed and nodded.

"Look homie," Meres said putting his phone down to look at Samuel, "Volunteer for a deployment. Hell, you don't even have to go to Iraq or Afghanistan. Go on a MEU. You are a meritoriously promoted, decorated combat vet. Those MEU CO's will nutt themselves if you tell them you want to go."

Samuel thought to himself that it really was not a bad idea.

The next day was Samuel's last full day of Corporal's Course. He started asking around about who was going on a MEU. He finally found out about a battalion who had gotten a warning order to go on one, but there was a catch, there was a rumor the MEU was going to make a stop in Iraq. They needed NCOs though. Samuel spent the next few days solely concerned about making that decision. On one hand he would definitely be leaving and not seeing Samantha for an extended period of time. On the other hand, he could stay and probably would be going on a combat tour and not see Samantha for a long time. He decided that the old cliché that "The devil you know is better than the devil you don't" had a lot of truth to it.

Samuel walked into the company office. He had resolved his fate. He could not let Samantha throw her life away her future following him, only to find out that he was going on another combat deployment. Samuel figured this solved both problems. He would at least be able to make plans for his life, even if they were not exactly what he wanted, and Samantha would have no excuse not to stay home for almost another year.

Samuel found it ironic that the reason this deployment was even possible for him was for the same reason he was going. Make no mistake about it, Samuel was a Marine through and through. Marines like to fight. But there were a ton of guys that just got sick of getting jerked around. The battalion that was going was a sister battalion that had gotten back from Iraq a few months before Samuel's. They had been told that they had a year of being home and then the workup process would start back up. But then some other battalion got plucked for Afghanistan off of the Marine Expeditionary Unit rotation. So, they just moved this battalion off of their year home side and on to the MEU rotation. Guys trying to be responsible adults had planned pregnancies enrolled in schools, whatever. All those plans went right out the window.

The result of this type of this "impossible to plan around" uncertainty was that the Corps was bleeding Marines. No one wanted to re-enlist. This meant that, particularly the NCO's and experienced combat vets were jumping ship. Thus, this MEU needed more NCO's desperately, and Samuel had the opportunity to volunteer. Samuel made his way through the company offices getting the form signed off, so that he could go to the battalion offices to get the form signed off so that he could tell their sister battalion that he was willing to go with them on their "float." By the time Samuel got done with all the leg work, he believed he had discovered yet another reason why no one wanted to re-enlist. Finally, a week or so later word came that he was approved.

Samantha sat silently on the phone. Samuel had sounded excited when he told her he was getting deployed. He had to explain a lot of new words to her. There was something called a Marine Expeditionary Unit, actually there were several of them. Apparently, they went around different parts of the world on ships making stops in random places and Samuel was going to be on one of them. Selfishly, she did not want him to be gone again. This ruined the plans she had been making. She had already started preparing transfer applications. But if there was a silver lining there was no discussion of Iraq. And Samuel explained that he would be coming to see her for a few weeks before they left. Samantha learned a new emotion in her life from the whole experience of the twisting reality of being a part of Samuel's life, melancholy.

She did not feel like there was any reason to be depressed and no reason to be happy. She had the greatest man she had ever known but could not be with him. The love of her life would be safe, but he would be absent from her life for an extended period of time. "Sam, I love you." was the only words Samantha could conjure up.

Samantha had heard her entire life from women she trusted that the key to love was sacrifice. And she was learning that the truth of that lesson was devastatingly accurate. Being in love with Samuel was the easiest thing she had ever done in her life. He was everything she ever wanted in a man, and a million things she never knew she wanted in a man. But loving Samuel was tearing her insides out and burning them in front of her. All she wanted was to be with him, but forces beyond their control were keeping him away from her.

Samuel had taken his leave and was back home in Samantha's bed. They were laying together when Samantha started sobbing.

"Sam?" he asked worried, "What is it love?"

Samantha was on the verge of hyperventilation. After a

bit of effort on his part she finally calmed down enough to answer.

"It's just not fair." Samantha said.

"I know," Samuel replied softly, "you did not sign up for this."

They sat in silence for a few moments. Samuel knew she was right this was not fair for her. Samuel considered to himself that this was the ultimate irony. He had been smarter at 18 years old than he was now. Samuel had been wise enough to not subject her to this before he knew the first thing about the Corps. Samuel had just assumed that he would go to war and if he survived it was over.

"This is not what I signed up for." he thought out loud. Samantha raised her head off his chest and looked at him with tears in her eyes.

"What did you sign up for?" She asked.

Samuel took a deep breath. He considered not answering. But he adored this woman. She deserved to know his reasoning.

"We grew up with everything," Samuel started,

"We had safety and security. We had vacations in Florida. Playground games. No fears. No wants. Our parents gave us anything we wanted. We did not have a threat of nuclear war. Our world was peaceful and serene. We did not have Nazis, or nations threatening us. And one day we watched it end. We watched a few people that never had any potential to ever be significant to us kill thousands of people. And we learned that we were not invincible. The whole world learned it that day. Four planes and men deciding to do evil, and evil was in our world for the first time. I watched you cry that day for the first time, and I couldn't do a thing about it. I could not make you un-cry those tears. I knew someday my grandchildren would ask me what I did to get that back-- the world without tears. What did I do to remove that evil? I would either have to say nothing, it was not that

important to me."

Samuel looked at her and said, "Or I could tell them I fought for it."

He stared at her for a second and finally said, "It felt like if I did not volunteer to go, I was betting that we could never get that back. Because getting that back is something worth dying for."

Samantha put her head back down on his head. Samuel ran his fingers through her hair as he said, "I never considered that fighting to better the world would mean hurting the best thing in my world."

CHAPTER 10
MANEUVER
WARFARE

Samantha was living letter to letter. Samuel got to call her occasionally, but she had given up hope on waiting for them because they were too sporadic. Samuel had been gone for exactly six weeks. Samantha and Lucy moved into an apartment together off of campus. Lucy decided that she needed something with an elevator or on the first floor, because Mac was visiting her frequently. They would not openly declare themselves for each other, but Mac had enrolled at Ole Miss for the fall semester.

Samantha attempted to keep herself busy with schoolwork. There was little that could keep her mind occupied enough to not think about Samuel. But Samantha had resolved to be strong for him. Samantha had made her life about countdowns. Samuel was coming home "no later than" eight months. He was getting out of the Marine Corps "no later than" seventeen months after that. She had found a new appreciation for the phrase, "no later than." When life is a countdown, the final date was the most important fact to know.

Samantha had entirely replaced the Corps as the center of Samuel's life. Ship life was not the worst thing in the world. Samuel wrote a letter to Samantha every single day. He considered it some form of a romantic diary. And to his surprise mail was surprisingly consistent. He figured his letters got out about every eight days. He got letters from Samantha every eight days or so. But the quarters were tight and being on the ship gave a new definition to boring.

They had stopped in Djibouti for a training exercise for a week. Then they had a liberty call in Dubai. Samuel thought that if anyone had some preconceived notion that the Middle East was just one giant shithole, they only needed to go to Dubai to crush that notion. Dubai sat like a monument to a pinnacle of civilization. It was foreign to be sure, but it displayed the heights of human civilization. Samuel had thought that this detour in his ultimate destiny of being with Samantha might turn out to be a great adventure. But when the fleet pulled out of port in Dubai everyone knew their fortunes had faded. The float was steaming north, full tilt, straight to the Persian Gulf. The civilizational highs would be contrasted by the civilizational lows soon enough; they were going to the cradle of civilization- Iraq. And much earlier than anyone expected.

Samantha was wrecked. She felt absolutely betrayed. If not by Samuel than by the Corps, by the war, by the country, or maybe by all of them. She was holding Samuel's letter laying in bed sobbing.

"Sam," Lucy said, "I brought someone to cheer you up."

Samantha did not even bother to look she knew no one could cheer her up.

"Good God," she heard Mac say, "You even look gorgeous crying."

Samantha was not having any of it. Mac walked over to beside her bed and got down on his knee so that he was nearly eye level with her. Samantha knew it was a sweet gesture especially from him as he had such a terrible time getting up and down. Samantha looked at his face and sobbed harder thinking that Samuel now suffered the risk of this in his fate. Samuel could be the man struggling to kneel on the floor to comfort her.

"Sweetheart," Mac said in a soft voice, "What's wrong?"

Mac was being sweet. He sounded like a man that was

talking to a child that was crying over some childhood tragedy. But this was not a childhood tragedy, this was potentially the end of her world.

"He's going to Iraq!" Samantha screamed.
Mac put his big hand on her face to wipe away the tears. Samantha closed her eyes. For a split second she felt like it was Samuel in the room with her. She shuttered trying to catch her breath.

Then she said, "He wasn't supposed to go to Iraq."

Mac softly replied, "Darlin' if he went on a MEU that's not going to push back his time at all. He's going to come home on time. Those ships don't change plans like that."

Samantha rolled over away from him and cried, "What if he gets killed or hurt? That will change the plans."

Mac laughed loudly. Samantha turned back. Her crying ceased instantly. She was angry. This was not a laughing matter to her.

Before she could utter a word, Mac started speaking in an almost scolding tone, "Do I look like a man that's easily scared?"

Samantha looked at him blankly. She was not going to answer him.

"I'm not. I assure you," He continued, "Samuel scares me. I know you know Samuel Parker better than any of us. But I know Corporal Parker."

"Sergeant Parker." Samantha said softly.

"Exactly," Mac said throwing his head back, "I only ever made it to Corporal. You know why he's a Sergeant already, a year before I got out."

Samantha shook her head in silence.

"Because he is the baddest man I've ever met." Mac said, "If Sam ain't the baddest dude in Iraq right now, I'll promise you the baddest dude doesn't want to fight him. Standing behind that man, that you think is the sweetest person in the world, is the safest place in the whole damn country."

Samantha was not sure if that was supposed to make her

feel better or not, but it kind of did.

"God built that man for combat," Mac said returning to his soft voice, "God's just got a sense of humor so he made him good enough at loving you that you still think he's some sweet boy who wouldn't hurt a fly."

Samantha slowly and gently put her arms around Mac. His words had helped some.

Lucy being Lucy had to make a joke, "If you need to borrow him to cuddle with, I'll allow it."

Samantha let out a giggle.

"He's no Samuel, but he suffices." Lucy said.

When they were getting off the ships to go into Iraq they had been told, "Two days getting everything that they needed off the ships, two days security for the elections, and two days loading the ships back up," That was the plan: outfit, ride, retrograde. The officers had passed word that they did not want to see Marines with a ton of personal gear. They were seeing guys carrying a ton of stuff and they would sneer, "You don't need all that it's only a week off the ship" The XO had said he wanted everyone to have seventy-two-hour gear and that's it. Samuel had just gotten promoted to Sergeant. He was basically the squad leader for first squad. Sergeant Vandersline, Van for short obviously, was the squad leader. But he was actively shadowing the Platoon Sergeant, Staff Sergeant Morris, because Morris was going to recruiting duty as soon as they got back. The three of them along with the other squad leaders all agreed not to enforce the seventy-two gear rule that strictly.

They were in Iraq for three weeks when the commanding officer told them that they <u>HAD</u> to be back on the ships next week because the fleet had a time hack to keep for a training mission in the Indian Ocean. It was four weeks after that before they went anywhere near a major installation so Samuel could buy more socks and underwear.

Samuel's first deployment had been a test of his willpower, and this was already proving to be a test of his character. Samuel knew what happened, it was a tale as old as officers.

The officers came out and showed off their toys and higher headquarters asked if they wanted to play with them some more. A mission or two later and their officers had realized what they had. A Marine rifle battalion all the way down to a rifle platoon is a finely crafted weapon. It is truly breathtaking what modern infantry formations can do, especially American, especially Marines.

So, their officers wanted to see what else they could do. Samuel did not blame them for it. No man has ever been handed a saber that did not have an instant desire to hack at something with it, at least a couple times. These officers had been handed the deadliest sabers ever crafted and they whacked a tree with it, no huge crime there. And then they hit it again, and again, and again. They were a fine saber, built to duel with any other saber in the world and their fine steel would hold its edge longer than the competitor. But a tree is a piece of nature. If someone is going to chop a tree down, get an axe. How long does it take before curiosity becomes criminal? Samuel's platoon, and he assumed entire battalion was getting chewed up by the environment and the pace. At a certain point when the young man hacks at the tree enough, it's his fault the blade is ruined, not the smith's.

Samuel blamed stupidity and braggadocious attitudes for what was happening, not sadism. But to most of the troops on the ground that's exactly what it was. The whole damn war was a practice of sadism. Bomb makers made bombs, bomb makers planted bombs, the troops found the bombs, they looked for the bomb makers, lots of people died, rinse and repeat. Every few months they would roll out some new way to overcome the bombs, usually with equipment. Up-armor the trucks, and then all the trucks started breaking down. Heavier flaks with groin protectors, neck protectors, throat protectors, thicker front, back, and side sapi plates, wear flight suits and NOMEX gloves, and then conduct modern infantry maneuver tactics in all that gear and with broken down trucks in a desert country and in a hellish urban terrain. Oh, and look out for bombs, because it turns out all that gear is not any more effect-ive at stopping them.

Samuel would later reflect that *this* was the beginning of the veteran counterculture for his generation. The society back home would complain about "the Great Recession" and various other inconveniences. But the veterans of this war felt like they faced the only real hardship that the last twenty years had to offer western civilization. The division between civilian and veteran ran deep. Veterans developed their own subcul-ture to indicate their place in the ranks of the baptized. They had their own language, music, and tribal customs. Veteran owned t-shirt companies supplied them with uniforms, vet-erans painted the art that they would admire, veterans wrote the books they read, and they would adopt just about any-thing else one could imagine to distinguish themselves. It was about a hipster advertisement of distinction. These counter-cultures had existed before, but unlike the Vietnam generation that banned together in solidarity against screaming college kids, this generation was the one screaming at the college kids. The world back home was wrought with plenty and this generation of warfighters was not going to let anyone forget that fact. They were the ones who, in a generation raised on boy bands, left their souls in the searing desert amongst the corpses. They were the only ones who knew what it was like to live in the sweat and the filth with murder on their minds and hopelessness in their guts. The rage born in the desert was going to come home with them. And God save anyone who asked why they were so pissed off.

Samuel's disgruntledness was most centered on his lack of Samantha not his lack of comfort. It was a cruel irony to him that the ship floating in the middle of the ocean had been able to keep up with the mail. But once ashore mail had basic-ally stopped running. He was carrying thirty-three letters that he simply had not gotten a chance to mail. They kept moving deeper and deeper into the desert. They had been in search of an area of operation, AO, that needed them. The battalion had fanned out to a few forward operating bases throughout Al Anbar. And, Samuel assumed, there was no real way for the mail to catch up to him. His company had found, "honest work" in their AO. They were picking up side jobs is what they were doing. One platoon had taken the best vehicles and was running with the artillery battery from the MEU on convoy ops back and forth on the Main Service Roads, MSRs.

The other platoons in the company were mercenaries, and no task was too small. They would sit on suspected IEDs until EOD would arrive or they would link up with some SOCOM unit and provide security while they snatched up some suspected "high value target." Once Samuel's entire platoon started combing the desert for five days looking for some unexploded ordnance, UXO, that some close air support had dumped that did not explode. It was not work befitting a group of infantrymen that fancied themselves elite death dealers. And the unit was ravenous and near mutinous. Proudly disciplined Marines were quickly becoming a rabble, only a few strong NCOs like Samuel were keeping the whole thing together.

Samantha was completing her daily ritual of checking the mailbox looking for a letter from Samuel while she left her daily letter to him to be sent. She had not received a letter from him in far too long. She was wearing his sweater today. She missed him even more than usual. Samantha had grown used to the disappointment of seeing the empty mailbox, but today it stung even more.

She trudged the distance to the apartment. She saw Mac's huge truck parked in front of the building. She felt guilty that she did not want to see him today, but it was too hard. She walked in the door and saw Mac sitting on the couch watching TV eating a burrito he had picked up from somewhere. He glanced at her momentarily and then looked back trying to find the remote. He was watching the News. Samantha actively avoided the News. Hearing about the war just made her nervous and scared. The image on the screen was a blown-up military vehicle. The headline said "Iraq Erupts with Violence." Samantha heard the anchor say, "Experts are saying this is on track to being the bloodiest week in Iraq since Fallujah..." Samantha felt her eyes well up with tears. She dropped her bag and covered her mouth with both hands.

Mac said softly, "I'm sorry I just-"

Samantha did not wait to hear the response. She raced to her room and slammed the door behind her. She could not help but feel like this was going to be the poetic end to the most poetic of men. He was a hero from a Greek tragedy. The audience would only feel sorrow for his loss. But for Samantha, Samuel being gone was a loss, Samuel dying would be the end of her life. She looked at the picture on her nightstand as she slowly fell to her knees. She had gotten the picture from Samuel's mother. Samuel must have been eight or nine. He was holding a plastic bucket and a plastic shovel on the beach, with the waves crashing behind him. He had a huge smile on his face. Samantha thought how much she wished she could have been there on that trip. She wished she could go back to the first time they met, whenever that was. First grade, before then, it did not matter. She wanted to tell that happy little boy, "Don't go! Let someone else go! I need you!"

Samuel had taken a deep breath and closed his eyes. It was his ritual. He would slow his heart rate and prepare for the murderous task ahead. Bullets were striking the low wall he and the other Marines had taken cover behind. He had his hand on Malone's flak to hold him down.

Samuel was waiting for the slightest change in tempo. Then they would strike. He knew when he opened his eyes it was go time. He was not nervous, not anxious, not full of belligerent rage, he was calm. He heard the Rat-tat-tat pause. He opened his eyes as he stood up to face the building. "Move!" he screamed.

Samuel made sure he was the first one up by not shouting until he had already taken the slack out of the trigger for his first shot. He was sighted in on the window on the second floor where the shots had first come from.

All of the Marines opened up. He did not hear his own shots, and was scarcely aware that he was shooting.

The Marines stormed across the street firing and moving--textbook. Samuel had a song playing in his head, the melody was guiding his pace.

The Marines stacked up on the door facing the street they had just crossed. Their mission, kill everyone in this house. Samuel quickly changed magazines. Malone was slightly back off the wall pointing his rifle up towards the second-floor window. Smith was on point, closest to the door. Phillips had the S.A.W. and was in the back of the stack covering their rear. Samuel saw his Marines were out of breath, which meant his enemy inside was recovering from the assault too. The melody drug on in his head pushing him to keep up the pace as he squared up on the door and kicked it with all of his force.

Instantly, Smith was through the door. Samuel was humming to himself as he entered right behind him.

There was a staircase to the right that led up to a landing. As Samuel followed Smith into the entry hall, he saw a man pop out from the right side on the second floor.

Samuel let out a few rounds until the undeniable color of blood had painted the wall behind the man and he slid down to a sitting position. Samuel did not take a millisecond to consider his kill. The melody kept driving, and that's what he was going to do, relentlessly keep the tempo.

"Malone stairs, Phillips door, Smith on me" Samuel barked when he was certain they had all breached the first funnel. Samuel and Smith set up on opposite sides of the first door on the first floor. Samuel was humming to himself when he nodded to Smith telling him it was time to go to work.

Malone had his rifle trained on the second-floor landing.

He could see down the short hall where Samuel and Smith had just disappeared. Phillips had taken a knee directly to his left and was pointing his belt fed weapon out the door they had all come through. Malone could see Samuel's kill sitting with the huge bloodstain behind him. Malone was shaken. Their fire team leader had been hit moments ago. Before anyone figured out what happened Sgt. Parker had physically snatched him up and drug him, and the rest of the fire team to this house. Malone heard shots from the hall. Then there was an audible scream from a man's voice and more shots. He cut his eyes to his left and down at Phillips. Phillips cut his eyes up to Malone. The two young Marines shared a moment of insecurity. They heared an audible "dat-dum dat-dum" from Sgt Parker in the back room. Then they heard a loud "Clear." This relieved their fear but not their anxiety. Suddenly, they heard Sgt. Parker from the doorway yell, "Two Marines coming out."

The song in Samuel's head was just getting to his favorite part as he emerged from the back hallway. He swiftly made his way to the Marines he left posted for rear security. He stacked up on Malone with Smith behind him.

He pointed his rifle up the stairs. He felt Smith knee him in the back of his thigh meaning he was ready. Samuel tapped Malone on the helmet to indicate it was time to get some. Then he put his hand back on Malone's shoulder. They made their way up the stairs.

The gruesome reminder of Samuel's earlier violence was at the top of the stairs. Samuel did not admire his work, but he did notice the figure had already assumed all of the qualities of a corpse.

When they reached the top of the stairs Malone abruptly and expertly turned to the right and Samuel did the same thing to the left. So that the two men were nearly back to back. "Door" Malone said. Samuel had a door on his side too. He knew that door led to the second-floor window.

That was the window where the shot had come from that hit Davis, one of his fireteam leaders. The other three kills had been business, but he was going to enjoy this one. For the slightest second he was worried he might have killed the shooter when they were crossing the street. Smith and he stacked up and they got to work.

Samuel went in first. The room appeared to be empty. He gave a quick scan of the room and his eyes were drawn to a couch in the center of the room centered on the window.

Samuel continued along the wall to the left while he kept his weapon trained on the couch. Smith had gone along the opposite wall. The song continued.

Samuel made it to the point where he could see past the couch. He saw his target. The man had his AK in his lap and was covered in gore. The man was holding a wound on his chest with a terrified look on his face. Samuel did not hesitate, he let out a volley. It was not that it was *that* personal to Samuel to kill this man, it was business too. Civilized men might scoff at Samuel for shooting this man who was already as good as dead. Hell, some gentle souls might try to render aid. But Samuel was not wasting his Corpsman's time on an insurgent with a sucking chest wound. And they had to get back to the rest of the squad on the perimeter. This man had died honorably with his weapon close at hand. He did not beg. Samuel thought it was an honor to kill him, and he hoped the man was honored to be killed by him.

Samuel suddenly heard Malone yell, "Mother fucker!" from the landing outside.

Samuel rushed to see what was the matter.

He found Malone tussling with a man. The guy was not getting the better of Malone, who had him pinned against the wall with his rifle, but Samuel was disappointed.

Malone could end this if he decided to be just a tad bit

more violent.

Samuel walked towards the men locked in gladiatorial combat while drawing his knife off the front of his flak. Samuel reached past Malone with his hand not holding the knife and pinned the other man's head against the wall. The man and Malone panicked at the new hand entering the fray.

The man was wearing Jihadist white like the others had been. But his face did not give the impression that he was ready to meet his God.

Samuel felt a little pity for him as he sank his knife into the man's kidney.

Malone shirked away as the man, reeling in pain, let go of his rifle.

Samuel looked back at Malone as if to offer him the opportunity to claim his kill. Malone's face told Samuel that he was not interested. Samuel pulled his knife out and stuck it in the man's neck at an upward angle to cut into the cerebral cortex. Samuel felt the confirmation of the man's quick death as he felt only a couple more beats of the man's pulse through the hilt of his blade.

Samuel pulled his blade out and wiped the gore on the man's white robes. Samuel let the fresh corpse slide to the ground as he walked over to Malone. Samuel sheathed his knife and stared at Malone for a second. After a beat or two, Samuel patted Malone on the helmet. "You two clear that last room," He ordered. Samuel turned his back and walked down the stairs confident he had vanquished every last soul in the house not wearing a MARPAT uniform.

Samantha was laying in bed. She had no tears left to cry. She was listening to the same sad song, one where a woman was singing about missing everything about her lover, on repeat. It was not loud enough because she could hear Lucy yelling at Mac from the living room, "New, rule. No news in the apartment!" Then she heard her yell, "I don't care. No war movies. No Marine talk. No news. Keep that shit out of this apartment!" Samantha could not even gather the emotion to feel happy that Lucy was being so protective of her. Suddenly the door flung open. Lucy was standing there looking at her.

Lucy walked over and opened the curtains letting in the light and said, "Get up we are going out tonight."

Samantha searched for the emotion of anger. But she could not find it. All she felt was sadness.

"I can't." Samantha said softly.

"Why not you have a long night of listening to this depressing shit planned out?" Lucy snapped back.

"I just can't." Samantha said.

One of the good things about Iraq was the ability to keep a comparatively regular workout routine. Marines treated physical fitness like a religion. And like zealous crusaders of old they built chapels everywhere they went. If a group of Marines was in place for seven days or more a makeshift gym would crop up. Two weeks and the gym would have a roof and some professional equipment. Eventually, there would be a functional temple to conditioning with walls, lights, some type of sound system, and, all things considered, an impressive amount of equipment of varying quality. Soon each Marine would be there attending mass at regularly scheduled intervals. Samuel was immersed in taking his daily sacrament of weightlifting, a gunfight earlier in the day was not going to interrupt that.

Torres was in the gym talking to the Marines from Samuel's squad. Torres had volunteered for this deployment when Samuel did. They had gone to Iraq the first time together. Samuel would forever remember Torres as the guy that went to post naked. Torres was assigned to another squad. Samuel knew all of the Marines thought his music was blocking out their voices, but he was doing bench-presses when his last song ended. So, Samuel could hear every word.

"Davis is good to go," Torres told them, "He might be going back to the ship or he might be going home. The shot was through and through in the calf."

"Solid." Phillips said.

"I didn't even realize he was hit," Smith added, "I heard the shot and got down. The next thing I knew Sgt. Parker was running like a mad man yelling, 'Let's go.'"

Torres started laughing.

"Pony Boy is a war junky." Torres said, "I wanted some extra money before I dropped and went home. Parker is home."

"I've never seen anything like it Corporal." Smith said.

Torres asked, "He went all god of death, did he?"

Phillips replied, "He went through that house stacking bodies while humming some fucking pop tune."

Samuel smirked at the inaccuracy as he completed another repetition.

"Would you have felt better if it was death metal?" Torres asked.

The Marines all laughed.

Malone said, "I don't give a fuck what it was, shit was unnerving."

Smith added, "Once we got in the house, I never got a shot off. He was like a fucking composer of death. He pointed like he was pointing at an orchestra. But people died in that symphony."

"Like I said killers," Torres added, "That man loves this shit. He says he has a demon inside him that comes alive when it's time to start killing. I fucking believe him."

Samuel felt his arm start to shake as his muscles failed. He had gotten distracted listening to his fast-growing legend and done a few too many reps. The Marines all rushed over and helped him put the bar back on the rack.

"That's disappointing." Torres said, "The god of death is mortal after all."

Samuel sat up and rolled his eyes.

"Aren't you supposed to be on QRF?" Samuel asked.

"I am on QRF." Torres said, "I was up at the COC when news came in Davis was good to go. I came here to tell you, but I knew better than to interrupt you when you were getting your swell on."

"Appreciate it," Samuel said standing up. He looked at the Marines from Davis' fire team. "Y'all go find the Platoon Commander and see if there's any way y'all can get out to see him before they send him off to wherever. Tell him I said I knew it would mean a lot to Davis. He'll figure a way out to get y'all out there."

They nodded as Phillips said, "Aye Sergeant."

Torres, Phillips and Smith all left to carry out their orders, but Malone stayed behind.

Samuel looked at him for a few seconds and then said, "Malone you know I am not some dickhead Sergeant. If you have something to say, say it."

The other Marines from the squad all scurried off to other gym equipment expecting to hear some ass chewing to happen soon.

Malone said, "Sergeant, I just wanted to say I'm sorry. I know I fucked up. I shouldn't have taken my eyes off that door."

"You shouldn't have," Samuel said plainly. Samuel took a drink of water and saw the shame on Malone's face.

Samuel put his hand on his shoulder and said, "Everyone that's supposed to be dead is, and everyone that isn't, ain't. Today goes in the win column."

Malone still had an ashamed look on his face. Samuel knew what this was really about. Samuel told all of the guys all of the time, "People do dumb shit in combat." He even provided examples from his first deployment of big fuck ups. Malone was ashamed about what came afterwards, not killing the man.

"Where you from?" Samuel asked Malone.

"Atlanta." He replied.

Samuel raised an eyebrow and said, "Rough city."

Malone nodded and said, "I always wanted to be a Marine. I was gonna' come back and show all the dope boys what a real tough guy looks like."

Samuel paused for a moment, then he said, "You aren't a pussy Malone. That's not why you didn't stab that man in the neck."

Malone looked at Samuel with uncertainty.

"I'll guarantee you, you've had a rougher life than me." Samuel said continuing his lesson, "but Torres was right about one thing. I do have a demon inside of me."

Malone looked at him in shock, both that he had heard them talking about him and that he was saying it was true.

"Every man does," Samuel continued

"You better find a way to wake yours the fuck up. It doesn't matter what hood or suburb you come from. These men we are fighting, they've awoken their demons. You are fresh meat and they will eat you alive. And the only thing that is going to keep, Demarcus Malone, the kid from Atlanta, that is going to do something with his life, off the dinner menu; is whatever fucked up demon you have lurking inside of you."

Malone hung his head briefly and then looked back at Samuel with understanding. Samuel continued,

"I don't love this shit. Samuel Parker is not home. I'm an upper middle-class kid that grew up in, what would probably pass for a mansion in your neighborhood. I should be in college studying for finals. That's home, curled up with the girl next door."

Samuel shook his head and scoffed as he said, "Hell, I should be in a bar with her right now. It's my twenty first birthday."

Malone looked at him with a surprised look on his face.

"That sucks," Malone chuckled, "Happy birthday Sergeant."

Samuel smacked Malone on his shoulder and said, "I'll

do whatever the fuck it takes to make sure my last birthday is not in this shithole country. If that means I have to let the demon out to eat, so be it."

Malone smiled at him.

Samuel turned around and put more chalk on his hands. He sat down on the bench.

"You doing another set Sergeant?" Malone asked.

Samuel replied, "Somewhere there is a man that wants to kill us that's doing another set. He's counting on us not doing another."

Samuel laid back and put his headphones in his ears and started another song. Samuel reached up and gripped the bar. A smile came to his face when he saw Malone's freshly chalked hands grab the center of the bar to assist him off the rack.

CHAPTER 11. UNITED FEDERATION OF DOOR-KICKERS, IRAQ LODGE 0311

"I just can't go out tonight!" Samantha exclaimed.

"Why not?" Lucy said.

"It's his birthday today!" Samantha said looking at Lucy. Lucy just stared at her.

"I can't go out because I'm going to miss him more." Samantha finally felt herself letting it out and it was therapeutic. She continued,

> "I can't go to a bar because I know he's not there. I can't just lay in bed because I know he won't be there when I roll over. I can't watch the news because it makes me scared to think what's happening to him. I can't study because I just read about these body parts and my mind starts thinking, Wow I hope Sam doesn't get shot there that will kill him. Oh if he gets blown up and that gets damaged he won't be able to do that anymore. I can't listen to songs because he's in every line. He's everywhere but he's not here. I can't touch him. I can't feel him anymore. His clothes don't smell like him anymore. He's not here but he's not gone either."

Lucy was staring at her. Suddenly in an unsympathetic tone Lucy said, "That is the dumbest shit I have ever heard."

Samantha looked up at her with a shocked face.

"If you are going to treat him like he's dead at least celebrate the man." Lucy said.

Samantha's mouth opened wide.

"It's his birthday-- " Lucy said, "I doubt he's having a good time. Celebrate it for him."

Samantha was speechless. She did not feel like she was wallowing in self-pity before this moment, her pain was real. But Lucy made a very good point, if he was here Samantha would be giddy with excitement for his birthday. There was no rule that said she could not be excited for his birthday while he was gone.

"I'm not changing out of his sweatshirt though." Samantha said as she sat up in the bed.

"That's fine." Lucy said, "We don't have to worry about you getting drunk and hooking up with anyone, because no one is going to hit on you lookin' like that."

Samuel was walking up to the COC, to find out what he could about the plan for tomorrow and listen to everyone's criticisms about the day. He walked in. Van spotted him and came charging at him with a scowl on his face.

Van grabbed him by the collar and yelled, "What the fuck are you trying to do?"

Samuel drove his knee into Van's gut. Van doubled over. Samuel reached under him and grabbed him by his uniform blouse. Samuel picked him straight up into the air and slammed him on his back. Samuel was crawling on him to start smashing his face in when the other two squad leaders grabbed him and pulled him off of him. Morris hobbled over to the scrum that had formed.

"Knock it the fuck off." Morris screamed. "Jesus Van. You don't even know what the fuck happened yet."

Samuel stood up and straightened out his camies.

Morris continued, "If you want to be a platoon sergeant someday you are going to have to learn to listen before you speak."

Samuel looked at Morris.

Morris had been one of the first "casualties." He was a good Marine and a solid leader. He made his rounds every day for the first few weeks. That was before they had an AO and no real billeting. They were roaming around the desert like nomads. He was always the first one awake and the last one asleep and always up and about checking on his Marines. Morris, like everyone else, did not have enough clean socks and nowhere to clean the dirty ones. He had gotten trench foot so bad Doc had said he was genuinely concerned they were going to have to amputate. Morris refused to go to some field hospital so the CO, Doc, and him compromised on a semi light duty assignment in the COC until his feet healed. Van was running the platoon day to day and Samuel was running first squad. There were a lot of stupid casualties like that chewing up their company.

"I don't trust boots or officers to tell me the truth," Morris said limping back over to a chair to sit down, "So tell me what the fuck happened."

Samuel looked around the room. There was a mix of expressions. Some were looking on in adoration and others had scowls on their face like Van. Samuel reached down and gave Van a hand up off the ground. Van begrudgingly took Samuel's hand looking over at Morris for approval.

"We got sent to that suspect device." Samuel said. "We were holding the perimeter for probably three hours by that point."

Morris looked at him and nodded as if to say go on.

"I looked over to where Davis' team was set up about the time he stood up. I guess he got bored or stiff or pissed the fuck off or all three." Samuel looked back at Van as he said, "I saw the muzzle flash out the window and then saw him go down. And I got pissed the fuck off. So, I snatched up his team and killed every mother fucker in the building."

Morris nodded and said, "Yeah we heard about you stacking bodies. All the officers want to pin another medal on you. My issue is you didn't radio a fucking thing to anyone here. Only thing I heard was your RO calling in a nine line out of nowhere."

Samuel thought back to the events, he was not sure he would do a single thing differently, but he saw their point.

Morris added, "Your days of being a war hero are over pimp. You have to stay in command and control of your squad. What if that was the opening shots of a multi-sided ambush?"

Samuel nodded at him acknowledging that he was right.

Morris said, "In the end though everyone that needed to die is dead, and all of our guys are alive."

Samuel smirked considering that he'd just said the same thing to Malone about an hour earlier.

Morris continued, "You're a damn good Marine Parker. I'm thrilled to have you. But if you think you can't control your urge to personally murder motherfuckers, I will put someone else in charge of that squad."

"Understood," Samuel said.

Van finally asked, "I heard you knifed a motherfucker in the throat and saved Malone?"

Samuel nodded.

"I guess I would have been pretty pissed if I saw the actual moment one of my guys got hit too." Vans said patting Samuel on the shoulder.

"It wasn't just that." Samuel said. All the guys in the room stared at Samuel as if to hear some secret to unleashing that kind of rage. Knife kills were a fairly rare occurrence in modern warfare, to have one put you in a club that was revered in the Marine Corps.

"While we were sitting on fucking perimeter," Samuel continued, "there was this little girl, probably about three or four, no more than ten feet from me. She was dead, and staring at me. But I couldn't move because that was the only fucking place I could see all of the teams posted up around that, trash bag or whatever the fuck it ended up being. So, I just had to sit there for three hours while she stared at me."

Samuel looked around the room, all the men had their heads hanging a little. Marines had a gallows humor for sure, but there was not going to be a joke about a dead kid. Every one of the men in this room was at least on their second deployment, they'd all seen at least one.

"I guess, I snapped from that," Samuel said. The room was quiet for a minute.

Morris was the first to speak up when he said, "Fuck Parker, next time just start off with the dead kid we'll get it." Everyone chuckled a little bit. Then Morris continued, "Or don't be such a fucking moron and move."

The chuckles grew a little louder that time.

Samuel snapped back in a joking manner, "Didn't you just say maintain command and control?"

Morris laughed at him and said, "Yeah, fuck that bro, my ass would have moved."

Morris, Van, Samuel, and the other squad leaders were back to joking and bitching about the deployment, their Marines, and mostly the officers. The subject came up about it being Samuel's birthday so at the evening brief their platoon commander brought him an MRE muffin top. They wrote "Fuck you" on it with chocolate peanut butter spread. That was how Samuel celebrated the all-important, American birthday milestone.

Mac had made all the girls resolve to only drink whiskey and sprite the whole night in honor of Samuel. Lucy had actually done a pretty sweet thing by calling quite a few of their friends and getting them to meet them at the bar. The girls had put up a banner that said "Happy 21st Sam, We're drinking for you." Samantha thought that Lucy must have put out an emergency call because they had gotten all of this together in about an hour.

Mac was in heaven. He was surrounded by women. He was devoted to Lucy, but he could not help himself from showering all the girls with flattery and hitting on them. Lucy did not seem to mind too much, occasionally she would say,

"Aaron," and slap his arm, in response to some ridiculous comment. A couple girls had brought their boyfriends but for the most part it was a girls' night out, and Mac. Samantha was glad that Lucy made her come. She did feel better. She was worried that she would be out when something happened to Samuel, but she had no way to know anyway.

Samantha had gone up to the bar to order another drink when a guy walked up and said, "Put that on my tab."

Samantha looked over at him and then back to the bartender and said, "No, please don't."

The bartender nodded he head and started to walk away.

The guy said, "Seriously, I insist."

The bartender threw his hands up, Samantha gave the bartender a slight nod and he finally walked away.

Samantha looked over and said, "Thank you."

"My pleasure," the guy said. Samantha turned back to the bar thinking that the conversation was over.

The guy leaned in very close to her and said, "It's really loud, do you want to come over to my table so we can talk."

"I'm sorry," Samantha said, "I have a boyfriend."

"Oh, my bad," the guy said.

"I'm Max," he said sticking his hand out.

Samantha started to get uncomfortable that the guy would not leave her alone. She looked to see if the bartender was coming and then looked back at the table to see that Mac was not even paying attention.

"Sam," She said. But she refused to shake his hand.

"Is that your boyfriend?" He asked, pointing at Mac.

"No, he's not here." she replied.

"Oh really, you did not make him up to try to get rid of me did you?" Max said.

"No, his name is Sam." Samantha said pointing at the sign.

"So, what's your name?" Max said laughing. Samantha felt herself getting really angry. She wished Samuel would walk through that door right now and smash this guy.

"Sam." She replied frustrated. The bartender walked up and sat the drink down.

"So, where is he?" Max asked.

Samantha picked up the drink with one hand and turned towards the guy and pointed towards the eagle globe and anchor on Samuel's sweatshirt she was wearing with the other.

Max got a smug look on his face as he said, "So he's not even here to care if you talk to me."

Samantha wanted to pour her drink on him. But somewhere inside of her she felt like she was channeling Samuel. It was not as quickly as Samuel did it, but she knew exactly what to say. Her mind was processing any response this guy might give her and formulating her statement ahead of time to deal with it. Serendipitously the song cut off and there was a moment of relative silence for her to deliver. Samantha felt like Samuel had cut the music for her to speak on his behalf.

"You know why he's not here?" Samantha shouted loud enough for the bar to hear. She continued,

"He's not here because he's fighting a war. He's fighting a war he already had to fight once. But he's there again and he may never come back. But he had to go back because if we had to count on you, we'd be waiting forever. So, I'm not refusing to talk to you because I have a boyfriend. I'm not talking to you because you are such a chicken shit you have to wait until he's five thousand miles away before you'll talk to his girlfriend. So, thanks for the drink, it's his favorite. I'll be thinking of him while I drink it, I'll be thinking of him tonight. And I promise when I walk away, I will never think about you again."

By the time Samantha turned around Mac was standing there. He was staring at Max. Mac put his arm around Samantha and walked her back to the table. Samantha thought that Samuel would have been proud of her oratory prowess. She was proud, it made her feel strong for the first time since she got the letter saying they were going to Iraq.

Samuel was sitting in a briefing about to fall asleep.

Van leaned over whispered, "You good bro."
Samuel said, "Yeah, I'm fine."
"You don't look fine, just slip out. I'll fill you in on anything you need to know, later." Van said, "I'll cover for you."
Samuel said back, "It's straight dude. We just had went and did that sweep yesterday, and then sat on that IED on the way back." Samuel yawned and said, "then last night we were QRF and that dickhead officer from CLB, or whatever it was, called in contact, probably just trying to get a CAR. So, we spent most of the night looking for a shooter that did not exist."
"Do you gentlemen have something to add?" The commanding officer said.
Van replied, "No sir. Sorry, sir."
Samuel heard a loud voice behind him say, "I do." It was First Sergeant Peterson. Now the thing that has to be understood about first sergeants, is that they tend to follow a very similar mold. They are the senior enlisted in the company. They are the commanding officer's right-hand man, and they usually act accordingly. They say things like "to piggyback off of what the CO just said." Translated that means, "I am about to say exactly what the CO just said." The other thing they do is run around and bitch at Marines about dirty camies and having their hands in their pockets. Well, everyone's uniforms were filthy and there was no way to fix it. So, Samuel assumed they were about to be subjected to either a long drawn out "Look like Marines" speech or a "Respect the CO when he's talking speech." But Samuel felt like he got a slight voyeuristic view of the reason that rank existed when he actually started his rant this time.

"Sgt Vans was asking him if he was good." First Sergeant Peterson said, "which was a legit question because he looks like shit." The CO looked back at First Sergeant, and then hung his head expecting to get the "Look like Marines" speech at an inopportune time.

But then he continued, "which I find shocking because he's an outstanding Marine. Hell sir, we saw fit to push up a meritorious package for him."

Samuel looked over his shoulder to see First Sergeant Peterson was red in the face, he was very angry as he continued, "But then I heard Sergeant Parker explain why. His squad was on missions since what-"

First Sergeant Peterson looked down at Samuel for an answer, but Samuel did not feel like it was appropriate for him to say anything.

"At least two days straight." First Sergeant Peterson continued. "These guys are broke the fuck off and were talking about increasing the tempo right now."

The CO looked at Samuel and then looked up at First Sergeant and nervously said, "We are all stretched pretty thin."

First Sergeant Peterson did not even wait a second before he replied, "Then why do we keep reporting to battalion that the men are good to go and can take more missions?"

The room fell silent.

First Sergeant went into full rant mode as he continued:

"I know the First Sergeants are telling Sergeant Major that the Marines are cracking at the seams. But he's telling us that all of the Company Commanders are telling the Battalion Commander that they are good to go ready for more work. We have twenty-four Marines that are medically unfit for duty right now and only two of those are combat related. Meanwhile we are sitting on a FOB full of Marines itching to get into the fight. There's a staff sergeant over in the supply section I'm considering putting on suicide watch because he's so depressed that his whole section has not left this FOB since they got here. They would love to get in this fight. The engineers here. I have watched them fill and dump the same two thousand sandbags, probably sixty times. Our

Marines need a break, sir. Maybe send a squad a couple squads to Al Asad for a couple days and rotate them. Let them wash some camies and eat real food. These other guys can handle, 'sitting on an IED' or 'sweeping the desert looking for UXO' in the meantime."

Every NCO in the room wanted to stand up and clap as First Sergeant sat down. He was right. First Sergeant, like most of them that get sent to rifle companies, was not a grunt. He was, well Samuel had no idea what his MOS had been. But none of these missions were high speed infantry missions, they were glorified busy work. It took a "pog" in a room full of grunts to tell them that there was an AO full of guys that would actually be excited to do some of this bullshit work. Because, no Marine wanted to be sent to a war only to be confined to a couple acre forward operating base until it was time to go home.

Samantha had felt much better since they had all gone to the bar for Samuel's birthday. Him being gone was hard, but She felt like she was out of her full-on depression. Samantha opened the mailbox at the apartment complex. There was a note on the door that said "Samantha Wallace: Delivered to" with the word "office" circled. Samantha was not sure what it could be as she did not order anything. Samantha was disappointed to see that there was still not a letter from Samuel. Samantha went into the front office of the complex and told the girl behind the counter her name.

"Oh boy," she said as she walked towards the back room. She came back with a gigantic stack of letters that were all rubber-banded together. There must have been sixty letters in the stack. Samantha's heart was overjoyed. This was definitely a good day.

Samantha walked into her apartment and took to the task of reading the letters. Each one always started with "Hey Sam." Her heart was floating reading his words. Some of them were angry, not at her but at the situation. Others were sad and told about his loneliness. Some were surprisingly funny. Samuel told her in one that he had adopted a son who happened to be an eighteen-year-old black kid from Atlanta. But he did sound like a proud father when he described how he had started molding the young man. He explained the young man was now a "beast" and he was happy to think it was due to his tutelage. But the ones she cherished the most talked about how much he loved her.

Samantha always knew Samuel had a way with words, but something about reading his flattery on paper in his handwriting made the words better. Samuel explained how he had come to share Mac's belief that he was touched by God. But, Samuel believed his purpose in life was to come home and love her in such a way that everyone that saw them together would be inspired. Samuel in another letter explained to Samantha that he did not regret joining or going to war because he knew that it had made him the kind of man that she deserved. Samuel swore that he would be the partner she needed for all her life because he had been forced to live without her for so long. There were some that Samantha preferred to keep secret, that reflected more, carnal desires.

Samantha reflected on all the letters. Mac had said that Samuel was the god of death. But to Samantha, Samuel was the god of life, and of love. Just his letters swelled her with happiness. When he left it was like a chunk of her heart left with him, leaving a hole. Then when she found out he was going back to Iraq there was another chunk ripped out. But each letter she opened was a bandage that she could wrap around her heart until he got home.

The Marines boarded the ship in near silence. It was a stark contrast to the last time Samuel left Iraq. That time everyone was cheerful and excited. This time every single Marine had developed some new pain that manifested itself in a new limp or hunch. Samuel's first deployment had been some of the most intense fighting anyone saw in Iraq. This deployment was not that type of deployment, and they weren't even there as long. This one was a grind. All of these men had been depleted. They had no motivation left, not even the motivation to be happy about leaving.

All of the sailors shuffled out of the way of the Marines as they made their way through the bulkheads and ladderwells to get to their birthings. Samuel almost flew into a rage when he got to his to find a huge stack of letters from Samantha strewn about his rack.

"You know the fucking Nazis even made sure the POWs got their fucking mail." Samuel yelled to Van.

"Are you asking me if I have trouble believing that the Nazis treated American servicemembers better than the Corps does?" Van replied climbing up to his coffin rack, "Because that's easy to answer, absolutely not fucking hard to believe."

Morris walked over and looked at the stack and said, "Too many of them for one to be a 'Dear John'. You're good bro."

Samuel wanted to read the letters in privacy, which he did not have at the moment. So, he and his squad made their way to the mess hall to sit down and relax for a moment. When they walked in some sailor was cleaning up.

"There's no mess being served right now." the sailor said. They must have all had an intimidating look on their face because the guy looked like someone who was preparing himself for an ass-kicking.

Samuel finally said, "We're not here for chow."

The squad sat down in small groups around the same long table. Samuel saw some SEALs sitting at another table laughing and joking looking back at his squad. He nodded to them and they nodded back.

SEALs were easy to spot, the beard was always a dead give-away. That and they wore, basically, Marine uniforms with the sleeves cuffed to almost the elbow. Samuel only ever envied the beards. He wished he would have been given the option. Risk dying in a gas attack or have a beard. That was easy, bring on the asphyxiating gas because he would grow the beard.

Samuel glanced over at the SEALs again, he was fairly certain he recognized them. His platoon had been regularly tasked with working with them while they were raiding and snatching high value targets in their area of operation. Samuel thought it was ironic that the war had devolved to the point that typical shooter jobs were now relegated to special operations. His first deployment the idea of any SF operators kicking doors looking for "high value targets" that no one had ever heard of would have been a joke. They went after the guys with their faces on the playing cards; grunts, the normal shooters, they went after bomb makers and guys that fit the Jihadist recruiter profile. In typical Marine fashion, someone had cards on them. The Marines started dealing out cards and playing spades. Samuel looked up to find the SEALs had walked over to where they were sitting.

"Glad y'all decided to join us, maybe we can get the fuck out of here now." One of them with a ginger beard said.

Samuel just tilted his head while he was looking at his cards to indicate that he was fine with them sitting down.

The guys sat down and the ginger bearded spokesman said, "You guys sure look like shit. Last time we were out your way there was not shit going on."

"Believe me dude," Samuel said looking to the guy who had sat across from him, "that was the biggest crock of shit I've ever experienced in my life. There is only one reason we look like this and it ain't got shit to do with combat."

The, now four, SEALs sitting with them started laughing.

"Yeah," the ginger beard said, "about the time y'all started looking for UXO in the desert we decided to get the fuck out of there."

Samuel looked as his cards, half listening to the SEALs.

"We reached out to some 'group' friends that were in country and heard that they had work around Mosul," he continued.

Samuel decided there were two things he was jealous of. He had beard envy, and he coveted the idea of shooters being able to find their own work, even on the other side of the country if they wanted.

"A lot of work out there?" Samuel asked confused.

"Hell yeah dude." Ginger beard said looking at the other SEALs like they had some inside joke, "They were churning IEDs out in that area like there was a fucking factory set up in the city somewhere."

"Huh?" Samuel said looking up from his cards. Samuel reflected that they had surprisingly few *actual* IEDs. Samuel stated, "The only thing getting churned out of our whole AO was working parties."

"Crazy isn't it?" Ginger beard said, "Two guys in the same war, at the same time, doing basically the same job, can have two totally different experiences." Ginger beard paused and said, "But still deal with the same bullshit at the same time."

"I doubt we were doing the same job." Samuel said looking up at the apparent spokesman.

Samuel knew the military was a weird place. A Marine infantryman, and an army infantryman for that matter, considered their jobs the toughest in the world. SEALs, Special Forces guys, and the rest of SOCOM believed they had the toughest jobs. The weird part is the grunts, or the shooters, only really respected the special operations guys, or the operators. And vice versa. It was a weird dichotomy where the operators were glad they did not have to deal with the bullshit that the shooters had to deal with, but the shooters respected the operators' abilities and training.

"Probably right." Gingerbeard said, "But at the same time, you'd be surprised."

It was not that Samuel had any animosity towards the SEALs, but at that particular time in his life, after seeing all the letters, and getting the bullshit deployment that he had ignorantly volunteered for, he had animosity towards everyone. SEALs were usually respectful towards everyone, especially

Marines, even though one would expect them to be overly arrogant. And Samuel knew these guys had probably been on the ship for a while with no one to talk to but each other and the sailors, and the sailors were not shooters or operators. But Samuel really wanted the conversation to end. He was just not in the mood to hear someone else's war stories.

But Malone ruined the opportunity of the conversation ending when he said, "Sergeant here is just salty because he only got to stab one motherfucker in the throat. To him it might as well have been a camping trip if he didn't get to stab more than one."

"Oh shit," The guy sitting next to Samuel with a dark beard said, "That was you."

Another one added, "Shit, I heard it was five. I was expecting a fucking samurai or some shit."

Everyone but Samuel laughed.

Malone replied, "He shot four in that house, he only stabbed one. I was there."

Samuel knew Malone was trying to talk Samuel up in front of the SEALs, but Malone did not realize Samuel really did not care. Everyone had their job, his was to stab some guy in the throat that day, later that week his job was to legitimately guard concrete drying on a roadway to make sure no one put a bomb in it. War is about doing your job.

Samuel was desperate to change the subject asked, "So did y'all ever find the factory?"

Ginger beard looked at him funny.

"In Mosul." Samuel clarified.

"Oh fuck no," Ginger beard said, "They brought in every asset they had and put us all over to try and catch the guys planting bombs. At the same time the army went building by building looking for the *factory*. I think the RCT found the factory. We didn't find shit."

The dark bearded guy laughed and said, "We might have found something until this one," pointing at ginger beard, "got a bright idea."

Ginger beard exclaimed in his own defense, "That was a fucking great idea, it just didn't work out."

Samuel put his cards down and looked over at them. He did not want to care, but he could not help it. He was addicted to tactics in this war. He wanted to know what did not work so that he would not repeat them, even though he was not a special forces operator and he had no intention of ever coming back to this shithole country.

Ginger beard said, "So look. They wanted us to look for bomb makers. There was this one fucking spot that they had bombed like five fucking times. So, I decided that was the logical place for us to sit, twenty-four seven."

Dark beard chimed in with obviously excited to tell this story,

"Yeah, so, we sit on this shit, in shifts twenty-four seven. And the first night we see this kid, probably about fifteen years old, come walking out of this fucking house on the west side of the street and walk over to the east side. He goes into this house looking all suspicious. And it's like zero two in the morning. He's not carrying anything, doesn't stop and look, doesn't appear to be giving any signals. He just rolls over to this house and dips out like two hours later. So, this fucking guy."

Dark beard pointed at ginger beard again and then continued.

"Is fucking convinced this dude is a bomb maker. He's making up wild stories like he's tunneling under the house and shit. Even though I'm like, 'bro the kid could just tunnel from his house if that's what he's doing.' But we watch this kid for like five days straight. Every night, same shit. Goes across the street late at night, leaves after a couple hours. We start building profiles and shit. The house on the east has one male and three females in it."

"Oh shit," Samuel says laughing understanding where

this is going.

"Exactly!" dark beard said laughing and pointing at ginger beard. Ginger beard just rolls his eyes as dark beard continued,

"So this house on the east is straight burka wearing mother fuckers. We got no clue how old any of these women are or anything. Finally, on the fifth night the kid goes over there. Twenty minutes later every light in the house turns on. Suddenly, suspected bombmaker jumps out of this window in nothing but his skivvies. This girl pops out the window, naked and titties flopping all around, and throws some clothes to him. She's blowing him kisses while he picks up his clothes and runs home. I'm laughing so hard he looks right up at our nest."

Everyone at the table was hysterically laughing.

"Five days of no sleep for that shit." dark beard added.

"She probably got stoned to death for that shit." Samuel said.

"Young love brother," Gingerbeard said, "You know how that shit goes."

Samuel did know how it went. He was ready to get back to his young love and leave the world of shooters and operators behind.

CHAPTER 12
LIBERTY CALL

Samantha was sitting in class when she felt her phone vibrate. She looked at the caller ID and saw it was a very strange number. She had a knot in her stomach. She was cautious to hope it was Samuel. But the possibility was there so she couldn't not answer it.

She answered the phone and said, "Hello." The professor and everyone else in the class turned to stare at her.

"Hey Sam," She heard on the other line.

Tears immediately started to form in her eyes, as she yelled, "Sam!" Samantha shot out of her seat and started making her way through the aisles tripping on other students' things and bumping into them. She did not even care. She heard Samuel chuckling on the other end of the line.

"Oh my god it is you." She said.

Samantha made her way to the back of the room and out into the hallway as she heard Samuel say, "Of course it's me."

Once she made it to the hall she just sat on the floor with her back against the wall. She was so emotionally overwhelmed she could not physically stand.

"Oh my god it's so good to hear your voice." Samuel said in a shaky voice.

A single happy tear rolled down Samantha's face as she said, "Baby, it's so good to hear your voice too."

Samantha could hear Samuel clearing his nose on the other end.

"Are you ok?" Samantha demanded.

If Samuel had bad news, she needed it now. The worst news was confirmed to not be true, he was alive.

"I'm- I'm fine love." Samuel said, "we're back on the ship. We'll be back in about a month or so."

Samantha's heart sang in triumph. The love of her life would be home soon.

"Oh my god," Samantha said, "if this is a dream I don't want to wake up."

Samantha could tell by the silence that Samuel agreed, and that he was very near to full on crying.

"I was just so scared Sam," Samantha said, "the news has not been good out of Iraq."

"I'm fine love." Samuel said, "I've been writing you every day have you been getting them?"

Samantha chuckled and said, "There was a time when I wasn't, but they caught up to me. Have you been getting mine?"

Samuel replied, "Same, they caught up to me eventually."

They sat in silence for a moment and just listened to each other breathe. This was the closest they had been to each other in almost eight months.

"I love you." Samuel said softly, "so much."

"I love you too." Samantha said.

"Well, we got the chance to make a call, so I threatened to fight everyone to get to the front of the line." Samuel said.

Samantha started laughing.

"But I know I can't take all two hundred of them, and they are starting to figure that out, so I've got to get off of here for now."

Samantha said softly, "I don't want you to go, fight for it."

Samuel laughed and said, "Seriously, you'll be greeting a corpse in a month if I don't get off of here. I will call you as soon as I get another chance."

"Promise?" Samantha asked.

"I promise, baby. I love you," Samuel said.

Samantha could hear some type of commotion going on, on the other end.

"I love you too," Samantha said as she heard the phone hang up. Samantha sat on the floor a little longer. He was not home. But they made it. It was all over but the waiting. Samantha breathed a sigh of relief as if the entire weight of a society at war was off her shoulders.

That was the reality of this war. The pressure was felt by very few. Previous wars, like World War II, everyone had someone gone. The whole nation rationed and followed the goings on as if their future hinged on the outcome. That meant everyone could lean on each other. But in this war very few people's future hinged on the war. Small pockets of people were totally enveloped by what happened in the deserts of the Middle East. Would they have a lover in a year? Would they lose a father, mother, sister, brother? Would their children grow up without a father? The pressure of those questions was faced by a relatively small segment. But Samantha had gotten the answer to the question, the gubernatorial pardon had reached executioner in time. Samantha and Samuel's future may still be delayed but it would eventually be able to continue unabated.

Samuel hung up the phone and turned around slowly.

"Let's go god of death," Van said, "She still worships you just like the rest of us." Some of the other Marines behind him were laughing and making kissing noises at him.

"Some of us have to find out how much of our shit our girls left with." Van stated as he pushed past Samuel to get to the phone.

In truth the stories of the "Dear John" letters were not exaggerated in scale or scope. Samuel had basically missed out on a whole segment of the Marine experience because he had not had a woman leave him while he was on deployment. Samuel wondered how many of these guys were going home to more loneliness. Empty homes and custody cases were in a lot of these guy's futures, that was not a question. Samuel pondered why that was. Was it that this generation of women were somehow less virtuous? Less dutiful?

That seemed like too easy of an answer. The sexual liberation movement and second wave feminism had certainly changed the relationship dynamic. Women were not beholden to men anymore. If they were unhappy, they would leave. What would make a woman more unhappy than her man leaving her to kill people in a foreign desert? What did it say about a woman that was just "ok" with that?

But Samuel thought it had to be something deeper than that. Samuel figured that there had to be a facet of this war that was different. Samantha had said that "the news" coming out of Iraq was bad. That was true the army had been getting fucked up. The truth had finally come out about the whole deployment once they got back to the ship. The commanders in Iraq had wanted to keep the MEU, and every available unit for that matter, close at hand to respond if the violence erupted across the whole country. And the MEU commanders wanted to stay in case another Fallujah popped off.

But the army had done a pretty damn good job at keeping the violence isolated in their regions. That was not a good story, though. The titanic American military being able to subdue a rabble of tenacious but otherwise ineffective Jihadists and insurgent fighters was not a story that sold ad space. The American story was one of an outclassed rabble bloodying the nose of a great world power. Samuel knew as well as anyone the war was hard fought and hellish, and it had devolved into a quagmire where the victory conditions were no longer definable. But the troops on the ground were battle hardened now. They may not have known how to win this war, but they knew how to fight it, and they knew how to survive it. But that was not the headlines they were selling the families back home.

"If it bleeds it leads."

That's as much a statement about the morality of journalists as it is about the values of the population consuming the media. The population expected to see pictures of blown-up trucks. But, for the families back home, nothing quite bleeds like their loved ones. Every picture of a blown-up truck had their loved one sitting in it. And Samuel wondered if it was even fair to judge the women that decided enough is enough. Those women may not be able to end the war, but they could end the relationship that brought them plenty of anxiety and heart ache, but very little comfort.

Samantha walked back into the classroom with a huge smile on her face. *All over but the waiting.* She thought to herself. The whole classroom looked back at her. The professor had stopped mid-sentence to stare at her. She was not embarrassed. She felt like the whole world should be as happy as she was, the greatest man in the world had survived and was coming home.

"He's coming home!" Samantha announced to the class in excitement.

In her mind the class was going to erupt in clapping and balloons would fall from the ceiling. They would all start partying and laughing with the same level of celebratory fervor she felt in her gut now.

But instead, all she got was the professor saying, "That's great!"

The class all laughed.

He added, "I'm sure we'd all be happy if you would take your seat so we can be done with this lecture before he gets back."

Samantha had the sad realization that not a person in the room knew Samuel. Maybe some had gathered that he was a Marine by her frequent wearing of his clothing. Some might have even divined that he was overseas, but at best he was just another soldier that had gone to Iraq. Samantha calmly walked back to her seat and tried to get her mind back on the lecture.

After class Samantha walked out to the aisle. The professor waved her to the front. She walked grudgingly up to the front. As she got a few feet from them she was preparing to defend her earlier interruption.

"What branch is he with?" The professor asked, "Your-boyfriend."

Samantha nodded to tell him yes it was her boyfriend. Then he held up a picture on his lectern of a young man in front of an American Flag in a blue uniform.

"My son is in the Air Force." the professor said, "I can recognize the look of someone that is taking a phone call from over there."

The professor tilted his head to indicate he was talking about overseas. It was as if he could not say the name of the place or it would breathe life into it.

"Sam's a Marine." Samantha said smiling.

"Do you know when yet?" He asked.

Samantha shook her head and said, "Not one hundred percent."

"When you find out let me know. I'll let you take whatever assignments early so you can be there when he gets off the plane."

Samantha smiled and nodded at the great courtesy. It felt good to know other people knew how it felt. When she turned around there were several girls waiting behind her. Samantha assumed they were all waiting their turn to ask the professor some question or another. So, Samantha hung her head and walked past them. But two of the girls started walking with her.

"That was so sweet," one of the girls said.

Samantha looked at her confused. She was not sure if they had heard what the professor offered her or not.

"You were so excited to say he was coming home." the girl added.

Samantha felt herself blushing.

"I just forget that not everyone had been waiting for him to come home like I have." Samantha said softly.

"How long has he been overseas?" the other girl asked.

Samantha looked at her with a dumbfounded look.

"We all knew that had to be your story." The girl said, "You always looked so sad, and you wore Marine t-shirts and sweatshirts all the time. We all figured that you had a boy-friend that was gone."

Samantha smiled nervously not realizing that she had advertised her depressed state so much.

"He's been gone almost eight months."

The first girl said, "I cannot imagine what that is like. It must be so hard."

Samantha was caught off guard. For a moment she had thought for sure these girls had been through what she had been going through. She had thought they must have been able to tell because they were members of the secret society of people with loved ones that were gone, like the professor and her.

"It's been rough." Samantha said sighing.

"You should get a photographer for when he gets off the plane." the other girl said. Both of them let out an "awe".

Samantha was not a fan of that idea. She wanted him all to herself. And there was no way she was not going to sob when he put his arms around her. It might make for a sweet picture, and it may be a happy moment, but Samantha thought that it would be like childbirth. Even if someone is the type that wants to have a picture of the moment, bringing a third party into the moment would spoil it, no matter how much better the quality of the picture would be.

"He'll be getting off of a ship." Samantha said smiling.

"So, he's like a sailor?" the second girl asked.

Samantha scoffed. She did not know why that offended her so much but the idea of someone getting his branch wrong was, well, offensive. Samantha did not really understand how it worked, but she knew sailors stayed on ships. Marines got off the ships and fought with the soldiers. But Marines weren't soldiers and were quick to correct anyone that referred to them as such. And Samantha had heard Sam and Mac talk enough to know that they didn't think the guys in the air force faced the same hardships they did. Samantha felt like she was compelled to defend Samuel's courage and point out that he was out there in the maximum danger.

"No," Samantha snapped, "he's Marine infantry. He's just getting back on a ship."

There was a brief silence. Samantha felt a little guilty. A year ago, she did not know the difference from any of the services, or servicemembers, or what they actually did. These girls were being sweet. and she was snapping at them when their only crime was ignorance.

"At least that's what he says whenever someone asks what he does." Samantha giggled to try and soften the effect of her scolding comment. She continued, "It's hard to keep up with what the difference is between all of them."

The group had made it outside.

One of the girls asked, "Which way are you going?"

Samantha pointed and said, "I have to go study for a test I have in a couple hours."

"Ok," the girl replied, "good luck. We're so happy for you."

Samantha hugged the girls and gave them thank-you's and good-byes. Samantha was comforted to know that they had a genuine sentiment of happiness. They may have been ignorant to the pain she had felt, but they were not oblivious to it existing, and she appreciated that they recognized it.

Samuel did not give a shit about the pageantry. If this ship did not dock and lower the gangplank soon, he was going to start throwing people off, starting with whomever thought it was important to line everyone up on the top deck and have them stand there while it slowly taxied in. Samuel would have been happy if they just beached the damn thing and everyone rushed off. Samuel felt like they were adding steps to them coming home and him getting to see Samantha again. Samuel thought back to the first time he got back. They flew in a commercial jet, chartered of course. As they approached the landing strip two Cobras took formation on either wing and escorted the plane to the ground. Samuel was looking out of the window and the pilot saluted him around the time the wheels touched the ground and then peeled off. That was how you come back home in style. This was a photo opportunity for some ship's captain. These Marines wanted to get off the ship and get drunk and have sex with their girls, and not necessarily in that order.

Samantha was scanning the people on the top of the ship trying to see if she could recognize one of them as Samuel. She had not ever realized that these ships were so tall, and it was hard to make out any of the faces. The ship was moving painfully slow. Samuel's mother, father, and Carrie were all there with Samantha. Samantha's father and mother had come as well, but they were standing off to the side to give them space. Her father had spent some obscene amount of money buying a new professional quality digital video recorder for the event, so he was busy filming the ship pulling in and the helicopters. She thought it was nice that they had chosen to come. She felt like it was a sign that Samuel and her were meant to be together forever and everyone knew it.

The ship had gotten close enough now its shadow was nearly covering the whole pier. Samantha gave up on trying to see Samuel now, as she could not crane her neck high enough to see to the top. There were a few sailors running around the peer doing various things. Samantha gathered that this had something to do with getting the ship moored to the pier. She was getting anxious. This was taking a very long time. When all the families arrived, everyone was cheering and clapping. Everyone was excited and pointing out to the ships. Now, after what had to have been hours, there were babies crying and people murmuring. But suddenly this big door opened. A ramp slowly extended and then lowered to the pier. Samuel's mother started crying and hugged Samantha.

Samuel was in a near rage. He thought that there had to be around three hundred Marines and twice as many sailors crammed into these hallways. Bulkheads were claustrophobic to begin with. To make matters worse, the Marines did not want to step foot back on this ship, so they had taken all their sea bags and gear with them. Either to avoid an uncontrollable mutiny or out of genuine reverence it was agreed the Marines were getting off first. But that was not coming "first" enough, for Samuel. He was imagining smashing people's heads into the bulkheads repeatedly until his path was clear so he could be the very first one off that gangplank. Samuel knew that this was supposed to be a happy moment, he was getting to see Samantha again in mere moments. But this moment was adding an exclamation point to the anger he felt for the entire deployment.

Samantha went from excited to concerned as the first Marines started walking down the ramp. She could no easier tell them apart now than when they were all up on the top of the ship. They all wore their hats low covering or casting a shadow across their face. Samantha was worried she would not be able to tell which one was Samuel. Most of them were not as big as he was and many of them were taller or shorter, but in general they all looked the same. Suddenly she saw someone that she was pretty sure was him emerge from the belly of the ship onto the ramp. He was the right size. He was carrying a few bags. There was another guy next to him that was a little smaller. They were talking back and forth as they shuffled down the ramp. But then Samantha saw a tall younger looking black guy behind him tap him on the shoulder, say something, and laugh. That must have been Malone, his "adopted child." Samantha was sure it was him. He had made it almost all the way down the ramp. Samantha could not hold back anymore, she went racing towards him.

Malone tapped Samuel on the shoulder and said, "Hey Sergeant! Let me know when you have your twenty second birthday. We'll actually get to throw down for that one." Samuel laughed and said alright. He was already feeling better being off that cramped ship. Samuel looked up to see the helicopters doing another pass. Every infantryman will tell you nothing makes you feel safer than the sound of air on station. So, something that seemed to be another part of the dog and pony show, actually made him feel like he could relax a little bit. Samuel looked down to see, whom he immediately recognized as Samantha, running towards the gangplank. They had all been told to go past this big yellow line before they stopped to make sure that there was enough room for everyone that was getting off the ship to get off. And the families had apparently been told to stay on the other side. But Samantha being Samantha ran right past it.

Samantha also, being Samantha, was not going to get stopped by anyone. She was wearing a bright red dress. Samuel thought to himself that she looked so gorgeous, objectively, that someone could put her picture on the album cover of any female country music singer of the time and no one would know that she was not one. She was that kind of southern classic beauty anyway, but she looked particularly glamorous today. She was running towards the gang plank from the left, which is what side he was standing on. Samuel knew he had a few more feet until he was all the way off.

But Samuel decided that was too long, so he thought and said out loud, "Fuck it." Samuel threw his bags over the side of the gang plank onto the pier and vaulted over the railing. By the time Samuel recovered from his jump Samantha was jumping into his arms. They locked lips as he held her in his arms off the ground. Now he was home. He heard Van yell from the gangplank, "See Marines, stab bitches in the throat and your girl will look like that." Samuel's kiss turned to a smile. He did not care that she had heard about stabbing throats, he just thought to himself *No, when your girl looks like this, you'll stab bitches in the throat to get back home.*

Samantha heard all the Marines laughing from the ramp. She assumed it was about him jumping off of the ramp. But she did not care, she was whole again. She could not decide what she wanted to do more, kiss him or look at him. She missed everything about him. She wanted his taste, his touch, his smell, and the view of him. She would stop kissing long enough to look at him and smile and then go right back to kissing him. America had a slight obsession with military homecomings. The videos of them had a wide-ranging viewership on the internet and with early morning "feel good" news shows. If anyone needed to smile and shed a happy tear those were always a safe bet to watch. But Samantha thought to herself that those still did not hold a candle to the feeling of being a part of one. There was a torrent of feelings. The best comparison she could think of was if someone had been told that the love of their life had a terminal illness. The closest that the person could get to their room was the lobby of the hospital. And after months of waiting to hear if they had succumbed to their illness, the patient just stepped out of the elevator healthy and smiling. If one could imagine the feeling of the person in that waiting room, they might be able to feel what it was like to have Samuel's arms around her now.

To Samantha's disappointment Samuel put her down as he said, "Johnathan."

Samantha turned slowly to see her father with a camera up in front of his face filming them, she wondered how long he had been there. Her mother was next to him with a camera taking pictures. Samantha thought back to the girls suggesting that she get a professional photographer for the homecoming and thought that it was definitely not necessary as she had two thoroughly embarrassing parents to do that.

"I got the whole thing." her father said proudly, "the jump, the first kiss, everything."

"Thanks," Samantha said, annoyed.

Her mother made them pose for a few pictures. Then Samuel finally got to hug his family and say hello. Samantha's mother took pictures of them together too, but Samuel never let go of Samantha. In every picture Samantha was on one arm. Samantha gathered that he was no sooner ready to let go of her than she was to let him.

Finally, Samuel said, "Let's get the hell off this pier."

He went to pick up his bags, but Samantha was not letting go of his hand.

He looked at her and said, "I have to grab the bags baby."

Samantha looked at him with a sweet and innocent smile and said, "No. I'm not letting go of your hand."

Samantha's father, Johnathan, said, "I'll grab them," as he picked one up.

He got one about half-way up when he said, "Jesus Christ!"

Samuel picked one up with his free hand. His father grabbed the other bag and they all made their way out to the vehicles. Samuel learned that the families had gotten condos on the beach in South Carolina. One for Samuel's family, one for Samantha's family, and one for Samantha and him. Samuel considered this the best news he had ever heard. It was if they knew that Samuel and Samantha were going to need some privacy.

"Let's head there now." He ordered.

Everyone but Samantha seemed to not understand what the rush was. They all wanted to take him to "get real food" or "grab a drink." Samuel and Samantha had business to attend to, they both knew it, but their families seemed clueless to the fact. Even so, the couple dutifully but grudgingly went with the families to eat and drink a few. They partook in the toasts to Samuel being home silently waiting and hoping for the moment that they could make this reunion "official" between them.

It was the first time since she had jumped into his arms that Samuel was not touching Samantha. But they had decided that it might be too obvious if they walked back to the table holding hands. Samuel did not feel guilty or ashamed that they had sex in the bathroom. Samuel did not like that he could not lay next to her as was their custom afterwards, and he felt bad that he was now not touching her at all. But the families may have had the slightest inclination that their relationship was going to be physical later that night, but his mother would be just as disturbed by her son having sex in the public bathroom of a restaurant as her father would be disturbed by her doing so. Samantha finally came walking back to the table. Samuel looked into her eyes and they shared a smile. Samantha sat down with him and put her hand on his inner thigh. Samantha's mother was looking at him as if she knew their secret.

Samuel leaned over and whispered, "I thought the point was for us to not be obvious."

Samantha kissed him and said, "oops."

Samuel felt like they had picked up right where they left off, but only more so. They were madly in love with each other, both of their families knew it, and now the future was bright and certain.

Samantha did not feel dirty about their bathroom rendezvous, she wanted it badly. But she never thought that their sex life would include that. Samuel was more ferocious than he'd ever been. The shy boy had entirely given way to a confident man that knew exactly what he wanted. He was still sweet and passionate and gentle with her though. Samuel had not lost all his best qualities. His shyness had been a cute quality, his confidence now was sexy, and a little bit dangerous. Samantha was looking into his eyes almost ignoring everyone else at the table. She bit her lip to tell him she had far from had her desires satisfied. Then she watched the devilish smile fade from his face. Samantha looked behind her to see a little girl with dark hair and big brown eyes running from her mother. She might have been about three years old.

"Sam." Samuel heard Samantha call to him. Samuel shook his head to snap out of it. Samantha had her hand on his face.

"What's wrong?" Samantha said softly.

Samuel had zoned out entirely. The laughing and playing little girl had taken him back. Samuel had thought that if he could get through the sight and sound and smell of Willy burning alive in the truck on his first deployment, nothing from his second deployment would bother him. But the little girl haunted him. She had since that day. Something about being there next to her for as long as he was. It gave his brain too long to contemplate her fate. The loss of her future. The death of her innocence; somehow Samuel felt like his innocence was tied to that little girl's. The war had taken them both and smashed them. Samuel got this sense of dread that anytime he started to get too happy she was going to show back up to remind him that she was dead and he wasn't.

"Was it something about the little girl?" Samantha said softly.

Samuel breathed a sigh of relief that there was actually a little girl that had just run by. He was not sure that there was.

Samuel nodded and softly replied, "She just looked familiar is all."

How long would it take before children remind him of the living and not the dead again? Or was this just the reality for Samuel now? Had his innocence become another casualty of war? It was mortally wounded the first tour, utterly murdered the second. Samuel got a cold chill as he thought that there was no going back to the boy from before, he had to remember that little girl forever. It was not even just for him to want to forget. That girl deserved to have a witness.

CHAPTER 13 YUT!

Samantha and Samuel made it to their condo in complete and total ecstasy. Samantha felt as though all the pain and heartache had been a penance to purify her soul for this time in her life. She was certain no one had ever loved anyone more than she loved Samuel. All distractions, from him and how much she loved him, had been purged from her life. School stress, young adult drama, the stress of trying to get ready for medical school, and any other stress seemed trivial. The love of her life was with her and she was never going to let him go again. Samantha pitied women who she knew would go their whole life and never experience a day as in love as they would be forever. She knew how easy it was for the world to cloud someone's vision of what was important in life. But Samantha vowed to herself to never take her eyes off what was most important to her, Samuel.

Samuel and Samantha finally stopped kissing long enough for her to show him the gift Mac had sent. It was the largest bottle of Crown Royal he had ever seen.

It had a note attached: "Didn't want to get in the way of y'all populating the world with beautiful people. Besides I'm a college boy now. Stay gold Pony Boy."

Samuel smiled and told Samantha, "So Mac is at Ole Miss. Never thought I'd see the day."

Samantha giggled and said, "He says he's going to be a P.E. teacher."

Samuel laughed and said, "I can imagine him hitting kids in the face with a dodgeball easy enough."

Samantha hugged him and said, "Let's go watch the sunset on the beach."

Samuel hated the idea of sand. He despised sand. If he never felt a speck of sand again in his life it would be too soon.

"Baby, we're on the east coast. We aren't going to see the sun go down on the water."

Samantha stuck her lip out imitating a sad child. Samuel thought to himself that if there was a single person in the world that could get him in the sand again it was her. He had done his duty to his country, twice now. His life was now devoted to Samantha. His duty was to do anything that would make her happy.

"Let's go." Samuel said with a smile as he picked up the bottle of Crown.

Samantha found a romantic spot for them to sit. Samantha noticed Samuel was not as spry as he had once been. As he sat down there were a lot of pops and cracks coming from his body.

"Old man," Samantha said to him laughing.

"Yep." Samuel replied as he started slipping his shoes off.

Samantha was in absolute horror when he got his socks off. She had nearly worshipped every part of Samuel's body, but now his feet were revolting. The nails that were not missing completely were black or brown. Each foot was nearly one giant callus and his right foot had a huge knot on the left side on the ball of his foot.

"Someone needs a pedicure." Samantha said.

"Not a chance," Samuel said laughing as he opened the bottle of whiskey.

Samantha sarcastically said, "What too tough to get a pedicure?"

Samuel looked at her and smiled as he said, "The only person allowed to touch me is you."

Samantha laughed and said, "Well alright then no pedicure, because I'm not touching those things."

Samuel smiled at her and then turned the bottle up. He was guzzling the whiskey. Samantha's mouth opened wider and wider as she waited for him to stop.

"Jesus baby." Samantha said to him.

Samuel stopped and held the bottle to offer her some.

"One of us needs to be sober enough to get back into the room." Samantha chuckled.

"Sorry, I needed that." Samuel said.

Samantha put her arms around his arm and said, "I'm so glad you're home."

Samuel thought about that word, home. Torres had said Samuel's home was Iraq. He had honestly probably walked more miles in that country than his own. He had not seen most of the United States, and he had fought in most corners of Iraq. He had only been driving for about two years when he left the states, he had spent about that much time in Iraq. Was that his home? What made a place home?

Samuel looked down at Samantha. If home was where you felt like you belonged, then home was here with her.

"I'll never be able to explain to you how much I love you Sam." Samuel said to her, "After all that I've done and all that I've seen, to become what I have become, you're the only thing that makes any sense to me."

Samantha looked up at him with stars in her eyes. Samuel felt like she did not know that was not just some line.

"You did not become anything Sam, you did what you had to do, but that is not who you are." Samantha said.

Samuel did not believe that. The boy was dead, he had become something. Something different. He was not malevolent but he was not like everyone else anymore.

"When you talk to our grandchildren about it, they will know what I know. You are the greatest man who has ever lived." Samantha added.

Samuel smiled as he caught that *our*. The thought of their future together finally did not seem like a fever dream, it was okay to think about forever.

"I will spend the rest of my life reminding you that you are the greatest man who has ever lived." Samantha added.

She saw a smirk come to Samuel's face as he took a pull from the whiskey bottle.

Then he looked at her and said, "Was that a marriage proposal?"

To Samantha the two of them spending the rest of their lives together was a foregone conclusion. They were meant to be together. She knew that Samuel was made for her.

"Would you say 'yes' if it was?" She said sweetly.

Samuel chuckled and said, "Not without a ring."

Samantha scoffed and rolled her eyes while she patted him on the bicep.

"And it better be a big one, I ain't some cheap hussy." Samuel added.

Samantha pushed Samuel into the sand and crawled on top of him. She was looking into his eyes. They were absolutely made for each other she thought.

"Hey Sam." she said softly.

"Hey Sam." He said back.

As they kissed, Samantha thought that *this* was their wedding night. A private beach wedding at sunset they had exchanged their simple vows, and they kissed as man and wife, with the stars, slowly taking their place in the sky, as the witnesses.

Samuel had resolved after their night on the beach that he was going to propose to Samantha before he went back to the fleet. The timing would be prodigious. In about a year he would be a free man. Free to spend the rest of his life with the woman he loved. Samantha may have been right, he may not have transformed into a monster. Or, he might have been right. He might have been consumed by the demon that he had unleashed so often to keep himself alive. But the one thing that was certain he was going to marry Samantha and spend the rest of his life paying her back for sticking with him through it all. Loving her was an easy task, and spoiling her with affection came so naturally. It did not matter to him who was in control the demon or the man, he would be able to be a great husband for her.

Samuel had followed the proper protocols. He met with Samantha's mother and father in a clandestine operation after coming up with some reason to leave her alone while in the condo. And he asked for their blessing. They both gave their emphatic support and embraced him as a son. Then Samuel told his parents who also gave their blessing. The only question any of them had was when. Samuel did not have a great answer for that. He had not really thought about it until their night together on the beach when Samantha had referred to their grandchildren.

Samuel had settled on the proposal happening back *home.* In truth Oxford had become their new home. Samuel had not even gone back home yet. But he knew women thought about things like getting proposed to, and the number one rule was to make it special. So, he decided that he was going to take her to the place that made the most sense, the place where everything started for them; he was going to take her to the old frozen yogurt store and propose over a pepperoni pizza from Luigi's. He had to wait for finals to be done. Samantha had always been brilliant and a good student. He hated that he seemed to be a big distraction from her schoolwork, so he decided that he would not add another distraction by proposing and filling her head with a million new thoughts when she needed to focus on finishing the semester. But the time was rapidly approaching.

Samuel had told Samantha that they were going back home for a special date to celebrate her finishing the semester. Samantha thought that it was odd that he wanted to celebrate such a mundane achievement. But he had become even more of a romantic than he had been before, even though that seemed impossible. Samantha counted that as one of the good changes though. Samuel had changed a lot. She would wake up covered in cold sweat most nights. Samuel's cold sweat. Sometimes he would jerk awake and scare both of them half to death. It was as though he was home, but his unconscious was not home. When he fell asleep, he was still fighting the war. Samantha considered that the price of war, and she did not know if it would ever change, but she thought it was such a small price for her to pay. She knew her sleepless nights were not as bad as his. She figured he was the one reliving his hell every night.

The other change that was much more unsettling to Samantha, was that Samuel seemed to hate children. This was extremely strange to her. Samuel had told her previously that after his first deployment he felt safer around children. He had explained that on his first deployment if they were moving through an area and there were no children around that they could count on a bomb or ambush coming up soon. But now if they went out to a restaurant and there were children sitting around them, he just stared at them with a scowl on his face. Samantha was uncomfortable with asking him about it. She figured he would talk about it when he was ready. But she had gone to Mac about it. Mac said he could not get Samuel to open up about it. Mac said if he had to guess, they had used a kid as a suicide bomber or something. He had heard of that happening and that it was probably enough to make any man suspicious of children afterwards. Samantha thought that she could understand that. There would probably not be anything more horrific than seeing a child blow up, but it had to be even worse if that child was used as a weapon against you and your friends.

Samuel was disappointed to see that the yogurt store had closed. He thought his whole plan had been ruined. But Samantha lit up when she saw where he had taken her.

"You are so sweet." She said nearly tearing up at the gesture.

So, Samuel knew that this was already perfect.

"Well we'll have to eat in the parking lot." Samuel said laughing at the luck.

Samantha kissed him sweetly.

"Just pretend like we're inside." He added.

They got out of the car and Samuel picked Samantha up and sat her on the hood of his car.

"Do I need to pretend to be cleaning a counter for full effect?" She asked him with a smile on her face.

"That's a really good idea, actually." Samuel said laughing. Samuel ran off to Luigi's to pick up the pizza and get everything ready.

Samantha saw Samuel walking holding a pizza box with a huge smile on his face. He was beaming with excitement and Samantha thought how the whole display was incredibly cute. Samantha pretended to be wiping down an imaginary counter. Samuel laughed as he closed the distance between them.

"Hey Sam." he said.

"Hey Sam" she replied.

Samuel sat the pizza box on the hood of the car next to her. Samuel turned the box so that the lid was facing her. Like he had always done when he brought her pizza in their youth, it was his way of making sure that she got the first piece. It was another subtle gentlemanly habit of his. Samantha smiled big at him. Samantha opened the box and saw the pepperonis were in the shape of a heart.

"Awe!" Samantha said, throwing her head back. It was the sweetest of all of his romantic gestures to date.

When Samantha looked back Samuel was down on one knee. Samantha suddenly felt overwhelmed. Was this really happening? Was he really proposing?

"Well?" Samuel said.

Samantha popped off the car and covered her mouth. Suddenly she felt a little confused, she looked around and did not see a ring. She thought for a moment this was Samuel's funny way of poking at her beachside "proposal" from earlier.

"What, so you have to get a ring, but I don't," Samantha said laughing.

Samuel's face went blank as he said, "Sam, the pizza."

Samantha looked back to the box that was mostly closed. Samantha had not opened the box all the way as she had thrown her head back at the adorableness of the heart on the pizza.

"The pizza is the ring?" Samantha said.

Samuel's face went blank again as he reached up with one hand and opened the box. Samantha saw the ring box in the center of the heart as

Samuel said, "The ring is in the pizza!"

Samantha picked up the ring box and stared at the ring for a moment. Samuel loved that it did not work out exactly as he had planned. He thought it was a great metaphor for how their relationship had been up to this point. They had had a few hiccups, but it was still perfect. Samuel reached up and took the box out of her hand and took the ring out.

Samuel slipped the ring on Samantha's finger and said, "Samantha Wallace, will you marry me, you goofball?"

Samantha looked down at the ring and then looked back at him and then back at the ring. There were a few short moments of silence.

Samuel finally said, "Uhh, Sam."

"Yes?" She said. And then as if she had snapped out of some strange trance she shouted "Yes!"

Samantha almost fell on the ground as she bent over to throw her arms around Samuel. Samuel stood up and picked her up off the ground. They kissed and Samuel wondered if there would ever be another moment in his life that would top this one.

As Samuel put Samantha back on the ground she looked back and saw that the entire staff from Luigi's and what appeared to be a few random customers had made their way out to the parking lot and were clapping for them. Samantha was in tears, the happiest tears she had ever cried. Samantha never had any doubt that they were going to be together, but it was official. And that was something no one could ever take from her.

Samantha kissed Samuel again and said, "This is the best day of my life."

Samuel took her hand and started pulling her to the car as he said, "It's not over yet. It's going to get better." Samantha got confused as she thought how it could get better.

"Wait!" She exclaimed. Samuel stopped in his tracks and looked at her with concern. "Are we not going to eat the pizza?" She said.

Samuel laughed and grabbed the box off the hood of the car.

Samuel was floating he was so happy. He stuffed his new bride to be in the car and handed her the pizza box as he walked back around to the driver seat. They headed to his parents' house. Samantha figured out where they were going rather quickly. So, they decided to play a prank on everyone when they got there. So, Samuel went in first and pretended that she had said no. Samantha made her dramatic entrance soon afterwards before the prank got out of hand. Her father was upset that he had cut the camera off before she walked in, but to Samuel and Samantha getting to prank both of their families was well worth not capturing the moment they announced that they were officially engaged to be married. Samuel resolved that this was the new beginning to a new chapter in his life, full of laughs and love and general mischief with the love of his life. They drank champagne while Samantha showed off her ring. Lucy and Mac made jokes about how hard it was to keep it secret for as long as they had.

Carrie was telling Samantha how excited she was to have a sister. Samantha was excited as well she had never had a sister either. Carrie was a sweet enough girl, but Samantha was ready to go. She wanted Samuel so badly. But Samuel was being the gracious man he was, saying his thank yous, and bragging on his future wife. If anything, that made Samantha want him even more. Samuel had always loved her, but now she was certain that there was never a person more in love than she was. She adored everything about him. He was sweet, thoughtful, strong, funny, intelligent, and sexy. Samantha did not care if it was rude to everyone else, she wanted to go.

"You know what we haven't done as fiancés yet?" She said to Samuel. He looked at her as if reading her mind.

He got a sly grin on his face and said, "What's that?"

Carrie was looking at them with a face of disgust as if she was about to hear something she did not want to think about.

Samantha said, "Watch TV."

Samuel laughed and said, "I do love watching TV." Carrie's face went from disgust to confusion as she studied the two of them.

"Do you think it's different as engaged people?" Samuel asked.

"Only one way to find out." Samantha said smiling at Samuel.

As Samuel loaded his bags into the car to return to the fleet, he did not feel as full of dread as he had before. He was about a year away from being done. Samantha had one school year left and she would be graduating. The two lovers had finally reached a good, sensible place. Samantha was not entertaining ideas of following him out to the Carolinas anymore. They had set a date for the next summer. Samuel was going to finish up his obligation and they would be together forever. Samuel gave Samantha a bittersweet goodbye and he was on his way to Lejeune. For the first time in his career he was taking a car to base. He thought it would be easier to drive back when the time came where he could get leave to come help with the wedding planning.

When Samuel got back, he found out that he was going back to his old battalion. Samuel thought it was a fitting way to end his career. He had "grown up" with a lot of those guys. It was his Marine Corps home. He loved most of those guys more than brothers. He had made a lot of lifelong friends in the battalion he had deployed with the second time but going back to his first battalion would be like a homecoming. And "like a homecoming" was exactly what it was like. Samuel was meeting new joins that rushed to meet the legend. Old comrades were slapping him on the back and reminiscing about the old days.

The word that was on everyone's tongue though was Afghanistan. Samuel had felt pretty stupid for his earlier volunteering as his battalion had not deployed at all while he was gone. Now they were slated for Afghanistan and had just gotten the warning order. It was a couple months out, and Samuel was going to hit his end of active service before the tour would end. Earlier in Iraq guys had their contracts involuntarily extended, it was called stop loss. But that was like an ancient tradition. No one knew of a recent account of that happening. That did not stop the Corps from trying to get him to stay though. Before Samuel even made it out of the battalion headquarters office the career planner was harassing him about reenlisting. The bonus was seventy thousand dollars. That was as high as anyone could remember it being. But Samuel had a life planned now, the money would not change his mind.

Samuel was excited to check in with the executive officer of his company. The executive officer had been his platoon commander on his first deployment. He was just a boot second lieutenant that was green behind the ears at that time. Samuel was fond of him.

"Sir, Sergeant Parker reporting as ordered, Sir." Samuel announced.

"Jesus Parker," the executive officer said, "stop getting medals some of us are still trying to catch up to your first deployment."

Samuel was in his service uniform as the regulation dictated and his ribbons were on full display. Samuel was proud of his "stack." He had been decorated again for his second deployment and was very highly decorated for someone with his time in.

"Well sir," Samuel said smirking, "some of us have to work for a living."

The XO stuck his hand out and shook Samuel's hand.

"Yeah," He said, "but there are very few who do work like you."

Samuel smiled and sat down. Samuel knew that this was going to be two old friends catching up for a while.

"We heard about your exploits all the way back here." The XO continued, "You represented the battalion well. When I heard Pony Boy got a knife kill I was not surprised. If Mac wouldn't have been so adamant that everyone call you Pony Boy, I think 'god of death' would have been all anyone called you."

Samuel smiled reflecting that he had actually missed being called Pony Boy.

Samuel said, "Mac says 'hi' by the way sir."

The XO laughed and said, "I'm sure he had a lot more to say than 'hi.'"

Samuel and the XO shared a smile.

"What's he up to?" The XO asked.

"Studying to be a P.E. teacher." Samuel laughed.

"Oh Jesus." The XO said as they both shared a laugh.

"And dating my fiancé's roommate." Samuel added.

The XO nodded his head and said, "Congratulations."

"Thank you, sir." Samuel replied.

"I'm sure she's outrageously beautiful," the XO added while packing a tin of tobacco.

"She is." Samuel said smiling.

The XO and Samuel both put a pinch of tobacco in their mouth. "Makes sense he'd be dating her roommate," The XO said as he spit into a bottle on his desk, "You two were always attached at the hip."

Samuel just smiled, reflecting on the old times.

"Well, I'm glad you're back we have a lot of boots that need to get schooled up before we deploy." The XO said.

"Look forward to training them," Samuel said and then smiled and added, "and maybe hazing them a little bit when you and your cadre aren't looking."

The XO smiled and said, "God knows most of them could use it. But of course, the staff does not condone that type of behavior."

Samuel noticed that his face went from a smile to a stern look as he said, "We're going to need your experience when we get over there."

Samuel chuckled as he figured there was another sales pitch coming his way.

"Well sir," Samuel said, "as much as I would love to show these kids why my nickname was almost the god of death, I'll be hitting my EAS before y'all get back."

"You aren't taking the money," The XO said with a blank look on his face, "I wish I had it like you have it." The XO started laughing. "Seventy grand tax free that's a lot of money."

"It's not about the money, sir." Samuel said, "I have a life to get back to."

"What life Parker?" the XO said, "You were built to end lives."

Samuel forced a smirk, "Sir, I was third in my graduating class. I'm ready to go on to being good at something else."

The XO's face twisted and he looked down at his desk with a face of shame, "That's not surprising. You being brilliant is just one other thing you're better at than the rest of us." Finally, the XO looked back up at him and said with a stern look, "You might want to reconsider taking the money."

Samuel got the impression he was not going to like what he was about to hear.

"Sam," He started.

Officers called each other by their first names sometimes. Men deployed called each other by their first names sometimes. But officers almost never called enlisted men by their first names, especially in the infantry community.

The XO continued with a somber look on his face, "This is straight from division. The 03 community is stretched too thin. All of you guys that are going to hit EAS halfway or more through the deployment are going."

Samuel felt his knuckles get white as he said, "They are going to stop loss me on a third deployment."

The XO nodded and hung his head. "There's no guy I'd rather this not happen to. You've earned the right to do whatever the fuck you want."

The XO could not even look at Samuel in the face.

Samuel took a long breath and closed his eyes. That was his "get ready to kill a lot of people" ritual. For a moment he was not sure he would be able to stop himself from doing that.

"Parker," The XO said, "We just don't have the experienced NCOs. These young Marines need guys like you. You might be the difference between them all coming home or not."

Samuel sighed. That was a low blow. Samuel loved the Marines. He would lay down his life for any of them, but he was ready to start his life with the one person that mattered. Samuel did not reply. He had nothing to say and he felt like he was going to explode.

"I'm going to feel safer with you there," The XO said, "Hell, remember that woman I was dating when we were in Iraq."

Samuel did not respond he just stared at him.

He continued, "Well she's my wife now. She knows all about you. I told her. She remembers your name and everything. Actually, I'm glad you never met her she probably would have married you instead of me."

The man looked like he was about to have a nervous breakdown trying to keep Samuel from exploding. Samuel was certain his face had the look of the man with murder on his mind.

The XO continued, "I told her you were going with us. She's glad you're going. She says it makes her feel better about it. That's the kind of presence you bring to this fight."

Samuel looked at him for a moment and then said, "How do you think it's going to make my fiancé feel when I tell her?"

Samuel did not even bother waiting or asking to be dismissed, he just stood up and walked out of the office, full of rage.

CHAPTER 14 "I LOOKED AND BEHOLD A PALE HORSE..."

Samantha hung up the phone exasperated. It was the first time in her life that she wished she was a man. If she had Samuel's physicality, she would find the person responsible for this outrage and strangle the life out of them. But the real frustration was she did not know *who* to be mad at. Samuel had not done this. Samantha was certain that the maddest she had ever heard him was while he was telling her about *them* making him go on a third deployment. Who were *they?* The Corps? Who was the Corps? Samantha only really knew Samuel and Mac. Who was the Corps if not the gracious and noble men like them that made it up? Was it the generals in the Pentagon? Were they responsible? Had they never been like Samuel? Had they not been noble youth once before? Had their wives never faced injustices like this?

Or maybe this is how the military was. Everyone that had ever been remotely associated with the military had been shit on, so when it came time to shit on a whole new generation no one batted an eye. It was completely unjust.

Samantha had always been a wholesome all-American girl. Samantha stood for the anthem, she said the pledge, she was engaged to be married to one of the nation's valiant defenders, a true war hero. And her reward for her patriotism was to be subjected to extra time as a fiancé. They were robbing her of days of happiness with Samuel. That crime was unforgivable. And how had this happened? Samuel had done more than his share. He could not leave to be with her because of a contract he signed as a young boy. But now *they* were changing the terms of the contract. They were not going to be satisfied until they used him up and broke him completely. She held the entire system responsible. She had always felt like a sweet person. She cared for everyone, and never had an ounce of contempt in her heart, not even for people that had wronged her. But she hated the whole system now.

Even now the politicians were celebrating that they had started the withdrawal from Iraq. They touted their achievement as some great peacemakers. But they were liars as far as she was concerned, every single one of them. She was disgusted with her naive faith that she had ever said the words, "with liberty and justice for all." Yeah, unless you decided to go the extra mile and swear an oath to the nation, then you were fodder for a foreign war, and your family was destined to be weeping widows and have their hearts ground to powder. Samantha felt guilty but she hoped Samuel used their rage and ended this war single handedly. If he had the strength left she wanted him to end this war and leave such a path of total destruction that the whole world would be at peace for a thousand years as everyone was too afraid another wronged lover would do what he did.

Samuel had no more time for anyone's bullshit. He wore his discontent like a badge of honor. He prepared for the coming war with fervor like a man crazed with bloodlust. The new Marines feared him. He ran them ragged. They all felt like he was pain incarnate. He demanded that they achieve the impossible. Training was all day every day. His squad may have been green, but they were going to be the fittest, most well drilled Marines to have ever donned the uniform. If he caught a man smiling, the next day's training would be that much more intense. There was no room for happiness. Everyone would be just as pissed off as him.

Samuel had only one thought to console him. They were going to the place this really started. He enlisted to avenge 9/11. To this point the closest he had gotten was to provide some Jihadists with the opportunity to find out if their god was real. Now they would get to fight the Taliban. There would be no finding God for them. He was bringing the demon, and he was training a whole company of men to unleash their demons too. They would be the nightmare. When they got done with them, men would talk about what they did there for centuries. He was bringing an apocalypse with him and there would be no shelter from them, there would be no quarter given.

Samuel basked in the irony. Today was his twenty-second birthday. He was not in Iraq as he had vowed. He was in Afghanistan. Samuel's company was completing a left seat right seat exercise. Basically, the outgoing unit was slowly handing over control of the missions in their area of operation to his unit, the incoming unit. Samuel walked up to the command post. The outgoing company commander was talking to his company commander making plans for the day.

"Good morning, gentlemen." Samuel greeted.

They both looked at Samuel and nodded.

His company commander said, "Can I help you with something, Sergeant?"

"Yes, Sir," Samuel said, "If there are some squads going out today, I'd really like to get in with one."

Samuel was asking to go out with one of the squads from the outgoing unit. That is part of "left seat right seat." The leadership of the incoming unit starts going out with the guys from the outgoing unit to learn the ropes.

"He's eager." The outgoing company commander said.

"You have no idea," Samuel's company commander replied, "I'm sure we can squeeze you in somewhere, Parker."

Samuel nodded but he did not leave.

"Something else?" his company commander asked.

Samuel looked past him to the outgoing commander, "If there's a squad that's going to get into some shit, I'd prefer to go out with them."

The outgoing commander got a dumbfounded look on his face.

He looked at Samuel's commander and asked, "Is he fucking serious?"

Samuel's CO just nodded.

"You're going to fit right in here," the man said, "but you'll get your chance to get that combat action ribbon I promise."

Samuel's commanding officer burst out laughing and began murmuring to the other commander. The outgoing commander's eyes got wide.

"If it's all the same Sir," Samuel said, "I'd consider it a birthday present."

Samuel had spent his last two birthdays in a warzone, and the one before that at the School of Infantry learning to kill. It had all but become a tradition for him to sacrifice enemy lives on his birthday. He was eager to get into a gunfight.

"Hell yeah motivator," the outgoing commander replied, "you make me sad I'm even leaving. Gung-ho Marines like you give me a hard on. I'll look around and try to guess where a firefight will break out."

Gung-ho, is what they called it. Tenacious, is how they would write about it if they were venerating his exploits in some hallowed history or award write up. Samuel knew the truth. He was mad. He did not even try to pretend there was anything left of the boy, he embraced the demon fully. The demon was always hungry for fresh meat.

"Thank you, gentlemen." Samuel said taking his leave.

To say that Afghanistan was a totally different war seemed obvious. But the difference could not be overstated. The terrain was entirely different. Gone was the torturous desert and the hellish urban terrain. Afghanistan was craggy peaks that reminded Samuel of some Tolkienesque description of the mountains of Mordor. These mountains faded into foreboding forested hills. Below that were valleys that could be covered in tall grass or nearly devoid of all vegetation, there was no in between. The only thing all of this terrain had in common is the enemy knew how to fight in it better than any of them. Samuel got his birthday firefight. It was short lived, but it happened. It did not quench his thirst though. Samuel needed more, and more is what he got throughout this deployment.

Samuel was proud of his men. He may have seethed with hatred for the war, the Corps, and the enemy, but he had trained up the finest group of warfighters the world had ever seen. Each one of them he had molded in his image and he loved them all like sons. And they looked to him like a father. They may have hated him back in Lejeune and 29 Palms, but here he was the captain of the ship. His squad was treated like a crack force. The mission was easy. The fighting season had started. The Afghani farmers traded in plows for AK's and RPGs and took to the hills and rock faces. Samuel respected that they were looking for a fight. But anytime the company was certain there was going to be a fight, they sent Sam's squad in first. And his men adored him as the winner of this reverence for their battle prowess.

Every few days they would get into a firefight. These firefights could last for hours. Eventually, every time they would kill or rout the enemy, to the last man. That was the only thing that was certain. It would seem to be to the last man. Samuel was learning that and many other lessons as well. They had more assets here. In Iraq someone damn near needed a presidential order to get indirect fire support. Here they sent artillerymen out with them to act like salesmen. One day the "cannon cocker" that was patrolling with his squad came running up to him with a big smile in the middle of a far ambush.

"Hey Parker," the man said, "You ever seen what a variable time fuze can do to enemy foot mobiles in the open like that."

Samuel smiled and shook his head.

"You want to see pink mist?" the man asked.

Samuel nodded. He did want to see that. He did not know why. The demon loved that kind of shit though. Samuel Parker would have found it a gruesome display, Sergeant Parker thought it sounded awesome. When the rounds fell Samuel made it a point to watch. Even though it exposed him a little. He had to watch.

Another day Samuel's squad was acting as the quick reaction force, QRF. He was hanging out in the command post listening to the radio traffic. A platoon in another company was in a pretty decent gun battle a few kilometers away. Samuel heard battalion clear close air support to hit the enemy up in the hills. Samuel went running out of the CP to gather his squad so they could watch. He got some binoculars and ran up to the top of a tower that was on the east side of their patrol base. All the Marines got up to the tower and looked out to the horizon. He heard the screaming of a jet engine echoing in the sky and got a smile on his face. Suddenly the sound shifted to a growl, Samuel imagined this is what a dragon would sound like right before it blew fire on some unsuspecting castle. That's what was about to happen anyway. The jet was nothing but a speck in the sky. Samuel suddenly saw the speck dive, and then peel off. There was a loud roar in the atmosphere as the jet kicked on the thrusters and started speeding away. Samuel saw the huge flash. Then he heard the loud boom. The earth began to tremble. That was miles off, miles and miles. Samuel was jealous he was not closer. In Iraq an explosion like that meant some vehicle full of Americans had been blown up. He wanted to be close enough to really enjoy the force of the destruction being wrought on the enemy, since he was not having to feel dread thinking about it being his allies on the receiving end of it. All the Marines cheered loudly. But then it was like Deja vu. The scream, the growl, the dive, the roar and the earth trembled.

This was the might of the American war machine on campaign. The first bomb had to have killed all of them. The second bomb was an exclamation point. That was just to show everyone in the region that they could do this over and over. But then Samuel heard the sound of two Super Cobra attack helicopters coming in at speed, full tilt. They roared overhead. Samuel started to feel angry. Not at the overkill. He was angry that all this destruction was not his doing. He was beginning to see his men and him were not the only predators on this savanna. They were lions, but there were all sorts of other violent hunters out there.

Samuel heard the rockets start with a loud SWISHHHH. Then each one in rapid succession echoed in the air as they exploded on the mountainside. The sound was like cloth furling in the wind. But this blanket flapping in the air must have sounded like more doom to the enemy. Samuel felt a scowl come to his face as he thought that the enemy might be more afraid of the air power than they were of him. Samuel did not even bother to watch the rest of the barrage. He climbed down and walked away.

Samuel's squad would spend the nights together as soldiers have for thousands of years. The campaign campfires were one of the romantic parts of war that had not lost any part of its luster. Granted there were no actual campfires, but the concept was the same. They were living a thoroughly expeditionary life. Their patrol base was earthen palisades and sandbags lined with plywood. Samuel was not sure if it was just because he had completely lost control of himself or if it was just that much better than Iraq, but he loved this war. He could not help it. He wanted to hate this war. It took him from the love of his life. He could not deny that he was back in harm's way. Maybe more so. The IEDs were still there and the ambushes were frequent. He woke up at least a few nights a week to the sounds of mortar alarms and sometimes to explosions relatively close to the base, but this felt like the war he was built for.

His generation might have been spoiled little kids before. This crop that was here with him now had almost entirely grown up in a post 9/11 world. And they were led by battle hardened veterans. The NCOs of the United States military of this time were the most experienced well-trained professional warfighters, perhaps, that the world had ever seen. Their being alive to be here now was proof that they were undefeated. These men, like Samuel, had been in more gunfights than anyone since Vietnam. And these kids here now had been the ones that joined long after the reality of modern warfare was common knowledge. Samuel was not home, but the demon was, and the demon was driving the bus. Samuel hoped he could rest control when the fighting was done.

Samantha heard a knock on the apartment door. It was late. She looked through the peephole and saw two uniformed police officers. Her heart filled with dread. She felt like she was going to hyperventilate as she slowly opened the door.

"Good evening ma'am," the officer started, "I'm Officer Vonlin and this is my partner Officer Wilkins."

Samantha could not catch her breath to respond. She was preparing herself for news about Samuel, but she could not face the reality.

"We had some questions about your neighbors upstairs," Officer Vonlin said.

"Are you serious?" Samantha said quietly.

The officer got a strange look on his face as he said, "Yes, ma'am. We are investigating a domestic that occurred tonight."

Samantha slammed her fist against the door as she yelled, "Are you fucking kidding me?"

The officer got a dirty look on his face as he started to say, "Ma'am I'm going to need you to calm-"

"No," Samantha yelled, "Don't you tell me to calm down." Samantha began crying as she said, "You scared the shit out of me." There was a long silence and she added, "My fiance is in Afghanistan and I thought you were here giving me bad news."

There was another long silence.

The officers looked at each other and finally Officer Vonlin said, "Ma'am I'm real sorry. I can promise if something happens to him there, it won't be us that comes to talk to you."

Samantha chuckled in her tears, "I should know that."

"Is this his first deployment?" Officer Wilkins asked.

"Third." She replied.

"Army?" Officer Vonlin asked.

"Marines," Samantha replied as she wiped the tears off of her face. "I'm sorry guys. They argue all the time" Samantha pointed towards the ceiling to let the officers know who she was referring to. "The truth is," Samantha continued, "I'm always distracted, and I just drown them out. I can't really tell you much."

The officers did not seem to care much about that anymore. They looked at each other and then Officer Wilkins started getting something out of his wallet.

"Ma'am," Officer Vonlin said, "Our wives always tell us how much they hate getting knocks at the door at night. I'm not going to pretend like it's the same thing because at least we see them at the end of our shift. But we get it."

Wilkins handed her a card with two numbers handwritten on it.

"Between the two of us one of us is always in this area at night," Officer Wilkins said, "I don't know what we could possibly do to make it better for you. But if you hear something go bump in the night, or you drink too much and need a ride, or hell, even if you just need some furniture moved don't hesitate to call one of us."

Samantha looked at them and back at the card. It was a nice gesture.

"I know it seems to help them to spend time together," Officer Vonlin said, "Maybe you can hang out with our wives one weekend."

Samantha gave the men a forced smile. They nodded and she closed the door. She envied the idea that those women got to see their husbands every night.

One night, Samuel was writing his normal letter to Samantha listening to one of the Marines strum around on the guitar. Young, one of Samuel's fireteam leaders was on the rack next to him throwing a football up in the air. Young was an example of this new generation. Young had started a tradition. An insane and entirely undisciplined tradition, but the Marines all loved it. Every morning he would wake up with the rising sun and climb up on the earthen palisade of HESCO barriers. Young had a bullhorn, no one knew where he got it, but no one bothered to ask.

But every morning he would face the sun and attempt to yell the intro to the Lion King into the bull horn. To a bunch of men that had spent at least a portion of their childhood in the nineteen nineties, everyone knew what he was trying to imitate. Samuel though, being a nerd, knew what the words meant. It was Swahili. Roughly translated it was announcing the coming of the lion. And that's what it had become, a ritualistic announcement to the locals that the lion was awake and ready to hunt. All of the Marines on the patrol base found it endearing. Samuel had even heard other units in the battalion had started imitating the tradition as a reveille.

"You writing your girl again Sergeant?" Young asked.

"Every night." Samuel replied.

"Goddamn you're so good." Young replied.

Samuel chuckled.

"I only write home when I am running out of dip or something." Young continued.

"The Corps will get you two things," Samuel replied, "knee pain and a girl that's way the fuck out of your league. Don't take the good thing for granted."

Young just looked at him and smirked. Samuel knew what Young meant. Young, like most of these kids, was just here because he wanted to go to war. That was it, there was nothing back home. Young knew the reality of modern warfare and, either he was crazy enough or bored enough, that he wanted to give it a shot. They had been in a fire fight a few days ago and Young was just shooting at the enemy, not behind any cover, just shooting. Samuel had yelled at him, "Hey bitch, get the fuck down. If you die out here, I'm going to tell your mother the truth, you died because you are a fucking idiot." But that's how these guys were, near suicidal. Samuel was concerned they were imitating him, and it was going to get one of them killed.

Young looked at Samuel from his rack and said, "You know you are the first legend I've ever met that lived up to the hype."

Samuel smirked.

Young continued, "I met Sylvester Stallone one time when I was a kid. He was at the airport and he was just like," Young tried to do a Stallone impression, "'Hey kid.'"

Samuel let out a laugh.

"I remember thinking he did not look like Rambo," Young stated, "I was disappointed."

Samuel went back to writing to Samantha.

"But you," Young said, "everyone told me you were the Pony Boy and the god of death rolled into one."

Samuel looked up to see Young staring at him, studying him. He could tell the kid was trying to have a father son moment with him, so he gave Young his undivided attention.

"When I heard you were going to be our squad leader I was pumped," Young added, "But then when you started training us, I thought it was a nightmare, that you hated us."

"I did hate you," Samuel laughed, "I still do. Y'all are a bunch of fucking savages."

Young smiled.

Samuel added, "But you are the finest group of infantrymen in the world."

Young's smile got bigger as he said, "Well that's because

you ran our dicks in the dirt making us as much like you as possible."

Samuel felt a sense of dread come over him. The last thing he wanted for these guys was for them to be like him.

"Don't be like me," Samuel said softly.

Young looked at him with a disconcerted look.

"Be better." Samuel ordered.

Young laughed and said, "Yeah sure, I'll get right on that. First thing to achieve, immortality."

"I'm serious," Samuel said. There was a long uncomfortable pause. Samuel looked around the hooch to see his whole squad was listening to him now. "They always told me I was a war junky." Samuel started, "I never believed them."

All of the Marines had a sullen look on their face.

"I used to say it wasn't me that loved this shit, it was the monster inside." He continued.

All of the Marines silently nodded. He had explained the demon to them. He encouraged them to embrace theirs.

Samuel hung his head and said, "Truth is the demon is in control now. I fed him too much too often. The only time I feel like myself is when I'm writing to my girl. The rest of the time it's just about finding the next person I got to kill."

You could have heard a pin drop on the plywood floors.

Samuel finally broke the silence by saying, "It's not worth doing what you have to do to survive if the person you are is going to die in the process."

The Marines all looked away in shame. This was the first time they had ever heard Samuel say anything like this.

"Lights out in twenty minutes," Samuel ordered, "We are going out tomorrow, I'm expecting trouble. I want everyone rested."

Samuel's squad was on patrol. They were approaching a battlefield from a few days prior. The Afghans were tough and vivacious, but they were not what Samuel would call creative. After a defeat they would leave and lick their wounds, and after a few days they would return. More often than not they would set up their next ambush very near the last one.

So, Samuel started to feel his senses heighten as they approached some corpses from a few days previous. There was a cloud of black flies that were making a meal of some dead man. Samuel felt sick to his stomach watching them. They were not like house flies from back home. These were gigantic flies, plump from the feast of rotting flesh. Samuel tried to make a path well clear of them. But it was all for nothing. A few of the pestilent monstrosities traveled the distance to Samuel. Soon enough he was being swarmed by them. Samuel shuddered with horror as they began landing on his face and flying in his ears. Samuel could take dead bodies and he could take insects but the thought of these insects feasting on a dead body and then landing on his face bothered him. For a moment he lost his icy cold composure. Samuel started swatting at the flies feverishly. Samuel trotted away as quickly as he could.

One of his Marines looked back at him and laughed. "You good Sergeant?" He asked Samuel.

Samuel was about to yell up to him, that he was good when he heard shots ring out. The sound was rapid, but it was not fully automatic, it was Marines shooting. Samuel looked to his right where the sound had come from.

"CONTACT RIGHT!" Echoed in the air. Suddenly, the air erupted with the sound of gunfire. It was the Afghan response to his Marine apparently getting the first shot off. Like a symphony his Marines responded in kind. Samuel moved and took cover behind a large rock. His Marines moved with expert precision, everyone taking position. Samuel closed his eyes to begin his murder ritual. He took a deep breath, but the flies had followed him to his new position. They buzzed around and Samuel's sacrament of death was interrupted. He tried to swat them away so he could start it again.

Suddenly, his radio operator came running up. Samuel was frustrated that his sacrament was going to have to wait. Samuel pulled out his map and yelled to his RO their present coordinates for him to relay back to the unit. Samuel then lifted up to take stock of the ambush and to pass that information to headquarters. Samuel started looking on the horizon for the enemy muzzle flashes. This was a decent size force he thought, maybe a platoon size or bigger. Samuel passed the information to his RO. Then he looked again and saw that they were too close for air support and too close for artillery. Samuel smiled and thought this was an infantry fight. But these guys had bitten off more than they could chew, they were going to learn what it was like to try to ambush the greatest infantrymen in the world. Samuel turned back around to his RO.

Suddenly, the greatest sound in the world joined the commotion. They had been expecting this fight, so, Samuel had two crew serve teams with him, 0331s, machine gunners. Every Marine infantryman was proficient with a machine gun. But 31s were fucking artists with a belt fed weapon. The average infantryman was just a pale comparison to the gunners when they were masterfully displaying their craft. The guns opened up with a long burst. Then they started making their guns "talk." Samuel always thought it sounded like singing. Like a beautiful opera of hate and discontent. It was glorious. This fight was already decided.

His RO called back to him, "Second squad is en route from their patrol route, and QRF is en route Sergeant!"

Samuel looked at his watch. QRF should be about ten minutes out.

"Good to go!" Samuel responded, "What do you say we get in this fight?"

Samuel rolled over and looked again. He directed his RO towards the left seeing it was the safer route towards the firing line. Samuel started making his way towards the center, he was going to get some action for himself, and check on his teams.

Suddenly, Samuel felt a rush of worry as he heard the gun on his right flank abruptly and conspicuously stop. Samuel cautiously popped his head up into the storm of lead to see if he could see what was the matter. A crack over-head verified that was not a safe course of action. Samuel waited for a few seconds considering it might just be a barrel change. After he was certain that there had been enough time for any immediate or remedial action to have been taken and there was still no machine gun fire from that flank he decided it was time to investigate for himself. Samuel sighed and got to his feet to run in that direction.

Samuel made it about seven yards before he felt a sharp sting through his left leg. Samuel's legs failed and he hit the ground. Samuel scanned quickly for some type of cover. There was a small boulder near him. It was scarcely good cover, but it was better than nothing. Samuel crawled towards it on his back. Samuel looked at the trail of blood he left behind him as confirmation that he had been hit. Samuel got to the rock and yelled, "Fuck."

Moments ago, he was eager to get into the fight now, he was a casualty. Samuel grunted as he pushed on the wound in his leg. There was a lot of blood. Samuel took his gloves off and felt for the wound. The bullet had gone all the way through his left leg. The hot liquid on his hand was a stark reminder that this was not a game as he had been treating it. All things considered though this was not that bad, it could have been a head or neck shot.

Samuel got his tourniquet off his flak and went to the task of putting it on. He had drilled this maneuver a hundred times and forced his Marines to do the same. He screamed out in pain as he used all his strength to tighten the windless. When it hurt, turn it more, then that meant it was tight enough. Samuel started to feel light-headed and his vision was getting blurry. He figured he had lost a lot of blood pretty quickly. This might be more serious than he thought. Samuel leaned back to raise his leg up. He might get his feet shot off, but he needed to get that life-giving blood back to his core so it could pump to his brain before he lost consciousness.

Samuel struggled with the seemingly simple task. He

looked down to his horror to see that his right leg was gushing blood too. *That's not good.* Samuel thought to himself. He grabbed that leg and pushed on it with every bit of strength he could muster.

Samuel wanted to scream out for help. But there are a few words that are universally known on a battlefield. The enemy as well as his men would recognize the word "Corpsman." Sometimes an enemy hearing the word corpsman or medic would stiffen their resolve. After hearing that shout, they would train their weapons on the next man they saw moving and unload on him. Not to mention the effect it might have on his men for them to hear him call for a corpsman. That might stir panic in his ranks. Besides that, for all he knew, the corpsman was on the right gun treating a wounded Marine. He would not risk the life of his corpsman or another Marine for his own benefit and his fate be damned.

Samuel started thinking of Samantha, and how much he was letting her down. He was trying to feed the beast with fresh carnage, and he had gotten himself shot. It was dumb luck at best, it was criminal recklessness most likely. Suddenly, like the sound of God answering a silent prayer, he heard the gun on his right flank join in the chorus again. Samuel then looked back towards the horizon away from the fire fight and saw the dust clouds from the vehicles of their quick reaction force coming to the fray, at speed. Samuel thought that if there was any chance he would survive this, this was it.

"CORPSMAN!" He screamed. It took more out of him to shout those words than he thought it would. But Samuel knew that in the chaos in a modern battlefield saying anything once was the same as not saying it at all. He had to find a way to muster the strength to say it again. He owed it to Samantha to fight to make it home to her. All the men he had killed, all the death he had been surrounded by, all the pain he had endured would not mean a thing if he could not find a way to scream one more time. The thought of Samantha in widow's garb filled his head as tears came to his eyes. "CORPSMAN!" He screamed with every last ounce of strength in his body. He felt the strength in his fingers fleeting away. His grip loosened on his leg. Samuel's eyes got heavy. His breathing started to slow as he thought of the flies.

The flies must have been clairvoyant. They chased him knowing he was their next meal. They recognized the smell of fresh food. The god of death was going to be the flesh that they dined on this afternoon. Samuel was going to share in the fate he had exacted on so many, and he was going to see his brothers. He hoped that Samantha would keep him waiting. Samuel faded away reflecting to himself, *I always thought it would happen so much quicker than this.*

It was one of those southern torrential downpours outside. One of those that seemed like they took the whole town and stuck it under a waterfall. Samantha was looking out the window reflecting on her life to this point. She had become so bitter. She should have been planning her wedding. But she lacked all motivation to do so. Samuel was going to be home soon, so they said. But they had lied before. She did not believe anything anyone said, anymore. As far as she was concerned, they would find a way to keep Samuel in a war until he was dead. He was a drug and they were going to use him up without sharing. She did not like being this negative, but she could not help it. Last week Mac and Lucy were celebrating their engagement. Mac had made a comment about them having a dual wedding. Samantha only replied sarcastically that he was too optimistic if he thought that her and Samuel would ever be able to get married. She was worried that she had not even told Lucy she was happy for her.

But Samantha had no grace left to offer anyone. She felt like she was being punished for some crime she did not even know she had committed. Samantha must have been a horrible person in a past life. Or perhaps this was karmic justice for some rude thought she had about someone years ago. Perhaps this was God's punishment for her skipping church or kissing that boy at vacation bible school forever ago. Like a sadistic deity he was taking his revenge on her. But the unrighteous part was that Samuel was collateral damage. He had never done anything to anyone, and he was being just as cruelly punished as she was, even more so in fact. She was depressed on his last deployment, she was just pissed the fuck off now.

Samantha's worries only got worse when she saw Mac's truck racing through the parking lot of the apartment complex. He whipped into a space and jumped out with the truck crooked. Samantha looked on with horror as he ran, ran towards the apartment. Mac's wounds had never fully healed. He had gotten more mobile, for sure, but, she had never seen him run.

Before she could get out of her room to go into the living room to see what was the matter, she heard Mac yell, "Where's Sam?" Before Lucy could answer, Samantha was standing in the room staring at Mac. He did not have his happy go lucky aura about him.

Samantha felt like she was in a dream. There is no way he was here to break horrible news to her. This was not real. If she had to put Samuel in the ground, she was going with him. There was only so much one woman could take, and that would be the proverbial straw that broke the camel's back.

"Sam," Mac said, "sit down for a second."

"Shut the fuck up Mac." Samantha said as she started to sob.

"He's alive" Mac said as he walked up to her and put his arms around her.

Samantha slapped him in her rage. He had just scared her to death.

"I can't-" Samantha said as she started sobbing. Mac pulled her close and she buried her face in his big chest. "I can't Mac." Samantha said, "I can't take this anymore."

Mac pulled her face away from his chest and looked into her eyes as he said, "He's alive Sam."

Mac had tears in his eyes. Samantha figured out that he did have bad news. This was not just her dread projecting on every situation that arose. This was not pessimism, something actually happened.

"What are you talking about?" Samantha said, "What happened?"

Mac ordered her in a stern voice, "Sit down."

Samantha sat down on the couch in shock. She was shaking considering what had happened that could have Mac behaving like this.

"Sam's alive." Mac said again as if he was reminding himself, "Ryan called me in a panic about eight hours ago."

Samantha knew Ryan was on his first tour in the middle east with the air force.

Mac continued, "He said that someone that had known he had a brother in the Marines had told him he caught wind of a Marine named Parker that had been airlifted. Ryan did the digging he could and found out that it was Sam. But he couldn't get any information about his status. So, Ryan called me to see if I could reach out to any old buddies and get some answers."

Samantha was certain she was asleep and having a nightmare. The military could not be trusted. They had been wrong about everything. She thought. He wasn't supposed to go to Iraq. Samuel was not even supposed to be in Afghanistan. They could be wrong about this too. He could be dead, or he could be just fine.

Mac continued as if to quash that thought entirely, "Finally, I got in contact with a buddy of mine from way back in the Fallujah days. Samantha, I talked to him myself, I trust this guy. He's a captain now and he made some phone calls. He said Samuel is alive and he had gotten taken to Ramstein in Germany. He didn't know what happened, but he was listed as a combat casualty and he was alive. That's all I know honey."

Samantha felt like she was going to hyperventilate. What did that mean? Combat casualty but alive. That was the most vague description possible, he could be a vegetable on life support for all she knew. He could have lost every limb in some violent explosion. Why had no one called her and told her anything? This was the greatest form of betrayal.

Mac put his arms around her and said, "Sam made me promise to tell you if something happened to him. He knew the Corps would only tell the next of kin. And Samuel had his mother listed as only to be notified in case of killed in action. That man was always so stubborn about protecting his mother, but he did not think this one through. They won't tell Ryan shit until he's off flight status."

Samantha sobbed and sobbed. She had not cried like this since Samuel told her he was leaving again. She had been too bitter and angry to really cry. So now it was like she had months of tears and fears and anxiety just pouring out of her.

A few hours passed when finally, Samuel's mother called. They had waited for Ryan to get off of mission status before they informed him. He called their mother and told her. She was now calling Samantha. Samuel had been shot, and it was bad. No one seemed to know how bad. They told Ryan he would be stable enough soon, that they were going to send him back to Walter Reed. Samantha prepared for the worst as she made plans with her future mother-in-law to get to Maryland to see him when he got there.

CHAPTER 15
NINE LINE

This was unlike any hospital Samantha had ever been to. Samantha knew that a part of the treatment at normal hospitals was a happy and positive atmosphere. But here, in the military hospital, the atmosphere felt like a monastery. There were people buzzing around in uniforms, people in lab coats that were obviously military types, and people in lab coats that were not. Their faces were sober. They were not unhappy, it was not a negative energy. This was sacred ground. These walls and the people in them echoed with the silent chant of reverence. The feeling was that if someone were to speak above a whisper, they would be committing blasphemy.

The very next thing that struck her was that the place was filled. The hospital staff crowded the halls moving room to room with diligent purpose. They were disciples to these patients. Samantha could not fight her urge to look into the rooms as her and Samuel's family passed by each one. Usually, she could not see anything. But occasionally, she saw curiously similar scenes. A military aged man struggling to take a step or sitting and moving a prosthetic. A family of various ages standing by a bed looking down. Samantha felt like that was the secret. This curious bedside manner was a pious devotion to a hospital filled to capacity with the valiant defenders of a nation at war.

Samantha felt tears come to her eyes as she realized she had never stopped to consider that war was nothing more than a million stories like hers. People consciously remember widows and orphans. Little thought is given to the new word she had learned, casualties. Mac had been wounded, but his force of personality hid the fact. She had met him during his road to recovery, but he was far from the starting line. That's what this place was, it was a starting line. These families were just starting like she was. These men and women had a long road ahead of them for the sons and daughters who had paid a sacrifice. Samantha had not thought about it before, but the term "ultimate sacrifice" implicitly states that there are other sacrifices that can be paid.

Samantha felt like she was getting a window display on all the things that could have been the sacrifice Samuel had paid. Any one or multiple of these could be in Samantha's future forever. Her mind started to ring with ideas as they passed the rooms. Amputation, disfigurement, coma, epilepsy each room foreshadowed a doom. Then she saw the sign on the double doors of the wing that led to Samuel's room and it read, "For the Peace of the Patients Please Silence all Cell Phones and Remain Quite." The whole hospital was basically silent. What did that mean for this wing? Samantha thought that sign might as well have said, "They Came Seeking Peace Here, Because They Cannot Find It Anywhere Else." Samantha now understood not all of these were going to be physical wounds.

Finally, they reached a man in a lab coat that was standing outside of the door. He turned to them with a stern look on his face.

"Can I help you folks?" He demanded.

"We're here to see Sergeant Parker." Samuel's father said.

The man looked them all over and said, "Can I speak to the next of kin for a moment please?"

Samuel's mother stepped over to the man. She grabbed Samantha by the arm and pulled her with her.

"Just the next of kin please." He said.

Samuel's mother said, "This is his fiance and the love of his life anything you tell me I am going to turn around and tell her."

The man sighed and said, "Very well. It has been my honor to serve as Sergeant Parker's doctor for the last two days."

Samantha was bracing herself to hear that he had passed while they were on the way.

"Sometimes I feel like I am a part of the military," The doctor said with a smile, "They even let me read some of these men's service record. When I read men like Sergeant Parker's record, I am reminded I have more in common with a lawyer than a soldier."

Samantha felt as though she recognized the bedside manner. Make a funny comment before you deliver the really bad news. A woman in a uniform walked up to the doctor and he whispered something to her. The woman scurried off.

"I am not sure how much you know." The doctor said.

"Basically nothing." Mrs. Parker said.

The doctor got a sullen look on his face, as though this was the worst part of his job.

"I can't tell you where, other than in Afghanistan," He started, "But, Sergeant Parker sustained a gunshot wound while engaged in combat."

He sounded very matter of fact, as though he was reading a news report.

He continued, "The bullet entered his left leg and traveled all the way to his right leg where it lodged into his femur."

Samantha's mother started sobbing. Samantha realized that this information about the love of her life was about her baby boy.

"Miraculously, the bullet missed both of his femoral arteries. But Sergeant Parker still lost a lot of blood." the doctor continued, "He was in a coma by the time he got to the field hospital."

Samantha could not hold back anymore, she joined in the sobbing.

"Sergeant Parker received multiple blood transfusions and was airlifted to Ramstein where he received surgery to remove the bullet," he said, "Sergeant Parker was stabilized there and then-" Samantha noticed that he paused, "He was transported here."

They stood there in silence for a moment. Samantha thought of the sign on the double doors. She was beginning to rack through her pre-med classes and remember the extent of brain damage that could occur from blood loss or a coma.

"Will he ever walk again?" Samuel's mother asked.

The doctor looked as though he was deep in thought for a moment, "I suspect he will."

Samantha looked at him with a very disconcerted face. They were not here for uncertainties.

"Most doctors," He started as he realized he needed to explain, "deal with patients that treat scrapes like broken arms, here we deal with the exact opposite. I have a soldier in another room that was brought in with fragmentation in his whole upper body from a grenade. I could not figure out how his leg was broken. Then we looked at the x-ray closer and realized it was months old. The man had been patrolling Afghanistan with a broken leg for at least two months. That's the story with all of these men. They come in for one injury and we find several old ones."

Samantha thought of Samuel trying to sit down on the beach.

"Sergeant Parker is no different. Quite frankly I am surprised he was able to walk at all. He has broken every tarsal at least once, he has virtually no cartilage left in his right knee, he has two herniated discs in his back, and his shoulder needs to be entirely reconstructed. But something tells me he will be outrunning me in no time." the doctor said in adoration.

Samuel's mother finally said, "Can we see him?"

The doctor let out a heavy sigh, and then nodded. "But no more than two at a time."

Mrs. Parker looked up at Samantha and then took her hand. The woman in the uniform returned and handed the doctor something and then walked away. The doctor handed

Samantha and Samuel's mother a folded yellow brochure. Samantha saw the letters on the top "PTSD" and a picture of a man in a uniform hugging a woman.

"Sergeant Parker is a fighter." He continued, "No doubt in my mind it saved his life. He just hasn't quite realized his fight is over."

The doctor turned towards the room and started to walk them towards it.

He lowered his voice to a near whisper, "I would not tell you not to hold your son or your fiance, but I would not stand too close to the bed when he is sleeping."

They walked into the room. Samantha saw him lying on the bed, restrained by all four limbs. He had tubes coming out everywhere and his skin was ashen white. This great man who had once had so much life force that everyone felt his presence when he walked into a room had been reduced to this. The only sign that he had life at all was the beep...beep...beep of the EKG machine.

"We've had to keep him sedated." the doctor said.

He looked like a science experiment. Something they had thrown together with spare parts to make this machine they were planning to bring to life eventually. Samantha sobbed in agony. The three of them sat in silence for a moment.

"We were going to wake him up soon to try to eat again. I'm certain he will be happy to see you too. Last time he was calling for Sam." The doctor said, looking at Samantha.

The doctor left the room and the two women collapsed into each other's arms.

Suddenly three very large men entered the room with the doctor. The doctor shut the door behind him. He looked at the two of them. Samantha and Samuel's mother must have given him a look that said they were not going anywhere, because he just looked away ashamed as he pulled the curtain around the bed closed.

Samantha saw that the three men had taken up positions around Samuel before the curtains closed. Suddenly she heard the EKG speed up beep..beep. beep beepbeepbeep. A loud roar entered the room. Samantha and Samuel's mother jumped with fright. They heard the sound of the chains tightening and twisting. Samantha could hear one of the men saying something softly. And the EKG started to slow down.

Samuel jerked to life. He had no clue where he was. He scanned around to see three men around him. There was a large black man next to him.

The man started saying softly, "I got you devil dog. You're good brother, you're safe now."

Samuel tried to pull his arms up, but he was strapped down. Flashes of the past started rolling through his head. He remembered, hospital staff. He had been in a hospital. Samuel looked up at the big black man and saw an eagle globe and anchor pendant on the collar of his shirt.

"You're good big dog. You're good." He said.

Samuel started to catch his breath. He was not certain where he was, but he had vague memories of the doctor at the foot of the bed.

The man with the eagle globe and anchor pin said, "You're at the hospital, Sergeant. In the States."

Samuel felt a little safer. He recognized that the man next to him was a Marine.

The doctor at the foot of the bed said, "Sergeant Parker do you remember me?"

Samuel nodded at him as he remembered more and more of his recent memories.

"We're going to take the restraints off, ok." the doctor said to him.

Samuel nodded, as he struggled to say "Sam." His mouth was dry. And his throat was sore. Samuel felt drowsy. He could tell he was on drugs, but he wasn't sure what. The men around him took the restraints off and looked at him cautiously. Samuel was not really able to think in coherent thoughts, but he realized he must have been violent in his sleep.

The Marine put his hand on Samuel's arm and said, "You're safe now Sergeant."

Samuel started to try to ask about his Marines and where they were, but he could not form the words.

The three men shuffled to the edge of the bed and the doctor announced with a smile, "Sergeant, we have some people who are very happy to see you."

The doctor pulled back the curtains. Samantha could not see past the wall of men. They shuffled out towards the door holding the restraints. Samantha noticed the last one to leave, the large black guy had a tear in the bridge of his eye. Samantha saw Samuel's face. He looked at her with a confused look. This would be the cruelest of punishments. What would she do if he did not recognize her, if he did not remember her? Before she could dwell on the thought too much, he formed a smile as a single tear rolled down his face. It looked like he was struggling to open his hand towards her. Samantha was scared to startle him, so, she walked slowly to his bedside. Samantha gently touched his hand. Samuel opened his arms slowly as if he was saying he wanted a hug.

Samantha smiled as she felt a tear roll across her face now. She was careful not to jostle him, as she was afraid to add to his pain, but she crawled into the bed with him and rested her head on his chest. Samuel wrapped his arm around her. Samuel's mother stood over them holding Samuel's other hand. There was nothing but silence in the room for a moment until Samuel finally said in a broken and scratchy voice, "Hey Sam."

Samuel was slowly gaining his wits back. He remembered a little more. He was not entirely sure he was not dead and in heaven. Speaking was still very hard. But some nurse brought him water. He guzzled it and he could feel his physical capacity to speak returning, but forming thoughts was not any easier.

He remembered being shot, calling for a corpsman. He

remembered grabbing someone in a helicopter. Then it was just a blur of hospital staff and hospital rooms. There was an unnatural quiet from everyone. Samantha would gently kiss his cheek from time to time but other than "I love you" She had not said much. Carrie and Samuel's father had taken turns coming in to see him after his mother. Samantha never left. When the nurse brought him food, he was not sure if he had been condemned to purgatory instead of in heaven. If this was purgatory, if he was paying penance for the men he had killed and all of his other sins, he was going to be here a long time he thought to himself. But at least he had his silent version of Sam with him. That was proof enough that God was merciful.

Samantha saw a man with a polo and slacks on walk in and shut the door behind him. He had a very big smile on his face. He looked at her and then at Samuel.

"Sergeant Parker," he said, "I assure you, you are very much alive. And if you cooperate with me you will be out of here in no time."

Samantha sensed that this man was on a mission and he did not make time for bullshit. She was eager to hear what he had to say.

"Sergeant we need to talk about what's going on in your mind." the man said. Samantha looked back at Samuel. She had gotten out of bed with him to let him eat but she was never going to be more than an arms-length away from him. Samuel gave her a look like he did not want her to be in the room. She was torn on what to do.

"No," the man in the polo said, "I'm your psychologist. I need you to remember why you want to get better. So, she stays."

Samuel looked up at the man with a scowl.

"You see Sergeant, I'm a glutton for punishment. So, I decided to be an army psychologist. Now I can order you to take medications, but I have been doing this for a while now." The man continued, "So I know that eventually you would stop taking them. Then you will go right back to whatever hell is in your mind now and then you will hurt her, then you will hurt yourself, and that would mean I am a very bad psychologist."

Samuel felt insulted that he would even hint at the fact that he would hurt Samantha.

"Sergeant when you are awake you are the picture perfect gentleman we expect our servicemen to be," the psychologist said, "but when you are asleep you are in a waking nightmare. We need to talk about that nightmare. Two nights ago, they thought you were having a heart attack in your sleep. When they woke you up you choked a nurse. She is still hospitalized."

Samuel felt sick to his stomach.

But the man continued, "Now really that's their fault, because you broke a doctor's nose in Germany when they brought you out of the coma. But that, of course, was after you tried to throw the flight nurse out of a helicopter."

Samantha felt nervous. She did not know what the proper feeling was to have. Was she supposed to be scared? It seemed entirely unreal to be afraid of Samuel. In Samuel's arms had always been the place she felt safest.

The psychologist started filling up a glass of water and said, "Sergeant, your war is over. You did more than your duty. You are a bonafide war hero. All we have to do is convince your mind your war is over, and you can go home and live happily ever after with this lovely woman."

The psychologist walked over to the tray and put the water down and said, "Now start from wherever you want and anytime you start to feel panicked take a sip of water."

Then the man pulled up a chair and sat down at the foot of the bed.

Samantha listened to Samuel talk softly to the psychologist. The guy was good. He had said all the right things to get Samuel to talk. He must have talked for hours. The psychologist had not said much after Samuel started. But towards the end of the session he explained to Samuel that his mind was like the cup of water. Every traumatic "fucked-up" memory was poured into the cup. Some memories were a lot of water, others were just a drop. But the goal was to walk around with the cup without spilling any. It might be easy when there's not much in the cup. But Samuel's cup was overflowing from three deployments and now he could not take a step without spilling water. And for one reason or another going to sleep was like running sprints while holding the cup. It made a lot of sense to Samantha. She understood he had reached a limit of human endurance she was amazed he had been able to carry so much for so long with relatively little effect she could see. Samantha vowed to herself that being faithful was how she would respond. She would not be afraid. She would stand by him and be a rock for him. It was his turn to feel safe in her arms.

Samuel would not say that he felt better after talking to the psychologist. But he was willing to do anything. The idea of hurting Samantha had scared him too much. Whatever was necessary he thought, drugs, therapy, anything. Samuel was fighting sleep as the night drew late. He was terrified of the idea of going to sleep. They had moved the recliner in the room to right next to the bed for Samantha. And Samuel knew that's where she was going to sleep. Too close for safety. So, Samuel breathed a sigh of relief as a man walked in holding the restraints.

"Time for bed Sergeant." the man said.

Samantha stood up and demanded, "What do you think you are doing?"

The man looked at her with a concerned look and then said, "It's orders ma'am."

"It's not my orders," Samantha snapped back, "I'm not a part of your fucked-up system. You break a man and then chain him up like an animal because you are worried you taught him to fight too well."

The man stood there for a minute not sure how to respond. Samuel was confused, he wanted the man to restrain him, but Samantha seemed so demanding that it not happen. Samuel gathered that this was point of dignity for her. She was not going to let them do it no matter what. If she had faith in him everyone else was required to.

Samantha stared at the man.

"I have to." the man said quietly.

Samantha shook her head and said, "I'll take them off."

The man looked at her with disbelief. She did not feel bad for putting him in a tough spot though. This was not right. Dogs used for fighting could expect to be treated this way, not a man.

"Ma'am there's a woman in the hospital right now."

Samantha felt her face twist as she said, "Pardon me, but I think it's safe to say he's been through worse. I'm the one that's staying in here, I'm not afraid. So, leave."

The man looked at Samuel and then looked back at her and his face got a stern look. Before he could say anything, Samantha cut him off by saying, "Oh, please. Please say you will make me leave. If you are afraid of him when he's asleep what do you think is going to happen when you try to get me out of this room? You want to find out if you have enough security in this building to stop him from stopping you from putting your hands on me."

The man's face went from stern to horrified. He shook his head and walked out. Samantha looked back at Samuel. He was looking at her with sad eyes. Samantha knew he was afraid of hurting her.

She knew he did not trust himself near her. She leaned in and said, "I have faith in you enough for the both of us." and she kissed him. She did not sleep much that night, but she held his hand the whole night.

CHAPTER 16 TAPS

To say that he was home was a half-truth. The love of Samantha's life was back, and he did not have to leave her again. But it was like a thousand pieces of him were missing. They were in the sands of god forsaken countries a thousand miles away. Samantha had resolved that she would do whatever it took to get him back, no matter how long it took. He had unceremoniously bore the cross of hellish battlefields and he now wore the scars on his mind and on his body. But Samantha determined that the memory of the man who had all of her heart deserved for her to bear the cross of putting him back together again.

Samuel had been home from the hospital for three weeks. They had not had sex in that entire time. He was a cold shell of the passionate loving spirit that had gone before. Her heart was filled with the happy memories of the time they had spent together before. She proudly believed she loved the greatest man to have ever lived. By comparison the Samuel that shared her bed and her home now, was a husk. But he was trying. He had quickly resolved to get help with very little protest. He was on medication now, and it seemed to be helping. But he was a zombie. His brilliant mind had abandoned him, and he struggled to form thoughts into sentences. Samantha spent most nights in the bathroom weeping as if she had been left an actual widow. But she was still proud of him and resolved to stand by her man until whatever bitter end.

Samantha was taking Samuel to some Veteran's Day celebration at her father's Country Club. Samuel could not muster the coherent argument to protest when she called to ask him if they could go. It was a cruel and ironic fate. He desperately wanted to forget the wars. He wanted to reclaim his identity. But to forget his men and to forget what he had seen seemed like a betrayal of the highest order. And what's worse his unconscious mind would not let him forget.

Samuel had always thought of the mind as a filing cabinet. The key to his intelligence was that his filing cabinet was pristine and perfectly organized. Anytime he faced any quandary he could immediately flip to the corresponding file containing all facts, thoughts, or experiences and could accurately predict future happenings from those files. The issue is there is nowhere to file absolutely horrific memories. The brain just stuffs those files wherever they fit in the cabinet.

The smell of Willey's burning flesh while he flailed, burning alive, while you lay half-conscious on the ground helpless. Yeah just stick that wherever that fits. Or, *that dead three-year-old's ghastly eyes staring at you for hours. Don't even try to find a place for that just open a drawer and drop it in.* Even the seemingly more mundane started to add up. *That cloud of black flies feeding on that dead Afghani and then swarming your face.* There's not a drawer for that.

After three deployments, Samuel could not open any drawer in his mind without some fucked up memory invading his thoughts. So, for Samantha's sake he had started medication.

The medication "helped." what the medicine really did was say: *ok the cabinets are fucked up.* So, the medicine took out all of the files sorted through all the horrible shit and put it in a new drawer at the bottom and put a giant label on it that said, "Do Not Open." The problem was *the medicine* had put ALL the files back after that, and Samuel had no control over where the files went. And now Samuel had no fucking clue where anything was.

Incredibly simple questions were impossible to answer. Samantha could ask, "Do you still love me?" *That's easy,* Samuel would think, *Second, drawer from the top is my undying love for Samantha.* But he would check the drawer and it would be memories of Carrie and Ryan and him as kids. Then he would frantically search the drawers looking for the file. He would finally find the file that said "Yes! You Do Love Samantha and This is Why." He'd open the file and it was one page that said, "All memories, facts, and statements about this subject have been assimilated into other files." That's what it was like to be on the medicine. And the worst part of it was he had no clue where the emotions drawer was, if those files still existed, they must be in the "Do Not Open" drawer. Until the night before, when he had that pistol in his mouth, he had not felt anything since starting the medicine.

Samantha had grown accustomed to the silence of being around Samuel. But she was still not comfortable with it. She believed she could count on one hand every word Samuel had said since they had gotten into the car. Her father had insisted that they come to this function today. Her family had not spent any time with Samuel since he got back, and she was nervous about it. It was like she was bringing a ghost to the land of the living. She felt selfish even to think of herself in this situation, but she was fairly certain that if anyone pointed out how different he was, *she* was going to burst into tears.

Her father genuinely loved Samuel. He had since the first time they met. He thought of Samuel as a surrogate son. This was a chance to show off Samuel to his cronies. And it was not some self-serving display. Her father was proud of Samuel. The whole community was proud of Samuel. Samuel was a true-blue war hero. Samuel's commanding officer had a page for all the family members to visit. It had a picture and bio for all of the Marines and sailors that had gone to Afghanistan. Samuel's bio was amongst the longest, listing out all of his medals and achievements. Samuel was one of a handful that had served three tours. Samantha did not know if what he had become was worth all of his accomplishments, but she knew all of his sacrifice was worth her steadfast dedication.

They pulled up to the country club a little before eleven.

There were red, white, and blue streamers everywhere. American flags, flags from the different services, and balloons lined the giant ionic columns of the Victorian style building. Samuel looked at Samantha and forced a smile. Samuel was as much in love with her as he had ever been in his life. Samuel had promised God that if he got him home, he would spend the rest of his life in peace and dedicate himself to the solitary task of making Samantha as happy as possible. Samuel had intended to be a man of his word. Samuel just could not remember how to make her happy. He remembered happy times, but it was like looking at pictures in black and white. But Samuel knew that this, spending time with her family, was one of the things that made her happy. Samantha gently brushed his hand and they got out of the car. As she made her way around the car, he stuck his hand out. She looked at him and her eyes got watery as she took his hand. He knew he had not been showing the kind of affection he wanted to. He felt like a prisoner talking to his love through the glass most of the time.

He took a deep breath and they walked towards the main door. The banner said, "Heroes Luncheon." Samuel felt it was an enigmatic description, all of the heroes were dead, only the ruthless had survived. Samuel was fairly certain he would find a time to complete his task and join the heroes soon enough.

Samantha was shaking with nervous excitement. Samuel did not offer up his hand anymore. His affection was broken and unintelligible. She had told herself every day to have faith that it would get better, and this was the first real sign that maybe it was. The doctors had told them that the drugs were cumulative, and it could take a while for them to *really* work. Maybe this was a breakthrough day. They walked in through the main hall she saw many old vets in their uniforms buzzing about. The dining hall was noisy and there was a clamor everywhere. Two weeks ago, Samuel would have had a panic attack the second they stepped foot in the room. This was another sign that things were getting better.

Her father was sitting clear across the room. He got a

huge smile on his face as he saw Samuel and her. He walked towards them with a quickness. Samantha saw Samuel stick his hand out to shake her father's hand while he was still a good distance away. These were the reminders that something was just not right. She felt tears coming back to her eyes.

Samuel was desperately trying to find the emotion. *Happy* he told himself, *You have not seen this man in a year. You are happy to see him.*

"Johnathan." Samuel uttered with his hand out as he got close enough to hear him. Her father got a confused look on his face as he walked past the hand he had sticking out and threw his arms around Samuel and gave him a big hug.

"I'm so glad you are here Sam." Johnathan said in a joyous tone.

Samuel realized it was appropriate for him to close his arms around him and hug him back.

"Thank you for inviting us." Samuel said awkwardly hugging him.

Johnathan pulled away from him and looked at Samantha.

"Hello angel." Jonathan said as he kissed her on the forehead.

Samuel could tell she was happy to see him because her eyes were watering as she leapt to throw her arms around her father.

"Daddy." She said in a sweet tone.

Samuel resolved that he would do everything he could to make sure Samantha knew he was happy to be here. After all his resolve to make her as happy as he could was the only thing that kept him suck starting a pistol the night before.

They all walked back to their table together. Samantha saw her mother had stood up and was grinning ear to ear as they walked up.

"Martha, it's so good to see you again." Samuel said, giving her a big hug.

Samantha thought it was much better than the greeting he had given her father. Again, she thought that this was progress. After the hugs were shared and greetings were over, her father insisted that Samuel come with him to meet some people and walked Samuel away with his arm around him like a doting father. Samantha sat down at the table. Her mother had sat down too. She was not smiling anymore.

She looked at Samantha and said softly, "How's he doing?"

This was what Samantha was afraid of. Her mother always knew. She had those maternal instincts that told her whenever something was wrong.

"He's doing... better." Samantha said looking towards Samuel being shuffled from person to person with her father.

She looked back to her mother who was still staring at her. It was as if she could look straight through her.

"How are you doing?" Samantha's mother inquired.

Samantha felt the tears well up in her eyes as she looked away in shame. The answer was too much for her to say. Samantha felt her mother's hand gently touch hers.

The tears streamed out of her eyes as she said, "It's so hard mom."

Her mother just gently caressed her hand as she said, "I can't imagine."

Samantha felt so weak. All she had to do was stay strong for Samuel and it would all get better. He was the one who had lost his friends and been blown up and forced to kill people and experience all the horror. All she had to do was love him unconditionally. But they never say that unconditionally includes the person you love fundamentally changing in their substance.

Finally, her mother broke the silence by saying, "Did you ever wonder why your uncle is so much older than me?"

Samantha looked at her mother confused. She wiped the tears away from her face as she shook her head.

"Your grandfather," she said as she took a sip of wine, "had gone to Korea. Your grandmother said that he came back a different man. It was like the man she had married and had a child with did not come back."

Samantha was in disbelief, she had never heard this story. Her grandfather was amongst the sweetest men she had ever known in her life. She knew he had served but she never considered that he might have had a similar experience to what Samuel had been through.

"So, what changed?" Samantha asked. She was expecting to hear how her grandmother had to fall in love with a new man all over again.

"Well," her mother began, "they did not have answers for things like PTSD back then. They just did not talk about it, that's how society dealt with it."

Samantha was intrigued. She leaned in to listen intently to every word.

"It took years," her mother said, "Your grandmother almost left him several times. But one night she found him sitting on the porch crying in the freezing cold weather."

Samantha felt a shudder come over her, she had found Samuel sitting on their patio a week before just staring out into the darkness.

"She hugged him," her mother continued, "and he looked up at her and asked how he was supposed to go on and have a happy life when so many of his friends would never get a chance at any life. She told him that she believed he was supposed to have a happy life *because* his friends did not have a chance at any life."

Samantha said in incredulity, "And that worked?"

Her mother laughed and took another drink of wine and then said, "I was conceived that night... so the story goes."

Samantha was dumbfounded, she did not see that working with Samuel.

"It did not change everything overnight," her mother added, "but love came back into their lives. Your grandfather always said that your grandmother pulled him out of the darkness."

Samantha felt her mother put her hand on hers again.

"Samuel's in a hell we cannot begin to imagine." Her mother said, "If you let him, he'll pull you down there with him. But you're the person who has to bring him out. I don't know how to tell you to do that."

Samantha felt strangely comforted by the conversation, even though she did not have any epiphany on what to do. Somehow knowing she was not the first woman in her family to deal with a man shattered by war was comforting enough.

Samuel had made the rounds with Johnathan and they were all sitting back at the table. The lunch was nice. Samuel thought to himself how society had been genuinely gracious to his generation. There was plenty of glad-handing and showing off the token veteran to go around. But for the most part the American populace seemed to be truly appreciative for their contribution. The Vietnam veterans had been treated like trash, the Korean veterans had been forgotten, and the Desert Storm veterans had been treated like a novelty. OIF vets and OEF vets were given some real reverence. The whole luncheon had seemed like a lot of pomp and circumstance, but it also seemed like a few filthy rich guys really just wanted to show their appreciation. They had tastefully set up a table of honor to the dead and missing. They reserved the head table for gold star families. Samuel could not think ill of any portion of the event. An old guy from the American Legion who was a club member got up and gave a speech about the club's appreciation to the veterans.

Samuel was one of five OEF/ OIF veterans in attendance. They had put pictures of them up on the projector. Samuel felt something as they started going through their bios. It was not a happy feeling, he was nervous. But for the first time since he had started taking the medicine, he did not feel like he was living in black and white.

His mind started wheeling through the filing cabinet as he started considering how best to respond once they got to his bio. Tears started forming in his eyes. They were happy tears.

He felt like he was living in color. He looked at Samantha and he felt warm. He was happy. He smiled at her and she smiled back as tears started forming in her eyes as well. He reached out and took her hand from across the table.

"Sergeant Samuel Parker." He heard the announcer say. "This Marine is humbling to say the least."

Samantha was bursting with happiness. Samuel had smiled and tears had formed in his eyes. She felt excited about the future for the first time in a while. Some flicker of the boy she had loved showed himself as he blushed while they read off his bio. Samantha thought back to the many nights from the first time he came to visit her in Oxford. She thought of their pizza dates in high school. She thought of the night he proposed to her before he left for his third deployment. She started crying she was so happy. The shy boyish charm she fell in love with seemed to be trying to make its way to the surface.

Samuel felt like they were reading a eulogy to Sgt. Samuel Parker, and to be honest Sgt. Samuel Parker had lived a very hard life. He deserved to be laid to rest with dignity.

"Sgt. Parker," the announcer continued, "deployed to Iraq where he received a Purple Heart after his vehicle was struck by an IED. He was meritoriously promoted to Corporal and he received a Bronze Star for his actions in a firefight."

Samuel reflected on what had been said.

"Sgt. Parker was deployed again to Iraq. He was meritoriously promoted to Sergeant and received a Navy and Marine Achievement medal with a V for Valor for his conduct throughout that tour."

Samuel hung his head thinking about all the hardships of his second tour. He thought of the girl. He thought about her eulogy that would never be read. But for the first time ever he questioned if she could be at peace with Sgt. Parker in whatever great beyond.

"And finally, Sgt. Parker served a tour in Afghanistan, where he was awarded another Purple Heart for after he was shot during an hours long firefight."

Samuel expected to hear: *He is survived by Samuel Parker.*

Samuel listened as they finished reading his non-combat decorations and achievements. Then Samuel heard the room start to clap. The announcer was looking right at him when he said,

"Sgt. Parker stand up please, be recognized."

Samuel shyly smiled and stood up. He hated being the center of attention, but he was so happy to *feel* like he did not like it. He looked at Samantha who had tears in her eyes as she clapped with the rest of them.

"Would all of our Iraq and Afghanistan veterans stand again to be recognized," The announcer said magnanimously.

Samuel felt like he was alone in the room with Samantha again. He leaned over and locked lips with her. He got butterflies in his stomach again like the first time they kissed so many years ago. Samuel knew that war had killed his innocence. He would never be the boy he was before. He did not think he would ever be able to function again without the medication. Samuel knew he would never forget his friends he had made, and especially the ones that did not make it back. But Samuel had learned that trying to regain that lost innocence was not possible. It was dead. But if his innocence could die, so could his guilt. He did not have to feel guilty for surviving or what he had done to survive or the way he felt about the wars. The sword drawn in violence could be sheathed again. Samuel thought to himself as he had so many times before when he needed to call the demon into service. *Goodbye old friend. On behalf of the President of the United States and a grateful nation...* but instead of feeling sorry for the loss of the demon, he just smiled to himself and thought, *thank you for your service.*

Samuel went to the bar feeling good about his new cleared conscience and clear resolve. He was determined to enjoy the rest of his day. There was a grizzled graybeard at the bar when he walked up. The man was well dressed, and he figured he was one of the members. His body emanated the smell of bourbon. Samuel nodded to him as he walked up and ordered a beer.

"Sounds like you had one hell of a fight." The old man said.

Samuel looked at the man's forearm and saw a Seventh Calvary tattoo, that placed him in a hallowed Vietnam unit.

Samuel replied, "Probably not as bad as yours."

The man patted Samuel on the back and said, "Hell, I don't know about all that."

The man tapped his glass to Samuel's as Samuel picked his up. They both took a drink.

"You know I always wonder," the man said, "if our wars weren't tough because we grew up with plenty."

Samuel knew what the man was hinting at. There is an old adage that soft times make soft men. Samuel thought to himself. He found himself formulating a response at his normal speed. It was refreshing to have his mind working properly again. "You know," Samuel started,

"I can't speak about Vietnam. I don't know what the men were like at Khe Sanh or Hamburger Hill. But I know the men I served with. There were no soft men in Fallujah. And the guys toiling through the rubble in Ramadi were tough as nails. I know driving through the deserts of Al Anbar looking for Mujahideen and Jihadist to fight was not for the faint of heart. The men I met who took Baghdad, Kabul, and a dozen other cities were lions. And in Marjah our enemies faced hardened warriors."

Samuel looked back at the old veteran. "We were not tough because we survived. We survived because we were tough."

The old vet's face morphed to a smirk as he nodded silently.

Samuel continued feeling as though he had delivered a thesis on his life, "I know I grew up in the softest times. But if soft times make soft men, they must have found every tough son of a bitch left in this country and put a rifle in our hands when these wars started."

The old vet looked at him glassy eyed feeling like Samuel had just given him reassurance about his own generation. The vet stuck his hand out.

Samuel shook his hand and said, "If you'll excuse me."

Samuel walked back towards their table. He felt like there was a magnet drawing him. Samuel may not have known who he was anymore, but he sure as hell knew who he wasn't. He wasn't the demon. He wasn't the boy. He would be the man. The man Samantha deserved.

The Corps taught him the mission comes first. His new mission was to live and let live, no more living like he was already dead. The Corps had taught him honor. He could could honor his dead by honoring his wife to be. The Corps taugh him courage. Not all courage was conspicuous. Maybe the bravest thing he could do was face the next day, and the one after that. The Corps taught him commitment. Samuel never had commitment issues, but he had never committed to himself.

He may never be the same, but he could be better. We are not simply the sum of our experiences. But experience, whether good or bad, is a part of who we are. Experiences are shadow and light. You can be over exposed or hidden in darkness. Finding the balance is what makes for a beautiful photo. Samuel resolved to himself that he would not continue in the shadows of his war story. He would step back into the light of his love story. And he would find the perfect balance for the picture of his life moving forward.

He saw Samantha glowing and laughing with her mother about something. She was the happiest he had seen her since he had gotten back. He sat his unfinished beer on a random table. All of the people sitting there looked at him in confusion. Samantha got a worried look as he walked up to the table. Samuel looked into her beautiful eyes and felt his heart overflow with love for her. Every fiber of his being ached for her. There was a long uncomfortable pause until finally he said, "Let's go get a pizza and watch TV."

ABOUT THE AUTHOR

P. S. Hunter

I think I tried to write my first piece at 8. I kept writing until I discovered girls and guitars. I was not very good at either of those but such is the fickle juvenile mind. I left high school and joined the United States Marine Corps. I came home and attended the Univerisity of Tennesssee at Chattanooga. (contractually obligated Go Mocs!) While there, my mother passed away quite suddenly and quite young. I don't know that there is ever an age where it is not devestating for a boy to lose his mother, however, I was certainly far too young. That's when I discovered writing again. I had a therapist tell me that it was normal to feel like i wanted to punch a hole in every wall I saw. But it was not ok to tell people I felt like I wanted to punch a hole in the wall in casual conversation about how I was doing. But I could write a story about a boy who lost his mother that wanted commence with the wall punching, and they would get it. And I have been writing for the past 12 years or so now. I really write for me and my own mental health. But truthfully I hope the stories that invade my brainhousing unit might help someone else struggling with something. I am married to my beautiful wife Emily. We have 3 dogs and our own slice of heaven in a pretty rural part of Tennessee. I am influenced by Faulkner, Anne Rice, Fitzgerald, Cormac McCarthy, and quite a few others I am remiss for leaving out. But if you want to read people that do what I do but alot better, check with them.

-Semper Fi

Made in the USA
Columbia, SC
06 June 2021